A Kiss for Colt

KISS A COWBOY SERIES BOOK TWO

Deanna Lynn Sletten

A Kiss for Colt
Kiss a Cowboy Series Book Two

Copyright 2014 © Deanna Lynn Sletten

ISBN – 10:1941212212
ISBN – 13:978-1-941212-21-9

Editor: Denise Vitola
Cover Designer: Deborah Bradseth of Tugboat Design

Excerpt from Kissing Carly Copyright 2014 by Deanna Lynn Sletten

A Kiss for Colt

KISS A COWBOY SERIES BOOK TWO

Chapter One

Colt Brennan paced the waiting area in the Missoula International Airport, unable to contain his excitement at the arrival of Carly Stevens, Andi's sister. It was only two days before Christmas, and Carly was flying in from Seattle to celebrate the holidays with the Brennan family and her sister, as well as attend the special event planned for New Year's Eve—Andi and Luke's wedding. Colt hadn't seen Carly since they'd first met back in August when she'd driven to the ranch and stayed a few days. Andi's car had broken down and she was staying with the Brennan's while it was being repaired, and Carly had come out to bring some of Andi's prints to sell at the county fair.

The first time Colt had laid eyes on Carly, his heart skipped a beat. She was the most beautiful woman he'd ever seen. Her long blond hair and captivating blue eyes had knocked him for a loop. And the fact that she'd found him, a simple cowboy, attractive and worthy of flirting with, had both surprised and humbled him.

Growing warm, Colt discarded his sheepskin jacket onto the empty seat beside Andi and began pacing again. He lifted his cowboy hat from his head and ran his hand through his short, sandy blond hair, then paced once more. Several women in the airport watched Colt with interest as he walked back and forth, but he paid them no mind. With his tall, muscular frame, long legs, square jaw, high cheekbones, and deep set blue eyes, he garnered attention from women wherever he went. But being the shy young man that he was, he rarely noticed when women looked his way.

"Colt, if you don't stop pacing, you'll wear a groove in the floor," Andi said with a grin.

Colt stopped short and stared sheepishly at Andi. "Sorry." He dropped into a chair beside her. "I'm just excited to see Carly again. We've been emailing each other for months now, and I'm finally going to see her."

Andi patted Colt's arm and smiled at him. "I know. But pacing isn't going to make the flight arrive any quicker."

Colt nodded, trying hard to sit still. At twenty-five years old, he was only three years younger than Andi, but since she was soon to marry his older brother, he felt like she was his older sister as well. Colt was different from most twenty-first century men. He'd grown up working on the family ranch and attended a small-town school. Unlike Luke, who'd left at eighteen to attend college in northern California before moving back to the ranch, Colt had never had any desire to leave. He was a strong, competent man when it came to working the ranch and he could break a wild horse like no one else for miles around, but when it came to women, he was shy and uneasy. Except with Carly, it had been different. Carly was confident and outgoing and knew exactly how to pull Colt out of his shell, and he'd fallen for her immediately. But now, as he waited for her plane to arrive, he worried if she'd still find him interesting or think he was an awkward, hayseed cowboy.

The twelve forty-five p.m. flight from Seattle was announced over the loud speaker as having arrived and Colt jumped up from his seat to stare out the window and try to catch a glimpse of it.

"Why don't we head over to the baggage carrousels and wait for her there?" Andi suggested as she stood and picked up Colt's coat.

Colt nodded and began walking quickly ahead of Andi with long strides. He stopped half-way there and waited for her to catch up.

"Sorry," he told her, taking his heavy coat from her. "I'm not being very polite, am I?"

Andi laughed as she looked up at him with twinkling, green eyes. "It's okay. It's hard being in love, isn't it?"

Colt felt his face heat up as he stared at Andi. When Andi had first been stranded at their ranch, Colt had a huge crush on her. Her long, wavy red hair, big green eyes, and soft curves had been hard to ignore. But very soon it became obvious that Andi was more like a sister to him. He felt comfortable around her and she teased him good naturedly. Then, when Carly showed up and immediately started flirting with him, he was like putty in her hands. But he adored Andi and was happy she and Luke were getting married. After knowing her for less than five months, he already felt like she was a part of their family.

"I'm not sure I'd call it love," he said, trying to sound convincing. "But I sure do like her." Deep down inside, he knew he was already madly in love with the vivacious Carly, he just didn't want to admit it and sound like a crazy, lovesick idiot.

"Colt! Andi! Over here," a sweet voice rang out over the noise from the small crowd of people that had formed near the baggage carrousels. Both Andi and Colt looked up to see a woman dressed all in white making her way through the crowd, waving at them.

Carly stood out from the crowd in a formfitting white, North Face jacket with faux fur trim on the hood and sleeves, a long, fuzzy sweater, a pair of white leggings, and mid-calf length white snow boots with fur trim on top. Her light blond hair swirled around her shoulders and her blue eyes sparkled as she pulled a small, brown Louis Vuitton bag behind her with a matching handbag attached to the handle. She looked like a snow bunny that had missed her flight to Vail or Tahoe. But on the lively, spirited Carly, the outfit seemed just right.

Colt's eyes lit up at the sight of her and Andi shook her head and grinned as Carly came flying into Colt's arms and placed a big hello kiss on his lips.

* * *

"My handsome cowboy," Carly exclaimed as she threw her arms around Colt and kissed him quickly on the lips, leaving a smudge of red lipstick behind. Carly pulled back and giggled before she ran her thumb across his lips to wipe the red away. Colt's face turned bright red to match the lipstick, which only made Carly giggle again. "I really missed you, Colt."

The one and a half hour flight from Seattle to Missoula was short, but for Carly, it had felt like hours. She couldn't wait to see her big sister or her hot cowboy. Ever since meeting Colt months before, Carly had thought about him often. Even though she'd dated a few men during that time, Colt stayed on her mind. He was unlike the men she usually dated, and she liked that. Where they were usually sophisticated and worldly, Colt was sweet and unaffected by possessions and status. He treated her like a true lady. The fact that he was dreamily handsome and a great kisser helped a lot, too.

"What about me?" Andi asked. "Didn't you miss me at all?"

Carly turned, smiled wide at Andi, and pulled her into a hug. "Of course, I did, silly. But who would you hug first? Your sister, or your cute cowboy?"

Andi laughed. "Definitely, my cute cowboy." She looked her

sister up and down. "That's quite some outfit you're wearing."

Carly stepped back and pursed her lips into a pout. "Don't you like it? You said to dress warm, and there's no reason not to look stylish and be warm, is there?"

"I'm just teasing you," Andi said. "You look adorable, as usual. You'd look stunning in a paper sack."

Carly grinned. "Goodness. Never a paper sack. Unless it's a designer one."

Andi laughed and Carly gave her another hug. "Show me your ring," Carly said excitedly. "I've been waiting months to see it."

Andi lifted her left hand and Carly held it, inspecting the white gold band with a solitaire brilliant cut diamond sparkling on it.

"It's gorgeous!" Carly exclaimed. "Not too gaudy and not too small. Luke did a good job."

"I'm glad you approve," Andi said, chuckling. "The minute I said I'd marry him, Luke insisted we go shopping for a ring. He wanted the world to know we were engaged."

"Smart man," Carly said. She looked up at Andi wistfully. "I'm so happy you're marrying Luke instead of Mr. You-Know-Who."

"Me, too," Andi whispered conspiratorially. Carly was referring to Derek Hensley, the man Andi had been engaged to when she started her drive across country. Carly had never really liked Derek, and had told Andi to fall in love with Luke, instead, because he was much cuter and nicer than Derek. In the end, Andi had to agree. Falling in love with Luke was the best thing that had ever happened to her.

"Do you have any more luggage?" Colt piped up.

Both women looked up at Colt, startled. They'd been so busy talking, they'd forgotten where they were.

"Oh, yes. I do," Carly said. "Would you be a sweetie and

grab it for me, Colt? It's awfully heavy. It looks just like my small bag here."

"Sure," Colt said, sounding happy to please her. He strode over to the carrousel and watched it intently.

"Louis Vuitton, huh?" Andi asked. "Did you win the lottery or something?"

Carly gave her sister a sideways glance. "Don't be such a spoilsport. I work. I should be allowed to splurge on nice things once in a while."

"Outlet mall?"

"Yes," Carly whispered. "But don't tell anyone, okay?"

Andi laughed and put her arm around her sister, pulling her close. "Oh, Carly. I sure have missed you."

"Me, too," Carly said.

Colt found Carly's bag and they walked out into the crisp winter air through the parking lot to Colt's truck. Once inside, Colt cranked up the heat and they headed west out of town for the hour long trip back to the ranch.

Carly had scooted into the middle of the seat so she could sit next to Colt and Andi sat by the door. Her luggage was tucked safely in the back seat of the truck.

"When you said it was cold here, you weren't kidding," Carly said. "I thought Seattle was cold in the winter, but this is ridiculous. Look at all the snow."

Andi nodded. "It takes some getting used to, but I don't mind it too much. I stay inside most of the time anyway, either painting or helping Ginny with meals."

"I can't wait to see everyone," Carly said. "And to see your wedding dress. It's so romantic that you two are getting married on New Year's Eve and by the fireplace in the house just like all the Brennans before you."

"Every Brennan since the 1860s when the house was first built," Colt said proudly. "It's a family tradition."

Carly smiled over at Colt and put her hand on his thigh. "Even you, Colt? Will you get married there?"

Colt glanced shyly at Carly. "I suppose, if anyone ever wants to marry me."

Carly's blue eyes twinkled. "I'm sure it won't be too difficult to find someone."

"Sheesh. You guys are too much," Andi said. "I hope Luke and I didn't sound so sickeningly sweet a few months ago."

Carly giggled. "No, you two were too busy pretending you weren't in love with each other to sound cute."

Colt chuckled. "Sorry, Andi. I have to agree with that."

Andi shook her head and turned to look out the window. When Andi's car broke down last summer and she stayed with the Brennans, she'd had every intention of leaving the moment her car was repaired. Her relationship with her fiancé had been strained already, and over the course of the three weeks she'd stayed at the ranch, it grew even more distant. But despite its rocky start, the relationship between her and Luke had grown, to the point where they could no longer deny their feelings for each other. Andi did try to leave, but couldn't. She'd fallen in love with the handsome Luke, and he'd begged her to stay. She did, and they'd been happily together every day since.

"Don't be mad, Andi," Carly said. "I think you and Luke's love story is beautiful. And I can't wait until the wedding. Wait until you see the dress I bought to wear as your Maid of Honor. Colt and I are going to look so cute together in the pictures, him in his tux and me in my dress."

Andi smiled. "Carly, you two would look great in pictures no matter what you wore. But I can't wait to see your dress."

Carly and Andi chatted about the wedding and what had gone on in their lives since they'd last seen each other until Colt pulled into the long driveway up to the main ranch house. Colt and his mother, Ginny, lived at the main house and Luke and

Andi lived in a cozy cabin just down the road. Everyone, including Randy Olson, a longtime family friend and their ranch hand, ate meals together at the main house.

Carly's eyes lit up with delight. "Everything looks so different here with snow everywhere. It's beautiful."

Snow covered the rolling fields and cattle dotted the pasture. The red horse barn had a blanket of snow on the roof as did the house. There'd been a smattering of fresh snow the night before, and today it glittered in the sun.

"It's magical," Carly exclaimed in awe.

"Yeah, until you have to shovel it," Andi said, bursting Carly's bubble.

Carly rolled her eyes. "Spoilsport."

Colt chuckled.

They pulled up near the house and got out of the warm truck into the twenty-five degree day. Carly pulled her coat closer around her as Colt lifted her bags out of the back seat. Just as they walked to the back door, it opened, and there stood Colt's mother, Ginny, smiling wide.

"Carly! You're here," Ginny said. She scrambled down the steps wearing only her jeans and sweater and her winter boots. Her dark blond hair was pulled back into a ponytail and her hazel eyes sparkled. Even with a few strands of gray streaking through her hair, Ginny looked too young to have two grown sons.

She pulled Carly into a warm embrace and gave her a kiss on the cheek. "My, but aren't you beautiful all dressed up in white. You look like a snow princess."

Carly beamed at Ginny. "Thanks." It was hard not to feel happy around Ginny. She was always so warm and loving, even to strangers.

Bree, their black and white Australian Shepherd, came bounding out the door to greet Carly, too.

"Bree," Carly cried, bending down to pet her. "I missed you too, girl."

"Well, come in out of the cold," Ginny said, leading the way. "There's warm chocolate chip cookies waiting and hot chocolate, too."

The group stepped into the mudroom and discarded their wet boots and jackets before heading into the kitchen. Bree followed them in and went to lie on her pillow over by the back staircase. To Carly, the cozy kitchen smelled like home should smell, with fresh cookies just out of the oven and hot chocolate warming on the stove. She picked up a cookie from the plate on the kitchen table and took a bite.

"Ah. Heaven," she said with a sigh.

Everyone laughed.

"Colt, dear. Take Carly's bags up to her room and then come back down and join us. I have no idea where Luke and Randy are right now, but maybe they'll smell the cookies and come running," Ginny said.

Carly sighed as she sat at the large kitchen table, sipped her hot chocolate, and nibbled on another cookie while watching everyone bustle around her. She and Andi had been raised by wonderful parents in a beautiful modern home and had been allowed to try everything that interested them. Andi's interest had been painting, and she was very talented at it. Carly's was managing and selling, and she did that well at the art gallery where she worked. She'd lived in Seattle her entire life and enjoyed the eclectic feel of it. But, even with everything she'd been able to experience throughout her life, this sweet, country kitchen at this ranch in the mountains of Montana felt more like home to her than anywhere else ever had. Maybe it was because of Ginny's kindness, or the fact that her parents had died when she was only fourteen and Andi was eighteen. Or maybe it was because everyone here was so real and down to earth. Carly didn't know why. She was just happy to be here with her sister and among the people she considered her family, especially her handsome cowboy, Colt.

Chapter Two

Colt had a big grin on his face as he put Carly's bags in the spare bedroom upstairs and headed back down to sit with the others. From the excited way Carly had greeted him, he was sure she had missed him, too, and was still attracted to him. There was no question how he felt about her. He had fallen fast for her last August and he felt the same way now as he did then. And while they'd never done more than steal a few hot kisses last summer, he still felt as if he were closer to her than any other girl he'd ever dated. Not that there had been many. Colt hadn't dated in high school, because he'd been too shy and there were very few girls in his small class anyway. As the years went by, he'd overcome his shyness a little, because he'd learned to dance quite well. He spent his weekends at the local honkytonk, The Depot, where he danced to live country music with the many single women who hung out there. He'd only had two semi-serious girlfriends, but neither one had lasted long. Most of the women who lived in these out-of-the-way towns wanted more than anything to get out, and they weren't going to hitch their wagon to a rancher who was certainly going to stay.

Luke was in the kitchen when Colt returned. He'd come inside for a moment to give Carly a big hello hug. Colt knew he and Randy were trying to repair a heater motor on one of the water tanks outside that the cattle used. The water would freeze without it in this cold weather, so it was imperative that they fix it. Soon enough, Colt would have to return outside to help with the evening feeding of the cattle and horses.

"I'm happy you're here," Luke said, helping himself to a cookie from the plate on the table. "I know your sister has missed you." He winked at Andi, his blue eyes sparkling. Luke stood a bit taller than Colt and had a chiseled face that belonged on a magazine cover, it was that handsome. Bundled up in his thick, sheepskin coat, the collar up, and with his dusty, black cowboy hat on his head, he looked like the Marlboro Man from the commercials of long ago. "She finally has a woman to talk to about the wedding instead of all us men."

"Hey, I take offense to that," Ginny objected.

"Sorry, Ma," Luke said, grinning. "You know what I mean, though."

Ginny laughed. "Yes, I do. A girl needs her sister at a time like this."

"I'm happy to finally be here," Carly said, smiling up at Luke. "I felt left out of all the wedding plans. I hope there are still some things I can help with."

"Oh, don't worry," Andi piped up. "We'll find plenty for you to do."

"I need to get back out to the barn," Luke said, grabbing a napkin and folding two cookies into it. "If I can't fix that heater today, then I need to run to town and buy a new one. I'll bring these out to Randy." He motioned to the cookies in the napkin. "He needs something to cheer him up after spending the day fighting with that heater." Luke waved and walked out the back door.

Colt sighed. He wanted so badly to stay and spend time with Carly, but he knew he had to get outside and start feeding the cattle before suppertime. "I have to go, too. I'll be in later, though."

Carly followed him into the mudroom and watched as he slipped on his boots and coat. "I hope we can see a lot of each other while I'm here," she said softly, looking up at him with her tantalizing blue eyes.

Colt's heart pounded. He wanted to spend a lot of time with Carly, too. "I do, too. We can go riding on warmer days while you're here. Tonight, I'll show you how the house looks in the dark. We've decorated for Christmas and for the wedding. It's really beautiful." *Like you.* He wanted to say it out loud, but couldn't get the words to come out.

Carly stood up on tip-toe and placed a soft kiss on Colt's cheek. "See you later, Colt."

Colt's face felt flushed as he walked outside. This was going to be the best week of his life.

* * *

After Colt left, Andi took Carly into the sitting room just off of the kitchen to see the Christmas decorations. The sitting room was actually their spacious living room complete with a floor-to-ceiling river rock fireplace on one side, enormous windows, a cathedral ceiling with exposed beams, and the main staircase on the far wall. Its name came from years past when the house was built in the 1860s and the first Brennans lived there. Since then, the house had grown larger and so had the sitting room, but the fireplace was still the same one that every generation of Brennans had been married in front of.

Carly gasped when she saw the room. A tall, full Christmas tree stood on the far side of the room in front of a large window. It looked at least seven feet tall and was decorated with beautiful white, blue, silver, and crystal ornaments with a sparkling silver star on top. Brightly wrapped presents sat under the tree. The rustic, wood block mantel was covered with evergreen garland that glittered with decorations similar to those on the tree. White candles in tall, glass holders sat in the garland. Decorated garland also hung around each of the side windows and the front windows as well. A round wreath decorated the door and garland had been strung all the way up the railing of the staircase. Everywhere, decorations sparkled and glittered, and the scent of evergreen filled the air. The fireplace held a crackling fire behind a decorative screen that protected the garland from wayward sparks. The room was warm and cozy, but festive as well, and it wasn't hard for Carly to imagine a wedding ceremony taking place here.

"I love it," Carly squealed. "Are you walking down the staircase for your grand entrance?"

Andi nodded. "I thought about it. I could come out of the office over there instead. What do you think?"

"Oh, the staircase for sure. Think of how dramatic that will look with you sweeping down the staircase in your white dress, your train trailing behind you." Carly stopped and looked at her sister. "Does your dress have a train? I can't believe I haven't seen it yet."

"Don't worry, you'll see it soon. It's down at the cabin, but we can stop by there later for you to take a peek. And yes, there is a short train, so a staircase entrance would be lovely. Of course, that is if I don't trip on my way down."

"I doubt very much that you will. I wish Mom and Dad were here to see you get married. Mom would have so loved decorating for you, and Dad could have walked you down the aisle."

Andi sighed. "I know. I wish they were here, too." Both women were lost in their own thoughts for a moment, remembering their parents. They had died in a car accident over ten years ago, and Andi had taken care of her younger sister until she was through college and had a good job. Their parents had left them with a load of debt and the first few years had been difficult, but they'd made it through, together. They both still missed their parents very much.

"Who's going to walk you down the aisle?" Carly asked.

"I asked Randy to," Andi said. Randy had been friends with Luke since childhood, and he had a strong bond with the Brennans. Over the past few months, Andi had grown fond of the tough, yet kindhearted cowboy.

Carly wrinkled her nose. "Randy? But he's so snarly." Randy was the only man Carly had ever met who hadn't succumbed to her charms, so she wasn't a big fan of his.

Andi laughed. "He's not snarly, he's a sweetheart. You just don't like him because he doesn't worship the ground you walk on like all the other men do."

Carly pouted. "Not all men worship me, you know. But most men at least like me, and Randy doesn't even give me the time of day. But I don't care. I have Colt."

Andi rolled her eyes. "You don't *have* Colt. You just shamelessly throw yourself at him. And as I've warned you a hundred times before, don't play games with him unless you're serious. He's such as tenderhearted person. I don't want to see him hurt."

Carly's eyes widened. "I'd never play with Colt's feelings," she insisted. "I do care about him. Do you really believe I'm that evil?"

Andi pulled her sister close. "No, I don't believe you're evil. I just think that, sometimes, you are having so much fun, you forget that others may be taking you more seriously than you are them. Let's face it, Carly. You love men and men love you. It's been that way for years."

"Geez, Andi. You make me sound like a slut."

"No, Little Sis. That's not what I mean. I know that you just love having a good time. Just make sure that while you're having fun, you're keeping in mind that Colt may be taking you more seriously, that's all."

Carly sighed. "Okay, okay. Enough with the lectures." She smiled wide. "Let's go upstairs and I'll unpack. I can't wait to show you my dress for the wedding."

Instead of using the main staircase, the women went through the kitchen to go up the back stairs. Once in Carly's room, they began unpacking her things and talking and giggling like years gone by when they were teenagers. Carly's room was the one Andi had stayed in months ago when she first stayed at the ranch. It was a lovely country-style room with a blue star quilt, blue rag rugs on the oak floor, and an antique dresser and bed set. Right down the hallway was a small bathroom and beyond that was Colt's room. Ginny's bedroom was downstairs behind the kitchen where generations of Brennan owners had slept.

Carly pulled out an evening gown that had been carefully folded in her carry-on bag and held it up against her body to show Andi. It was a full-length, satin gown in a deep red color. It had a sweetheart neckline, and a body-hugging bodice that fell down from the waist in a soft, flowing skirt to the floor. Glittery rhinestones embellished the waist and straps of the dress.

"It's beautiful," Andi exclaimed. "And it's the perfect color. It'll match the roses in my bouquet."

"I'd hoped you'd like it," Carly said, beaming with delight. "When you said your flowers were going to be deep red and white roses, I knew I just had to have a red dress. And I bought silver shoes to match the decorations on the dress."

"You'll look beautiful," Andi said, giving her sister a hug. "Standing next to Colt in his black tux, you both will look lovely in the pictures."

They quickly hung up Carly's clothes and put some of her other things in the dresser drawers. Carly changed into a pair of jeans and a thick, pink sweater so the white outfit she'd been wearing wouldn't get dirty. Even dressed simply, Carly still looked gorgeous. She was just one of those lucky women who'd been born to shine, and it brought attention to her wherever she went.

The women went downstairs to the kitchen and helped Ginny make supper. Carly peeled potatoes while Andi cut up carrots to boil and Ginny put the finishing touches on an apple pie for dessert. A beef roast was already cooking in the oven. As they worked, the women talked about Christmas, the wedding, and all the preparations needed to be done for the dinner they planned on serving to the small wedding crowd that evening. Ginny's two friends, Mary and Sharon, who she shared a fair booth with each year to sell their homemade preserves, had offered to help with the dinner so Ginny could enjoy the evening. Ginny planned on making up most of the food ahead of time and the two women would cook and serve it to their guests.

"That way Ginny can spend more time with her new beau, Glen," Andi teased.

Ginny playfully shook a finger at Andi. "Don't you start with me, now," she said. "It was your idea that I go out with him in the first place." Glen Parker was a retired real estate developer who split his time between his home in Montana and his winter place in San Diego. He was a good-looking man in his late fifties, and he had a kind, thoughtful way about him. He'd bought preserves from Ginny at the fair every year and this year he'd purchased one of Andi's original paintings. He'd invited Ginny out on a date, and Andi had encouraged her to go. Ginny's husband had died several years earlier from cancer. Even though Luke and Colt had been uncomfortable at first about their mother dating, they were getting used to it, and they both liked Glen.

Andi laughed. "No, it was Glen's idea that you go out with him. I just gave you a little push. You deserve to have some fun. You've worked hard enough around here all these years. It's your turn for romance."

"Romance," Ginny snorted. "You're talking like a crazy woman. But I do enjoy Glen's company."

"I feel left out," Carly said as she cut up the potatoes she'd peeled. "Ginny has a new romance, and Andi's marrying her hot cowboy. What about me?"

Andi laughed. "What do you mean? It's obvious Colt adores you. I thought he was your hot cowboy."

Ginny shook her head. "I don't want to hear this. My sons—hot cowboys? Sure, they're good looking men, and hard workers, and I raised them right. But hot cowboys? A mother doesn't need to hear that."

They all laughed as they finished their work and the conversation continued to flow.

The men soon came in for supper and they all sat down and dug right in to the delicious meal. It was already dark outside. The days were short in the winter, so the men had to work faster to get everything done before the sun went down.

Randy gave Carly a courteous nod and then immediately ignored her. Carly scooched closer to Colt on the bench seat and listened as the men talked about finally fixing the heater for the water tank and how they had to move more hay bales closer to the feeding areas tomorrow. She watched Andi and Luke across the table smile at each other, their eyes twinkling. *Ah, love.* Carly was so happy that her sister had finally found her perfect soul mate. To think that Andi almost married that awful Derek instead of Luke made Carly shiver. She liked Luke immensely, and she knew he'd always take care of her sister. Maybe someday she'd find the perfect man for her, too. She just wasn't in a hurry yet to settle down with anyone.

Chapter Three

Colt impatiently waited after supper until Carly was finished helping his mother and Andi with dishes. He'd been waiting all day to spend time alone with Carly, and it was hard to contain his excitement. He sat at the table, pretending to play a game of solitaire, but his attention was on every move Carly made. She was so beautiful. It was hard for him to keep his eyes off of her.

"You can't put a red queen on red king," Luke said, looking over Colt's shoulder.

"Huh?" Colt looked up at his brother.

Luke chuckled. "Guess you're mind is on something else, huh?"

The three women turned and looked at him. Colt felt his face grow warm.

"Ready to go?" Luke asked Andi, walking over to her. She smiled up at him and nodded.

"Are you leaving already?" Carly asked. "When are you going to show me your dress?"

"I can show you tomorrow," Andi said. "Right now, I think Colt wants to spend some time with you."

Colt nervously ran his hand over the back of his neck. "Well, uh, I was just going to see if Carly wanted to look at the Christmas lights outside. That's all."

Andi smiled and winked at Colt. "Goodnight, Colt. See you in the morning."

"Goodnight," he said, trying to still his pounding heart. He watched as Andi said goodnight to Carly and Ginny, then walked out to the mudroom with Luke's hand on the small of her back.

Carly sprung up in front of him. "I'm ready," she said. "Let's go outside."

They bundled up in their coats and boots and headed outside. Colt grabbed Carly's gloved hand and pulled her toward the barn.

"Don't look yet," he said. "I know the perfect spot where we can see the lights."

Carly ran beside him and they soon entered the barn. They stopped in front of the ladder that led up to the loft.

"Up there?" Carly asked, pointing to the loft.

"Yep. You can see everything from up there." He moved to the side and let Carly begin the climb first, and then he followed behind her. Up through the opening in the floor they went and soon they stood among bales of hay.

Carly sneezed.

"Sorry," Colt said. "The hay is dusty." He led her to the front of the barn and then he pushed aside the big, sliding door that faced the house.

Carly gasped in delight when she looked outside. "Oh, Colt, you're right. This is the perfect view."

The inky black sky shone with a multitude of glittering stars. Below them, the house was lit up with twinkle lights outlining the roof, windows, and doors. The decorated tree shined through the window of the house. Icicles hung from the eves and the lights made them sparkle. The white snow that blanketed the rolling pastures around them shone under the stars. It was a picturesque view that belonged on a Christmas card.

Colt came over and stood beside Carly. It was warm in the loft, even with the crisp air drifting in through the open door. He looked down at her tenderly, remembering the first time they'd come up to the loft in August. Carly had asked to see a genuine hayloft, and he'd obliged. What he hadn't counted on, and was thrilled by, was the passionate kiss she'd given him that day, standing here amidst the hay bales.

"Do you like it?" Colt asked.

Carly smiled up at him. "Oh, yes. It's beautiful." She stepped closer to Colt and ran her hands up the front of his coat. Slowly, she unbuttoned his coat, and then opened it. Running her hands slowly across his chest, then around to his back, she snuggled in close to his warmth. "I forgot how strong you feel," she whispered as she looked up at him with sparkling eyes.

Colt wrapped his coat around her small body and hugged her in tight. She felt so good, tucked up against him, even with her puffy coat on. Her hair smelled of lavender, and it felt soft as it tickled his neck. They stood there, looking out into the winter night, and Colt swore he heard Carly sigh.

"Remember the last time we came up here?" Carly asked, her voice teasing. "Of course, it was hot then."

Colt's heart pounded. He glanced down and saw Carly gazing up at him. Slowly, he bent his head and tentatively touched her lips with his. He felt Carly's hand pull out of his coat and reach up behind his neck. He ran his own hands up her back and into her long, silky hair, and pulled her closer. She opened her lips to his and their tongues danced with delight as their kiss became more passionate.

Pulling away, Carly slipped off her gloves and coat, and Colt pulled off his own and dropped it to the floor. Carly slowly ran her hands up Colt's strong arms as she continued to hold his gaze with hers. She ran her fingertips along his strong jaw, and then up through the back of his hair. Every touch, every movement of her hands, caused Colt's breathing to grow heavier.

"You are my handsome cowboy," Carly whispered, running her hand down his neck again and across his strong chest. "Hold me, Colt. I want to feel you next to me."

Colt placed his large hands on her narrow waist and slid them up her sides, under her sweater, and around to her back. Her skin felt warm and silky to the touch. He pulled her closer, so close, there wasn't a sliver of light between them. He dipped his head and claimed her lips, this time without hesitation.

Carly responded, her lips eager for his. Colt's breathing quickened. He pulled away and dropped his lips to the sweet spot at the base of her neck, making Carly gasp with pleasure. Once again, he kissed her while his hands roamed freely under her sweater.

Carly pulled away, chuckling softly, and spoke in her sultry voice. "Andi said I should be careful not to lead you on, but I think I'm the one who should be wary of you stealing my heart."

Colt swallowed hard as he gazed down at Carly. He raised his hand and gently swept her hair away from her face and behind her ear. Her eyes were bright and her checks were flushed with passion. She was the most beautiful creature he'd ever known, and he wanted her right now more than he'd ever wanted any other woman in his life. But good sense told him to step back and wait. When he made love to Carly, if he were ever so lucky, he didn't want it to be on the floor of a hayloft. He wanted it to be special, like her.

Carly cocked her head and looked at Colt. "Something the matter, Cowboy?"

Reluctantly, Colt slipped his hands out from under her sweater and took a step back. "Maybe we should just sit here a while," he said, motioning to a square hay bale on the floor. "Before things get too heated and out of control."

Carly frowned for just an instant, but then she nodded. Colt laid his coat over the hay bale and they sat on it, cuddling up close.

"Are you playing hard to get?" Carly teased.

Colt chuckled. "Nope. I think I'd be pretty easy right now." He turned and kissed the tip of Carly's nose. "But you deserve better than a hayloft."

Carly looked up at him, surprise clearly written on her face. "You are so sweet, Colt. I've never known anyone else like you." She wrapped her arm around his waist and dropped her head on his shoulder.

"Is that good or bad?" Colt asked, enjoying her body snuggled up against his.

"Oh, it's a good thing. You know how to treat a lady. I love that."

Colt smiled as they sat close together watching the stars twinkle over the white, blanketed earth.

* * *

Carly awoke on Christmas Eve morning with a smile on her lips. Thinking about Colt and the night before made her feel warm and tingly all over. She thought it was so sweet of him not to give in to his desire the night before and to have the self-control to pull back and wait. Most men she knew wouldn't have thought twice about taking her right there on the hayloft floor. And, if she were honest with herself, she'd have to admit that if Colt had tried, she'd have probably given in to him. He was so damn sexy, how could she resist? But that was what made him different. He treated her respectfully, even though she knew he had strong feelings for her. That made her want him even more.

Despite what her sister and friends thought, Carly didn't sleep with every man she dated. Yes, she had a longer track record than some, but she never slept with men casually or had one-night stands. She had to feel connected to them and know them well, first. She wasn't ready to settle down in a permanent relationship with anyone yet, and she was far from wanting to be married, but she did enjoy having a steady boyfriend. She just hadn't found the right guy, yet.

Carly quickly showered, dressed, and headed downstairs to the kitchen. Everyone had already eaten breakfast, because work on the ranch started early, even when the sun didn't come up until after eight in the morning. Ginny was in the kitchen, prepping a turkey for supper, and Andi sat at the table decorating sugar cookies. Bree was on her pillow, so Carly bent down and patted her on the head before heading into the kitchen.

"Good morning, sleepyhead," Andi greeted Carly. "You missed breakfast, but there are muffins left on the table and coffee on the stove."

Ginny gave Carly a quick hello squeeze before returning to stuffing the turkey. Carly poured a mug of steaming coffee, grabbed a plate and the butter out of the fridge, and came over to sit near Andi at the table. She took a blueberry muffin out of the basket and slathered it liberally with the farm-fresh butter.

"I'm going to get fat while I'm here," Carly said as she took a bite of her muffin. "But everything is so delicious, I can't resist."

Ginny laughed. "You can stand to gain a pound or two. No one will notice."

"You probably burned off all your calories in the hayloft last night anyway," Andi said, giving her sister a sideways glance.

Carly's eyes opened wide. "What?"

"Oh, don't act so innocent. That's where Colt took you last night, isn't it? To see the Christmas lights?" Andi rolled her eyes.

Carly pursed her lips. "That's what we did. Looked at the lights. And that's all." She popped the last bite of muffin into her mouth, and then she snitched one of the iced sugar cookies and took a bite. "Yum."

Andi laughed. "If you're going to eat them, you're going to decorate, too."

They spent the morning decorating cookies and inhaling the tantalizing aroma of the turkey cooking in the oven.

After lunch, Carly and Andi drove down to the cabin so Carly could see the wedding dress.

"You finally gave in and bought a new car," Carly said as they rode down the driveway toward the cabin. It was only a short distance from the main house.

"I needed a new one out here," Andi said. "Four-wheel drive is a must here in the snow and even with the new transmission, my old car wasn't reliable anymore."

"So, last summer wasn't really about the car after all," Carly said, her eyebrows raised. "It was more about not wanting to marry Derek." When Andi broke down last summer on her way to marry Derek, she could have easily left her car and flown to Buffalo, which was what Derek had wanted her to do. He'd said he'd buy her a new car. But Andi had been stubborn and insisted her car be fixed, which meant staying longer at the ranch. The longer she stayed, the more she realized she didn't love Derek, and that she was falling in love with Luke.

Andi bit her lip. "Yeah, I guess that's true. But I'm happy with the way things worked out."

Carly patted her sister's shoulder. "Me, too. Luke is perfect for you. It was fate."

Andi chuckled. "Can't argue with that either."

They pulled up in front of the cabin and went inside. Luke had built the cabin a few years before when he was married to his first wife, Ashley. She'd been from California, where Luke had met her while going to college, and she'd missed it dearly, so she left. Luke had sworn off "city girls" after that, until he met Andi. Now they lived here, and Andi didn't mind that he'd built it for another woman. She loved the cabin with its tall ceilings, river rock fireplace, and open floor plan. Even the furniture that Luke had picked out was fine with her. She'd only added a few feminine touches to give it a cozier feel.

Andi led Carly to the spare bedroom that she was currently using as her paint studio. She opened the closet and pulled out her dress, encased in a cloth bag.

"I thought Luke was going to build you an actual paint studio with a lot of windows," Carly said, looking around the room. An easel sat by the window with Andi's current painting sitting upon it. A table with paint tubes and paint sticks sat beside it.

"He is, next spring. There wasn't enough time before winter for such a large project this year. This room is just fine, though."

Carly walked over and looked closely at the unfinished painting. She gasped with glee when she recognized the scene. "That's the view from the top of the riding path at sunset, isn't it?"

Andi nodded. The riding path led up the hill above the ranch, and at the top, there was an amazing view of the ranch, the river, and the hills in the distance, covered in evergreens. At sunset, it glowed. When Carly had come to visit last summer, they'd all ridden up the path and watched the sunset.

"I also finished one of the valley by the cabin in the summer pasture," Andi said. It's over there, on the table."

Carly walked over and stared at the painting. The colors

were glorious, the scenery lifelike. It made her want to come back next year and visit the summer pasture with Colt. "Andi, this is gorgeous," Carly told her. "Are you going to have prints made so you can sell them around Missoula?"

"Probably. I'm going to wait until I have a couple more paintings done first, so I have a good selection. Come on. Let's go in the living room so I can show you my dress."

The two women walked out into the living room where natural light came in through the large windows from both the living area and the dining room. Carly held up the dress hanger while Andi unzipped the bag and pulled it off the dress. Then Andi took the hanger and turned it around for Carly to see.

Carly gazed at the lovely white, satin dress. It was an off-the-shoulder design with a scoop neck that gathered softly. The bodice was form-fitting and then fell from the waist to a full skirt with a short train. Sequins decorated the bodice on one side and crossed over and trailed down the dress in a delicate pattern, lining the hem to add just enough sparkle. It was the perfect dress for Andi. Richly feminine and eloquent, but not garish.

"I love it," Carly exclaimed. She looked from the dress to Andi, her eyes filling with tears. "This is really going to happen, isn't it? I can't believe it. You're getting married."

Andi carefully laid the dress over the back of the sofa and pulled her sister close. "Yes. It's really happening. And I'm the happiest I've ever been in my life."

Carly pulled away and wiped her tears, careful not to smudge her mascara. "I don't know why I'm crying. I knew this was happening, but seeing the dress makes it all so real. My sister, Adrianna Stevens, is going to become Adrianna Brennan. It's so unbelievable after all these years when it's just been the two of us."

"I know," Andi said, patting Carly's back. "But someday

you'll find your perfect match, too, and it will happen to you."

Carly laughed. "Not for a long time. I'm not ready to marry anyone, no matter how perfect a match they are."

Andi shook her head. "Come on. Let's put this dress away and go back to the house. The men will be done with work soon and our Christmas Eve celebration will begin."

They slipped the bag over the dress and hung it back in the closet. Then the two women hopped back into the car and headed to the house.

Chapter Four

Colt worked quickly all day so he could finish up and spend time with Carly. After feeding the cattle and horses, he strode back to the house, but was disappointed that Carly wasn't there. He went upstairs and took a quick shower so he didn't smell of dusty hay and horse manure tonight.

All day long his thoughts had been on Carly and last night. How she'd felt, her sweet scent, and the passionate way she'd kissed him. He couldn't believe how lucky he was that a woman like Carly could ever feel that way about him. At least, he hoped she felt the same way about him that he felt for her.

By the time Colt returned downstairs, everyone was in the sitting room, waiting for supper. Carly wore a baby blue cashmere sweater that had flecks of silver running through it and a pair of skintight jeans. Colt's heart beat faster at the sight of her. She smiled when he entered and ran over to him, slipping her arm through his.

"Hmm. You smell delicious," she whispered as she pulled him over to the sofa to sit beside her.

Luke and Andi sat close together on the other sofa and Randy sat in the big chair. Ginny stood behind Randy's chair, poised to rush into the kitchen if she heard something boil over. She wore a new, silky, royal blue blouse with black pants and her hair was down and nicely styled, something she didn't do often. Carly had helped her style her hair so it looked nice.

"We can eat as soon as Glen gets here," Ginny said, and then took a lot of ribbing from everyone about her boyfriend coming. "I'm going to sit in the kitchen if you all keep this up," she told them with mock sternness.

There was an open bottle of red wine on the coffee table between the sofas, along with empty glasses. Luke poured wine for everyone, except Randy, who had grabbed a beer from the fridge instead.

"To Christmas and family," Luke toasted, raising his glass. The others did also and the glasses clinked.

The tree lights sparkled, the fire crackled warmly, and the house smelled of evergreen and cooked turkey. Christmas music played on the stereo, and Colt sat with Carly by his side. He couldn't remember when he'd had a better Christmas.

Glen showed up with his hands full of presents and soon they all sat at the large kitchen table and enjoyed the feast that Ginny and the girls had prepared. Roast turkey, cornbread stuffing, homemade cranberry sauce, mashed potatoes, candied yams, and home canned green beans filled the table and their plates along with freshly baked buns and homemade butter. There was no formal dining room—just the big, kitchen table, and that suited everyone fine. At this Montana ranch, everyone was treated like family.

After they were all full from eating too much food, the women quickly put away the leftovers and cleaned up the dishes. Randy said his goodbyes, even though Luke and Ginny both asked him to stay. His mother lived in a nursing home just outside of Missoula and he would be visiting with her tomorrow. He thanked Ginny for supper, and carrying a bag full of presents given to him by the Brennan family, he left.

They all gathered in the sitting room with a plate full of cookies and wine glasses all around. Even Bree had joined the party and lay near the fire with her ears perked up with interest. Luke pronounced himself the official Santa Claus this year and began handing out gifts from under the tree.

Colt sat next to Carly, anxiously waiting for her to open his gift to her. He'd brought Andi along for her opinion when he purchased it. Now, as Carly opened a sweater from Ginny and a pair of leather ankle boots from Andi, Colt became nervous about his gift. What if she didn't like it? Maybe he should have bought her something more practical.

"Here's one hiding in the tree for Carly," Luke said, handing the small, rectangular box to her and winking at Colt.

Carly looked at the tag to see who it was from and then gave Colt a sly smile. "Mmm. Good things always come in small packages."

Colt felt like every eye was on him, when in fact, the others were busy opening their own presents. He held his breath as he watched Carly carefully slip off the glossy blue ribbon and the silver paper. Slowly, she lifted the lid of the black, velvet box and her eyes lit up when she saw what was inside.

"I love it!" she exclaimed. Sitting on the velvet was a teardrop shaped, London blue topaz stone set in white gold and hanging from a serpentine chain.

Colt let out the breath he'd been holding in.

"Help me put it on." Carly lifted the necklace from its case and handed it to Colt. She turned and lifted her hair so he could hook it around her neck. Now, everyone was watching him as he unhooked the clasp, placed the chain around Carly's neck, and tried to hook it again. His large fingers were awkward and clumsy, but he managed to finally hook it.

Carly dropped her hair and turned to Colt. "How does it look?"

Perfect. Just like you. Colt wanted to say out loud, but with everyone staring at them, he said shyly, "Very nice."

"It's my birthstone," Carly said, touching it gently with her fingertips. "It's lovely."

Andi had told Colt that it was her birthstone, but the reason he'd chosen it was because it matched the color of her eyes.

Carly wrapped her arms around Colt's neck and kissed him right there, in front of everyone. "Thanks, Colt. I love it."

"Aw," everyone said in unison. Colt felt his face heat up.

Carly had sent presents out ahead of her so she didn't have to pack them. She gave Colt a new, black cowboy hat with a silver band around it, and it fit perfectly. She told him she'd asked Andi to look inside one of his hats so she'd know the size. She'd given Andi a beautiful pair of garnet earrings, and Luke a very expensive pocket knife. For Ginny, she'd given her a beautiful turquoise necklace, and a pair of cufflinks for Glen. She'd even brought a gift for Randy that she'd hoped he'd like, even though she wasn't a big fan of his.

It was a wonderful evening. Glen left soon afterwards, but promised to return for the Christmas day brunch that Ginny always made for the family. Andi and Luke left after him. Ginny said goodnight, and even Bree went off to her pillow and fell asleep.

Colt reached for Carly's hand and they walked up the stairs together. He stopped when they were outside her room.

"I love my necklace," Carly said again, a small smile on her face. "You are such a sweetheart."

Colt looked from the stone lying nestled on her sweater up to her eyes. He'd been right. It matched them perfectly. Slowly, he lowered his head and placed a gentle kiss on her lips. Carly reached up and ran her hand across his strong jawline and down to the back of his neck. Shivers ran down Colt's spine.

Carly pulled away and smiled. "Goodnight, Colt."

"Goodnight."

She turned, walked into the bedroom, and flashing him her

most brilliant smile, she closed the door.

Colt grinned and headed to his own room.

* * *

The week after Christmas flew by for Carly as she helped Andi and Ginny with last minute preparations for the wedding. She also spent as much time as she could with Colt. They went riding several times on sunny days. Even though it was cold and she had to bundle up, she enjoyed riding and being with Colt. Paths around the pastures where kept plowed so they could get through with their trucks to feed the cattle. It gave her and Colt plenty of places to ride.

The day before the wedding, Luke, Randy, and Colt moved the furniture out of the sitting room and onto one side of the enclosed front porch. They were careful to leave plenty of space open for guests to walk through when they arrived at the front door. Tables and chairs that Ginny had rented came that day and the men set them up on the far side of the room, leaving space by the fireplace for the ceremony and a space open near the Christmas tree for the two-piece band that would be playing and a small dance floor. The women covered the tables with red table cloths and added white cloth napkins. Red and white rose centerpieces with candles were being delivered the day of the wedding for each table. There were also going to be roses placed among the evergreen boughs on the fireplace and down the staircase railing. It would be simple yet elegant. A perfect setting for a New Year's Eve wedding.

A red runner was placed on the floor leading from the foot of the stairs to the front of the fireplace. Two tall vases of flowers would be set on either side of it where Andi and Luke would be standing with the minister. Photos would be taken during and after the wedding, because Andi didn't want Luke to see her in her dress until the moment she walked down the stairs.

Ginny was busy in the kitchen making up several types of hor d'oeuvres that she could store in the fridge and her friends could bake before serving. Baked chicken with cream sauce and roast beef with gravy were on the menu for the wedding dinner along with roasted potatoes and asparagus tips. They set up a side table where the food would be kept warm and guests could serve themselves buffet style. Since they wanted the actual wedding to take place at eight o'clock, they were going to serve dinner first, and then have the ceremony. After that they would serve dessert and celebrate. It was an unusual twist to a traditional wedding, but it was how Andi and Luke wanted it.

The wedding day dawned bright and sunny despite the cold temperature outside. A light dusting of snow had fallen overnight and it glittered in the sunlight. Carly couldn't wait for the festivities tonight. It was not only her sister's wedding night, but also New Year's Eve, and Carly always loved the start of a new year. She loved the thought of everything starting over with a fresh start.

She quickly showered and dressed, and then ran downstairs to see what she could help with. Ginny was preparing the food, and her two friends, Mary and Sharon, were already in the kitchen helping her. Mary was older than Ginny and was slightly plump with short, gray hair while Sharon was tall, slender, and had a sensible blond bob. Both women were kind and easy going and Carly liked them immediately.

Carly found Andi in the sitting room placing white covers and red ribbons over each of the chairs. She began helping her and it didn't take long for them to finish. Including the immediate family and Glen, there were only going to be about thirty people at the dinner and wedding. Some were old friends of the family who lived on nearby ranches, a few were old school friends of Luke's, and the rest were Brennan cousins who still lived in the area. Andi and Carly were the only ones from their side. Over the past ten years, Andi had been so busy going to school, working, and taking care of Carly, that she'd lost touch with old school friends. They had no other relatives who were close to them, and any couples Andi had known had been connected to Derek. Carly knew Andi wasn't sad about it, though. She'd made a place for herself in the Brennan family, and she'd make new friends here.

The flowers arrived and Andi and Carly placed them on the tables and in the garland. Then the four-tiered wedding cake arrived and everyone stopped a moment admire it. It was a creamy white frosting with gorgeous red and white fresh roses running down it in a spiral motion. Everything was coming together beautifully and the anticipation of the wedding grew among the women.

At two in the afternoon, Andi, Ginny, and Carly headed down to Luke and Andi's cabin to meet up with the hair stylist. The woman came over from a hair salon in Superior and began right away on Ginny's hair, then Carly's, leaving Andi's hair for last. Ginny asked to have her hair pulled up in a simple French twist, and it looked very sophisticated on her. Carly's long hair was pulled up loosely with spiral tendrils falling about her face. She had small rhinestone clips in it that sparkled when she moved her head. Andi wanted a simple style for her long, thick red hair. It was pulled up loosely like Carly's, but curls still touched her shoulders. Her short veil would be placed near the back of her head and hang down over her shoulders.

The three women and the stylist all joked and giggled while their hair was being done. Carly painted her nails the same red color as her dress. Andi settled for clear gloss, as did Ginny. By the time their hair was ready, it was time for them to dress for the dinner before the ceremony. Andi and Carly had regular dresses they were wearing for dinner and then would change for the ceremony. The men were going to wear regular suits for dinner and then change into their tuxes. Ginny had a burgundy, knee-length, V-neck satin dress she would wear for the dinner and ceremony.

Andi stayed at the cabin to dress and wait for Luke, and Ginny and Carly rode back to the house, careful not to ruin their new hair styles. They brought along Andi's wedding dress which she was going to change into in Carly's room. The kitchen smelled delicious as Carly walked through it to the staircase. Bree lay on her pillow by the stairs, watching all the commotion, but staying out of it. Carly walked up to her room with the heavy wedding dress hung over her arm. The shower in the bathroom was running. She grinned and wondered what Colt would do if she walked in on him. "Better not," she told herself, laughing. She didn't want to ruin her hair. Instead, she went into her room and dressed, filled with anticipation for the night ahead.

Chapter Five

Colt came out of his bedroom just as Carly stepped out of hers. He stopped and stared at her with wide eyes.

Carly smiled at him mischievously. "What's the matter, Cowboy? Cat got your tongue?"

Colt slowly shook his head. "You look stunning," he finally managed to say.

Carly made a slow circle to show off her dress. It was aqua blue, sleeveless, with a scoop neck, tight in the bust and billowing out to a full skirt that fell high up on her slender thighs. She wore silver heels, but she still only came up to Colt's shoulder. Sparkling earrings dangled from her ears and the necklace Colt had given her glittered on her creamy skin.

"You'll be the prettiest woman in the room," Colt said.

Carly giggled. "Well, except for the bride, of course." She gave Colt the once over and grinned. "You don't look too shabby yourself." Carly walked over to him and ran her hand down the lapel of his navy suit. She raised red lips up to him in offering of a kiss.

Colt didn't resist. He dropped his lips to hers ever so lightly so as not to smudge her lipstick.

Carly giggled. "I'll let you get by with that kiss for now," she said. "But later, you're in for trouble."

Colt grinned.

Carly took his proffered arm and they walked down the length of the hallway to the front staircase and descended. Waiting for them below were Luke and Andi, Glen, Ginny, and Randy. The two musicians were already setting up their small amps and placing out their guitar and violin in the corner. Colt told Carly they were musicians who played regularly at The Depot and he nodded to them in greeting.

Soon, guests began to arrive. The minister arrived first and then a few of the local ranchers and their wives came next. The photographer, a sweet woman who dressed like a flower child from the 1970s, arrived and began setting up to snap photos of the dinner and the ceremony. The next hour was spent greeting guests, serving drinks, and passing out hor d'oeuvres. Carly met two of Colt's cousins who lived in Missoula and one second cousin who lived in Butte. They were all connected through the original two Brennan brothers who had homesteaded the ranch in the 1860s. It amazed Carly that the Brennan family tree was so big.

Dinner was set out and the guests served themselves and enjoyed the delicious meal. It wasn't long before Andi and Carly snuck away to change for the wedding and the men did as well. Luke changed in Ginny's room so he wouldn't see Andi until the actual ceremony.

The dishes were cleared and the wedding cake was placed on the table where the food had been served earlier. Luke joined the minister in front of the fireplace. Everyone downstairs waited in anticipation for the bride to arrive.

Upstairs, Carly helped Andi into her wedding dress and carefully zipped it up, mindful not to step on the train. She had already changed into her red gown. The photographer came in when Andi was dressed and snapped pictures of the sisters as Carly placed the veil on Andi's head. Mary had brought up the bouquets for both women, and more photos were taken of them and the flowers. Soon, they stood in the charming ranch bedroom, just the two of them, waiting for Randy to arrive and escort Andi downstairs.

"This is it," Carly said, barely able to contain her excitement. "This is really happening."

Andi smiled sweetly and nodded. "Yes, it is."

Carly grew serious. "Are you sure, Andi? Are you one-hundred percent positive that you want to spend the rest of your life with Luke?" It seemed like such a huge commitment to Carly. Even though she adored Luke, she couldn't imagine committing to anyone forever.

"Yes. I'm absolutely certain," Andi said calmly. "I've never been more certain about anything in my life as I am of this. I love Luke. I want to spend my life with him."

The sisters hugged, and then there was a knock on the door. "Are you ready?" a deep voice asked through the closed door.

Carly opened it and in walked Randy dressed in a black tux with a white shirt and bow tie. Carly's mouth dropped open. The rugged cowboy looked absolutely dashing. His brown hair was trimmed nicely, his broad shoulders stretched the limits of the tux jacket, and his brown eyes sparkled with delight when he looked at Andi. He walked right past Carly and over to Andi.

"You look like an angel. I'm so proud I get to be the one to escort you to Luke," Randy said warmly.

Carly stood there, staring at Randy, hardly able to believe that he was the same ranch hand who purposely ignored her during meals.

Randy turned and winked at Carly. "You look beautiful, Carly."

Carly smiled back. "Thank you." She was surprised Randy even acknowledged her.

Randy turned back to Andi and offered her his arm. "Shall we?"

Andi nodded.

Carly handed Andi her bouquet of red and white roses tied together with a thick, white ribbon. She picked up her own small bouquet and followed the two out the door into the hallway.

Colt waited at the top of the stairs. He turned as Carly came up behind him, and smiled appreciatively at her. Carly gave him a dazzling smile. He looked so handsome in his tux. *My, but these cowboys look good in tuxes.*

The music drifted upstairs. Carly quickly straightened Andi's dress train one last time and gave her sister a soft kiss on the cheek. Then she slipped her arm around Colt's and carefully descended the wide staircase with everyone's eyes upon her.

When Andi entered, the guests gasped at how lovely she looked and Carly noticed that Luke's eyes sparkled when he saw her coming toward him. It warmed Carly's heart to see such love emanating from Luke for her sister.

The ceremony was short, but lovely. Carly watched as Luke and Andi vowed to love, honor, and cherish each other, till death do they part. She glanced over at Colt a moment, and saw he was watching her, too. She smiled softly and he did also. She wondered if she'd ever be able to commit to a man as completely as Andi was to Luke. It was a daunting thought.

* * *

Colt watched Carly throughout the ceremony. He couldn't keep his eyes off of her. When he'd kissed her earlier, he'd done so gently, because he was afraid of smudging her lipstick. "Later, you're in for trouble," she'd told him. His heart had practically leapt from his chest. Was she just teasing or did she mean it?

As he listened to Luke and Andi's wedding vows, he

wondered if he'd ever be able to commit to a woman the way Luke was to Andi. The idea was scary, yet, when he looked at Carly, he could imagine them living a long and happy life together. Could she possibly be the one? She certainly made his heart skip at every turn and he was so darned attracted to her. But what could he ever offer her besides a ranch house and a lot of hard work? Carly needed more than that, he was certain.

After the ceremony ended there were congratulations all around. Champagne was served and everyone toasted the new bride and groom. Music began to play softly and the cake was served. Then, Luke and Andi danced their first dance as man and wife, and to everyone's surprise, it was to the Eagles song, "Desperado." Colt and Carly both smiled. They knew that it was the first song they'd ever danced together to, and it was special to them.

After Luke and Andi's first dance, others slowly joined them on the dance floor. Colt led Carly to the small space in front of the two-piece band and pulled her close. They danced smoothly, as if they'd danced together for years. Carly reached her arms up around Colt's neck and he dropped both arms down around her waist. Her hair tickled his neck as she laid her head on his chest. His spine tingled when he felt her fingers run through the back of his hair. Everything about Carly made his heart skip a beat. He wished she lived closer so he could see more of her. But most of all, he wished tonight would never end, and that he and Carly could dance like this forever.

For the next couple of hours, people danced and drank and had a wonderful time. Randy danced with Carly once, and Colt actually felt a tinge of jealousy when he saw Carly smile up at Randy and laugh. Luke danced a quick two-step with his new sister-in-law while Colt danced with Andi. They even line-danced to a couple of fast songs until everyone was laughing and feeling overheated.

Colt stepped away from the dance floor for only a minute to grab a beer for him and a glass of wine for Carly when he noticed his mom and Glen dancing together to a slow song. They made a nice-looking couple, and he was surprised when that thought hit him. He smiled. It was time that his mom found happiness again, and if that was with Glen, then so be it. Glen was a good man and he liked him. Things were changing, and he had to accept that. Luke was married. His mom was dating. But what about him? Would things change for him, too?

"There's my handsome cowboy," Carly said, walking over and snuggling up against him. She glanced in the direction he was looking. "They make a cute couple, don't they?" she asked dreamily.

Colt handed her the glass of wine. "Who?"

"Ginny and Glen, silly," Carly said. "Well, Luke and Andi, too, but we already knew they were cute together. But look at your mom. She looks so happy. And Glen, he's such a sweetie, too."

Colt wrapped his arm around Carly and pulled her closer. He gazed down at her and smiled. "I'm happy for them. But truth be told, I'm standing next to the prettiest woman in this room."

Carly's eyes twinkled and her full lips smiled up at him. "Are you flirting with me, Colt?"

Colt dipped his head and kissed her softly on the lips. "You bet I am."

Carly laughed.

A few of the couples left as the evening wore on, but the majority of people stayed until midnight. Sharon and Mary had finished working in the kitchen and had long since joined in on the party. Ten minutes before midnight, the two women filled champagne glasses for all and passed them around. Everyone gathered around the fireplace as the guitar player started counting down the last ten seconds of the year. When the clock struck midnight, everyone cheered, glasses clinked, the band started playing "Auld Lang Syne" and people were giving kisses all around.

Colt and Carly had been standing together, face to face when midnight struck. He clinked glasses with her, and then without hesitation, drew her in for a kiss. To his delight, she wrapped her arms tightly around his neck and kissed him back with a deep passion. When they pulled apart, she winked at him, and then left to give hugs all around to her sister, Luke, Ginny, Glen, and even Randy. Colt just stood there, in a daze, until Luke elbowed him and said, "Nice shade of lipstick you're wearing." Colt quickly drew the back of his hand across his lips and saw a gloss of deep red come off. He laughed. He didn't care. Tonight was the best night of his life, and he was going to enjoy every last minute of it.

* * *

Carly was in her room, waiting for the sound of Colt coming up the stairs. After midnight, the party began to disperse quickly. The band packed up and left, Andi and Luke headed to their home, and the guests drifted off into the cold, winter night. Carly had helped Ginny pick up glasses and stray plates and they'd covered and stored the last of the cake in the refrigerator. Colt had taken the covers off the chairs and then stacked the chairs up and out of the way. He'd also taken off all the table cloths and folded them. Finally, Ginny had told Carly to go along to bed and said they'd finish working in the morning. When Carly went upstairs, she'd heard Colt still moving tables around in the sitting room.

Now, she sat quietly on the bed and waited. She'd taken off her shoes, but she still wore her red dress. She'd also pulled the pins out of her hair and shook it to fall freely around her shoulders. She'd been flirting with Colt all night, and in truth, all week. She was not a tease. If she flirted, she meant it. And tonight, she could no longer resist Colt.

A few minutes later, she heard footsteps in the hallway, and then a door shut softly. Carly took a deep breath, walked quietly out of her room, and went to Colt's. Without knocking, she gently opened his door and slipped inside.

Colt stood beside his bed, pulling the bowtie from its knot. His jacket was off and hung over the chair of his desk. He looked up at Carly in surprise when she walked through the door.

"Thought you might want some help," she said softly.

She walked over silently and stopped in front of Colt, running her hands up his muscular chest. Reaching up, she unknotted his bowtie, then slid it out of his shirt collar and dropped it on the bed. Ever so slowly, Carly slid her hands down Colt's arms, stopping at his hands. She pulled one hand to her and undid his cuff buttons, then reached for the other hand and undid those. Running her hands again up his chest, she slowly began unbuttoning his shirt, her eyes gazing into his.

When Carly's fingers reached the last button, she gently pulled the shirt out of his pants and undid the last two buttons. Reaching up again, she slid her hands inside his shirt and slowly pushed the shirt off so it came loose of his arms and fell to the floor.

Colt stood still as Carly continued, tugging his T-shirt up out of his waistband and then running her hands under it, feeling the tight muscles of his back. Hungrily, she pushed his shirt up and he obliged by taking it off over his head and dropping it onto the floor.

Carly sighed when she looked at him.

Colt reached down to draw Carly to him, but she took a step

back and smiled up at him. "Hold on there a minute, Cowboy," she whispered. She turned around and slowly lifted her hair up, pulling it over one shoulder to lie on her chest. "Unzip me, please," she purred.

Colt reached up and gently unzipped her dress all the way down to the curve of her bottom. Underneath, all Carly wore was a pair of panties and a strapless bra. She heard a sharp intake of breath come from him, and she smiled.

Turning again to face him, Carly let the dress drop to the floor. Colt reached over and ran his strong hands down the curve of her waist. Carly arched her back and pressed her breasts against his bare chest. That was all it took. Colt pulled her close and dropped his lips to hers, kissing her deeply. She responded in kind.

Colt pulled back a moment and ran his hands through her hair, locking her eyes with his. "You're so beautiful," he said, his breathing ragged. "I've never wanted any woman as much as I want you right now."

Carly smiled up at him. "I'm yours," she said. And with that, they fell on the bed in a tangle of arms and legs, kissing, nipping, and caressing until neither one could hold back any longer.

* * *

Colt lay in his bed with Carly curled up beside him, her head on his shoulder and one arm and leg draped casually over him. He couldn't believe he'd just made love to her. He'd never been with a woman before who was so passionate and could drive him over the edge like she just had. Yet, he felt so completely comfortable with her. There was no awkwardness with Carly.

Colt felt her hand run gently over his chest. He reached for her hand and brought it to his lips, placing a soft kiss on her palm. Carly sighed, making Colt's heart swell.

"You're so different from anyone I've ever known," Carly said softly. "Always the gentleman, but so damned sexy."

Colt's eyes widened. Women in the past had called him cute, hot, and hunky, but he'd never in his life been called sexy. Nor had he ever felt he was.

"I wish I didn't have to leave the day after tomorrow," Carly said.

Colt wished she didn't have to either. "You could stay longer."

Carly snuggled in closer. "I can't. I have to be back at work."

Colt's heart sank. He wanted so much to spend more time with Carly.

"Wouldn't it be nice if we lived closer?" Carly asked.

Colt nodded. "I was just wishing that earlier tonight. Then we could be together more."

Carly tilted her head back and smiled up at Colt. "You were?"

"Yeah. But I can always come visit you. And you could come here, too."

Carly sighed. "I suppose. But it would be so much better if you lived near me. Have you ever thought of living anywhere else besides the ranch?"

Colt blinked. He'd never thought about living anywhere else. He'd grown up here, and had always worked on the ranch. What would he do in another place? Ranching was all he knew.

"You mean in Seattle?"

"Yeah. You could come and stay with me for a while. We have a small den with a pullout sofa. You and I could see more of each other then."

Colt chuckled. "Aw, you don't really mean that, do you? Don't you have a roommate? What would she say if I showed up there all of a sudden?"

Carly cocked her head and looked at him. "I do mean it. And yes, I have a roommate, but she's always working odd hours at the hospital and wouldn't even notice you there. It's just an idea. You should think about it."

Colt laid there a moment, deep in thought. Seattle. He'd never been there or anywhere for that matter. He wondered what it would be like to live somewhere other than the ranch. He wondered what it would be like to be able to see Carly all the time. The more he thought of it, the more the idea grew on him.

Carly rose up on one elbow and placed a kiss on the hollow of Colt's neck, causing chills to tickle his spine. She ran kisses up his neck, across his jawline, and to his lips where she kissed him deeply. Grinning at him, she pulled away. "Want to go for another ride, Cowboy?" she asked.

Colt was more than happy to oblige.

Chapter Six

Two days later, Colt drove Carly to the airport and watched her plane fly away with a heavy heart. His every dream came true with her spending the last three nights in his bed, and now she was gone.

Yesterday, Luke and Andi had flown to Florida to spend a week in Key West for their honeymoon. That meant Colt and Randy would be very busy for the next few days on the ranch without the extra help. But that wasn't going to be enough to keep Colt's mind off of Carly. In fact, he knew that while attending to all the mindless chores, he would be thinking of her constantly.

After leaving the airport, Colt stopped at a cell phone store and purchased his first phone and plan. He'd never really needed one before, because there was no reception at the ranch, but he'd decided that he wanted his own phone to talk to Carly privately. He could drive the short distance to The Depot where there was reception and talk to her. Emailing her was no longer enough. He wanted to hear her voice.

After purchasing the phone and setting up a plan, he headed home.

The next week was filled with endless chores that gave Colt too much time to think. As he lay in his bed alone each night, he thought about his life at the ranch and wondered if he'd be able to leave it. Luke had left for six years when he'd gone to college and worked in California. But, he had come home when their father was diagnosed with cancer and eventually passed away. Colt wasn't much for school, never had been, so he knew he wouldn't want to go to college like Luke had. He wondered what he could do to support himself in a big city like Seattle.

As Colt gazed around his room, he realized his life had been the same since he was a child. His furniture was different from when he was younger, but the room was the same. And he still lived in the same house as his mother. He'd never really thought of it before, but at the age of twenty-five, he had never experienced anything other than his small life here at the ranch. Maybe it was time he tried something new.

Each night after supper, Colt drove to The Depot, sat in his truck in the parking lot, and called Carly. Sometimes she was at home when he called, but most of the time she was out to dinner or at a bar with friends. She always sounded happy that Colt had called and she made a point of going off to a quiet place so they could talk, but Colt felt a twinge of jealousy that she was out having fun and he wasn't there with her. What if she met someone new and forgot all about him? He never voiced his concerns to Carly, because he didn't want to sound like a jealous idiot, but it weighed heavily on him. His feelings for her were so intense that he didn't want to wait to see her again. He had to see her very soon.

Luke and Andi came home, relaxed and tan from their honeymoon. Colt saw how happy they were together, and it made him even more heartsick that he wasn't with Carly. He wanted the same happiness his brother had. He was ready to be with only one woman, and that woman was Carly.

* * *

The night after Luke and Andi returned home, everyone sat at the table for supper like they did every night. Colt had made his decision and he decided that the sooner he told his family, the better. Mustering up all his courage, he spoke.

"I'm going to Seattle to see Carly."

Andi looked up at him with raised brows while Ginny looked at him curiously. Luke and Randy just kept eating, although Luke did ask, "You mean for a vacation? A week or two?"

Colt swallowed hard, but kept his tone steady. "No. I was thinking of living there for a while. Maybe a few months, maybe longer."

Everyone at the table stopped eating and stared at Colt.

Andi found her voice first. "You mean you're moving there? Where will you live?"

Colt cleared his throat. "Carly invited me to stay at the townhouse. She said there was a den with a pullout sofa bed that I could use."

Luke snorted. "That's ridiculous. You've never lived anywhere else but here. You don't belong in a place like Seattle." He shook his head and went right back to eating.

Randy kept his head down and continued eating. He looked like he'd rather be anywhere else but at the table.

Colt felt his face grow hot with anger. "You left the ranch and you did okay. Why shouldn't I try living somewhere different?"

Luke sat back in his seat and stared at Colt. "Are you going to go to college?"

"No. You know I don't like school."

"Then why in hell would you want to leave here?" Luke asked angrily. "You aren't trained for anything else. You earn a good living here, between your percentage of profits for cattle sales and the horses you raise and sell. No, it's out of the question. You're not going anywhere. You're needed here."

"Luke," Andi said quietly, shaking her head and placing her hand on his arm.

Colt's heart pounded as his anger exploded. "It's not up to you to tell me what I can and can't do. I think it's time I go and try something else. I'm twenty-five years old. I can do whatever I want."

"Boys," Ginny interjected. "Settle down. There's no need to get angry. We can discuss this calmly."

Luke frowned at his mother. "Are you okay with him leaving the ranch?"

Ginny took a deep breath. "You know I'd love for both of my boys to be here, but Colt has to make his own decisions about his life, just like you did, Luke. If he thinks he needs to try something new, then we all have to support his decision."

Luke glared at Colt. "I think you're crazy. You're going to run off after a woman who will probably dump you in three months. Then what will you do?"

"Luke!" Andi exclaimed.

Colt stood and slammed his fist on the table. The plates and silverware jumped and clanged. "Don't talk about Carly like that. You don't know her the way I do."

"I know her well enough to know that she gets bored with her boyfriends quickly," Luke yelled back. He turned to Andi. "You know how your sister is. Tell him."

Colt stared at Andi.

Andi sighed. "Colt, it's true that Carly isn't very good with commitment. You have to know that before you change your whole life for her."

"I don't care what any of you say. I'm going to Seattle," Colt yelled. He stormed out of the room and slammed the back door.

* * *

Colt sped out of the driveway and onto the highway, his heart pounding in his chest. He finally made himself slow down when his tires slid on the icy road. It wasn't long before he saw the lighted up sign for The Depot, and he exited the highway and parked in the near-empty parking lot.

Taking a couple of calming breaths, he sat there in the heated cab and pulled out his phone. Carly's phone rang three times before she answered.

"Hi, sexy Cowboy. What are you up to?"

Colt smiled. It didn't matter that he'd just had a fight with his brother. Carly always made him feel better. "I just wanted to hear your sweet voice," he told her.

"Oh, you're such a cutie," Carly said. "How did I ever get by without you?"

Colt hoped she meant that. He heard what sounded like jazz music in the background and wondered if she was out again with friends. He put it out of his mind. "I have to ask you a question."

"Shoot," Carly said, then giggled.

"Did you mean it when you said I should come out there and live in the townhouse with you?" Colt took a deep breath and waited for her answer. He didn't have to wait long.

"Of course, I meant it. Why? Are you really going to move here?" she asked, her voice rising with excitement.

"Yes, I want to. If you want me there."

"Whoo whee!" Carly squealed. "My cowboy! Yes, I want you here. When are you coming? I can hardly wait."

Colt sighed, relieved. He'd been afraid she'd already found someone new and wouldn't want him to come out to Seattle. Now more than ever, he knew for sure that all he wanted was to be with Carly.

"As soon as I can leave the ranch," he told her.

"That's wonderful," Carly said. "I'll warn Beth that you're

coming so she won't be surprised when you show up. Just come as soon as you can, okay?"

"Okay. I'll call you tomorrow night," Colt said.

"I'll be thinking of only you until then," Carly said seductively.

Colt grinned as they hung up. He couldn't wait to see Carly. He sat there awhile, thinking about their conversation and then remembered the music he'd heard in the background. It seemed like Carly went out a lot, but that was probably because she didn't want to sit home alone. Once he was there, they could spend all their time together.

Together, Colt thought. He loved how that sounded.

* * *

Carly's phone rang again and she smiled when she saw it was Andi. She clicked the button, but before she could say hello, Andi said, "What have you done?"

Carly frowned. "What kind of a hello is that?"

"Okay. Hello, Carly. Now, what is this about you inviting Colt to live with you?"

Carly sighed. She'd been having a fun night with her friends, and then had the good news about Colt coming. Now her sister wanted to ruin her fun. *Typical.*

"Geez, Andi. You sure know how to turn a good night into a downer. What's the problem? Colt's just going to stay with me for a while."

"Carly, it's not that simple. Colt made it sound like he was moving to Seattle. Forever. And from what I can tell, he's doing it just to be with you."

"Why is that so bad?" Carly asked, offended. "What's wrong with a guy wanting to be with me?"

Andi sighed. "That's not the point, Carly. The point is, Colt has fallen hard for you, and now he wants to be with you. He's giving up a lot to move out there, in case you didn't know. Do you love Colt? Is he the guy you want to be with for the rest of your life?"

Carly rolled her eyes. Her sister always made such a big deal out of nothing. "I don't know if I love him, but I really do like him. How am I supposed to figure out if we are meant to be together if I never get to see him? If Colt comes here, we can get to know each other better."

"I have a feeling you two know each other pretty well, otherwise Colt wouldn't leave the ranch to follow you out there."

"Hey, you're supposed to be on my side. You're my sister, remember?" Carly said, angrily. "You act like I'm trying to ruin Colt's life. He's a big boy. He can make his own decisions. I only asked him if he'd consider coming out here for a while so we can be together more."

"Carly, I am on your side. It's just that sometimes you forget that men are so drawn to you, they will do stupid things just to be with you. And sweetie, I'm sorry for having to say this, but you don't have the best track record with men. You lose interest after a few months. I just don't want to see that happen to Colt. He's such a sweet guy, and he's not exactly worldly, you know?"

"Hey. This coming from the woman who broke off a three-year relationship to marry a man she knew for only three weeks," Carly said snidely.

There was a long pause on the other end of the line and Carly suddenly felt bad for what she'd said. "Listen, Andi. I didn't mean that. I'm sorry. It's just that you don't know what's going on between Colt and me. I really like him, and I know he really likes me. Is it so wrong that we want to explore this relationship further?"

"No, it's not wrong. I just hope you'll be completely upfront with Colt and not lead him on."

"I'm not trying to lead him on," Carly whined. "He said he wanted to spend more time with me and that's why I invited him out. Who knows? Maybe we are meant to be together, eventually. That's what we're going to find out."

"Just be careful, okay?" Andi said. "He's really got it bad for you."

"I'm not going to lead him on," Carly insisted. "I really care about him, Andi. He's unlike any guy I've ever known."

"Okay," Andi said, sounding defeated. "I didn't mean to imply that you would hurt Colt intentionally. I just don't think you know how hard men fall for you sometimes. I love you, Little Sister. You know that, don't you?"

"I know," Carly said softly. "I know you're just looking out for Colt. I don't intend on hurting him. I'll be as upfront with him as possible. I love you, too, Andi."

After Andi hung up, Carly sat back and thought about their conversation. She had to admit, Andi was right. She hadn't ever had a relationship last longer than a few months. But that didn't mean she and Colt weren't good for each other. *Andi's just making a lot out of nothing. It's not like Colt is coming out here to propose marriage.*

"Hey, Carly. You coming back out here to dance, or what?"

Carly's friend, Adam, was waving at her to follow him back into the main area of the bar where the music was playing. Carly smiled. Enough drama for one night. It was time to have fun.

"I'm coming," she called.

Chapter Seven

Colt worked in the barn feeding grain and fresh hay to the horses in the stalls. It was late afternoon, and he'd managed to avoid Luke all day by eating breakfast and lunch long after Luke had finished. He didn't want to argue with his brother again. He'd made up his mind to leave, and that was that.

Just as Colt finished his work, he heard footsteps coming up behind him. He stood straighter and squared his shoulders. He knew instinctively that it was Luke.

"Can we talk a minute?" Luke asked, stopping directly behind Colt.

Colt turned. Luke was a bit taller than him, and built broader. He was all muscle, just like Colt, from the physical demands put upon them running a cattle ranch. Colt had always had a good relationship with his older brother and he'd always been fine with the fact that Luke ran the ranch and he took orders from him. But today, he didn't want to be told again that he was an idiot for going to Seattle. And if it came down to a fight, he was more than ready.

"I'm not talking if you aren't listening," Colt said with determination.

Luke's brows rose. "I didn't come in here to fight with you. I just want to find out what's going on."

Colt leaned the pitchfork against the stall and turned back to

Luke. "I already told you what's going on. I'm going to Seattle for a while to stay with Carly."

Luke nodded. "Okay. If that's what you want."

Colt just stood there, dumbfounded. He hadn't expected Luke to give in so easily.

"When do you plan on leaving?" Luke asked

"I guess as soon as I can."

Luke nodded again. He put his hands in his jacket's pockets. "Is there anything I can say to make you change your mind?"

Colt crossed his arms. *Here it comes.* "Nope."

"I just want to make sure this is what you want," Luke said evenly. "It means more to me than you just working on the ranch. You're good at what you do here. I don't know a better guy around here who can break a horse like you do. And you're excellent at calving time when there are problems. This is what you do. This is who you are. It's hard for me to believe you'd be happier somewhere else."

Colt dropped his arms and slipped his hands in his jeans' pockets. He'd expected an argument from Luke, not compliments. "It won't be forever," he said. "I just want to try something different, that's all."

"And it's about being with Carly, right?"

Colt narrowed his eyes. "Yeah. So."

Luke chuckled. "Don't get your shirt tied in a knot. I'm just asking. Listen, Colt. I know how it feels to want nothing more than to be with the woman you love. I get it. And by the sound of it, Carly is looking forward to you coming there, too. I just want to make sure this is what you want."

Colt frowned. "How do you know what Carly thinks about this?"

"Andi talked to her last night." Luke lifted his hands to stop Colt from protesting. "And don't go yelling at me for butting into your business. It was Andi's idea to call her, not mine.

Andi said she's serious about you, too, to an extent."

"To an extent?"

"Colt, you know as well as I do that Carly likes to have fun and she isn't ready to be tied down. If I'm wrong, then I apologize, but she even said as much to Andi last night. So, I just hope you aren't going out there with unrealistic expectations about where a relationship with Carly may go."

Colt crossed his arms again. He was tired of people telling him what Carly was like. They didn't know her as well as he did. She wasn't as flighty as they made her out to be.

Luke put his hand on Colt's shoulder. "Enough said. You do what you need to do. Can you wait to go until I find someone to fill in for you? Randy and I can't do all the work alone."

Colt nodded. "I know Randy's cousin, Jake, is looking for work. He was doing construction, but he hated it. He's been working ranches as long as I have."

"I'll ask Randy about him. Can you give me a week or two? That way you can show whoever we hire what you do on a daily basis."

"Sure," Colt said.

Luke took a step back. "You realize that your share of the yearly earnings will be less if you leave. Since you won't be working the ranch, and we have to pay someone else, your profits will be a lot less."

Colt nodded. He, Luke, and his mother each owned a third of the ranch and earned their money by splitting the yearly profits. Some years were good, some not so good. But it usually gave Colt a nice income, especially since he didn't have to pay rent or bills. "I understand," he told Luke.

"Will you try to come back in the spring to help move the cattle up to the summer pasture? I really need your help with that," Luke said.

"I'm sure I can do that."

"Good."

Luke turned on his heel and walked to the back door of the barn. He stopped a moment, and then turned around again. "I hope things work out the way you want them to, Colt. I really mean that. And if they don't, I won't say a word, okay? I'll just be happy to have you back here."

Colt nodded and watched as Luke walked out the door.

* * *

Two weeks later, Colt was on his way to Seattle. All he'd brought along was a large duffle bag packed with his clothes and personal possessions. He left everything else behind. He wasn't sure how much room he'd have, or how long he'd stay, so he didn't bring too much.

Luke had hired Randy's cousin, Jake Olson, and Colt had spent a few days working with him so he'd learn his daily routine. Jake was twenty-six, built similar to Colt, with short brown hair and brown eyes. He was quiet and very serious, sometimes not even reacting to Colt's jokes. But he was a good worker and seemed grateful to have a full-time job near his home. He had a wife and a baby on the way, so being close to home was important to him.

Leaving home this morning was tougher than Colt had anticipated. Andi was practically in tears as she gave him a hug goodbye, and his mom, usually the strong one, also held back tears. Luke had slapped him on the back and wished him well, but Colt could tell that his heart wasn't in it. By the time Colt bent down to pet Bree goodbye, there were tears in his own eyes. He'd lived here his entire life, and he was suddenly questioning if he could live anywhere else. But his desire to see Carly was strong, and that was what made him hop into his truck and head out.

Colt had left early so he didn't have to rush his drive to Seattle. He knew he could easily make it in one day. He felt like it was a good omen that the day was sunny and highway 90 was clear. His anxiety about leaving slowly melted away with each mile he drove, and he grew excited by the fact that he would soon be able to hold Carly in his arms.

It was a Monday, so he hadn't called Carly all day, because he didn't want to bother her at work. He'd talked to her the night before to let her know he was on his way and she'd squealed with excitement. Andi had set up the map directions on his phone to take him directly to the townhouse, so he knew exactly where he was going. He figured he'd call Carly when he was getting closer. She'd be off of work by then and waiting for him.

The drive through the mountains around Coeur d'Alene was, thankfully, uneventful and he was relieved there was no ice on the roads. His heavy pickup truck handled well on ice, but he didn't really want to encounter any today. He was eager to get to Seattle and didn't want anything to slow him down.

He stopped for gas several times along the way and the closer he got to Seattle, the warmer the temperature became. When he'd left the ranch, it was twenty-five degrees. As he came closer to Seattle, it had risen to the high forties. He'd shed his heavy coat and slipped on a fleece jacket instead. One thing he wasn't going to miss was all the snow and the cold temperatures in Montana.

Just outside of Seattle, Colt stopped for gas and grabbed a fast food burger. It was early evening and the sun had long since gone down. He wasn't too comfortable about driving in heavy traffic in a big city after dark, so he wanted to make sure he wouldn't need to make any stops. Mustering his courage for the last leg of his journey, he continued on.

The roads grew busier and the lights grew brighter all around him. Colt drove through what he thought must be suburbs, and as the traffic grew more congested, he figured he was getting closer to downtown Seattle. The two lane highway turned into four, and then six lanes. Cars sped by him as if he were a turtle, even though he was driving over the speed limit. Everywhere around him, Colt saw sparkling lights. He thought it would have been beautiful if he hadn't been so terrified by the heavy traffic whipping past him. He hung on tight to his steering wheel and tried his best to keep up with the flow of traffic while watching the signs above.

Still on highway 90, Colt drove across one bridge, and then a little while later, a much longer bridge. He tried to see the water below, but all he saw was darkness. He followed the signs to highway 5 north and then followed that until his phone told him to exit. He then began to drive through a maze of streets. The roads were hilly, and he had a hard time reading the street signs in the dark. As he drew near a cluster of homes that all looked alike, his phone told him he had arrived at his location.

Colt stopped the truck in the middle of the quiet neighborhood street and looked around him. He had no idea which one of these homes was Carly's. They all looked alike in the dark.

A horn honked and startled Colt. He looked around for a place to park, but didn't see one. He drove on, circling the block, looking for somewhere to park. Finally, he pulled into what looked like a driveway so he wouldn't block the street, put his truck in park, and called Carly.

Carly answered on the third ring. Loud noise came over the phone making it difficult for Colt to hear her. Finally, the noise grew quieter and Carly said, "Colt! Are you here yet?"

Colt smiled. Maybe she had the television on. "Yeah. I'm somewhere near your townhouse, but I don't know which one is yours and I can't seem to find a parking spot."

Carly giggled. "Silly. You have to park on the street. Give me a few minutes and I'll be right home. I can show you which house is mine."

Colt frowned. *She isn't home?* "Where are you?"

"I'm just a few minutes away at a little pub with my friends. We had dinner here. I'll be right there." She hung up.

Colt sat there a moment, wondering why Carly was out with friends instead of at home. He looked at his truck's dash. It was almost ten o'clock. That meant it was nine o'clock Seattle time. He played with the buttons a moment and reset the time. Then he sat back again and looked around. Except for streetlights and a few lit up windows, it was dark out. He couldn't see much of anything.

Colt felt disappointed. He'd thought that Carly would be excited about his coming and be waiting at home for him. Maybe that was silly to expect, but it made him feel bad. He'd been so anxious to see her. Maybe she didn't feel the same way. Doubt crept up inside him as he sat there. He wondered if he'd made a mistake coming here. Were Luke and Andi right? Would Carly just dump him after a few months? A few weeks?

A loud knock on the window made Colt jump and he turned quickly to look. There stood Carly with a big grin. Colt rolled down the window.

"Hey, Cowboy. You lost?" Carly stepped up on the truck's runner board and reached inside the window, pulling Colt to her and planting a kiss on his lips. Colt's heart flipped. He shouldn't have doubted her. She was happy to see him.

"You can't park here," she said matter-of-factly. "There's a spot behind my car just up the street. I'll wait right here for you."

Carly jumped off the runner and moved out of the way so Colt could back out. In the headlights, he noticed she was wearing the same white coat she'd worn in Montana along with a tight pair of jeans and high-heeled ankle boots. Her hair was loose and blowing in the cold breeze. Colt sighed as he drove the truck up the street and parked in the empty spot. She was as gorgeous as always and she was happy to see him. That was all that mattered.

Colt grabbed his heavy duffle bag out of the truck's back seat, slung it over his shoulder, and then headed to where Carly stood. She slipped her arm around his and led him down the driveway into a courtyard.

Colt looked around as they walked on the circular path around the courtyard. Small, decorative street lamps lit the way. There was an oval patch of grass in the center and large pots all around that he supposed were filled with flowers in the summer. Two long buildings flanked the courtyard and there was another grassy area straight ahead with a fence bordering it. The buildings each looked like four smaller homes connected to each other with peaked roofs. They were alternately painted light cream and dark beige. Except for the two different colors, they all looked the same to Colt.

Carly led him to the last door on the left. There was a small, cement porch with an overhang. A collection of pots of various sizes sat near the door for flowers. An embossed number four was attached on the siding beside the door. Carly pulled out her keys and unlocked the door.

"We're home," she said cheerfully.

Colt followed her inside, directly into a living room. He watched as Carly turned on a lamp that sat on a glass-topped table between a cream colored chair and sofa. There were soft blue throw pillows on the sofa as well as a blue fleece blanket lying on the back. A glass-topped coffee table sat in front and a large, blue and cream rug lay under it all. Even with the dark wood floors throughout the living room, dining room, and kitchen, the place looked completely feminine with all the light colored furniture, glass tables, and accessories. Colt wondered how he'd fit into such a womanly place.

"You can throw your duffle bag in here," Carly said, walking a short way down the hall and pointing to a door.

Colt followed Carly and looked inside the room. She'd been right. It was very small with only a beige sofa on one wall and a small desk on the other. He dropped his bag on the carpeted floor by the sofa and slipped off his coat as well. Not knowing where to hang it, he laid it on the sofa along with his hat. When he walked back out into the living room, Carly had already taken off her coat and was standing near the sofa. She smiled seductively and walked up to him, running her hands up his chest.

"Hmm, I missed you," she said. Her arms went up around Colt's neck, pulling him down to her. Their lips met. Colt felt the passion rise quickly as his tongue explored Carly's mouth. She tasted lightly of wine, but she tasted delicious to him. It had only been a month since he'd held her and that had felt like an eternity.

Carly pulled back and quickly undid the buttons on Colt's shirt, pulling it off of him and tossing it on the floor. Then she tugged on the ends of his white T-shirt so he pulled it over his head. This, too, ended up on the floor. She ran her hands greedily over his taut muscles and her eyes sparkled when she looked up at him.

Colt's heart pounded as his hands explored Carly's curves. After another deep kiss, his passion-induced fog cleared a little and he looked around. "What about your roommate?" he asked.

"She's not here. Beth is working overnights all this week," Carly said as she tugged at Colt's belt buckle. "Eleven to seven. We have this place all to ourselves and can make all the noise we want."

Colt's pulse quickened. He let Carly unbuckle his belt and unbutton the top button of his Levi's.

"Come on, Cowboy," Carly said with a wicked smile. She grasped his hand and pulled him down the hallway. "Let's go riding."

Colt happily followed Carly into her bedroom. He couldn't have imagined a better first night in Seattle than this.

Chapter Eight

Colt awoke the next morning to the light filtering in through the closed blinds over the bedroom window. He turned and saw the pillow next to his was empty, and frowned. Then he remembered that Carly had kissed him lightly on the lips an hour earlier before leaving for work. He'd meant to get up then, but had fallen back to sleep.

Colt rolled over and looked at the clock on the nightstand. Eight-thirty. He sat straight up in bed. Eight-thirty! He hadn't slept that late in his life. At home he was up at five-thirty each morning and eating breakfast by six. And here he was, his first day in Seattle, already sloughing off.

He ran his hands over his face and through his hair. A slow smile spread across his lips as he remembered last night. Carly had proved to him over and over that she was happy he was here. There was no longer any doubt in Colt's mind as to whether he'd made the right decision to move here. Carly had made it perfectly clear with her actions last night that he had.

Colt slipped out of bed and went into the attached bathroom. As he washed his hands, he noticed a note on the counter in Carly's flowery handwriting. "Come have lunch with me," it read. Colt couldn't think of anything else he'd rather do.

He walked back into the bedroom, found his jeans, and slipped them on. Looking around, he couldn't find his shirts, and then he remembered they'd been left on the floor in the living room. He quickly made up the bed as best he could and placed the ruffled throw pillows on it, although he was sure it wasn't done right. Carly's room was about as girly as it could be. The bedspread was puffy white cotton with pink stripes and the sheets were a soft pink. The headboard and nightstand were white and there was a flowery pillow on the bay window seat. Teddy bears and frilly-dressed dolls sat on the seat. A white dresser was on the opposite wall next to a small desk, and an oval, full-length mirror trimmed in silver stood in the corner. A miniature crystal chandelier hung in the middle of the room, over the bed. Carly's clothes were draped over furniture and some were left in a pile on the floor, but other than that, the room was neat.

Colt's stomach growled as he walked down the short hallway to retrieve his shirts. He thought he smelled coffee brewing and his taste buds came alive. Sunshine poured into the dining room through the patio window, practically blinding him, but he spied his T-shirt on the floor and bent to pick it up. When he rose, his eyes met a set of deep brown eyes with gold flecks. Colt gasped.

"You must be Carly's cowboy," a soft voice said from the sofa.

Colt stared, his eyes wide. A woman was curled up into the corner of the sofa, her legs pulled up against her and her hands hugging a large, green mug. Her thick, dark brown hair hung straight and skimmed her shoulders. She was dressed in blue scrubs. Her face was fresh looking, free of makeup, and her eyes were framed in thick, dark lashes and shapely brows. Her full lips smiled slightly in a teasing way as her dark eyes stared back at Colt.

Colt swallowed hard as he tried to regain his composure. He stood up straight and smiled, forgetting that he was only wearing jeans. "Yes, I guess so. I'm Colt."

Beth's smiled grew wider. "Colt, huh? Funny, but you don't look like a baby horse."

A confused look crossed Colt's face and suddenly he remembered he wasn't wearing a shirt. Clumsily, he slipped his T-shirt over his head. "Sorry about that," he said, feeling his face and neck grow hot.

Beth laughed lightly as she stood up and walked over to Colt. "I've seen more skin than that in my line of work," she said. She offered her hand to Colt. "I'm Bethany Owens, but you can call me Beth."

Colt raised his hand and gently took Beth's. Her handshake was firm, but her hand felt soft. He noticed she was slightly taller than Carly, but the baggie scrubs she wore disguised her build. Colt liked her smile though. It was warm and welcoming. "Nice to meet you, Beth."

"Nice to meet you, too, Colt." She cocked her head. "So, is that your real name or a nickname?"

"It's a nickname, but it's what everyone calls me. My real name is Cole."

Beth looked like she was considering his name, and then nodded. "Cole. I like that. But if you like being called Colt, then that's what I'll call you."

Colt watched as she made her way to the kitchen. Her scrubs made a swishing sound as she walked. There was a long counter with stools that separated the kitchen from the dining room, but otherwise, the entire area was open. The tall ceiling gave the rooms an airy feeling. A light oak dining table and chairs sat behind the sofa and near the large patio doors. The kitchen was to the left of that. Colt took a step toward the kitchen and nearly tripped on his plaid shirt, lying on the floor. He quickly picked it up, embarrassed that his clothes were in the living room. When he looked up, he saw Beth staring at him as she stood by the kitchen sink.

"Sorry about the clothes," he said.

Beth just shrugged as if it were no big deal. Colt wondered if finding men's clothing on the floor was a typical occurrence around here. He didn't really like that thought.

"There's fresh coffee made," Beth said, nodding towards the coffeemaker. "It's decaffeinated. Sorry. I didn't want a caffeine high when I went to bed."

"Oh, that's okay," Colt said. "Thanks."

"There's not much around here for food, though. I have some hard-boiled eggs in the fridge that you're welcome to, and some bread for toast. Carly eats all her meals out, so I'm the only one who buys groceries."

Colt didn't realize Carly only ate out. He was used to a fridge full of food at home, so he hadn't thought there wouldn't be any here. "I can pay you for the food," he said, trying to be a good guest.

Beth waved her hand through the air. "Don't worry about it. If you end up staying, we can work something out about the food."

"Okay." Colt watched as she rinsed out her mug and set it in the dishwasher. Beth turned and yawned, covering her mouth with her hand. Colt smiled. "It must be hard working all night."

"It's not so bad," Beth said, walking over to Colt. "I just sleep all day. My shifts change a lot. Next week I'll be working three to eleven. Sometimes I work seven in the morning until three. You get used to it."

"I suppose you do," Colt said.

"The mugs are in the cupboard by the stove. There's milk in the fridge if you need it for your coffee," Beth told him.

"Okay. Thanks."

"So, do you have plans for your first day in Seattle?"

"Carly left a note asking me to meet her for lunch, so that's where I'm headed later," Colt said.

"Do you know where she works?"

Colt stood there a moment, thinking. He didn't have her work address or directions. "No," he answered sheepishly. "I guess she forgot to tell me where. I suppose I can call her."

Beth put out her hand. "Here. Give me your phone and I'll type in the address for you. Then you don't have to bother her at work."

Colt remembered his phone was still in his coat pocket in the den. "Just a minute." He walked quickly to the small room, set down the shirt he was holding, and grabbed his phone. He turned to walk out of the room and nearly bumped into Beth as she stood in the doorway.

"Oops. Sorry. Here's the phone."

Beth chuckled. She quickly typed in the address to his map app and then handed it back to Colt. "It's only about a fifteen minute drive down to the gallery where Carly works, if traffic is good. It's downtown, near Pike Place Market."

"Thanks," Colt said, smiling. "I really appreciate the help."

"Not a problem." Beth turned to leave.

"If I shower, will it bother you?" he asked.

Beth turned. "Nope. I'll be dead to the world." Her face broke out in a wide smile. "It's nice meeting you, Colt. I hope you stay for a while."

"I hope I do, too," Colt said, wondering why she'd question whether or not he'd stay long.

"Oh, and Colt?"

"Yeah?"

Beth gave him a mischievous grin. "Your T-shirt's on inside-out."

Colt looked down and felt the back of his neck for the tag. Sure enough, it was hanging out. When he looked up, Beth had already disappeared into her bedroom. Colt grinned. *Well, I couldn't have embarrassed myself more than I've already done.* Hopefully, it was all uphill from there.

* * *

Colt took Beth up on her offer and ate a couple of the hard-boiled eggs and some toast and drank a mug of coffee. He rinsed his dishes and put them away in the dishwasher the way he'd seen Beth do. He'd never done much in the way of housekeeping before. His mom had always done all the cooking and cleaning, as well as the laundry, so he had a lot to learn.

He unpacked some of his things and, unsure as to which room to hang his clothes in, he decided to place them in the small closet in the den. Then he went into Carly's bathroom and shaved and showered, being careful not to leave a mess. Carly's bathroom counter was filled with hair products and makeup, so he had to be very careful not to knock all the bottles over. Colt usually had the bathroom at home to himself except when guests stayed, like Andi last summer and Carly more recently. Now, he'd have to get used to sharing, which meant being careful not to upset Carly by being messy.

Colt dressed as he usually did in Levis and a cotton, long-sleeved shirt with a T-shirt underneath. Looking at the weather on his phone, he saw it was forty-two degrees out, so he wore a black, fleece jacket instead of his heavy coat. After slipping on his boots and hat, he headed out to his truck. He locked the door behind him, but wondered how he'd get back in when he came home. He'd have to ask Carly for a key.

Following the directions on his phone, Colt was soon out of the neighborhood and driving down highway 99 toward downtown Seattle. The traffic was heavy, and it made Colt nervous. Cars swerved in and out of traffic all around him and he felt like he was constantly on the verge of hitting one.

Driving around Missoula, even at its busiest, hadn't prepared him for city driving.

He crossed a bridge over a waterway and noticed boats docked in a small harbor. A little while later, he drove through a tunnel and soon he saw open water to his right and a tall Ferris wheel straight ahead in the distance. He had trouble keeping his eyes on the road, he was so mesmerized by the scenery around him. He forced himself to watch the road and the signs so he wouldn't miss his exit for the art gallery where Carly worked.

Finally, he turned off the highway and headed slowly through the maze of streets until he spotted the building with the sign that said Bayside Gallery. He had to drive up and down the block several times before he found a parking space, and when he did, he had to walk two blocks back to the gallery.

Walking along in the cold afternoon, Colt looked around him with interest. People dashed in and out of shops with arms full of bags. He walked past restaurants, coffee shops, dress shops, and hair salons. Tourists with cameras hanging around their necks walked by in groups. No one seemed to notice the tall cowboy walking among them.

The large glass window outside Bayside Gallery displayed an arrangement of sculptures. Colt stopped a minute to look inside. He smiled when he saw Carly, dressed in a tight, knee-length skirt, black sweater, and high-heeled shoes. Her long hair was pulled up into a ponytail, but still hung down past her shoulders. Colt thought she looked sexy and sophisticated. She was talking seriously to a man and woman as they all stared at a big sculpture in the middle of the store.

Colt entered through the glass door and a chime sounded, announcing his arrival. An older man in a dark suit standing behind the counter on the right wall looked up at him curiously and nodded. Colt smiled back and walked directly over to

Carly, who had turned to see who'd entered the shop.

"Hey, good looking. Ready for lunch?" Colt said when he drew close to Carly.

Carly frowned a little and spoke quietly to the couple beside her. "Excuse me a moment." Then she herded Colt a short distance away. "I can't go, yet. I'm with a customer right now."

Colt's smile faded. He wondered if he'd embarrassed her. "Sorry. It's noon, so I thought I came at the right time."

Carly's eyes darted between the customers and Colt. "Just give me a few more minutes and then I'll be ready," she whispered. "Why don't you take a walk and look around outside? I'll come out when I'm done."

"Oh. Okay." Colt turned and walked out of the gallery with less enthusiasm than he'd had coming in. He hoped he hadn't made her look bad in front of the man in the suit who he assumed was her boss. He had to be more careful how he acted. He wasn't on the ranch anymore.

Walking down the street, his steps a little heavier, Colt looked in shop windows with little interest. Some shops had "Help Wanted" signs in the windows. This reminded him that he needed to look for a job soon. He didn't want to be the only one living in the townhouse who wasn't working.

The damp wind cut through him as he made his way down another street in the direction of the bay. He pushed his hands into his pockets to ward off the chill. Even though the temperature was in the forties, he hadn't realized how damp the air was here. He made a mental note to wear his heavier coat the next time he came down near the water.

Walking down another block and around the corner, he nearly ran into a woman carrying a grocery bag out an automatic sliding door. Instinctively, he tipped his hat and said, "Sorry, ma'am," as he stopped to let her pass. She stared at him strangely, but kept on walking. Colt sighed. He couldn't seem to do anything right today.

Colt walked past the door and looked up above the awning that shaded the long row of windows on the store. It read O'Hannan's Market. When he looked down again, he saw a "Help Wanted" sign in the window. Colt stopped a moment and stared at the market. It took up half the block in length and looked very busy inside. He wondered what type of job was open here, but didn't have time to go in and inquire. He noted the name of the street and then kept walking, heading back to the gallery.

Carly was waiting outside for him when he returned. She'd slipped on a long, black wool coat and looked very chic and stylish. Colt felt self-conscious about how casually dressed he was. But his worry faded when Carly smiled at him, her eyes sparkling.

"Sorry about earlier," she said, slipping her arm around his and leading him down the street. "I have to act all grown up and sophisticated in front of the clients. They were trying to decide if they wanted buy that five thousand dollar sculpture. The good news is, they did."

Colt stopped and stared at her. "Five thousand dollars?"

Carly giggled. "Crazy, huh? But that's what people will pay. Andi's original paintings sell for five to eight thousand, so it's not so unusual."

Colt nodded. He remembered when Andi had sold an original painting to Glen before he'd started dating his mother. He'd paid eighty-six hundred for it. It sounded like an awful lot of money to him for something to decorate your home.

"I'm starved. Let's go eat," Carly said, leading him into a small pub.

They sat in the crowded pub and ate sandwiches and seafood chowder. Colt ate all of his and half of Carly's sandwich. Carly had a glass of wine with her meal and Colt drank soda. He didn't want to drive through Seattle after drinking alcohol. The last thing he needed was to get arrested his first day here.

Carly entertained him with stories of clients at the gallery and some of the artists who sold their work there. She had funny anecdotes about both groups.

"But you like your job, don't you?" Colt asked.

Carly nodded. "Oh, yeah, I do. It's just people get so stuffy there sometimes. I just want to tell them to loosen up."

Colt walked Carly back to the gallery after lunch and then remembered to ask about getting a key for the townhouse.

"I forgot about that," Carly said. "Just take the one that's above the door on the ledge. I leave it there in case I lock myself out."

Colt stared at her, aghast. "You leave a key outside your door? Is that safe?"

Carly shrugged. "I've never worried about it. Just don't tell Andi or Beth that I leave one there. They both would have a fit. By the way, did you meet Beth yet?"

Colt nodded. "She was home when I got up. She gave me the directions to your work. She's really nice."

"Yeah, she is, I guess. I hardly ever see her. It seems like she's always working. At least she pays her rent on time," Carly said.

Smiling, she reached her gloved hand up around Colt's neck and pulled him to her. Their lips met for just a second, and then Carly pulled away and gave him a mischievous grin. "I'll see you later," she purred.

Colt watched Carly enter the gallery with a smile on his lips. She was always able to make his blood boil with just the simplest gesture. He rode the wave of euphoria he felt all the way back to this truck and drove home to the townhouse.

Chapter Nine

Colt found the extra key up above the door and entered quietly so as not to wake Beth. He was surprised to find her in the kitchen when he walked in.

"Hi," Beth said. "Did you two have a nice lunch?"

Colt nodded. "I figured you'd still be sleeping." He noticed she wore a baggie sweatshirt, jeans, and sneakers. Her hair was pulled back in a ponytail and her face was still devoid of makeup. Her skin was flawless and her lashes framed her eyes nicely. She didn't need makeup to enhance her features. She looked pretty just the way she was.

"I don't need that much sleep," she said. "I'm going for a walk."

"Oh, okay," Colt said, hesitantly. He wanted to go along, but he didn't want to be rude and invite himself.

Beth cocked her head and grinned at him. "Would you like go for a walk?"

"Sure," he answered quickly. He was used to being busy all day and the thought of just sitting around the house sounded boring to him.

"Do you have any sneakers to wear?" Beth asked, pointing to his boots. "I walk pretty fast. It's the only exercise I get, so you'll have to keep up."

Colt stared down at his boots a moment and then

remembered he'd packed some running shoes. "Yes, I do. Give me a moment." He went into his room, changed his shoes, and was out in a flash. "Better?" he asked.

Beth smiled. "Better. Let's go."

They walked out the door, through the courtyard, and onto the sidewalk. Beth didn't pick the easy downhill route. She chose to go uphill instead, and Colt kept pace beside her. It was easy, since his legs were much longer and she had to take two steps for every one of his, but he found she set a quick pace.

They walked several blocks before turning the corner. The day was still chilly, but the sun was out, which Carly had told Colt was a rare treat this time of year. Colt glanced around as they walked. There were homes and apartments and they passed a small park where young children played while their parents sat and watched. The streets were fairly busy, though, for a residential area. At least they seemed busy to Colt.

"How did you like downtown Seattle?" Beth asked as they walked along. They had turned a corner again and were heading downhill now.

"It was pretty along the water," Colt told her. "And that big Ferris wheel looked interesting."

"Yeah, that's a big tourist attraction. It's only been there for a couple of years, but people flock to it. I went up in it once, at night. It was pretty to see all the city lights from the top."

"That would be fun," Colt said. "I'm not sure of the height, though. I've never been in anything so high before."

"Then you should try going up in the Space Needle first. There's a beautiful view of the city from up there. And you won't be going up and down."

"Maybe," Colt said. "I guess I have a lot of sightseeing to do."

"You should ask Carly to take you around. She knows where all the good places are."

"Have you lived in Seattle all your life?" Colt asked.

"No, I grew up in Spokane. I came here to go to college. That's when I met Carly. We both went to the same college for our general education, but then I went on to nursing and she went to school for business."

"Do your parents still live in Spokane?" Colt asked with interest.

"My mom still does, with my stepfather. My father died the year after I started college. He had a heart attack."

Colt grew serious. "I'm sorry."

"Thank you, Colt. It's still hard to believe he's gone. And then my mother remarried a few years later, and that was hard, too. But I'm used to it now."

"My father died when I was fourteen," Colt said quietly. "He had cancer for quite some time before he died. It was hard. My mom recently started dating a new man, and it seems strange, but I'm happy for her."

Beth reached up and gently rubbed Colt's arm. "I'm sorry, Colt. I guess we both have something in common."

Colt smiled at her. He changed the subject. "So, you must know Andi, too?"

Beth shook her head. "No, I've never met her. Carly and I knew each other in college, and we had mutual friends, but I never really hung out with her. We don't exactly have the same interests."

Colt frowned. "So, you two aren't really friends?"

"Well, not like best friends, but we get along. We just like different things."

"Like what?"

Beth paused a moment before answering. "Carly likes to go out and have fun, which is fine for her, but I'm more serious. I don't go out much and I like to do physical things like walking and biking. I love going hiking. There are a couple of state parks not too far out of town where I hike and there are hiking trails in Mount Rainier National Park that I love to go to."

"That sounds interesting," Colt said. "You don't go alone, do you?"

"No. I usually go with a couple of friends from work. I haven't had much time to go lately, though, since my work hours are so crazy."

"How did you end up renting from Carly if you're not friends?" Colt asked.

"Basically through a friend of a friend. I heard she was renting out a room and I work at the hospital nearby, so it was perfect. I could rent my own place, but then I wouldn't be able to save as much money. I'm hoping to buy a house someday. I don't want to rent forever."

Colt glanced at Beth. She looked so young, yet she was already thinking of buying a house. He hadn't even thought of having his own house until lately. And he was twenty-five. "Aren't you kind of young to be thinking of buying a house?" he asked.

Beth laughed. "I'm twenty-four, the same age as Carly, and she owns the townhouse."

"Hmm. I never thought of it that way."

"What about you, Colt? I know you came out here to be with Carly, but what's your story? Have you always worked on the family ranch? Do you like ranching? Did you go to college?"

"Well, yes, yes, and no," Colt said.

Beth rolled her eyes. "That's it?"

Colt chuckled. "I don't really have a story. I've always worked on the ranch. I live in the same house and room I grew up in, and I've never done anything else. Until now."

"Well, what do you do for fun when you're not riding the range and roping cattle?" Beth asked with a grin.

"Is that what you think I do all day? Riding and roping?"

"I have no idea. It just sounded good," Beth said.

"Maybe someday you can visit the ranch and we'll put you to work. Then you can see what we do. Do you ride?"

Beth shook her head. "Nope. Never have. I'd like to try, though."

"Then that's the first thing we'll have to teach you," Colt said.

They had circled another corner by then and were headed back uphill toward the townhouse. Even though they'd kept up a steady pace, Colt wasn't even winded. Beth wasn't either, he noticed.

"So, what else do you do in Montana?" Beth asked.

"Well, on Friday and Saturday nights, I like to go dancing at the local bar."

"Dancing? Really? Now that is a surprise."

"Why? Don't you think a cowboy can dance?"

Beth chuckled. "I suppose it's to country music."

Colt nodded. "Is there any other kind of music?" he teased. They were walking into the courtyard by then. Beth pointed to a bench in the center and they sat down.

"I doubt you'll find many honkytonks to dance at here," Beth said. "Are you any good?"

Colt shrugged. "A few women have told me I'm pretty good."

Beth's brows rose and she gave him a mischievous grin. "We are still taking about dancing, right?"

Colt stared at her a moment before her words hit him. He shook his head and laughed. "You have a wicked sense of humor. I'll have to watch myself around you."

Beth laughed, too. "You know, I really like you, Colt. It's funny, though. You're nothing like any of Carly's other boyfriends I've met. You're more down to earth."

Colt sobered. "You say that like there have been a lot of them."

Beth shook her head. "Sorry. I didn't mean it that way. There hasn't been. I just meant that you're a whole lot nicer than the few I've met."

Colt nodded, but he still didn't like the idea that he was one of many. Even though Andi had warned him that Carly had dated a lot of men, he'd hoped she'd been exaggerating. Now, he had to admit she'd probably been right.

Beth stood and stretched. "I'd better go in and shower. Carly should be home soon. You might want to clean up, too. She usually eats out every night."

Colt followed Beth into the townhouse.

"Thanks for walking with me," Beth said. "It was fun talking with you. Maybe we can do it again sometime."

Colt brightened. "I'd like that." He had enjoyed spending time with Beth.

"And don't take what I said about Carly to heart. She's a nice person and she really doesn't bring men home all the time. I hadn't meant it that way."

Colt nodded. He knew he shouldn't be surprised about Carly having many boyfriends before, he just hoped he was the last.

* * *

Carly came through the door at five forty-five and smiled wide when she saw Colt sitting on the sofa, waiting for her. Her day had been long and the traffic home was busy. All she wanted to do now was change into jeans and a comfortable sweater and go out and show off her hunky cowboy.

"Did you miss me?" Carly asked, dropping her coat over a chair and falling onto the sofa beside Colt. She snuggled in close and kissed him on the lips before kicking off her heels.

"I sure did," Colt responded. He wrapped his arm around her shoulders and played with her silky ponytail.

"I'm starved," Carly said. "It was a long day. I'm going to change my clothes and then we can go eat."

Colt pulled her to him and kissed her again, soft and teasing at first, then turning into a deeper, more passionate kiss. When he pulled away, breathless, he asked, "Are you sure you don't want to stay home instead?"

Carly traced a finger down the side of his chiseled face and looked into his baby blue eyes. He was so adorable, it was hard to resist him, but they had time for playing around later. "Go and eat," she said, giggling and pulling away from him.

Colt chuckled.

They rode in Colt's truck the few blocks down to a little bar that served basket-style food. When they entered, Carly looked around the dark room a moment before spotting her friends in a corner booth. "There they are." She grabbed Colt's hand and led him to the booth.

"Hey, everyone. This is Colt, my hot cowboy," Carly announced to the people in the booth.

Three sets of eyes stared up at Colt. His face turned a deep shade of red.

"This is Adam, Chelle, and Everly," Carly said, waving her hand from left to right. She pulled Colt to the booth and they both slid in, joining the others.

"Nice to meet you all," Colt said.

Adam's blue eyes gave Colt the once over through a pair of oblong, black glasses. His light blond hair was short on the sides and long on top, combed back away from his angular face. He looked thin, even with the loose, long-sleeved, button-down shirt he wore. The two women did the same, staring at Colt with only mild interest. Chelle was slender and had straight, very black hair with thick bangs that fell into her dark brown eyes. Everly was the opposite of Chelle, plump and curvy with short blond hair and blue eyes.

"Well, you certainly look like a cowboy," Adam said in a soft voice. "Boots, Levi's, and hat included."

"Oh, sorry," Colt said, pulling off his hat with one hand and running his other hand through his hair, pushing it back. He set the hat on the back of the booth.

"Nothing to be sorry about," Everly purred. "But you do look adorable without the hat."

"Okay you guys, be nice," Carly said, pulling a menu from the stand in the middle of the table. "And hands off, Everly. He's mine. Same goes for you, Adam," Carly said, teasing.

Carly turned to Colt. "Everly works with me at the gallery. Adam is a sculptor and sells his work at the gallery, and Chelle sells her paintings there, too."

Colt looked at Chelle with interest. "What do you paint?"

"I work with colors and shapes," Chelle said, taking a sip of her wine. "My style is classified as Modern Art, but I'd like to think that what I create is unique and shouldn't be boxed into any one category."

"Snob," Adam said under his breath.

Chelle threw him a nasty look. "Jealous."

Carly sighed. She'd heard all this a million times before. "Ignore them," she told Colt. "They're artists."

Carly ordered a gin and tonic and Colt had a beer on tap and then everyone ordered food. The drinks kept coming and the talk flowed around the table effortlessly. People came by the table to talk to Carly and the others, and more drinks were brought. At one point, Colt shook his head when he was offered another beer. "I'm driving," he explained.

Carly told the waiter to go ahead and bring another one. "Don't worry," she told Colt. "Adam will drive us home if you have too much. He hardly drinks at all. You can pick up your truck tomorrow morning. It's only a few blocks from the townhouse. I do it all the time."

It was after eleven and several drinks later when the group started to disperse. Adam drove Carly and Colt home, and they stumbled into the townhouse. No sooner had they made it to the bedroom, Carly slipped off her sweater and pulled Colt up against her.

"Want to play, Cowboy?" Carly asked seductively.

Colt was more than happy to comply.

Chapter Ten

Colt awoke the next morning with a dry mouth and a splitting headache. He slowly turned and saw that Carly wasn't in bed next to him. Looking at the clock, he saw it was nearly eight-thirty. He sighed. He'd slept late again, but after last night, he could understand why.

Colt slowly pushed himself up in bed, and then regretted it when his head pounded even harder. He got up anyway, walked into the bathroom, and splashed cold water over his face. Looking in the mirror, he saw bloodshot eyes staring back at him. How many glasses of beer had he drunk? And how on earth did Carly get up and go to work this morning? As far as he knew, she'd drunk much more than he had, and her drinks had been hard liquor.

He found his briefs and jeans on the floor and slipped them on. His head was hurting so bad, he had to find some aspirin and get a mug of coffee, fast. He walked down the hallway, rubbing his eyes, and turned toward the kitchen. He was relieved to see a fresh pot of coffee in the coffeemaker.

"Do you always walk around shirtless?" Beth asked from the sofa.

Colt jumped. He turned and saw Beth, once again sitting curled up in the corner of the sofa, mug in hand.

"Sorry," Colt said sheepishly. "I really needed coffee. And

aspirin."

Beth chuckled. She stood and walked past Colt into the kitchen and dug into the cupboard for the Tylenol. "Fun night, huh?"

Colt accepted the pills and headed for the coffee. "Thanks. Yeah, I guess I hadn't realized I'd drunk so much. It just kind of hit me."

"I hope you didn't drive," Beth said, frowning.

Colt shook his head. He popped the pills into his mouth and downed them with a gulp of coffee. "One of Carly's friends drove us home. Adam. I'll have to get my pickup later, after my head stops pounding."

"You want some toast?" Beth asked, already heading for the fridge.

"I'd love some, thanks," Colt answered. He walked over to the counter and sat on a stool.

"I'll fry you up some eggs, too," Beth said, pulling what she needed from the fridge. "Food can help settle a hangover. I only have one request, though."

Colt looked up, his brows raised. "Okay."

"Put a shirt on. You're distracting me."

"Oh, sorry." He hastily left the room and found his T-shirt, and then slipped it over his head before returning. "Better?"

Beth laughed. "Better."

Colt watched Beth as she moved around the kitchen. She wore scrubs again, but today her shirt had pictures of kittens and puppies on it.

"Over easy or hard?" Beth asked after cracking two eggs into a pan on the stove.

Colt's brain was working slowly. He had to think a moment before he realized what she'd meant. "Over easy," he finally answered, laughing.

"What's so funny?" Beth asked, looking over her shoulder.

"Nothing. I just didn't hear you right at first. All I heard was "hard", and I had to think a moment."

Beth rolled her eyes. "Watch yourself there, Cowboy."

Colt grinned as he watched Beth flip the eggs and put down the toast. Soon after, she brought him the plate of food.

"Jelly?" Beth asked.

Colt nodded. "Yeah, thanks."

She brought over a jar of strawberry jelly, and then sat one stool over from him with a freshly poured cup of coffee in hand.

"Don't get used to being served every day," she told him. "I'm just doing this because I feel bad for you and I'm in a good mood this morning."

Colt scooped up a bite of eggs and bit into his toast. It tasted wonderful. Almost as good as his mom's cooking. "I appreciate it. I don't know much about cooking. My mom did all that on the ranch for me, my brother, and Randy. I guess I was spoiled."

"Sounds like it," Beth said.

"I sure wish I'd brought along some of my mom's homemade jam, though. You'd love it. She makes the best jam in the state."

"Maybe when you go visit, you can bring some back. I'd like to try it."

Colt looked over at Beth. "What exactly do you do at the hospital? I mean, do you work with patients or in surgery?"

"I work on the children's floor with kids up to age twelve."

Colt nodded. "Ah. That explains the kitties and puppies."

"What?"

"Your shirt. I noticed it had kitties and puppies on it."

"Oh, yeah. I have a lot of cartoon and animal print tops. It gives the little kids something to smile about sometimes."

"Is it hard working with sick children?" Colt asked. "Seems

like it could be sad sometimes."

Beth nodded. "Sometimes it's hard. I'm not supposed to get too attached, but with some children, you just do."

"I'll bet you're really good with them," Colt said, finishing up the last bite of his food.

"Based on what?"

Colt stood and carried his plate and mug over to the sink. "You've been really nice to me, and I'm a stranger to you. I'm sure with kids, you're amazing."

Beth smiled. "Thanks. It's easy being nice to you, Colt. You actually appreciate it."

Colt rinsed his dish and silverware and put them in the dishwasher, then filled his mug with more coffee. He felt much better now that the Tylenol had taken effect and he had food in his stomach.

"Let me know when you go grocery shopping so I can reimburse you for the food," Colt said. "I've already eaten a lot of it in the past two days."

Beth nodded. "I will."

Colt looked at her a moment, catching her brown eyes with his blue ones. "Thanks, Beth. For the food and for being so nice."

"You're welcome."

Colt turned to walk back to the bedroom, but stopped and looked over his shoulder when Beth called out.

"Hey, do you want me to drive you to your truck before I go to bed?"

"No, that's okay. You need to get your sleep. It was my fault I drank too much to drive home, so it's up to me to get the truck. Next time, I'll drink a lot less. Thanks, though." He smiled at her, and then walked to the bedroom so he could shower.

By the time Colt was cleaned up and dressed, his headache

had subsided and he felt almost normal. The living room was empty when he walked through it, so he guessed that Beth had already gone to bed. Quietly, he closed and locked the door, then started walking the five blocks down to the bar where his truck was parked.

The day was cloudy and cold. Colt pulled up the collar of his coat to ward off the chill. His thoughts turned to Beth as he made the trek down the city blocks. She was so nice to him, even though she hardly knew him. He wondered if it was because she was used to seeing people come and go in the townhouse, mainly men, or if she was just being nice to him. "You're nothing like any of Carly's other boyfriends I've met," she'd told him yesterday. This made Colt wonder what her other boyfriends had been like. Were they more sophisticated than him? Probably. Better looking? Rich? He had no idea. But if he kept thinking about Carly with other men, it would drive him crazy, so he finally pushed those thoughts aside. He was just happy that he got along well with Beth. Otherwise, it would have been awkward living there.

Colt finally arrived at the bar parking lot where his truck was and walked up to it. There was a long scratch on the driver's side door that hadn't been there yesterday. It was very noticeable on the shiny, black paint. Colt ran his finger over it, hoping it would rub out, but it didn't. It looked like someone had purposely keyed it.

"Damn," he muttered. The truck was only a year old and he'd always been so careful with it. He sighed and hopped into the cab. "That'll teach me for drinking too much and leaving it in a parking lot overnight," he said out loud.

Colt realized that he'd never had to worry about drinking and driving back home because Randy or Luke always looked after him when they were out. Neither of them ever drank too much, so Colt was free to drink all he wanted and he knew he had a ride home. Well, those days were over. It was high time he took responsibility for himself, and for Carly, and be more careful so he could always get them home safely.

Colt sat in the parking lot, wondering what he should do. He could go back to the townhouse, but there wasn't much to do there. It was only ten o'clock, so it was too early to meet Carly for lunch. Then he remembered the Help Wanted sign in the window of the market near the gallery, and he made up his mind. He'd go there and ask what type of job they had open. If he was going to stay here for any length of time, he needed to work. That was as good a start as any.

He followed the same directions he had yesterday and was soon in downtown Seattle. Driving through the streets near the gallery, he finally spotted the market and drove around the block twice until he found a parking spot. As he stepped out of his truck, rain began to drizzle from the gray sky. Colt hurried to the market so he wouldn't be dripping wet when he walked in.

The glass doors swished open automatically as Colt entered O'Hannan's Market. He stopped and looked around the busy store a moment. Spotting a service counter to his left, he walked over and waited until the man behind the counter acknowledged him. Colt couldn't tell if the man behind the counter was fourteen or forty. He was short and thin, and his light blond hair was cut very short. He looked no older than a teen, but his eyes looked tired like an older man.

"Can I help you?" the man asked, looking at Colt with disinterest.

"I wanted to ask about the job opening you have," Colt said.

The man snorted. "Which one?"

Colt stared at him a moment, not sure what he meant.

"Here," the guy said, reaching down under the counter and pulling out a sheet of paper. He slid it on the counter towards

Colt along with a pen. "Fill out an application and I'll see if the boss wants to talk to you today or another day. We have warehouse and stocking jobs open and also cashier jobs." He looked Colt up and down a moment, and then said, "You look more like a warehouse type of guy than a cashier. You should put that on your application." With that, the guy turned away and picked up a phone.

Colt took the application to the end of the counter where he'd be out of the way. He stared at the sheet of paper. He'd never filled out a job application before. He put the date in the corner and started to write his name, then stopped. Maybe he should use his real name, the one on his driver's license. The name Colt might seem odd to these people since they didn't know him. Yet, using Cole seemed odd to him. *Crap. I didn't think it would be this complicated.*

Colt decided to use Cole and began filling out the application. From time to time, he'd stop and look around at the busy market. There were several cashier counters to his left, all in a row, and beyond that were aisles of groceries. He watched men and women stocking shelves, and then watched the cashiers work the registers. He was terrible with computers and wouldn't even know the first thing about running a register, so maybe he should only consider the warehouse or stocking. Colt tried imagining himself standing in the store aisles stocking shelves wearing a green apron like all the other workers. He frowned. It wasn't what he'd pictured when he'd thought about applying for a job.

"What's the matter, Cowboy? Something on the application stumping you?" the counter guy asked.

Colt shook his head. He hadn't seen him walk over. "No, I'm fine."

The guy leaned over the counter and looked at the application upside-down. "Cole, huh? Funny name for a cowboy. I'm Connor. The owner is my uncle. He said he'd be out here in a minute to talk to you. I told him you were tall and looked strong, and he was eager to speak with you right away. You can sit on that bench over there and wait if you want."

"Okay. Thanks," Colt said. He finished filling out the application and then sat down.

"So, are you a real cowboy or do you just wear the boots and hat to look like one?" Connor asked, leaning his elbows on the counter.

"I'm a real cowboy, I guess," Colt answered. "My family has a ranch in Montana that I've worked on all my life." Colt wondered if he should stop wearing his hat so he didn't stand out so much. Everyone was always mentioning it.

"Then what on earth are you doing here?" Connor asked. "If my family owned a ranch, I'd be there, not here."

Colt just stared at Connor, unable to believe he'd ask such a thing. People here seemed to say whatever was on their minds. "My girlfriend lives here and I came to be with her," he said.

"Ah, I get it. Well, I hope she's worth it," Connor said. He turned away as a customer approached the counter.

Colt sat there in utter amazement. How rude was that? He hoped Carly was worth it? Of course, she was worth coming here for. This guy didn't even know her.

Colt looked up when an older man approached him.

"Are you the strong guy Connor told me about?" the man asked. He was much shorter than Colt, stocky built, and had short, reddish-brown hair and facial scruff. When he looked Colt right in the eyes, Colt was startled by their deep green color.

Colt stood and offered his hand. "Yes, I guess I am. I'm Colt…I mean Cole Brennan."

The man took Colt's hand and shook it hardily. "Ah, a good Irish name. I'm Gerard, the owner. You're a tall one, aren't you?"

Colt nodded, not quite sure how to answer.

"Come along to my office where we can talk," Gerard said. He turned and headed through the store. Colt followed.

Customers and workers waved or said hello to Gerard as he passed by. Colt thought that was a good sign. He seemed to be friendly with everyone.

They walked through swinging double doors into the back area. Colt looked around while he continued to follow Gerard. There were rows of floor-to-ceiling shelves holding pallets of every type of food items imaginable. People were walking about, filling carts with items to restock shelves. Down the way, he heard a machine running and wondered what it was.

"In here," Gerard said, waving Colt into a small office just off the stock room. "Have a seat."

Colt sat in a black plastic chair while Gerard took the chair behind an old, scratched, wooden desk. The desk was piled with papers and folders on one side and there was a computer in the other corner. Filing cabinets stood against the wall behind Gerard.

Colt handed Gerard his application, but the older man just set it down on the desk and kept his eyes on Colt instead.

"So, tell me about yourself, Cole. What type of work experience do you have?"

"Well, all my experience has been working on my family's ranch," Colt said.

Gerard glanced at Colt's application. "Ah, so you're from Montana, eh? That explains the cowboy hat."

Colt quickly pulled the hat off his head and ran his hand through his hair. "Sorry about that," he said. He kept forgetting to take it off when he was indoors.

Gerard chuckled. "Nothing to be sorry about. So, what brought you here to Seattle when you have a permanent job in

Montana?"

Colt cleared his throat. "My girlfriend lives here. I moved here to be with her." Colt waited. He hoped Gerard didn't say he hoped his girlfriend was worth it, like Connor had, or else he'd just walk out.

"A girl, huh? Well, it must be serious then. So, what kind of work are you looking for?"

"I'm not really sure," Colt said honestly. "I guess I'd be good at stocking or something."

Gerard nodded. "You look pretty strong to me. Guess you'd have to be, working on a ranch. I tell you what, Cole. I have an opening in the warehouse for someone to help with unloading trucks every morning and then moving the heavy pallets around in the stockroom. It would be a lot of heavy lifting and also running a small forklift. Have you ever driven a forklift before?"

Colt shook his head. "No, sir, but I'm sure I could learn."

Gerard slammed his hand on the desk, making Colt jump in his seat. "Now, that's what I like. Someone who's honest and willing to learn. You just can't imagine how many times I've hired people who say they can do stuff and then I find out that they can't. At least you're honest."

"I try to be," Colt said.

"Good," Gerard said. "I like you, Cole. I have a good feeling about you. The only other thing I need to know is if you'll be around the area for the entire spring and summer. I want to hire someone who'll stay a while. I get so tired of having to hire people every couple of months."

"Oh." Colt hesitated. He wasn't sure how long he'd be here. If things worked out well with Carly, he figured he'd be here a long time, unless he could talk her into moving back to the ranch. But that was a long way into the future.

"Well, listen, Son. I have a full-time job in the warehouse

working seven to three, five days a week. The pay isn't great, but it's not too bad either. If you can promise me you'll be around until the end of summer, it's yours. What do you say?"

"That sounds good," Colt said. "But, I'd have to be gone for a week in May. I promised my brother I'd help move the cattle from the winter pasture to the summer pasture."

"My God, you're a genuine cowboy, aren't you," Gerard bellowed. "And you keep your promises. I like that. So, will you take the job?"

Colt thought for only a moment. At least he'd be working while he was here, and the market was close to Carly's work. That was a plus. "Yes, Sir. I'll take it."

Gerard smiled wide as he stood. "Great. You'll be working with my son, Quinn. I'm sure you two will get along just fine." He came around the desk and shook Colt's hand. "Can you come in tomorrow at seven so Quinn can show you around?"

Colt nodded. "Sure."

"Wonderful." Gerard looked down at Colt's boots. "By the way, you'll want to wear some good, sturdy work boots. Steel-toed. For your protection."

"Okay," Colt said. He had no idea where he'd get a pair of boots between now and tomorrow morning.

Gerard walked Colt back to the swinging doors that led into the market. "Glad you'll be working here," he said. "See you tomorrow."

"Thank you," Colt said. He watched as Gerard turned and walked back into the warehouse.

Colt walked through the store toward the exit. Just as the sliding glass doors opened to let him out, he heard a voice holler at him.

"Hey, Cowboy. Did you get the job?"

Colt turned and saw Connor looking straight at him. He nodded yes.

Connor gave him a thumbs up. "See you around."

Colt left the market and headed to his truck. The realization of what had just happened hit him. He had a job. A job he got all on his own. He smiled wide. He couldn't wait to tell Carly the good news.

Chapter Eleven

Carly stood behind the counter at work going through last week's sale slips. She had to enter them into the computer under the artists' names so they could be paid their commission at the end of month, which was only three days away. She sighed. She'd drank way too much last night, and her head still ached despite the Tylenol she'd taken and all the coffee she'd consumed. She knew she shouldn't drink so much on a weeknight, but she'd been having so much fun, she hadn't wanted to stop. And then when they'd gotten home, yum. Having Colt in her bed every night was a treat. It just wasn't a good idea when she had to get up early in the morning.

Everly came in from the back room just as the clock above the door hit noon. Good, Carly thought. She could go eat lunch. Just as she wondered if Colt would come and have lunch with her, the front door chimed and he walked into the gallery.

"Hey, beautiful," Colt said with a smile. "Can you leave for lunch yet?"

Carly smiled wide. *Goodness, but he was adorable.* "Yes, I can. We're not busy anyway. Let me get my coat."

Carly came out from behind the counter and Colt grabbed her around the waist, picked her up effortlessly, and swung her around in a circle before setting her down and placing a kiss on her lips.

Carly giggled. "What was that all about?"

"I'm just so darned happy, that's all. And I have good news. I'll tell you at lunch."

Everly walked by and rolled her eyes. "God, you two are sickening." But she was smiling when she said it.

Carly tossed her head, her loose hair flying. "You're just jealous."

Everly nodded. "Of course, I am. I admit it."

Colt laughed and waited while Carly retrieved her coat from the back.

They walked a short way to a small cafe. Colt ordered a burger and Carly ordered soup and toast. As they waited for their food, Carly asked, "So, what's the exciting news?"

Colt grinned. "I got a job."

Carly blinked. She hadn't expected he'd get one so soon. "Really? Where?"

"At the big market a couple of blocks from here. I'll be working in the warehouse, unloading trucks and moving stock around."

"Oh." Carly sat quietly a moment. She'd known he'd wanted to get a job, but she'd figured he'd wait to see if he was going to stay first. Cripes, she didn't even know how long she wanted him to stay. And in a market? In the warehouse? She frowned.

"What's the matter?" Colt asked, looking concerned.

"Oh, nothing," Carly said quickly. "It's just, well, is that the type of job you wanted?"

Colt shrugged. "Oh, I don't mind. I'm not sure what else I can do around here. Unless you know of a ranch nearby that needs someone to break horses," he said, a twinkle in his eyes.

Carly smiled slowly. It was hard to resist Colt when he was so darned cute. "No, I don't. I guess you can try it for a while and see if you like it."

"There is one thing," Colt said. He'd stopped eating and

looked at Carly seriously. "I had to promise the owner that I'd work there throughout the summer. I hope you don't mind. I mean, we get along so well, I thought you wouldn't mind if I stayed the whole summer."

Carly's eyes grew wide and her head began to pound again. *All summer? It was only the end of January.*

Colt's face dropped. "I guess I shouldn't have taken it, huh? I can go right back there and tell him I can't take it if you want me to."

Carly suddenly felt guilty for making Colt feel bad. *Sheesh! Since when do I feel guilty about anything?* She made herself smile. "No, it's okay. I want you to stay. I just hadn't thought that far ahead. Take the job if you want to. You're right. I do like having you here. That's the point, right? To see where things lead?" Carly knew she was rambling and she didn't even know what she was saying. She was just happy to see Colt's eyes perk up.

"Great. Besides, this way I can pay rent and help with the bills. I don't want to be the only one living there who doesn't work."

Carly nodded and stirred her soup. Maybe it wasn't such a bad idea. She did have strong feelings for Colt. So, why did the thought of a long-term relationship scare her to death?

Colt interrupted her thoughts. "Say, do you know where I can get a pair of leather work boots? I need them for tomorrow."

Carly wrinkled her nose. The only shoe stores she knew about sold designer shoes—at a discount, of course. "You should ask Beth. She'd probably know since she buys uniforms and sensible shoes."

Colt nodded. "Yeah. Good idea. I'll ask her. She'll probably be up when I get back to the apartment. She was yesterday. Did I tell you we went walking together?"

Carly stared at Colt. Walking? "No, you didn't."

"Yeah. I like Beth. She fixed breakfast for me this morning when she saw I was a little hung over. She's really nice."

Carly watched Colt finish up the last bite of his burger and eat his fries. She wondered why Beth would make breakfast for him. Then she pushed aside that thought. What did it matter? After all, there was really no comparison between her and Beth. *Oh, my God! Now, I'm jealous? What is wrong with me?* She decided that she was just tired.

After Colt walked her back to the gallery, Carly went into the back room and pulled her phone out of her pocket. Panic hit her again. All summer. Colt was going to be here all summer. Did she want him to be there that long? She quickly dialed her sister's home phone and hoped she'd be at the cabin to answer it.

Andi's voice came over the line. "Hello?"

"Hi, Andi. I'm glad you're home," Carly said, relief filling her voice.

"Is something the matter?" Andi asked instantly.

Carly smiled to herself. Andi's radar had kicked in immediately. They may not live together anymore, but they'd always have a close connection.

"Everything is okay," Carly told her. "Except...well, I'm kind of having a panic attack and I need to talk to you."

"What's happened?" Andi asked.

"Colt got a job."

"That's worth a panic attack?" Andi asked, sounding confused. "I thought that was the idea. He'd move out there, live, and work. What's the problem?"

Carly's heart pounded faster. She started pacing. "He got a job where he promised the owner he'd work there the whole summer. As in, staying here, with me, the entire summer," she nearly shrieked.

"Oh." There was a pause on the line. Finally, her sister

asked, "Wasn't that what you wanted? Didn't you want Colt to stay a while so you could see if you two were meant to be together?"

"Well, yes. Kind of. Oh, I don't know." Carly stopped pacing and dropped down in a chair. "I just didn't know he'd get a job so quickly. He's only been here two days. I guess I figured he'd wait to see if we last at least a month before he committed to the entire summer."

"Carly. You said you wanted Colt there. You invited him. Are you telling me that now you don't want him to stay with you? That you just don't want him?"

"No," Carly insisted. "I do like Colt and I want him to be here. But I don't know how I'll feel in month. Or two months. Let alone six months."

"I told you before he moved out there to make sure you were serious about him," Andi said, frustration lacing her tone. "I told you he was serious. Now, after only two days, you're telling me you're not sure you want him to stay? If that's true, then you have to tell Colt to not take that job. The more attached to the area, and to you, that he gets, the more hurt he'll be when you let him down."

Carly stomped her foot. She couldn't help it. She was so upset already and her sister wasn't making her feel any better. "I didn't call to be lectured to. I called because I'm in a panic about this, and you're not helping at all."

"Okay," Andi said, sounding calmer. "Tell me why you're panicking?"

"I don't know," Carly whined. "I do want Colt to stay longer, but when he said the whole summer, I panicked. What if we don't last all summer? Then I'll feel even worse. Six months is a big commitment."

"Calm down, Carly. It's not like Colt proposed to you or anything. He just got a job. You two can still explore your relationship over the next few weeks and if it doesn't work out, it just doesn't. But, if you know right now that it won't work between you two, tell him now. Don't lead him on. That will make it much worse."

Carly took a deep breath. Her heartbeat slowed back down to normal. "I'm not leading him on," she said calmly. "I do still want him here. I guess the fact that he committed to the entire summer just kind of freaked me out. You're right. It isn't that big of a deal."

"Carly. I don't want to see either of you get hurt. Promise me that you'll be completely honest with Colt, okay? It will be easier for both of you that way," Andi said softly.

"I know. I'm better now. I really do care about Colt. Things will be fine."

After talking a little longer about everyday things, Carly hung up. She stood, stretched, and ran her hand through her hair to smooth it down. She realized there was no reason to freak out about Colt committing to a job. Like Andi said, it wasn't like he'd proposed marriage to her. He was just staying all summer. Who knew? Maybe their relationship would still be going strong by then.

Carly walked out to the gallery showroom and over to the counter to continue entering the sales slips into the computer. She passed Everly on her way there.

"Trouble in paradise?" Everly asked. "You didn't look so happy when you came back from lunch."

Carly closed her eyes. Her headache was returning. "No. Everything is fine." She turned to her paperwork. *I think I need a drink.*

* * *

When Colt returned to the townhouse, Beth was already up

and dressed, curled up on the sofa watching television. Except for finding the long scratch on the truck's door this morning, Colt's day was going pretty well. He'd found a job and he was going to stay in Seattle at least until fall. The thought of spending the entire summer here with Carly made him very happy.

Although Carly had looked a bit stunned when he'd told her about the job, she seemed to be okay with his staying that long. In fact, she'd said that she wanted him to stay. Colt couldn't think of anything better than going to sleep and waking up with Carly beside him for the next few months. Heck, if it were up to him, he'd do it forever.

Forever. Wow. The thought of getting married used to scare him, but now he could actually picture himself spending the rest of his life with one woman. Carly.

"What's that grin on your face for?" Beth asked.

Colt looked over at her. She wore a sweatshirt and jeans again. Her hair was pulled back in a ponytail and her face was free of makeup. She was the exact opposite of Carly, yet, Colt thought she was really pretty.

"I had a good morning," he told her, walking over to sit beside her on the sofa. The volume on the television was low. Colt glanced at it. He saw a young couple walking through a house. "What are you watching?"

"House Hunters," Beth said. "And don't make fun of me like Carly does. I like watching all these house shows. It gives me ideas on the type of house I want someday."

Colt sat back and watched the show a minute. "I don't really watch much T.V. What is this show about?"

"They go to different parts of the country and real estate agents show a person or couple some homes for sale and then the people pick the home they want."

Colt made a face. "That sounds boring."

"It's not," Beth insisted. "It's annoying sometimes when they whine about all the little things wrong with a house, but I enjoy watching it. You find out a lot about the real estate market from watching it. I also watch Property Virgins, and the shows where they flip houses. I get a lot of good ideas from them."

"Flip houses?" Colt asked. "What's that?"

Beth laughed. "It does sound funny, doesn't it? It's when someone buys a run-down house and fixes it up to resell for a profit. I learn a lot from those shows, like what problems to look for when buying a house."

"Huh. So, what type of house do you want to buy?"

Beth shrugged. "I'm not sure. I wouldn't mind an older home that I'd have to fix up. I'm sure that's all I'll be able to afford anyway. Definitely something with character, like bay windows, old woodwork, and a working fireplace. I guess I'll know it when I see it. What about you? What type of house would you like to own?"

Colt thought a moment. "I never really gave it much thought, but I guess I'd have a cabin style home like my brother Luke's, except I'd like a second story with a loft. And big windows."

"I'd love to have a house with a loft. What would you use it for?" Beth asked.

"I'm not sure. I just like how they look. Maybe an office, or a playroom for the kids, or even the master bedroom. I guess I'd have to think about it."

Beth grinned. "Kids, huh? So, you assume you will have kids someday?"

"I just figured I would. Doesn't everyone want kids when they settle down? Don't you?" Colt asked.

"Sure, I do, but I'm not sure that everyone does. You'd better run that by Carly first to see what she thinks. I'm not sure children are high on her list now, or ever. Although, I may be wrong."

Colt pondered what Beth had said. He hadn't thought much about Carly and kids. Seems like there was a lot he hadn't thought through.

"Say, speaking of Carly, she said you might be able to help me. I need a pair of work boots for tomorrow. Do you know where I can buy some?"

Beth cocked her head. "Why do you need work boots?"

Colt smiled proudly. "I got a job today. It's at a market near Carly's gallery. I'll be working in the warehouse, unloading trucks and stocking shelves. The owner said I should get some good work boots."

"Well, congratulations. Wow, a job so soon. I guess you really do plan on staying here for a while."

"I promised the owner I'd stay until the end of summer. Carly was okay with that. I hope you are too," Colt said.

"Sure. I have no problem with that. And I do know where you can get a pair of boots. There's a place in the outlet mall not too far from here where I buy my uniforms. They sell boots, too." She stood up and stretched, then snapped off the television. "Come on. We can go there right now so I can show you where it is."

"Great," Colt said. "Are you sure you have time, though? Don't you want to sleep some more?"

"It won't take long. You can drive, though. Your long legs will never fit in my tiny car."

Colt was so happy that when he stood, he gave Beth a hug without even thinking about it. "Thanks, Beth. You've been such a big help to me. If you ever need anything, just tell me, okay? I want to return the favor."

Beth stood there a moment and stared at him funny, but then finally smiled. "You're welcome, Colt. Being nice to you is easy."

They took off to find Colt a pair of boots.

Chapter Twelve

Colt was back at the townhouse by the time Carly came home. He'd found a good pair of leather, steel-toed boots that were actually comfortable for a good price. He was so excited about starting his new job, he wanted to take Carly out to dinner to celebrate. He'd invited Beth to come along, but she'd declined and said she wanted to grab a nap before her shift. She wished Colt good luck on his first day of work tomorrow.

"Hey, cutie," Colt said, getting up from the sofa to give Carly a hello kiss. "Did you have a good rest of the day?"

Carly shrugged. She slipped off her coat and hung it in the closet, then kicked off her heels. "It was okay. I'm going to change and then we can meet up with the gang for dinner."

Colt stood there a moment, unsure. He hadn't realized they'd be eating with her friends again. "I was hoping I could take you out to eat, just the two of us. You know, to celebrate my new job."

Carly walked into the kitchen and pulled a bottle of water out of the fridge. "But I always eat with my friends. I already told them we were coming. Besides, I hardly think getting a job in a warehouse is worth celebrating. It sounds like hard work."

Colt's shoulders slumped. *Had she really just said that?* He turned away toward the sofa. "Yeah, I guess it's no big deal to most people, but it's the first job I've ever gotten on my own and it's important to me."

Carly quickly walked over to him and wrapped her arms around his waist, laying her head on his back. "I'm sorry, Colt. I didn't mean it that way. I know it's a big deal for you. I just had a bad day and I'm being bitchy. We can celebrate. We'll go eat with my friends and celebrate, okay?"

Colt tried to understand. He knew she was tired from working all day, especially after being out late drinking last night. "It's okay. I know you didn't mean anything by it. Sure, let's go eat. I can't stay out late anyway. I need to get up early for work tomorrow." He turned around and pulled her to him, running his hand through her silky hair. His heart melted when he heard her sigh.

Carly pulled away and looked up into his eyes. She smiled. "I'll just go change, okay? Give me a minute and I'll be right back." She placed a quick kiss on his lips and then ran off to the bedroom.

Colt watched her go. She was just tired, he told himself again. She didn't mean to talk to him that way. Still, it was hard not to feel hurt from what she'd said.

They met up with Adam, Chelle, and Everly at a bar halfway between the townhouse and downtown Seattle. Carly had recovered her mood quickly and was laughing and teasing not long after they sat down at the table. Everyone ordered wine, except Colt who ordered a beer. Tonight, he wasn't going to drink more than one. He had to be able to drive home and he didn't want to feel sick tomorrow morning.

They ate dinner and the others continued to drink. Around nine o'clock, a DJ started playing music, and it blasted throughout the place. Colt gently reminded Carly that they needed to leave soon, but she pouted and said, "I want to dance." Then she grabbed Colt's hand and pulled him out onto the dance floor.

Colt obliged, although dancing to this loud, banging music wasn't easy. After a couple of dances, he finally declined another and soon Adam was out on the dance floor with Carly while Colt sat at the table and watched.

Everly slid her chair next to Colt until their shoulders touched. Colt tried to politely move away, but she kept moving closer. She pointed to Carly. "Don't worry about her dancing out there," she said into Colt's ear. "You know Adam's gay. He just likes to dance. And those three other guys around her are gay, too. She has a lot of gay friends. Many of them are artists from the gallery."

Colt looked across the room and stared at the guys Everly had pointed to. He hadn't really been too worried about everyone dancing around Carly anyway. People just seemed to dance in one big group around here. He guessed their being gay was a good thing. At least he didn't have to feel jealous.

"So, you got a job unloading trucks at the market," Everly said. "I don't know many men who are laborers." She ran her hand up Colt's arm and squeezed his bicep. "You must be very strong. I'll bet you look amazing with your shirt off," she purred.

Colt stared at her, surprised. He gently pulled his arm away and looked at Everly closely, noticing her eyes were glazed over. He figured she must be really drunk and that was why she was flirting with him. He tried ignoring her, and it must have worked, because Everly got up and wobbled to the bar on her stiletto heels to buy another drink.

Carly came back to the table and downed her glass of white wine. Colt noticed her balance wasn't too good, either. He reached out and gently took her hand. "We should leave," he said, leaning into her so he could talk into her ear.

Carly pulled back. "But I'm having fun. Come on. Dance with me some more. You know I love how you dance." Carly pulled him toward the dance floor.

Colt danced again with Carly through one more song and then gently pulled her from the floor. It was after eleven, and he had to go home. He picked up her coat as she drank down more wine, and helped her into it before she could protest. Then he slipped his own on. He had no idea where everyone else was, and he didn't care. He just wanted to get Carly home.

As they headed to the door, Carly got her second wind. "Hey, why are we leaving? I want to stay and have fun."

Trying to avoid a scene, Colt pulled her to him. "Let's go home," he whispered in her ear. "I want you all to myself." He kissed her softly on the lips.

Carly smiled back. "Yeah. Let's go home, Hot Cowboy."

Relieved, Colt steadied her up as he walked her to his truck. He hoped when they got home she'd pass out, because there was no way he'd be able to get up early tomorrow if she suddenly found a burst of newfound energy.

* * *

The next morning, Colt dragged out of bed at five o'clock after only five hours of sleep. He showered and then quietly made himself eggs and toast before leaving the house. Luckily, last night when they'd come home, Carly had dropped in the bed and fallen asleep. Colt had gently undressed her and covered her up, then kissed her goodnight before falling fast to sleep. He left her a note by the alarm clock telling her he'd stop by the gallery after his shift. For one instant, he'd thought about signing it, "Love, Colt." But he hesitated. Maybe it was too soon to use that word. So, he'd just left it unsigned. After all, who else would be leaving her a note beside her bed except him?

Colt followed the early morning traffic into Seattle and was happy that it wasn't too busy yet. He supposed that after seven o'clock it would get heavier. Going to work before rush hour was one good thing about working so early. He knew he'd have to go to bed earlier on a regular basis though if he was going to work at this job.

Colt arrived at the market and found a parking space. He noticed a sign that said three hour parking only. He figured he'd ask where he should park once he got inside. He didn't want a parking ticket his first day.

When he walked up to the door, it didn't open. Colt looked around. The market hours didn't start until eight o'clock. Peering inside the window, he caught site of Connor, who was already behind the customer service counter. Connor came over and let him in.

"Next time come in through the alley," Connor told him as he locked the doors again. "Where did you park?"

Colt pointed to his truck down the street.

"You can't park there all day." Connor went behind the counter and pulled a piece of paper out of a drawer. "Here," he said, handing it to Colt. "Put that on your dash and move your truck to the parking lot one block over from here. You'll have to buy a parking permit for all day parking later. After you move your truck, come in the back way from the alley."

Colt nodded. He wasn't used to so many regulations just to go to work.

"Hey? Where's the cowboy hat? You look like a regular guy today," Connor asked as Colt turned to leave.

"Didn't need it," he told Connor. There was no need to wear it here while he worked.

Connor grinned. "Shoot. Then I can't call you Cowboy. See you later, Cole."

Colt nodded. He went out to his truck, found the parking lot, and placed the parking permit on the dash. He'd have to ask how to buy a permit later. He walked down the street and saw the alley, and then he went down it until he reached the entrance to the market. There was already a truck unloading at the platform. He quickly walked inside. Gerard was waiting for him at the door.

"Connor told me you were on your way," Gerard said. "I'll introduce you to Quinn and let him show you the ropes. First, though, you'll have to punch in."

Gerard showed him where the time clock was and how to use it. Colt punched in and placed his card in a slot beside the time clock. It seemed strange to have to clock his hours. At home, he just worked until the work was done.

Gerard led him back to a room where he could hang his coat. It was a large room with tables and chairs and a small kitchen with a microwave oven and a refrigerator. There were small lockers in there, too, and he was assigned one and given the combination. He must have looked confused about the locker because Gerard explained, "The women use them for their purses and everyone uses them for their lunches and stuff they don't want left out. You can also put your lunch or drinks in the fridge over there. Everyone is pretty honest here. But it's best to put valuables in the locker."

Colt nodded. That was another thing he had to think about—bringing a lunch. He'd never had to do that either since his mom served lunch at the ranch every day.

Colt followed Gerard back out to the loading dock. People were milling around the back room opening up boxes and carting out items to restock the shelves.

"Quinn," Gerard yelled. A young man standing over by the truck looked up and came over when he saw Gerard wave. "This is Cole, the new worker I was telling you about. He's here and he's raring to go. You just have to show him what he needs to do, okay?"

"Hi Cole," Quinn said, offering his hand. "Happy to meet you."

Colt shook his hand. Quinn was almost as tall as he was, slender, but his arms were muscular. His hair was brownish red like his father's and cut short. When he smiled, his light blue eyes twinkled.

"Glad to be working here," Colt said.

"See you both later." Gerard turned and walked away.

"Come on." Quinn waved Colt in the direction of the loading docks. "We really need an extra set of hands around here. Hope you're ready to do some heavy lifting."

Colt nodded. "Yep."

"Great."

Quinn set him to work right away helping the truck driver unload large boxes onto hydraulic hand pallet carts, moving them to their designated area, and then unloading the carts so they could use them again at the truck. Another employee then moved those pallets to their proper location with a small forklift that ran up and down the aisles of the back room, stocking and retrieving items. There were two loading docks side by side, so Quinn worked one while Colt worked the other. Once those trucks were unloaded, Quinn filled Colt in on what he'd be doing every day.

"We get several trucks in here every day. The dairy and fresh produce trucks come most often, as well as the meat and fish deliveries. Then there are all the dry goods that come on a regular basis. You will be busy each morning unloading trucks, and then when I get a chance, I'll teach you how to run the forklift so you can help stock and retrieve items. We also bring out requested pallets to the main floor on the pallet carts so people can restock the grocery shelves. Believe me, your day will go fast."

"That's fine with me," Colt said. "I'm used to being busy all day."

"Good," Quinn said. "My dad says you're from Montana,

but you moved here to be with your girlfriend."

Colt nodded.

"She must be quite some woman for you to want to move out here for her," Quinn said.

"Yes, she is. She's really special."

"Well, that's good," Quinn said. "Seattle is a great town to live in. I like it. I'm sure you'll like living here."

"I do so far," Colt said. Quinn seemed like a nice guy. He was glad about that. It would make working here so much easier.

Colt's day went by quickly, even with a half-hour lunch break. He'd bought a sandwich and pop from the store's small deli and ate it in the break room. Connor had come in to grab his coat and asked Colt how his day was going. He seemed like a nice guy, too, even if he teased Colt a little. For a first day, Colt thought things went pretty well.

Colt left at three and walked up the few blocks to the gallery to see Carly. He wanted to ask her how he could buy a parking permit for the next day. When he walked in, though, she was busy with a customer, so he went back outside to wait. There was a coffeehouse two doors down, so Colt bought a coffee and a cookie and sat on a bench outside to eat it.

The day was chilly, but the sun kept peeking out from behind the clouds, warming the air. At home, there'd be snow everywhere and the temperature would be ten to twenty degrees colder. Colt didn't miss the cold, but for the first time since he'd arrived here, he missed the ranch. He wondered how everyone was, and what they were doing at this very moment. He supposed his mother was already starting to prepare supper and Andi might be helping her. Luke, Randy, and Jake would be working outside, feeding the herd and the horses. The sun would be down in less than two hours there, so they'd be working hard to get everything done before dark.

"Hey, handsome, what are you daydreaming about?" Carly walked over to Colt and sat down beside him. "Oh, coffee. Can I have a sip?"

Colt handed over his large cup. "I was just thinking about the ranch and what everyone would be doing right now."

"I talked to Andi the other day. She said everyone was fine and they already missed you."

"That's good to hear," Colt said, a smile appearing on his lips. "It's hard to believe it hasn't even been a week since I left. So much has happened." He raised his arm around the back of the bench and Carly snuggled up against him.

"How was your first day of work?" Carly asked.

"It was good. Quinn, the guy I work with, is nice. The owner is, too. I'm sure we'll get along fine. It's really a workout though. At least I won't grow soft while I'm here."

Carly turned and gave him a wicked grin, her eyebrows raised. "I doubt you'll ever get soft," she said.

Colt felt his face flush. "You're a little devil, you know that?"

"I try." Carly handed Colt the cup. "I have to get back to the gallery." She kissed him lightly on the cheek, running her hand behind his neck, and then giggled. "You need a shower."

"Yeah. I'll take one as soon as I get home."

"Sorry I have to miss that," Carly said. This time Colt pulled her to him and kissed her on the lips. She winked at him, snitched a chunk off of his cookie, and stood to leave. "See you, Cowboy."

Colt watched as Carly walked away and entered the gallery. He was tired, hungry, and needed a shower, but he felt like the happiest man on the planet.

* * *

Colt was dozing on the sofa when Carly came home that night. She changed clothes and said they were meeting the gang at a restaurant in downtown Seattle that was next door to a dance club. A new DJ was going to start tonight, and Carly couldn't wait to go dancing.

Colt yawned. "Aren't you tired from last night? I really need to sleep tonight. I only slept five hours last night."

"Oh, don't be such a big baby," Carly said, her voice teasing. "We won't stay out too late."

They ended up staying out again until after eleven and by the time they got to bed, it was after midnight. Colt was shot. But when Carly curled up next to him as he fell asleep, he couldn't stay angry. So, she liked to have fun. At least she included him. After all, she could be going out without him. He'd have the entire weekend to catch up on his sleep so he'd be rested up again by Monday morning.

But as January turned into February, each week went on as the one before. Carly wanted to go out every night with her friends, sometimes staying out so late that Colt could barely get up in the morning. When he'd tell her that he had to get more sleep, she'd carelessly say to just quit his job. She didn't have to be at work until nine, so if she went to bed by midnight, she'd still get at least seven hours of sleep. Colt, however, was lucky if he'd get five hours. But, since he didn't want to take away Carly's fun, and he wanted to be with her, he just went along with the crazy hours.

Every day at work, Colt had to fight to stay awake. A couple of times, he fell asleep in the break room during his lunch, only to be awoken by a loud noise out in the warehouse. Quinn came upon him sleeping in the break room one afternoon.

"Hey, Cole, is it your naptime?" he teased.

Colt woke suddenly and almost tipped his chair over. "Uh, just resting my eyes," he said, running his hand over his face.

"Do you always snore when you rest your eyes?" Quinn asked.

Colt chuckled. "Okay, you caught me." He knew Quinn was just ribbing him. He'd been working with Quinn for over a month and they got along really well. Colt had told Quinn about his family in Montana and about Carly, and he'd learned more about Quinn, too. Colt was fitting in with the other workers as well, and he liked Gerard, too. The market was a large place with a lot of employees, yet everyone acted like a family there. Colt liked that.

"You should get more sleep," Quinn told him as he sat down and ate his lunch. "It's dangerous working around all this heavy stuff and equipment when you're tired."

Colt nodded. "I know. I'm not used to living on such little sleep. But Carly loves going out every night. She did it before I moved here, so it's not really my place to tell her she can't now."

"Just stay home and let her go out then," Quinn said matter-of-factly. "You need your sleep. She should think of you, too."

Colt knew that was true, but he was afraid of upsetting Carly. She was used to getting her way. But he also knew if he didn't stop going out so much with her, he was going to end up getting hurt on the job.

Chapter Thirteen

One Friday afternoon when Colt got home at three-thirty, he was happy to see Beth was home and awake, working in the kitchen. Her work hours had been changing every week since he moved here so he hadn't had a chance to see much of her. Plus, he was often asleep on the sofa in the afternoons after work, so he rarely heard her come and go.

"Hey, stranger," he said, putting his coat away in the closet. "I almost forgot you lived here."

Beth laughed. "Yeah, me, too. It's hard to believe we live in the same house. I never run into you anymore."

Colt sniffed the air. "Something smells delicious. What are you cooking?"

"A lot of stuff," Beth said. "I have chicken in the oven, lasagna, and meatloaf."

"It smells great. Just like home."

"Well, I take that as a compliment after hearing how good a cook your mom is."

"Are you having friends over?"

Beth shook her head. Her hair was once again up in a ponytail and she was wearing a pair of sweat pants and a baggie T-shirt. Colt hadn't yet seen her in anything but baggie clothes. "I make up food in advance for my work week and freeze it in separate meals. That way I can take it to work for lunch or heat it up here at home."

"Why haven't I seen you do this before?" Colt asked. He grabbed a pop out of the fridge and sat at the counter.

"You've either been at work or out with Carly. I do this once a week on my day off. I have today and this weekend off and then I start a seven to three day shift next week. I figured today would be a good day to do this. Then I can enjoy my weekend."

"You'll have the same shift as mine," Colt said. "Maybe I'll see more of you next week."

"Maybe."

Colt went off to shower and by the time he came out again, the food was out of the oven. It smelled heavenly. "I'll pay you for a slice of meatloaf," he told her.

"You can have it for free," Beth said, laughing. She took a plate down from the cupboard and placed a slice on it, then also put a piece of baked chicken on the plate. She set the plate on the counter for Colt, and then got him some silverware. "Have at it."

"Thanks," Colt said before digging in. After a bite of the meatloaf, Colt sighed. "This is so good. I feel like I'm at home."

"Wow, if I'd known meatloaf would make you this happy, I'd have given you some sooner."

Carly walked through the door just as Beth had finished speaking. "What would you have given him?" she asked. She kicked off her heels and walked over to the kitchen.

"Meatloaf," Colt said. "It's so good. Do you want to try some?"

Carly wrinkled her nose. "Uh, no thanks. I'm not really a meatloaf kind of person."

"It's really good. I haven't had homemade food since I came here," Colt said, savoring every bite.

"What's wrong with eating out?" Carly asked, her hands on her hips. "It's not like you've been starving."

"Oh, I know. I just miss my mom's cooking. And this tastes just like her meatloaf."

Carly rolled her eyes. "Your mom is an amazing cook, but I like eating out. Don't fill up too much. I'm going to change and we're going to meet the others for dinner."

Colt kept quiet and continued eating his food. Even though he didn't feel like going out tonight, it was Friday, so he could sleep in tomorrow. It would make Carly happy.

He finished up his food and thanked Beth.

"If you'd like, I can make extra so you have food to heat up at work for lunch," Beth offered.

Colt didn't even have to think twice about it. "That would be great. Thanks, Beth. Just let me know how much I owe you for the groceries, okay?" He was already paying for his half of the eggs, toast, and milk that he used.

"Sure," Beth said. "Happy to do it."

Carly and Colt drove into Seattle to meet the others for dinner. They ate at a sushi bar that night, something Colt really didn't enjoy. He was happy he'd eaten some of Beth's delicious food earlier. Afterwards, they walked along the street toward a dance club. Carly was pressed up against Colt to keep warm from the cool breeze coming off the bay. Colt thought the breeze felt wonderful. The temperatures had been in the high fifties every day this week and they were only in the forties right now, so to him it felt good.

In the distance, he saw the Ferris wheel lit up and slowly spinning around. "That looks like fun," he said to Carly, pointing up to it.

"Really? It's such a touristy thing to do," she said.

Colt shrugged. "I guess I am sort of a tourist around here still."

Adam piped up. "There's always a crazy long line for that thing. If you want a good view of Seattle, you should go up in the Space Needle."

"I'd like to do that, too," Colt said.

"Well, maybe we can play tourist some weekend," Carly said offhandedly.

Colt could tell that she didn't really want to.

They entered the bar where the music played loudly. Colt loved music and dancing, but he didn't enjoy this loud, thumping music. Plus, the dance floor at these places was always so crowded that it was difficult to move on them. He missed The Depot and the fun country music he used to dance to every weekend.

Despite his distaste for the music, he danced a few times with Carly, and then went to buy more drinks at the bar while she danced with Adam. Chelle was dancing very close to a man she'd just met an hour ago, and Everly had followed Colt to the bar to help carry the drinks.

Colt pulled out his wallet and looked at his dwindling cash. Going out every night was taking a toll on his bank account. He had old-fashioned ideas of the man having to pay, but he was beginning to think he couldn't do it much longer. With a sigh, he pulled out a twenty. After waiting for over twenty minutes, they finally got their drinks and made their way back to the tiny table they'd managed to secure.

Everly nudged Colt with her elbow. "Remember when I said that most of the men Carly knew were gay?"

"Yeah."

"Well, that guy she's dancing with isn't. He's been after Carly for a few months now. You might want to keep an eye on him."

Colt scanned the dance floor until he spotted Carly. Her long, blond hair swayed side-to-side as she moved, and her short dress rose even higher as she raised her arms when she danced. The man in front of her was running his hands up and down her waist, and she wasn't doing anything to stop him.

Colt was not a jealous man, but at that very moment, he could have easily punched that guy.

He looked down at Everly who'd sat down and was nursing her red wine. "Should I be worried?"

Everly looked up at him with her big, blue eyes and shrugged. "Normally with Carly, no. But that guy? I'd say yes. He's very persistent."

Colt strode off across the room and made his way through the crowded dance floor until he stood next to Carly and the man. He had at least four inches on this guy. Both Carly and the guy stopped dancing and looked up at him. Trying to stay calm, Colt said, "May I cut in?"

Carly cocked her head and smiled up at him, but the man frowned. "Buzz off, kid," he said.

His heart pounding, Colt took another step closer to the guy. "I'm dancing with my girlfriend," he said, staring hard at the man.

"Oh, now, don't start anything, you guys," Carly cooed. "Come on, Colt. Let's dance." She wrapped her arms around Colt. The man glared at Colt, but walked away.

"What the heck was that about?" Carly asked Colt as they swayed together to the slow song that had begun to play. Her eyes were bright and her face was flushed. Colt knew she'd had too much to drink already.

"I didn't like the way he was touching you," Colt said.

Carly shook her head. "We were just dancing, Colt. This isn't Montana. You don't have a claim on me, so don't be so protective. I can take care of myself, okay?"

Colt swallowed his pride and waited for his anger to recede. Finally, he bent his head down and whispered into Carly's ear,

"I just don't like seeing another man touch you. I want to be the only man who touches you."

Carly smiled up at him. "Don't worry, Cowboy," she whispered. "I won't let anyone else but you touch me."

That night when they got home, Colt made sweet, tender love to her. He slowly undressed her, placing kisses over every part of her body as each piece of clothing dropped to the floor. His desire for her grew every day he was with her. He'd never felt this way about a woman before, the deep desire to protect her, care for her, and love her in every way imaginable. Afterwards, when they lay in each other's arms, he whispered, "I love you, Carly."

Carly reached over and kissed him softly on the lips before falling asleep in his arms. Colt didn't mind that she hadn't said she loved him back. Her actions told him everything he needed to know.

* * *

Carly awoke with a pounding headache and the feeling of cotton in her mouth. She lay in bed a moment before opening her eyes. Sunlight filtered through the cracks around the window shade. She turned her head and saw that Colt wasn't in bed. She figured he must have already gotten up and let her sleep in.

Slowly, Carly pulled herself out of bed. She found one of Colt's cotton, button-up shirts on the floor and slipped it on along with a pair of yoga pants. She needed aspirin and coffee right away.

Walking out toward the kitchen, she saw Colt and Beth lounging on the sofa in front of the television. The sun coming through the patio window was so bright, it practically blinded her. She squinted as she made her way to the kitchen.

"Hey, sleepyhead," Colt said. "How do you feel this morning?"

Carly ignored him while she poured coffee and downed two Tylenol. After her eyes had adjusted to the light, she answered. "Like a truck ran me over. Did I really drink that much last night?"

Colt chuckled. "You had a few. It was probably the mixture of wine and gin and tonics that did it to you. It's always better to stick to one type of alcohol."

Carly rolled her eyes. She didn't need drinking advice from a beer drinker. "What the heck are you two watching?"

"House Hunters," Colt said. "I figured I should let you sleep in, so Beth has been keeping me entertained with her favorite show."

"Goodness," Carly said. She couldn't understand why anyone would want to watch stuff like that. "I'm going to shower."

"Do you want some breakfast?" Beth offered. "It might make you feel better."

"Ugh, no," Carly said. "It'll make me puke. I just need to wake up with a hot shower."

Carly dragged herself into the bathroom, undressed, and stepped into the shower. As she stood under the warm water, her blood began to pump and her mind started to wake up. She washed her hair and stood under the water for a long time, trying to remember last night. They'd eaten sushi, and then gone out dancing. She remembered having a couple glasses of white wine. She didn't remember drinking gin and tonics, like Colt had said. She remembered dancing with Adam and Colt. Had she danced with another guy? She thought so. And hadn't Colt cut in at some point? Maybe. She didn't remember coming home, but she remembered Colt undressing her and caressing her so lovingly. Did they make love? Sheesh, why couldn't she remember?

The longer Carly stood under the warm water, the more her memory returned. Yes, they had made love. And then, right as she was falling asleep, Colt had said he loved her.

Carly's eyes grew wide. *Oh, my God. Colt had told her he loved her!*

Carly squeezed her eyes shut and tried to remember if he'd said it for sure or if she'd dreamt it. No, it hadn't been a dream. He'd actually said it.

She got out of the shower and dried and styled her hair, the entire time worrying about what Colt had said. She hoped to God she hadn't said it back to him in her drunken haze. She really liked Colt, but did she love him? Maybe, in a way she did. In the, he's so adorable, cute, and cuddly way. But she had a feeling that it wasn't the same way he had meant it.

Carly dressed and picked up her room. She felt a lot better, now that she'd cleaned up and the Tylenol had taken effect. She just wished she felt better about Colt having said he loved her.

Who says that after only a month of being together?

Carly wanted so badly to call Andi for advice, but she didn't dare. If Andi knew that Colt had professed his love for her, and that Carly didn't feel the same way, she'd tell Carly to tell him the truth. But Carly didn't know the truth. She'd thought they were just having fun. She hadn't expected him to say he loved her so quickly. Or, at all.

Carly walked into the hallway and opened the closet doors that hid the washer and dryer. She tossed a handful of her underthings in the washer and started it. She decided it was time to change the sheets on her bed, so she headed back into the bedroom. Just as she pulled off the top sheet, she felt someone standing behind her.

"Want some help with that?" Colt asked, wrapping his arms

around her from behind and placing a kiss on her neck.

Shivers went up Carly's spine. Colt's touch did that to her. But, was that love?

"Sure, if you want to help. Do you know how to make a bed?" Carly asked, pulling away.

"I'm sure I can learn," Colt said, grinning.

Carly smiled. Colt was so darned cute, it was hard not to smile. Together, they pulled off the bottom sheet and then put on the new one. Carly snapped the top sheet in the air and it fell perfectly over the bed, then she showed Colt how to tuck in the corners. They finished putting the blanket on and then the bedspread. Carly picked up the bundle of dirty sheets and headed to the washing machine again, setting them on top of it.

"I'll do these later after my other stuff is done," she told Colt, who had followed her out into the hallway. "By the way, have you been able to do laundry?"

Colt chuckled. "I would hope so. I've been here over a month. Beth showed me how to use the machines, so I've been doing my clothes when I get home from work before you come home."

"Oh." Guilt crept up on Carly, because she hadn't noticed this. Why hadn't she even thought to ask Colt about his laundry before? Was she so wrapped up in herself that she didn't even notice?

"Do you want to do something today?" Colt asked. "It's beautiful out. We could go walking, or take a drive. Anything you want."

Carly didn't enjoy walking and her stomach couldn't stand to ride for a long time right now. "I'd really like to go to the mall and shop," she said. "But I suppose that would bore you."

Colt shrugged. "I don't mind. What are you shopping for?"

Carly giggled. "Women don't shop for anything in particular, silly. We just shop."

They spent the day at the local mall going from store to store. Carly never tired of trying on new clothes, or buying them. Colt dutifully carried her shopping bags for her while she perused the racks, tried on clothes, and tried on dozens of pairs of shoes. Colt had dressed as he usually did, in jeans, boots, and a blue, button-down shirt that made his blue eyes stand out. He'd left his hat at home and had only worn a light jacket. Carly noticed he garnered attention from women everywhere they went. Of course, in many places, he was the only man standing around, but still, it irked Carly that women stared at him openly like he was available. But to his credit, Carly noticed that he wasn't even aware of the stares from other women. He only kept his attention and on her.

They had a quick bite to eat in the food court before walking toward the exit where Colt had parked the truck. By now, Colt carried several shopping bags for Carly, but he didn't complain. She liked that about Colt. Other men would have been annoyed with her, but not him. He was always willing to help and to please her. So, why wasn't she completely in love with him? He was good looking, sweet, a great kisser, and loving in bed. What was wrong with her?

They passed a small jewelry store and Carly couldn't resist pulling Colt in. "Just for a quick look," she told him. Colt obliged without a word, just as she thought he would.

Carly walked around the glass cases, looking at all the beautiful diamond and gemstone jewelry. She loved jewelry, but usually only bought cheap stuff. The few items of real gold and gemstones that she owned had been given to her as gifts or were pieces her mother had owned that she and Andi had kept. And of course, the lovely necklace Colt had given her for Christmas.

Carly reached up and touched the blue topaz that hung around her neck. She loved it. So many people at the gallery had given her compliments on it. Stopping at the glass counter that held blue gemstones, Carly looked at the selection of earrings. There, in the middle, was a pair of teardrop, London blue topaz earrings set in white gold.

"Look, Colt. They match the necklace you gave me," she said excitedly.

Colt looked where she pointed. "They do. They're really pretty."

"Can I help you?" A woman came up behind the counter and smiled at them.

"I was just looking," Carly said automatically.

"Can we see those earrings?" Colt asked, pointing to the ones Carly had just showed him.

Carly looked at Colt in surprise. She'd only pointed them out. She hadn't meant to actually look at them.

The woman nodded and pulled out the earrings. Colt lifted them up and handed them to Carly to inspect. "They are exactly like your necklace," he said.

Carly nodded. She noticed the tag hanging from the box they sat in. The earrings were very expensive. It made her wonder just how much Colt had spent on her necklace.

"They are very pretty," she said, handing them back to the woman. "Thank you." Carly turned and walked out of the jewelry store with Colt close behind.

They walked out into the fading sunlight. It was almost sunset and the air was growing chilly. As they drew close to the truck, Colt asked, "Didn't you like the earrings?"

Carly turned and smiled at him. "I loved them. But they were way too expensive. I like to spend money, but I have to draw limits somewhere. Clothes and shoes I can justify, because I need to dress nice for work. Jewelry, I can't."

Colt placed the bags in the back seat of his truck and climbed up in the cab. "Then why do you look?"

"Because, it's fun."

Colt shook his head. "I guess I just don't understand women that well," he said.

Carly laughed. "You understand them well enough," she said, reaching out to pull him to her and kissing him softly.

Chapter Fourteen

That night, instead of going out, they had food delivered and ate it in front of the television while watching an old romantic movie. Beth had left a note on the kitchen counter saying she'd gone hiking with friends and wouldn't be home until Sunday afternoon. So, Carly and Colt took advantage of the privacy by turning out the lights and watching television by candlelight as they ate.

Colt was happy to finally spend some time alone with Carly. Ever since he'd come here, they'd spent every night out with her friends. Tonight, they could relax and talk, and cuddle up together. It felt like the time they'd spent together at the ranch when there was nothing else to distract them. He wished they'd have more nights like this together.

When the movie credits rolled, Carly turned off the television and pulled Colt to her. They made love on the sofa, softly caressing each other until they could no longer hold back. Then they headed for the bedroom where their passion continued. It was the most romantic night of Colt's life, right up there with the first time they'd made love the night of Luke and Andi's wedding. As they lay curled up together in bed, Colt lovingly brushed a silky strand of hair from Carly's face and kissed the tip of her nose. He couldn't believe he was lucky enough to be with a woman as beautiful, smart, and sophisticated as Carly. He fell asleep, content that he knew where his life was heading, and who he wanted to spend his life with.

* * *

On Sunday, they had brunch at a restaurant near downtown Seattle with Adam and Everly. The day was fairly warm, so they sat outside in the sun on the upper deck where they had a nice view of the bay. Chelle hadn't joined them. Colt figured it had something to do with the man she'd met at the bar the other night.

"My birthday is almost here," Carly said excitedly. "And it's a big one. I'm going to be twenty-five."

"You're getting old," Adam chimed in.

"Hey, you're thirty-two, so watch it," Carly teased him.

"How are you going to celebrate?" Everly asked. "We should have a big party."

"I know exactly what I want to do. I want to eat dinner at that restaurant where they have the heavenly seafood, then go to the bar downtown with all the glass and mirrors and the great DJ. We can invite all my friends, everyone from the gallery, and the artists who sell there, too. It will be a blast."

Colt sat and half-listened to the three of them discussing Carly's party as he stared out at the bay. The sparkling blue water gave him a wonderful idea for a present for Carly. He couldn't wait until later this week, after he got paid, when he could go and buy her gift.

* * *

Later that week, Colt came home from work a little later than he usually did. He'd had an errand to run before heading back to the townhouse. Beth was relaxing on the sofa, eating an apple when he entered.

"Hey, there," she said. "Did you have to work late?"

"No. I went to buy something." Colt walked over and sat next to Beth. He pulled a small box out of the bag he was carrying and handed it to her. "I bought these for Carly's birthday. What do you think?"

Beth carefully opened the box and slid out the black velvet jewelry case. She looked up at Colt with wide eyes. "You didn't buy her a ring, did you?"

Colt frowned. "What? No. Open it."

Beth opened the case and sighed. "Geez, you scared me. It looked like a ring case." She moved the earrings back and forth in the light. "These are beautiful, Colt. They match the necklace you gave her. Carly will love these."

"Yeah. She saw them last week at the mall, so I know for sure she'll like them." Beth handed him the box and he slipped it back in the bag. "Why were you so freaked out about it being a ring?"

Beth bit her lip. "I didn't freak out. I was just surprised. I mean, it would be a little soon to propose, wouldn't it?"

Colt shrugged. "I suppose."

Beth laughed. "Don't look so serious. I didn't mean anything by it. You and Carly have plenty of time before you start thinking of marriage."

Colt wondered if Beth thought that Carly would dump him in time, like everyone else thought. He decided he didn't want to know if she did, so he changed the subject. "Are you coming to Carly's big birthday party? It's the Saturday after her real birthday. She's inviting all her friends."

"I hadn't heard about it yet," Beth said. "But I doubt if she'd invite me anyway. It's not like we're good friends."

Colt's face dropped. "But you have to come. I want you to.

After all, you're her roommate."

"Well, we'll see," Beth said.

Colt found out later that week from Carly that she hadn't invited Beth and hadn't planned to, either. "She hates that kind of thing," Carly told him. "She isn't much of a drinker and she doesn't fit in with my gallery friends."

Colt persuaded Carly to let him invite her so they wouldn't hurt her feelings, and Carly relented. "Go ahead," Carly said. "She probably won't come anyway."

The next week went by quickly and before he knew it, the day of Carly's birthday party had arrived. Colt had invited Beth to the party, as well as to dinner, and she'd accepted, although Colt could tell she was reluctant about coming.

Saturday night, Colt sat on the bed and watched as Carly applied her makeup and styled her hair. She slipped into a short, white, sleeveless dress that scooped low at the neck and showed off her long slender legs. Turning, she asked Colt to zip up the back for her. He did so willingly, first carefully brushing aside her hair so it wouldn't get caught. He bent down and placed a kiss at the base of her neck. "Hmm. You smell wonderful," he said.

Carly giggled. She slipped on a pair of high, shiny red pumps and then brought her necklace over for Colt to clasp behind her neck.

"I should let you help me dress all the time," she told him as he clasped the necklace. She turned around. "How do I look?"

"Beautiful," Colt said, delighting in her curvy figure in the tight dress. Carly looked gorgeous in everything she wore.

"You have to say that. You're my boyfriend." Carly ran her hand over his chest. "You look pretty good yourself, hunky Cowboy. I like that shirt on you." Carly had bought him a black dress shirt that he wore with his jeans. He had a black leather jacket to wear over it, too.

"You have to say that," Colt said with a grin. "I'm your boyfriend."

Carly giggled. She walked over to her jewelry box on the dresser and rummaged through the earrings.

Colt came up behind her. "Maybe you'd like to wear these tonight," he said.

Carly looked up into the mirror at Colt. He stood close behind her, holding a small, black, velvet box.

"Happy Birthday," Colt said, offering the box to her.

Carly turned around and accepted the gift. When she opened it, her eyes grew wide. "You bought the earrings! I love them. Thank you." Carly reached her arms around Colt's neck and pulled him down for a kiss.

"You're welcome," he said, inches from her lips.

Carly turned around and put on the earrings. "They're so beautiful," she said, admiring how they glittered as she turned her head.

"You're the beautiful one." Colt wrapped his arms around her waist.

Carly smiled into the mirror. "We do look good together, don't we?"

Colt laughed. "I look good because of you."

Carly reapplied her lipstick and slipped on a short, white, faux fur jacket that had strands of silver running through it that glittered in the light. "Let's go. I can't be late to my own party."

By the time they'd headed out the door, Beth still hadn't come out of her room. She'd already told Colt she'd meet them at the restaurant. Colt had offered for her to ride with them, but she'd declined. "I can drive myself," she'd told him. "I'm sure Carly will want to stay late."

When Colt and Carly arrived at the restaurant, Adam, Chelle and her date, and Everly were waiting for them, as well as two other women who worked at the gallery. Colt recognized

Chelle's date as being the man she'd met last week. The dinner party was going to be small, and then everyone else was coming later to the bar for the real party.

As they waited for their table, Beth walked in. Colt looked up when the door opened and was about to turn away when she smiled at him. His eyes grew wide. He hadn't even recognized her. She wore a sleek black dress that sparkled with tiny rhinestones around the waist and v-neckline. Her heels made her taller than he was used to, and her legs were long and shapely. She'd pulled her hair up, and loose tendrils framed her face. She was even wearing makeup, something Colt wasn't used to seeing on her. She looked stunning.

Beth looked up at Colt and smiled. "Better close your mouth before you start catching flies," she teased.

Colt quickly did so. "I didn't even recognize you at first," he said.

Beth's brows rose. "You mean I usually look so terrible that you didn't know I could look nice?"

"Yeah. Uh, no. I mean…" Colt snapped his mouth shut. His words weren't coming out right. "You always look nice," he finally said. "But tonight, you look beautiful."

Beth smiled. "Thank you, Colt. You look pretty good yourself. But then, you always look handsome."

Colt's face felt flush. *What the heck is going on? This is just Beth.* He couldn't understand why he was tongue-tied all of a sudden.

"Hi, Beth," Carly said, turning around from talking to her friends. "You look very pretty tonight. I'm glad you came."

"Thanks, Carly. You look lovely, as usual."

Carly introduced everyone to Beth and then they were led to their table. Colt trailed behind Beth, still amazed at her transformation. He was used to seeing her in baggy scrubs and clothes. But all along, under all those baggy clothes, she had an incredible figure. She looked incredible.

They sat at a table that overlooked the bay. Small boats sparkled on the water, lit up with twinkle lights. The moon shined high above, casting a silvery glow upon the water. Colt sat next to Carly and made sure that Beth was on his other side so she'd feel more comfortable.

"I see you gave Carly the earrings," Beth said quietly to Colt as everyone studied their menus.

Colt nodded. "She loved them."

"She'd be crazy not to," Beth said with a grin.

They ordered drinks and dinner, and then everyone around the table chatted. Beth talked easily with Chelle, who sat on her right, while Colt sat and listened to Carly telling Adam and the others about a difficult customer she had the other day. Carly was definitely the center of attention, but Colt couldn't help but glance at Beth often, marveling at how lovely she looked and how at ease she seemed. He'd thought she'd feel awkward around Carly's friends, but she didn't look it. He was happy he'd invited her.

After their meal, everyone gave Carly gifts, much to her delight. She opened each one, expressing how much she loved each gift. Adam gave her a beautiful turquoise, designer scarf that complimented her eyes and Chelle gave her a silver bangle bracelet with purple and clear crystals set in it. Carly squealed with delight over the scarf and quickly put on the bracelet, announcing how much she loved it. Everly gave her a designer handbag that Carly loved. Beth had been more practical. She gave Carly a gift card to her favorite clothing boutique downtown.

"I figured you'd rather buy your own gift," Beth said.

Carly thanked her, smiling wide. "I can't wait to spend it," she said, which made everyone laugh. It was no secret that Carly loved spending money.

They left the restaurant soon after that and walked the short distance to the dance club. Colt had run the gifts to the truck so they wouldn't have to worry about them.

Colt heard the music pounding before they even entered the club. The DJ had the speakers blasting so loud that it filtered out into the night. Carly had consumed three glasses of wine with dinner, so she was already dancing before they walked inside. Colt braced himself mentally. It was going to be another one of those crazy nights.

The club was like no other Colt had ever seen before. It was dark, but spinning spotlights shined everywhere in colors of blue, purple, and pink. Everything from the long bar to the tables and chairs, was silver, glass, or mirror, and crystals hung from the ceiling, reflecting the colors of the lights. The entire place glittered and sparkled. It felt like being inside a huge disco ball.

Colt stood there, dazed a minute, trying to adjust his eyes. It seemed crazy to him that a place where people drank would have mirrored walls. He wondered how many times people walked into the glass each night. But he had to admit, the effect was impressive.

The group squeezed through the crowd and found a corner in the back of the room where all of Carly's friends had gathered around several tables. Carly squealed with delight when she saw them and ran over, giving everyone a hug. In the middle of the table sat a large cake decorated with a pink champagne bottle pouring liquid into a glass, all made up of frosting. Around it stood real bottles of champagne and glasses for everyone.

"I love it!" Carly exclaimed. "You all know me so well."

Colt glanced down at Beth and she looked up at him. He could tell from the look in her eyes what she was thinking. This was going to be a very crazy night.

Carly tried introducing Colt to all her friends over the

blaring music, but soon gave up. That was fine with Colt. He wouldn't remember all their names anyway. Drinks were ordered, champagne was poured, and the cake was cut and served. Between the sugar high from the cake and the tossing back of the champagne, it didn't take long for many of the guests to become loud and cheerful.

Colt sat with Beth at the end of the table and watched in awe as Carly came alive from the champagne and all the attention her friends were bestowing upon her. He offered to get Beth a drink, but she declined. She'd had a sip of champagne, but that was all. Colt knew it was because she had driven here, and she was too sensible to drink much before driving home.

Carly soon grabbed Colt's hand and pulled him to the dance floor where they attempted to move together amidst all the bodies. The streaming lights and the banging music gave Colt a headache, but he wanted Carly to have fun, so he danced. Carly's eyes glistened in the lights and her body swayed seductively. Colt noticed many of the men around them stared at her as she moved unabashedly to the music. It was impossible not to rub up against the other people on the dance floor, but Carly didn't seem to mind. Many of Carly's friends were also around her on the floor, which made Colt feel better. At least strangers weren't groping his girlfriend. At least he hoped they weren't.

Colt went back to the table several times to check on Beth. Sometimes she'd be talking with one of Carly's friends, other times she'd just be sitting there, alone. He felt responsible for keeping her company even though she'd told him several times not to worry about her. She looked so beautiful tonight that he felt protective of her. He didn't want any of the men in the club bothering her. At one point, Colt saw her dancing with one of Carly's friends, and it took everything he had not to go out on the floor and cut in on them. It was a slow song and Colt thought the man was holding her too close. *Cripes. What is the matter with me?* There were men surrounding Carly, yet he was more worried about Beth. Carly could handle herself. She did this all the time. But Beth wasn't Carly. She was a homebody, not a party girl.

That thought made Colt pause. He'd never thought of Carly as a party girl before. But if truth be told, that was exactly what she was.

"Who are you glaring at?" Beth asked, coming up beside Colt.

Colt snapped his head around, startled. He'd been so wrapped up in his thoughts that he hadn't heard the music change or seen that Beth had stopped dancing.

"I didn't know I was," he said. "I was just watching everyone dance."

Beth chuckled. "If you're going to glare at anyone, glare at the men around Carly. Have you noticed all of them dancing with her out there?"

Colt stared out at the dance floor. There was a circle of men and right in the middle was Carly. Adam was there, and so was another man that Colt knew was also gay. He figured as long as Adam was with her, she was safe.

"She's okay," he said. "She's with friends."

Beth nodded. The music grew louder so she had to pull Colt down to her level to yell in his ear. "I think it's time for me to leave. It's getting late."

"Don't leave yet," Colt insisted. He regretted his tone immediately. "I mean, I haven't even had a chance to dance with you. Won't you stay for a few more minutes?"

Beth nodded. "But if we dance, it can't be to that stuff. We'll wait for a slower song."

Colt agreed, and soon after, the DJ began playing a slow

tune, "All of Me" by John Legend. Colt led Beth out to the edge of the floor where they wouldn't be smashed up against the other dancers. He slipped one hand around her waist and raised his other for her to hold. Soon, they were swaying gracefully to the soulful tune.

Colt looked down into Beth's brown eyes. The gold flecks he'd noticed that very first day he'd met her glittered in the light. She smelled lightly of orange blossoms. Her hand was warm and soft in his. He'd noticed before how pretty she was with her thick, dark lashes and creamy skin, but he'd never realized just how beautiful she really was. She smiled up at him, the most genuine smile he'd ever seen, and his heart melted.

They danced without saying a word, listening to the lovely lyrics. When it ended, Colt just stood there, gazing down at Beth. All he'd wanted was to dance one dance with her. Now, he didn't want to let her go.

Chapter Fifteen

The music blared out of the speakers, breaking whatever magic had held Colt's gaze with Beth's. It snapped Colt back to reality, and reluctantly, he let go of her hand. They walked together back to the table where Beth retrieved her coat. Colt held it while she slipped it on.

"Thanks for inviting me," she told Colt. "I had a good time."

"I'll walk you to your car," Colt said, grabbing his own jacket.

"You don't have to do that. I'll be fine."

"I want to do it," Colt told her. Beth nodded and walked ahead of Colt toward the door.

Right before they opened it, a spotlight hit the bar behind them and people began clapping. Both Beth and Colt turned to see what the commotion was about. There, standing on the glass bar was Carly, swaying to the music, her eyes shut, a smile on her red lips. People below crowded around her, cheering her on. Her motions were fluid and sensual. She was absolutely mesmerizing.

"That's our Carly," Beth said. "Always the center of attention. Always the shining star."

Colt looked down at Beth, surprised. "That's what Andi always calls her. The shining star. How'd you know that?"

Beth shrugged. "I didn't know she called her that. It's just true. Look at her. Anyone else dancing drunk on a bar would look pathetic. Not Carly, though. She looks stunning. She'll always be like that. A shining star."

Colt glanced around and saw Carly's friends by the bar. He knew she would be fine. Besides, even if he went over to her, she wouldn't come down. Carly did what she wanted to do. He opened the door and led Beth outside.

The air felt cool and refreshing after being in the stuffy club. Colt inhaled deeply, relishing it.

"Shouldn't you stay with Carly and make sure she's okay?" Beth asked.

"She'll be fine. Her friends are with her." Colt crooked his arm, offering it to Beth. She laughed and accepted, slipping her arm though his.

"Forever the gentleman cowboy, aren't you?" she said.

"My mama raised me right."

"Yes, she sure did."

They walked down the lit up streets passing people here and there. It seemed everyone was in a hurry, but not Colt and Beth. They took their time, enjoying the cool evening.

"I noticed you don't wear your hat much anymore," Beth said. "Why?"

Colt's brows rose. "I didn't know you were keeping tabs on me."

"I'm not," Beth said quickly. "It's just, you wore it a lot when you first came here, and now you never do. It seemed right on you. I just wondered why you stopped."

"I felt out of place wearing it here. Plus, I don't wear it at work 'cause it would get in the way, so I guess I just stopped."

"Do you wear a hat when you work on the ranch?"

"Yeah, almost all the time," Colt said. "But there, I'm outside, so it shades my face in the summer and keeps my head warm in the winter. Here it's different, I guess."

"Do you miss the ranch?" Beth asked, glancing up at him.

Colt's face softened at the thought of home. "Yeah, I do. I miss working outside in the fresh air and spending time with the horses. And I miss my family and sitting around the table, eating my mom's homemade cooking. I don't miss the cold winter temperatures, though. It was thirty-five degrees there today, and almost sixty here."

Beth laughed softly. "No, I wouldn't miss that either, I guess. But the ranch sounds wonderful. I've never ridden a horse before, but I wouldn't mind trying someday."

"Riding's not so hard. I could teach you. If you can ride a bike, you can ride a horse."

Beth looked up at him. "Really? A bike? How are they similar?"

Colt laughed. "They aren't. But it's still not so hard. Maybe you can come to the ranch someday and we'll make a cowgirl out of you. You can even wear a hat."

They had reached Beth's car and stopped beside it.

"You'd better be careful there, Cowboy. I may take you up on that offer," Beth said, a mischievous glint in her eyes.

"I'd be happy if you did. I never say anything I don't mean." Colt opened her door and stood aside so Beth could slide in behind the wheel.

Beth cocked her head and looked at Colt. "You really are different from anyone else I've ever known."

Colt leaned on the door and bent down closer to Beth. "Is that good or bad?"

"It's most definitely good," she said softly.

Colt gazed down at Beth. The streetlight gave off a soft glow around her and made her eyes sparkle. He leaned in closer. Their eyes met. Slowly, he reached up his hand and ran a finger gently across her cheek and behind her ear, brushing away a loose strand of hair.

Beth's eyes widened.

"A strand of hair was in your face," Colt said, suddenly realizing how intimate the gesture was.

"Oh, okay. Thanks," Beth said. Then she smiled. "See you at home, Colt. Drive safely, okay?"

Colt swallowed hard and nodded. "Yeah. See you at home." He carefully shut her door, then stepped back and watched as Beth drove away.

A light breeze picked up and chilled Colt, making him realize he'd been standing on the sidewalk a long time. He turned and walked back toward the bar. Back to Carly.

* * *

When Colt awoke the next morning, he rolled over and checked on Carly. She was sleeping peacefully, so he quietly slipped out of bed and went to take a shower. As he stood under the warm water, he replayed last night in his mind. Getting Carly to leave the bar had been difficult, and it wasn't until last call at one-thirty that he'd been able to talk her into leaving. By then, most of her friends had left, except for Adam and Everly. Adam said he was going to drive Everly home since she was clearly as drunk as Carly. As Colt walked Carly toward the door, his arm tight around her waist to keep her from stumbling, she kept insisting she was fine.

"I want to go somewhere else. It's my twenty-fifth birthday. I want to celebrate," Carly whimpered. But Colt knew she'd celebrated enough, and she passed out after only minutes of riding in the truck. Colt carried her into the townhouse and Carly awoke and suddenly became very sick. Colt had barely got her to the bathroom in time before everything she'd drank that night found its way up and out of her. He'd held her hair back until she finished, then helped her undress before she passed out in bed.

Colt hadn't minded taking care of Carly. He loved her, and he'd do anything for her. But now, as the water streamed over him in the shower, his mind wandered to Beth. Carly's birthday dinner and party had been fine, but for him, the best part of the night had been spending time with Beth. She'd looked so beautiful, he still couldn't get over it. He'd enjoyed dancing with her, and the walk to the car together had been easy and comfortable. Being around Beth had been easy and comfortable from the first day he met her. It was the same type of ease he'd felt around Andi after only a few days. He'd thought of Beth as a sister, but when he'd leaned over her and brushed aside that strand of hair, his mind hadn't been thinking brotherly thoughts. In that instant, he'd thought about kissing her.

What in the hell am I doing? I'm with Carly. I love Carly. Why am I thinking of Beth?

Colt wiped those thoughts away and finished showering and dressed. Beth was his friend. It had just been one of those things. That's all.

When Colt came out of the bathroom, he saw Carly stirring. He knelt down beside the bed and gently ran his hand through her hair to push it off her face. Carly opened her eyes and looked at him, then squinted.

"My head is pounding. I need some water," she whispered.

"I'll get you some. And some Tylenol," Colt said.

He went into the bathroom and filled a paper cup with water, then rummaged through the medicine cabinet and found some Tylenol. He took it out to her and helped her sit up to drink.

"I feel like crap," Carly moaned, sliding back down in bed.

Colt chuckled softly. "That doesn't surprise me. After all the champagne, wine, and shots you drank, you're lucky to be alive."

"I need to sleep," Carly said, curling up under the covers and closing her eyes again.

Colt bent down and kissed her softly on the cheek. "You sleep. Let me know if you need anything, okay?"

Carly didn't answer. She was already asleep.

Colt walked out into the living room. The patio window drapes were wide open and Beth sat at the table with piles of small baskets, tiny stuffed animals, candy, and other trinkets all over the table.

"Good morning," Colt said. He'd worried that after last night things might be awkward between them, but when Beth looked up and smiled, he knew everything was back to normal.

"Hi. I see you survived last night." She wore a big sweatshirt and jeans and her hair was once again in its trademark ponytail. Her face was free of makeup, but her eyes sparkled.

"Oh, yeah, I did just fine. I only had two beers all night. Carly isn't doing very good though. She was sick the minute we came home," Colt told her.

"I know. I heard her last night. I figured you'd come get me if you needed help."

"I've been around grosser stuff than that on the ranch. I could handle it," Colt said.

"I suppose you have. Make sure Carly drinks a lot of water today. She needs to keep hydrated."

"I'll try. She had some water and Tylenol. She's sleeping now. That's probably what she needs the most." Colt stood there and stared at Beth, a frown on his face.

"What?" Beth asked when she looked up.

"You said you heard Carly last night. Does that mean you hear everything that goes on in her room?" he asked hesitantly. He wasn't sure he wanted to know the answer.

Beth broke out laughing. "Goodness, no. I don't. It was just so quiet in here last night that I heard her being sick in her bathroom. Don't worry, Colt. I don't hear anything else."

Colt let out a breath. "That's good. You scared me for a moment."

"Well, just don't do anything too loud in the bathroom. I'll probably be able to hear that," Beth said, grinning.

"Thanks for the warning," Colt said, grinning. "So, what are you doing with all this stuff?"

"I'm making baskets for the kids at the hospital for Easter. The nurses on the family floor do this every year."

"Wow. Is it almost Easter?"

"It's coming up fast. It's early this year," Beth said.

"That's such a nice thing to do. I'll bet the kids love it."

"It's just a way to keep their minds off of being there, at least for a little time," Beth said.

"Do you buy all that stuff yourself?"

"Oh, no. We have a yearly fundraiser that helps pay for everything. We just volunteer our time to pick up the items and put them together. We also do stockings for Christmas."

Colt watched as Beth put together the small baskets. He thought it was so sweet of her to do this for the sick children. "You must really love your job," he said. "Most people wouldn't take the time to do this for others."

Beth nodded. "I do like working with children. It's amazing how resilient little children can be no matter how sick they are. Sometimes, it's hard not to get attached to them. It can be sad at times, but it's rewarding."

"You get attached, because you have a good heart," Colt said.

Beth smiled up at him. "You're sweet, Colt. Thanks."

Colt ducked his head. He felt his face growing hot. He hated that his emotions always showed so easily on his face. He turned around toward the kitchen. "Have you had breakfast yet? I could cook up eggs."

"You can cook, too? I'd say you're a keeper."

Colt turned around and grinned. "Smartass."

Beth laughed out loud.

"Do you want to eat or not?"

"You bet I do. I'm not going to miss out on you cooking for me for a change," Beth said.

Colt made up scrambled eggs and toast and they sat and ate at the counter. Colt had brought a small plate of eggs and toast to Carly, but she'd waved him away. "No food," she'd groaned. "The smell alone makes me sick."

Colt left her alone so she could sleep some more. After he cleaned up the dishes, he sat with Beth and helped her fill baskets. He left the ribbon tying to her, though. "I can't do pretty bows," he told her.

They talked about the party the night before, about the weather being so nice outside, and other topics. Colt was relieved he didn't feel awkward with Beth after last night. Maybe it had just been his imagination. They were just friends, nothing more.

After working on the baskets for over an hour, Beth sat up straight in her chair and stretched. "My back is getting sore sitting here. I need more ribbon, too. I should go to the craft shop and run by the grocery store and pick up a few things."

Colt glanced out the window. The sun was shining brightly. He thought it would be nice to get outside. "Mind having some company? I'll drive."

"Sure," Beth said, getting out of her chair. "Give me a moment and I'll be ready. You should go check on Carly, too, before we leave."

Colt nodded. "Is there an auto or hardware store on our way? I need to buy some rubbing compound to rub out a scratch on my truck."

"There's one near the craft shop. How'd it get scratched?"

"Looks like someone keyed it when I left it overnight at that bar parking lot last month. I'm never doing that again."

Beth shook her head. "It's a shame people do stuff like that. I'll be ready in a flash."

Colt went to check on Carly. She was sleeping soundly, so he left a fresh glass of ice water beside her bed and a note saying he'd be back soon. He figured she wouldn't miss him anyway, since she was sleeping.

He saw his hat on the back of the chair in the bedroom and grinned. He grabbed it and put it on.

"Hey, you're wearing your hat," Beth said when they met in the living room.

"Yep." Colt smiled wide. "You said it suited me, so I'm wearing it just for you."

Beth nodded. "It does suit you. You're a cowboy. You should flaunt it."

They took off in Colt's truck a few minutes later. The day was sunny and warm with temps in the sixties, and it felt good to be out, even if they were in the truck. Beth gave Colt directions, and soon they were at the craft shop. She pointed out where the hardware store was, and Colt ran in there while Beth went to buy ribbon. They met back at the truck within minutes and drove toward the exit.

"Say? Do you mind making a stop at the Home Depot over there?" Beth asked, pointing toward the store. "I need more floor cleaning product and I like the brand they sell. It works wonders on the wood floors."

Colt drove down the road and into the Home Depot parking lot. They walked inside and Beth headed directly to the cleaning supplies. She found the cleaner she was looking for immediately and picked up a bottle.

"You knew exactly where to look. You must come here often," Colt said. He offered to carry the heavy bottle for her and she let him.

"I like coming here sometimes and looking at light fixtures and cabinets and things like that. I imagine what I'd buy if I were building or remodeling a house. It sounds crazy, but it's fun."

"Show me what you've picked out," Colt said.

"Really?" Beth asked. When Colt nodded, she smiled wide. "Well, okay. Follow me."

They walked first through the light fixtures and Beth showed him all the ones she liked. Then they looked at the wood floors, tile for the bathrooms, and then the countertops for both the bathroom and kitchen.

"I love the quartz countertops for the kitchen," Beth said, running her hand over the smooth surface of the sample. "Most people still want granite, but quartz is a harder surface and much easier to care for than granite. And I love these honey-colored cabinets with the glass doors. Don't you think this glass tile backsplash is so beautiful, too?" She looked up at Colt with dreamy eyes, and he smiled down at her. Her passion for home decorating was evident.

"It's all beautiful," he said, looking into her brown eyes. *As beautiful as your eyes.* The thought came to him out of nowhere, surprising him completely. He hoped he hadn't said the words out loud.

Beth started laughing softly.

Colt panicked. He had said it out loud and she was laughing at him.

"I'm sorry. I must be boring you to death with all of this," Beth said. "Your eyes look all glazed over."

Colt let out a breath. *Whew! I hadn't said it out loud.* "No, you're not boring me. Go on. Show me what else you like."

Beth looked around the kitchen area and pointed out a

kitchen island. "I absolutely love this," she said, walking over to it. The island was long and wide and painted a distressed black with a honey-colored, butcher block countertop. There were cupboards on one side and a place for stools on the other.

Colt looked at it with interest. He liked it, too. "How does that fit in with the cabinets you like, though? Wouldn't the island and the countertop have to match the kitchen cabinets and counters?"

"That's what I like about it," Beth said excitedly. "Everything doesn't have to match. The island's countertop matches the cabinets, but the black color gives the kitchen a more lived in feel instead of everything being exactly the same."

Colt considered that. He didn't have much experience with decorating a new house. Luke had picked out all the finishes for his cabin and the main house where Colt lived had been built long ago. His mother hadn't even had a say in how it was built, but she had replaced the appliances with updated versions.

"You don't like it," Beth said, sounding disappointed.

"No," Colt said. "I do like it. I've never had to decorate a house before. You're giving me a lot of good ideas for when I do build a house."

"Well, if you build a house, give me a call. I'd love to help you pick out the finishes."

"I may hold you to that," Colt said with a wink.

Beth laughed. "Yeah. Right."

They left soon after that and went to the grocery store. Colt pushed the cart while Beth picked out what they needed. It felt like such a normal thing to do together, and Colt enjoyed it. Carly didn't go grocery shopping. She didn't wander home improvement centers picking out fixtures for her dream home. But Beth did, and Colt found that endearing. As they drove home with their bags of groceries in the back seat, Colt felt happy, even though he didn't completely understand why.

Chapter Sixteen

It was late in the afternoon when they arrived home and Carly was up, showered, and lying on the sofa looking tired, but better than she had this morning.

Colt walked over to her with his arms loaded with grocery bags and bent to give her a quick kiss on the cheek. "Are you feeling better?"

"A little," Carly said, pouting. "I woke up and you were gone. I didn't know where you were."

Colt set the bags on the counter. "I'm sorry," he said automatically. He noticed Beth frowning and wondered why, but kept talking to Carly. "You were sleeping so soundly, I didn't want to wake you. I left you a note, though."

"Well, I didn't see it," Carly said, her voice whiny. "I'm hungry. Did you bring home anything to eat?"

Colt chuckled. "We have bags of groceries here. There must be something we can eat in them."

Carly wrinkled her nose. "Can't we order take-out or something? I don't want homemade food."

Out of the corner of his eye, Colt saw Beth roll her eyes. He wanted to laugh, but didn't dare. Carly sounded whiny to him, too, but laughing would only make her mad. "We were going to bake chicken and make mashed potatoes. Can you wait an hour to eat?"

Carly slumped down in the sofa. "I guess I can, if I have to.

But I'm hungry right now."

Beth reached into one of the bags and pulled out a bag of potato chips. They were greasy and salty, and definitely not what Carly would normally eat. She walked over and handed them to Carly. "Here. The salt will settle your stomach while you wait."

Carly glared at Beth, and then at the potato chips. But her hunger apparently won out. She opened the bag and began eating them.

They ate supper together that evening like a family—sitting at the dining room table. Colt had cleared away enough of the basket items so they could all three sit together. Carly complained about getting up off the sofa at first, but then joined them. After eating, she looked better, and even admitted the food tasted good. Colt cleared away the dishes and put them in the dishwasher so Beth could work on her baskets again. Carly sulked on the sofa, watching an old movie on television.

Just as he finished doing the dishes, Beth got up from the table and grabbed a padded manila envelope from the small table by the front door, then brought it to Colt. "I keep forgetting to give this to you. It came in the mail yesterday."

Colt looked at the package in his hand. He had no idea what it was, but the return address was Montana. He opened it and pulled out a USB flash drive and a note. The note read, "Wedding pictures."

"Oh, it's Luke and Andi's wedding pictures," Colt exclaimed.

Carly squealed. "I can't wait to see them. Get my computer, will you Colt? It's on my desk in my bedroom."

Colt strode off into the bedroom and retrieved the laptop from the desk. He handed it and the flash drove to Carly, who sat cross-legged on the sofa with a pillow in her lap. Colt sat down beside her and waved Beth over. "Come see the pictures," he said.

Beth leaned on the back of the sofa so she could watch as Carly scrolled through the photos.

The first few pictures were of Luke and Andi posing in front of the fireplace, he in his tux, and she in her wedding dress.

"Oh, my goodness, Colt," Beth said. "They are such a beautiful couple. You didn't tell me that your brother is so handsome."

Colt shrugged. "Yeah, everyone says that. I think Andi makes him look good. She's beautiful, just like Carly." He glanced at Carly and smiled, but her eyes were on the photos.

"Well, I shouldn't be so surprised," Beth said. "After all, you look like a male model, too. You must come from good genes."

"They're both hot cowboys," Carly said, giggling. A picture of her and Colt came up next and she stopped there. "Look, it's us. Don't we look adorable?"

"You do," Colt said, his eyes sparkling.

"You both do," Beth said. "You really make a beautiful couple."

Colt pointed out pictures of his mother and Glen, and then there were more of the flowers, cake, and the reception. After they were done scrolling through them, Carly sighed.

"It was such a beautiful wedding. I need to get some copies printed up so I can frame them."

"You all looked wonderful," Beth commented, returning to the table to work. "And that ranch house is to die for. The fireplace is so beautiful. Are you going to get married in front of the fireplace, too, Colt?"

Colt stared at the first picture of Luke and Andi in front of the fireplace. It was such a heartwarming photo. "Yeah, maybe, someday. I guess I'd like to keep up the tradition."

"I want to get married on a beach somewhere," Carly blurted out. "Maybe on an island in the Caribbean, where it's nice and warm."

Colt looked at her and smiled. Yeah, that sounded just like Carly.

That night, Colt lay curled up beside Carly in bed, content with the quiet evening they'd shared together. It had been nice staying home for once, eating homemade food and just laying around, watching television. He thought about Luke and Andi's wedding pictures, and he felt nostalgic for the ranch. He remembered at the time of the wedding that the idea of marriage had scared him, but now, he could picture himself settling down. He saw himself and his wife living in a house he'd build on the ranch property, and him working the ranch alongside Luke. They'd all eat supper together at the main house, but there'd be children running around, too. It was a happy thought to fall asleep to. A dream he hoped to fulfill someday.

The rest of the week was quiet compared to the past weeks since Colt came to live with Carly. They still went out to dinner with her friends each evening, but instead of staying out late, Colt and Carly headed back to the townhouse early. Colt wasn't sure if it was because Carly didn't want a repeat of being sick, or if she understood he needed sleep in order to get up early each morning. Whatever the reason was, he enjoyed curling up in bed with her each night and making love to her most nights. He loved running his hands over her soft skin and through her silky hair. She and he fit together so perfectly, it was as if they were made for each other. And Carly made love with such passion, it made each time feel new and special. Colt was happier than he'd ever been, and hoped that life would continue like this, forever.

* * *

Carly stood at the counter at work, sifting through the weekly sales slips, getting them ready to enter into the computer as soon as Everly came back from lunch. The sales all week had been slow, and between that and the quiet week she'd had at home, she felt bored and antsy. It was Friday, and she planned on staying out late with her friends tonight. She knew that Colt wanted to go home early during the week so he could get his sleep, but she was already tired of it. She was too young to be a homebody, so tonight she'd make up for a long week of no fun.

Carly looked up when a man in a black pinstriped suit with a charcoal silk tie on his crisp gray shirt entered the shop and slowly glanced around. She studied him a second, noticing his handsome face and dark, neatly trimmed hair. He looked like he had money to spend. Carly hoped he'd buy something and make this day a little less dull.

The man looked directly at Carly with a pair of intense brown eyes. She smiled slowly. "Can I help you find something?" she asked, walking out from behind the counter.

The man took his time scanning Carly from head to toe. Carly actually felt her face heat up. She wore a tight black skirt that didn't quite make it to her knees and a sapphire-colored cashmere sweater that she knew made her eyes an even more brilliant blue. She also wore the necklace and earrings that Colt had given her, because they went so well with the sweater. She knew she looked good, and she made sure this handsome stranger took all of her in.

The man's intense eyes stopped when they met hers. "I think I found exactly what I'm looking for," he said in a deep, sensual voice.

Carly laughed softly. "If I had a dime," she said.

"Ah. I'll bet every man who walks in here flirts with you," he said, coming closer to her. "If they don't, they're fools."

Carly loved attention from handsome men, and this guy piqued her interest. She cocked her head and smiled coquettishly. "Are you looking for a gift for someone?"

The man chuckled. "Yes, I am. My sister. She just purchased a house up the coast on Puget Sound and I want to give her a housewarming gift. Any suggestions?"

"Oh, I have plenty of suggestions," Carly said, running her hand through her hair and pushing it back, off her shoulder. "Shall I show them to you?"

The man laughed, and Carly did, too. She enjoyed flirting with someone new. She walked slowly toward the back of the gallery, knowing full well that the man was watching her intently. She stopped at a glass case that held a black and white marble sculpture of a nude couple embracing. It was sensual and erotic, a very beautiful piece.

"How do you like this piece?" Carly asked.

"It's stunning," the man said, his eyes never leaving Carly. "But the gift is for my sister, so maybe we should find something a little less suggestive."

Carly laughed lightly. She offered the man her hand. "I'm Carly. And you are?"

"Jordan." He took Carly's hand in his and held it gently for longer than necessary.

Carly showed Jordan several sculptures and paintings that his sister might like, and he finally settled on a watercolor of Puget Sound. After he'd paid and given Carly the address it was to be delivered to, Jordan leaned in closer to her and asked, "Where will you be tonight, Carly?"

He was so close, she smelled his aftershave. It was musky and very masculine. "Out dancing," she said. "With my boyfriend."

Jordan nodded. "Boyfriend. I see. Well, I certainly hope he knows how to treat you."

"Oh, he does," Carly said.

"Maybe I'll see you around, then," Jordan said.

"Maybe," Carly replied, smiling.

Carly watched as Jordan made his way out the door. She sighed. He was so good looking, and it was fun flirting with someone new. She adored Colt, but she certainly wasn't ready to be tied down to just one man. Not by a longshot.

She went back to her work, wondering if she'd ever run into Jordan again and hoping that she would.

* * *

Colt was tired Friday afternoon from working all day and couldn't wait to get home and relax. He would have liked stopping by the gallery to see Carly first, but he'd quit doing that after the first week he worked at the store. She'd told him she was usually busy in the afternoon and couldn't always take a break when he came by, so he'd decided not to bother her there anymore.

When he arrived home, Beth was just getting home, too, and they talked a little while before he went to shower and change. Beth had applied for a position at the hospital where the hours would be set at seven to three, five days a week. She'd been offered the job today, and she was thrilled she no longer had to change shifts every week.

"Maybe now I can have a more normal life," she told Colt.

Colt was happy for her. He was also glad that the new hours meant he'd see more of her. He really enjoyed spending time with her. Spending time with Beth was a nice change from the chaotic life that Carly led. It felt more normal. More real. He liked that.

Colt wasn't surprised when Carly came home and wanted to go out that evening. It was Friday night, so he didn't mind, but he had so enjoyed spending the past week with her and not staying out late. They met Adam, Everly, and Chelle at a pub downtown to eat, and then were off to a dance club after that. Chelle had already stopped seeing the man she'd brought to Carly's party, so she was revved up to go out and find someone new.

They entered a loud, crowded dance club, squeezed through the throngs of people, and found an empty table where they all barely fit. Colt offered to get the first round of drinks, and Chelle went along with him. Carly was already on the dance floor with Adam, and Everly volunteered to guard the table.

Colt and Chelle waited in line at the bar for almost twenty minutes before they were finally able to order. Chelle said they should order two of each, and she offered to pay for the second round. Not wanting to wait in line again, Colt agreed it was a good idea. They stood there, pushed close together because of the crowd. Chelle eyed every young man at the bar and Colt was just trying to keep his spot so he could pick up the drinks. Suddenly, a hand clasped Colt's shoulder and a loud voice said, "Hey, Cole, what are you doing here?"

Colt quickly turned around and there stood Quinn and Connor from the store. Colt smiled wide. "Hey, guys. How'd you ever see me in this crowd?"

Quinn laughed. He looked different in his jeans, black dress shirt, and suit jacket. Colt had never seen him dressed in anything besides dirty jeans and a T-shirt. But then again, that was the way Colt dressed at work, too.

"It's not hard to find you in a crowd," Quinn said. "You're taller than everyone else. It was easy to spot you."

Colt nodded. "I suppose. So, you two are out together?" He nodded at Connor who was scanning the people around the room.

Quinn shrugged. "He's my cousin. I have to let him tag along."

"Hey, you invited me," Connor replied, but he was grinning. Colt noticed he was dressed hipster style with tight black pants, checkered shirt, a scarf around his neck, and a derby style hat tipped sideways on his head. He didn't look anything like he did at work.

Quinn turned toward Chelle. "Hi. Are you Cole's girlfriend, Carly?"

Chelle stared at Quinn quizzically. "Who's Cole?"

Colt quickly interrupted. "No, this is Carly's friend, Chelle. She's helping me carry the drinks. Carly is dancing with a friend." He pointed to the dance floor where Carly and Adam were moving to the pounding music. "She's the one in the short, silvery dress."

Quinn and Connor both stretched as tall as they could to look over the crowd. When they finally caught sight of Carly, both men's eyes grew wide.

"That's your girlfriend?" Quinn asked. "Geez, Cole. Now I know why you moved here for her. She's gorgeous."

Colt smiled. He felt so proud to be with Carly.

"Who in the hell is Cole?" Chelle yelled over the music. "Colt? Who are these guys and why do they keep calling you Cole?"

Quinn and Connor both looked confused. Colt rolled his eyes. "My real name is Cole," he told Chelle. "That's what they call me at work."

"You're name is Cole? Really? I'd have never guessed. You look like a Colt to me," Chelle said.

"Your name is Colt?" Connor blurted out. "I knew it. Cole just didn't sound right for a cowboy."

"Yeah," Quinn agreed. "I like Colt better. We're calling you that from now on."

Colt sighed. He guessed it didn't matter either way.

"So, you two cuties work with Colt?" Chelle asked, putting

on her best smile and batting her eyelashes. "Are either of you single?"

Connor raised his hands up as if to ward off Chelle. "Don't look at me. Quinn's the guy you want. I'm more interested in that cute guy dancing with Colt's girlfriend." He nudged Quinn. "I'll see you later. I'm going to wander around and see who's here." He waved at Colt and took off through the crowd.

Colt turned and stared at Quinn. "Connor's gay?"

Quinn nodded. "Yeah. Didn't you know that?"

Colt shook his head. "Never even occurred to me."

Quinn laughed.

The drinks finally came and Quinn ordered two beers for himself. As they walked back to the table, Chelle sidled up alongside Quinn and started flirting shamelessly. Colt chuckled. Poor Quinn wasn't going to know what hit him.

Colt introduced Carly to Quinn when she and Adam came back for their drinks and they all sat and talked over the loud music. Connor caught up with them, and he and Adam started up a conversation while Chelle did her best to latch on to Quinn. To Colt's surprise, Quinn seemed interested in Chelle. They danced several times and Colt and Carly danced, too. He enjoyed dancing the slow songs with her more than the fast ones. He loved the feel of their bodies swaying together to the music.

Later that night, Colt sat at the table while the other's danced. Quinn and Chelle came back and dropped into their chairs, so Colt stood to find Carly. Across the dance floor, he saw her dress glittering in the light, and he smiled. He told Chelle and Quinn he'd be back, and headed toward Carly, but halfway through the crowd, he stopped. Carly wasn't dancing with Adam. In fact, Adam was only a few feet away from Colt, dancing with Everly. Carly was dancing with a dark-haired man in a suit, and even though the music was fast, they were slow dancing to it, their bodies close and their faces only inches apart. And Carly was smiling.

Colt stood there, uncertain as to what to do. Anger rose inside him, but he wasn't sure if it was directed at the man or at Carly.

"Hey, what's wrong?" Adam had stepped over beside Colt.

Colt tried staying calm. "Carly. Over there. Do you recognize that guy?"

Adam stared at the man, and then shook his head no. "Never saw him before, but I can tell you one thing for certain. He's not one of her gay friends."

Everly walked up next to them and stared in the direction they were looking. "I know who he is," she said, slurring her words.

Colt looked over at her. "Who?"

"He was leaving the gallery today when I came back from lunch. He bought a painting or something."

Colt's anger began to fade. "So, he's a client from the gallery?"

Everly shrugged. "I think it was the first time he'd ever come in. I've never seen him before."

Adam put his arm around Everly to keep her from tipping over and patted Colt's arm with his free hand. "Don't worry, Colt. Carly's just a flirt sometimes. But she's going home with you."

Colt thought Adam was being a smartass, but when he turned and looked at him, he saw compassion in his eyes. Colt nodded, and they headed back to the table. Making a scene wasn't going to make things better between him and Carly, so it was best if he just walked away. Adam was right. Carly would be going home with him. Yet, somehow, it didn't make him feel any better.

Chapter Seventeen

Colt didn't mention to Carly that night about seeing her dancing with the other man. She was tipsy and silly as they drove home, and Carly kissed him so passionately when they went to bed that all his reservations flew out the window. Adam had been right. She did like to flirt sometimes, but in the end, she was with him.

They spent Saturday doing Carly's favorite thing—shopping—and Saturday night at a club again. Chelle and Quinn were the only ones who joined them and Colt thought it was nice for a change to be out with just another couple instead of a whole group. Carly didn't drink much, and she danced only with Colt. It reminded Colt of the times they had gone out to The Depot at home with Luke and Andi, just the four of them, and how much fun they'd had. He thought about home, the wedding, and the very first time he and Carly had made love in his room at the ranch. By the time they got home that night, Colt was feeling nostalgic for those first days with Carly, and content in their relationship now.

He lit the candles Carly kept around the bedroom and slowly undressed her, the way he had the first night they'd made love. Every kiss, every touch was slow and enticing, and Carly responded with deep passion and pure delight. Colt purposely took his time, bringing Carly's desire to its peak until she cried out, and only then did he pull her to him and share with her the sweet release they both desired.

Lying together afterward, with the moonlight streaming through the bedroom window, Colt's heart swelled with love for Carly. She was lying on her side, facing away from him. He ran his hand over the curve of her hip and around her waist, gently pulling her to him, nuzzling her neck with his lips. He just couldn't get enough of her.

Carly giggled softly. "Don't tell me you're ready for more, Cowboy," she teased.

"I am ready for more," Colt said huskily, his lips close to her ear. "I want to spend the rest of my life next to you." Colt rose on his elbow and looked down at her. "Carly. Let's get married."

Carly's eyes flew open. "What?"

"I know it's not the most romantic proposal, but it's from the heart. I love you, Carly. Marry me. Let's spend the rest of our lives together. Just like this."

Carly quickly pulled away and sat up. "Colt, you're kidding, right?"

Colt sat up. He looked seriously into Carly's eyes. "I'm not kidding. I love you. I want to marry you."

Carly's mouth dropped open. She pulled the covers up around her and turned to snap on the bedside lamp. "We can't get married. We haven't even known each other for very long, let alone long enough to make a lifetime commitment to each other."

Colt grinned. "Andi knew Luke for only three weeks and she knew he was the right one for her. This feels right to me."

"Well, that was fine for Andi and Luke, but I'm not Andi. She was ready to settle down and be with one man for the rest of her life. I'm not."

Colt's smile faded. "But you are with just me, aren't you?"

"Well, yeah, for now. But, you and I are just having fun right now. We're not serious. I'm not ready to be in a serious relationship yet. I'm just having a good time."

"I thought this was a serious relationship," Colt said. "I'm living with you. We're sleeping together. Isn't that as serious as it gets?"

Carly nervously ran her fingers through her hair. "Well, yeah, we're serious that way. But that's different from actually settling down. I'm not ready for that."

Colt reached out and took one of Carly's hands in his. "Carly, don't you want to get married someday? Have your own house, and maybe even have children?"

"I have a house. I don't need to get married to have a house," Carly said, her voice rising.

Colt chuckled, receiving a sharp look from Carly in return. "I'm not saying we have to get married tomorrow. But we can get engaged. We can start planning our future together."

"No!" Carly blurted out. She took a deep breath and let it out. In a calmer voice, she said, "Listen, Colt. I do care about you. I enjoy being with you. But maybe I misinterpreted the type of relationship we're in. Maybe we should slow down a little."

Colt frowned. "Slow down?"

"Yeah. Maybe we're going too fast. We both want different things from each other. I thought we were just having fun and I didn't realize how serious you felt about us. Maybe we should take this a little bit slower and get to know each other better before we start thinking about something as serious as marriage."

Colt looked at Carly, confusion etched on his brow. "I don't understand. Are you saying you want me to leave?"

"No, no, I'm not saying that at all. But maybe we shouldn't spend all our time together, like we've been doing. In fact, I'd been meaning to ask if you'd mind sleeping in the den during the week. Not that I don't love having you next to me at night, but you get up so early that it wakes me up and I don't sleep that well. But we'd still be a couple. We'd just be slowing it down a little to see if we really want to be together."

Colt felt like his world was crashing down around him. Just minutes before, he'd proposed because he wanted to spend every night for the rest of his life with Carly. Now, she had him sleeping in the den. What had happened?

"Carly, listen, we can forget I said anything about marriage. I didn't mean to scare you. I was just feeling so close to you, I thought we were both feeling that way. I still want to be with you," Colt said, panic rising inside him. He didn't want to lose Carly.

Carly sighed. "We're both tired. Let's get some sleep and talk about this tomorrow, okay?"

Colt nodded. They blew out the candles and Carly turned out the light. They'd had such a beautiful night together, and then he'd ruined it by proposing to her. *I'm such an idiot!* Colt moved closer to Carly, wanting to hold her, but she rolled over and moved away. A heavy sadness fell over him as he lay in bed and tried to fall asleep.

Colt awoke the next morning with a heavy heart. He'd hardly slept all night and he was exhausted. He turned and saw that Carly was already out of bed, and that's when he realized the shower was running. He lay there a moment, listening to the sound of the water, surprised at how early she was up considering how late they'd gone to bed. Normally, he'd join her in the shower on a Sunday morning, but today he thought he might not be welcome. Sadness enveloped him. In one fell swoop, he'd ruined everything between Carly and him. All because he was stupid enough to propose to her.

Carly came out of the bathroom partially dressed and Colt

turned and glanced at her. She smiled at him, giving him hope that things might still be fine between them. But then she spoke and he knew everything wasn't fine at all.

"I forgot I promised to meet up with the girls this morning for brunch," Carly said as she pulled on a lavender sweater and a pair of skinny jeans. The sweater dipped low, showing off Carly's ample cleavage, and Colt thought how beautiful she was, despite everything. "It's just us girls and I'm sure we'd bore you with our talk about clothes and stuff," she continued. "You don't mind, do you?"

Colt shook his head. He wondered if she was really meeting with the girls or if she just wanted to get as far away from him as possible.

Carly leaned toward the mirror, carefully applying her makeup, then ran her hands through her loose hair. She picked up a pair of high-heeled ankle boots and slipped them on and grabbed her purse. "You're a sweetie," she said, dropping a quick kiss on Colt's cheek before hurrying out the door.

Colt slid out of bed and walked into the bathroom. Maybe he and Carly could talk this out when she came home. He hoped so.

Shaved and showered, he went out into the kitchen and found Beth up and already cooking her meals for the week.

"Hey, there," she said, smiling up at him. Her smile faded. "Is something the matter? You look like you barely slept."

Colt shook his head as he poured a mug of coffee. "We were just up late."

"Oh. Well, there's batter in the fridge if you want me to make you some pancakes. How does that sound?"

Colt glanced at Beth, and gave her a small smile. "That sounds absolutely amazing."

Beth laughed. "They're just pancakes."

"I know. It's the fact that you'd offer to make them for me

even though you're busy," Colt said. "You're always so nice to me. I really appreciate it."

"It's easy to be nice to you, Colt," Beth said, and then she grinned. "Besides, I'm bribing you with pancakes so I can put you to work later."

"Ah, so that's the plan. Bring it on, lady."

After eating a pile of pancakes, Colt helped Beth separate the food she'd cooked into containers that would be stored in the freezer and then heated up later. She made enough for both her and Colt's lunches and for her suppers, too. After that, they cleaned up the kitchen and then Colt went on a walk with Beth since Carly hadn't come home yet.

"Why didn't you go with Carly to brunch this morning?" Beth asked as they made their way uphill.

"She was meeting up with her girlfriends. Guess it was no boys allowed," he told her, trying to keep it light.

"Well, her loss is my gain," Beth said with a smile. "I got free labor out of it."

Colt laughed. It felt good to be outside in the nice weather and spending time with Beth. "It wasn't free, remember? I got pancakes out of it."

When they returned to the townhouse, Colt did laundry and even picked up the pile of clothes in Carly's room and washed the things Beth told him he couldn't ruin. He folded all the other clothes she had lying on the floor and put them in a pile for her to take to the dry cleaners. Then he changed the bed and washed the dirty sheets, putting them neatly away in the closet. Carly wasn't much for housework, so he thought he'd surprise her by doing these things for her.

"You're going to make someone a really good wife someday," Beth teased him as he folded the last of the towels that he'd washed.

Colt laughed. "I wouldn't know how to do all this if you

hadn't showed me. I'm ashamed to say that I let my mother do this for me all these years. Boy, will she be surprised when I go home and can do a load of laundry."

Beth glanced at him. "Home. That's the first time I've heard you say you're going back to the ranch."

Colt shrugged. "I guess I figured I'd go back home someday. I can make a better living there than here. There're only so many boxes you can unload from trucks before you get tired of it."

Beth nodded, but stayed silent.

Colt went out to his truck and worked on rubbing out the scratch in the door with the rubbing compound. It was late afternoon and still Carly hadn't come home. He'd hoped she'd be back by now and he could take her to supper so they could talk about what happened. He didn't want this awkwardness between them. He wanted to know that they were still okay.

By early evening, Carly was still not home, so Colt ate supper with Beth and helped her clean up afterwards. They sat and watched television, but Colt couldn't keep his mind off of Carly. Where could she be? What was she doing? And most importantly, who was she with? He hated that the last question came to mind, but after seeing how she'd danced with that man last night, it was hard to push that thought away.

"Well, I'm off to bed," Beth said at ten o'clock. "I start my seven to three shift tomorrow and I don't want to be tired."

Colt nodded, but he felt lost. He should go to bed, too. The only problem was he wasn't sure which bed he was supposed to sleep in.

As Beth stood, Colt asked sheepishly, "Do you know where the sheets are for the pull-out bed in the den? I thought I'd make that up tonight."

Beth stared at Colt, surprise evident in her eyes. "Uh, sure. They're in the hall closet. I'll show you."

They got the sheets and Colt headed into the den. He pulled

off the cushions and put them aside, then pulled out the bed. It wasn't very long or wide. It was certainly not long enough for his tall frame. He just stood there, staring at it.

"Colt? What's going on? Why are you sleeping in here?" Beth asked from the doorway. "I know it's not my business, and you can tell me to butt out, but it doesn't make any sense."

Colt turned slowly and looked at Beth with sad eyes.

Beth came into the room immediately and stopped in front of Colt. "What's wrong? Did you and Carly have a fight? I'll listen if you want to talk."

Colt did want to confide in Beth. He knew she'd listen without judging, but he needed to speak with Carly first. He took a breath and tried to keep his voice light. "It's nothing. Carly isn't sleeping too well, because I have to get up so early, so I'm going to sleep in here a few nights."

Colt could tell by the way Beth studied him that she didn't believe him, but she didn't say another word. She helped him make up the bed and she found extra blankets for him to put on it. When they were finished, Colt said, "Thanks, Beth. You're always there for me."

Beth surprised him by hugging him. He wrapped his arms around her and held on tight, holding back tears that threatened to fall. Until the very moment they touched, he hadn't known just how much he needed to feel someone's arms around him. At home, his mom or Andi would have hugged him without hesitation the moment they saw something was wrong. The warmth of Beth's body next to his, for the briefest second, made him feel like he was home.

Beth pulled away and smiled. "I'm here to talk anytime you need me, okay?"

Colt nodded. He was too choked up to speak. He watched as Beth headed out of the room and a moment later, her door closed softly.

* * *

Carly had stayed away from the townhouse all day on purpose, hoping to avoid an awkward scene with Colt. This morning she'd lied when she'd told Colt she was meeting girlfriends for brunch so she could disappear without inviting him. She knew it was the cowardly thing to do, but she'd needed time to think about what had occurred last night and what she was going to tell Colt.

Damn. Their relationship had been going just fine until he'd brought up the idea of marriage. They'd been having fun and Carly had enjoyed lying beside him at night and waking up with him every morning. Colt was sweet, kind, and surprisingly passionate under his shy exterior, and she loved feeling his strong arms around her. The only problem was she wasn't in love with him. At least not the way he seemed to be with her.

Carly compared her relationship with Colt to her past relationships. If she were honest with herself, she'd never truly been in love with any of the men she'd dated. Lust, yes. Love, no. And the moment any of them had grown serious, she'd bolted. Being married just didn't interest her right now. She thought that most men would like that—a woman who wasn't pressuring them to get hitched. But in every case, she'd been wrong. It simply confounded her.

But, she had to admit that with Colt, everything was different. She should have seen this coming. He was more than a fling. He'd want to be in a serious relationship. And now, she'd really messed things up.

Carly drove around a while before finally parking at the mall and aimlessly wandering the shops. She'd wanted so desperately to call Andi and ask her advice, but she already knew what Andi would say. She'd lecture her on inviting Colt out to Seattle in the first place if she weren't serious about him. The problem was, Carly had truly believed at the time she'd invited Colt that she might possibly be falling in love with him. How was she supposed to pursue the relationship to see where it might lead if he lived in Montana and she in Washington? Inviting him to come to stay a while had seemed like a good idea at the time. Now, she knew it hadn't been.

Carly had called all her friends, including Adam, to join her at the mall, but each one already had plans and couldn't. Chelle was obsessed with Quinn, Adam was out with some of his artist friends, and Everly didn't answer her phone. She'd tried a few more friends, but to no avail. Then, she'd remembered the phone number on a slip of paper in her purse. Did she dare call him?

Carly thought back to last night when Jordan showed up at the dance club and surprised her. She'd been out on the dance floor just as the music had stopped for a second between songs and there he stood, only inches from her.

"I had to go to eight different clubs before I found you," he'd said huskily. Carly had thought that was so romantic.

The music had begun its pounding beat again, and Jordan had reached his arms around her and pulled her to him, dancing slowly, their bodies touching. While everyone around them was flailing their arms and legs to the beat, they were moving in a slow, steady rhythm. Carly's pulse had pounded in delight. In that moment, she'd forgotten she was there with Colt. She'd forgotten everyone and everything. She'd lived in that moment of time, feeling very sexy and desired by this mysterious man.

Without giving it a second thought, Carly had called Jordan and met up with him for dinner and drinks at a small pub downtown. And it was from there that she'd finally headed home. She hoped Colt was already in bed, asleep, so she wouldn't have to talk to him yet. She was still at a loss as to what to say, because despite everything, she didn't want to hurt him.

Chapter Eighteen

Colt was sitting on the sofa, half asleep, when Carly came into the house at eleven-thirty that night.

"Hi," she said, looking surprised to see him waiting up for her. "I thought you'd be in bed already."

Colt looked at Carly with hooded eyes. "I wasn't sure which bed I was supposed to sleep in."

Carly sighed softly and didn't answer. She put her jacket away, then slipped off her boots and left them on the floor. She walked over to the sofa and sat down next to Colt, curling her legs up under her and dropping her head on his shoulder. "I'm sorry about last night," she said quietly.

Colt draped his arm around her and kissed the top of her head. "It's my fault. I shouldn't have pushed you so soon. I just felt so close to you at that moment, I wanted you to know I never wanted it to end."

Carly looked up into Colt's eyes. "Colt, I really care about you. You have to know that. I don't sleep with every guy I meet despite what everyone thinks about me. Being with you these past few weeks has been really special. But, I'm not ready to get married. I don't want to be tied down yet. Can you understand that? It's not that I don't want to be with you, it's just if you're looking for something more serious, then maybe it isn't me you want."

"But, I do want you," Colt said emphatically. "I understand. I pushed too soon. Can we just go back to the way we were and forget this ever happened?"

"I don't think we can just forget this," Carly said. "Maybe we should slow things down like I suggested last night. We're going way too fast. I don't want to make life altering decisions unless we're sure that's what we want."

Colt's gaze dropped. "So, you want me to move into the den after all?"

"Would you mind? I love having you beside me every night, but it is interfering with my sleep when you get up so early every morning. We can just slow it down a bit and still be together. We should have done this at the start, but I was just so excited having my cute cowboy here that I couldn't resist you," Carly said, giving Colt an irresistible smile.

"But I'd still need to shower in your bathroom. Won't that wake you up?"

"Why can't you shower in the other bathroom?"

"That's Beth's bathroom. I don't want to disturb her."

"Oh, she won't mind," Carly said with a wave of her hand.

Colt wasn't sure of that. No woman wanted to share a bathroom with a man she wasn't dating.

"Please, Colt. Pretty please," Carly said.

Colt couldn't resist Carly. That was the problem. "Okay, I guess. But we're still together, aren't we? We're still a couple?"

Carly ran her hand along the side of Colt's neck and up through the back of his hair. "Of course, we're still together," she said seductively. "This will just give us a chance to explore where our relationship is going." She kissed him lightly on the lips.

That night, Colt went to sleep in the den on the uncomfortable fold-out bed that squeaked every time he rolled over. He missed Carly's warm body beside his, but as long as he knew they were still together, he could live with it.

* * *

The next week went by quickly and March turned into April. Easter was the first Sunday in April, and after spending half the night out with her friends, Carly just wanted to sleep in Easter morning. As promised, Colt did stay in Carly's room over the weekend, and he wasn't looking forward to returning to the den for the next week.

On Saturday, Beth had asked Colt if he'd like to help her pass out the baskets they'd made for the children in the hospital. She'd already given away several on that Friday and Saturday, but there were new patients who hadn't received one yet. Colt had agreed to help, so he slipped out of bed quietly and went to shower in the guest bathroom while Carly slept. Beth had said she didn't mind his using the bathroom as long as he picked up after himself, so he was always careful to wipe things down when he was done.

Before leaving the house that morning, Beth suggested Colt pick out one of the baskets for Carly and leave it on the counter. He picked one with a pink stuffed bunny in it and left a note, "To Carly, Love, The Easter Bunny." Then, carrying the large basked full of the smaller baskets, Colt and Beth headed for the door.

"Wait," Beth said. "You should wear your cowboy hat."

Colt looked at her quizzically. "Why?"

"You'll see. Please?"

Colt shrugged and went to retrieve his hat from his room, and then they headed out to his truck.

Colt was given a visitor's pass at the hospital and he and Beth headed up to the children's section on third floor. Beth let the nurses at the desk know she was there, then took the list of new patients and walked to the first room. Colt followed, carrying the large basket for her.

"You're going to be my Easter Cowboy today," Beth teased.

Colt smiled back. It sounded silly, but he didn't mind.

In the first room, a little girl no older than four was sitting up in bed watching cartoons. She had tubes strung into her right arm and a few nasty looking bruises on her arms and face. Her mother sat in a chair by the bed, dozing. Both looked up with tired eyes when Beth and Colt entered.

"We've brought you a present from the Easter Cowboy," Beth said cheerfully, motioning for Colt to bring the basket over to the side of the bed so the little girl could choose one.

"Howdy, little girl," Colt said, playing along. "Would you like to pick a basket?"

The little girl's eyes grew wide as she looked from Colt to the pile of baskets with toys and candy in them. "Aren't you 'spose to be a bunny?" she asked.

Colt chuckled. "The bunny was tuckered out from all his work last night. I'm taking his place this morning."

The little girl smiled and reached in to pick out a basket with a spotted puppy inside it.

The mother sat there, looking amused. "What do you say, Jenny?"

"Thank you, Mr. Easter Cowboy," the little girl said.

"You're so welcome, Jenny," Colt said. The little girl had already stolen his heart and they still had a whole list of rooms left to visit.

Beth led Colt from room to room and in each one the children were delighted by the Easter Cowboy. One little boy about nine years old looked at him seriously and asked, "Are you a real cowboy, or are you just dressed up like one?"

"I'm the real deal," Colt said, tipping his hat. "I break bucking broncos, go on cattle drives, and even know how to rope a steer."

The little boy looked up at him in awe. "That's so cool," he said, making Colt laugh.

For an hour and a half they went room to room drawing smiles and giggles from children who were sick or had broken bones. Parents enjoyed their visit, too, and thanked them for being so kind. When they were finally finished delivering the gifts, they left the remainder of the baskets at the desk for the nurses to give out to new patients and then headed out of the hospital.

"See why I asked you to wear your hat? The children loved it. It's not often they get to meet a real cowboy," Beth said with a grin.

They had just stepped outside into the warm spring day. Colt stopped and turned to Beth. "You're amazing, you know that? To give up your own holiday to bring smiles to those children is so sweet."

"You gave up your holiday, too," Beth told him.

"I couldn't have done anything more rewarding than this today," Colt said. There was a vendor on the street selling pink, orange, and white lilies. Colt walked over and bought a bouquet, then walked back to Beth.

"Pretty," Beth said, looking at the flowers. "Carly will love them."

"They aren't for Carly." Colt handed them to Beth. "They're for you. Happy Easter."

Beth's mouth dropped open as she looked up into Colt's eyes. "Thank you," she said softly, taking the flowers.

"They're from the Easter Cowboy," Colt told her, grinning. Then he bent down and kissed her lightly on the cheek. "That is from me," he said.

Colt offered Beth his bent arm, and she accepted it, and they walked together back to the truck to drive home.

The three of them spent a quiet Easter evening together. Beth cooked a large ham garnished with pineapple rings, mashed potatoes, and fresh green beans and they had chocolate cake for dessert. Everything was delicious, and it helped to make Colt a little less homesick for the ranch and his mother's cooking. At home, he knew they'd all be sitting down to Easter supper, and Colt wished he could have been there, too. But Beth's supper certainly made up for it.

Colt called home later that night and talked to his mom and Andi, and then to Luke. Carly talked to Andi, too. When they hung up, Colt announced, "Luke thinks we'll be able to move the cattle up to the summer pasture the second week in May." He looked over at Carly, his eyes sparkling. "You should come along. Andi isn't riding, she's going along in the truck with Ma and helping with the meals. We could ride together, herding the cattle."

Carly grimaced. "I don't know, Colt. How many days would we be riding?"

"It takes four days to move the herd that distance. We'd be camping every night, but we'll have tents we can pitch and bring sleeping bags. Ma carries it all in the truck."

Carly wrinkled her nose. "Yuk. Camping? That doesn't sound like fun at all. I think I'll pass."

Colt was disappointed. He'd really hoped that Carly would come along.

"You know, Beth likes that sort of thing," Carly said offhandedly, glancing over at Beth who sat in the chair in the living room. "You should invite her to go along."

Beth looked up, surprised. "I'd be in the way. I've never even ridden a horse before."

Colt's face lit up. "I can teach you. We can go a day or two early and you'll be an expert rider by the time we head out. Would you like to go? We need as many riders as we can get.

Besides family, Glen, Randy, Jake, and a couple of neighbors are going to help out. It takes a lot of people to watch over that big of a herd. It'll be fun."

Beth sat there, undecided. "I'd have to ask for the week off at work. Are you sure it will be that week for sure?"

"That's what Luke said. He's done this for years, so he should know."

"Well, it would be fun to help with a cattle drive," Beth said. She looked over at Carly. "Are you sure you don't mind my going?"

Carly shrugged. "I don't care. It will be cold, dirty, and everyone will stink when they're done. If that sounds like fun, go for it."

Beth sat quietly in thought for a moment. "Okay," she finally said, her eyes lighting up. "I'll see if I can get the time off or change shifts with someone else for a few days." She looked at Colt. "But remember, I warned you. I can't ride."

"You'll learn. I'm a good teacher," he said grinning.

As the weeks went by, Colt tried to persuade Carly to come along on the cattle drive, but each time she refused, saying that camping wasn't her thing. And throughout the weeks, she became more and more distant from him. There were nights when she didn't come home from work and Colt ended up eating supper with Beth instead. Sometimes, Carly would call and say she was having dinner with her friends downtown and ask if Colt wanted to drive down and meet them. Occasionally, he did, but more often than not, he opted to stay home and eat. He got too tired staying out late on weeknights with Carly, so he preferred staying home.

Several times Colt asked Carly if everything was fine between them, and she just kept saying it was. She explained that tourist season was starting up again and she was extremely busy at the gallery, which was wearing her out. Colt accepted her explanation. But when weekends came and went and he was still sleeping in the den, it saddened him.

The week before he was to leave for Montana, Colt made the effort to eat out each night with Carly and her friends. Quinn and Chelle were still dating, and Colt enjoyed spending time with them. Quinn was very down to earth and had a great sense of humor. He teased Colt about being a cowboy and the fact that he went on actual cattle drives. "People still do that nowadays?" he'd asked in surprise when Colt had asked for the week off. Colt had just laughed.

When he and Carly would get home, Colt tried becoming intimate with her, but Carly always had an excuse. She was tired. It was that time of the month. She was stressed. Colt began to worry that she was pulling away from him and he had no idea how to fix it. She insisted they were still a couple, but he didn't feel like it anymore. He hoped that by the time he came home from Montana, Carly would have missed him and their relationship would go back to the way it had been before he made the mistake of proposing to her.

* * *

Carly was trying everything possible to gently let Colt down without hurting him. She knew the right thing would be to just come right out and tell him she no longer felt the same way about him as she had at the beginning, but she just couldn't bring herself to do that. He already looked hurt every time she rejected his advances and she hated seeing the sadness in his eyes. Breaking up with him was going to be difficult, but she had to do it eventually.

Over the past several weeks, she'd been seeing Jordan for lunch, and even met him twice for dinner when Colt didn't join her. None of her friends knew she was seeing Jordan. Now that

Chelle was dating Quinn, she had to be careful that she, or any of her other friends knew nothing about Jordan.

Jordan intrigued her. He was handsome, sophisticated, and fun to be around. He was in his mid-thirties, worked at an investment firm near the gallery, and had an incredible fifth floor apartment downtown with a view of the bay. She'd only been to his apartment once, and only for a moment. She wasn't sleeping with him, yet, but she couldn't lie to herself. She wanted to. First, though, she had to find a way to break it off with Colt.

Carly hoped that the week Colt spent back at the ranch would make him realize he missed home and that he'd want to go back there permanently. If that happened, it would be easy to gently let their relationship go. He already knew she didn't want to get married, and she certainly wouldn't move to the ranch to be with him. It was the coward's way out, but it would be the easiest way to break up with him without totally breaking his heart. Or at least, she hoped it would be.

Chapter Nineteen

Colt and Beth left Seattle early on a Friday morning in May. It was a beautiful day filled with sunshine and temperatures in the sixties. Colt already knew the weather was about the same in Montana, because Luke had kept him abreast of the weather. The last report had been that the snow was nearly gone in the summer pasture and the grass was fresh and green, so it was the perfect time to move the herd.

Colt had warned Beth to bring along warm clothing that she could layer. Mornings would be chilly and afternoons might get warm, especially since they'd be working hard. He'd also gone with her to buy her a good pair of riding boots. He showed her the difference between a riding heel and a work heel, and told her the riding heel was best. Beth had looked down at her feet when she found a good fitting pair of light brown boots and laughed. "I'm becoming a cowgirl," she'd exclaimed.

On the ride there, Colt told her all about herding and how they'd keep the cattle moving and together. He explained that Luke, Randy, and Jake had already tagged and branded the calves as well as gave them the required shots. The cows with calves were tagged so they knew which calf belonged to which cow. The calves that had been born a little later would stay with their mothers in the fields by the ranch, but the others would be fine at the summer pasture.

"There really is a lot to ranching, isn't there?" Beth asked, interested in what Colt was telling her.

Colt shrugged. "I guess. It's all second nature to me. Since we sell the beef cattle, then there are a lot of regulations we have to follow. But the cattle drive is one of the fun parts of ranching. It's as close to the old days as you can get."

They arrived at the ranch just as the sun fell behind the distant hills. The days were longer now, and the sun didn't set until nine o'clock.

Beth stepped out of the truck and turned to watch the golden sunset. "Oh, Colt. It's beautiful here. How could you have ever left this place?"

As Colt watched the sunset, he wondered the same thing. Now that he was here, he realized just how much he'd missed home. But then he thought of Carly, and remembered how desperately he'd wanted to be with her. He wondered if he'd still make that same decision if he knew then what he knew now.

"Colt! You're home!" Ginny came running down the porch steps with Bree at her heels and flew into her son's arms. Colt laughed and lifted her up, swinging her in circles.

"Stop it, crazy boy," Ginny said, laughing. "You'll make me dizzy." She hugged him hard. "It feels like you've been gone forever."

"I was just thinking that, too," Colt said. He reached down and hugged Bree. "Hey, girl. I missed you." Bree responded by wagging her docked tail vigorously.

Andi came down the steps and hugged Colt, too. "I've missed you so much," she told him.

Colt hugged her back, and then pulled away. "You're as beautiful as ever," he said.

"Hey, stop flirting with my wife. Get your own gorgeous woman," Luke teased as he walked up from the barn with

Randy behind him. He grabbed his brother and pulled him into a hug. "I hope you haven't gone soft on us after all these weeks in the city. We're going to work you hard."

"Soft?" Colt said. "I've been moving boxes around for weeks. If anything, I'm stronger than you now."

"Good to see you home," Randy said, slapping Colt on the back. "We've really missed you here."

"Thanks, Randy."

Beth had been standing on the sidelines, watching everyone greet Colt.

Colt gently pulled her over beside him. "This is Beth," he said. "She came to help us with the cattle drive. Beth, this is my mom, Andi, Luke, and Randy. Oh, and Bree, too."

"It's nice to finally meet you all," Beth said. "I've heard so much about everyone, I feel like I already know you."

"It's all lies, whatever he said," Luke blurted out with a devilish grin.

"Ignore him," Ginny said, coming over to Beth and giving her a welcoming hug. "I need to hug the girl who's been keeping my son fed. Looks like you've done a great job of it."

"Thanks," Beth said. "It's not all me, though. Colt's been learning how to cook, too."

"Did I hear that right?" Ginny said. "My son can cook?"

"Only a little," Colt said, shyly.

"He can do his own laundry, too," Beth added, smirking at Colt. "So, don't let him get away with giving it all to you, Mrs. Brennan."

"Just call me Ginny, dear. We're all family here."

Beth nodded.

Andi came over to say hello to Beth, and Luke and Randy did, too. After everyone welcomed Beth, Ginny told them to head into the kitchen. "I made your favorite tonight, Colt. Fried chicken, mashed potatoes, and my homemade bread and jam. I saved some to reheat for the both of you. Let's go inside."

Colt retrieved both his and Beth's bags from the truck and followed the group into the house. He ran the bags upstairs to the bedrooms and came down, inhaling deeply. The kitchen smelled of chicken, homemade bread, and chocolate chip cookies. It felt so good to be home.

They all sat around the kitchen table as Beth and Colt ate their late supper. Beth said it was the best fried chicken she'd ever had and the bread and jam was to die for. Colt grinned. He'd missed his mother's jam and this kitchen and sitting around the table with his family. Nothing compared to being home.

"I hear Colt is going to teach you to ride this weekend before the drive," Luke said to Beth.

Beth nodded. "I've never ridden before, so I hope I can pick it up fast. Colt promised he was a good teacher."

"He's the best," Andi said, smiling. "Maybe Beth could ride my horse, Abby, since I won't be riding her."

"I don't know," Colt said. "She's kind of spirited. We may need one a little milder. I'll have to think about it." He cocked his head and looked at Andi. "Why aren't you riding? You did for the winter cattle drive."

Andi bit her lip and looked over at Luke. He shrugged in response and slipped his arm over the back of Andi's chair.

Colt frowned. "Is something going on? Tell me."

"Well," Andi said. "I wanted to tell you and Carly at the same time, but since she didn't come with you, I guess I'll let you in on it. I'm not riding because I'm pregnant. You're going to be an uncle, Colt."

Colt's mouth dropped open.

Beth smiled wide. "Congratulations!"

"Thanks, Beth," Andi said.

"A baby? A little Luke or Andi? This is amazing," Colt said excitedly. He got up and wrapped his arms around Andi, then backed away, afraid of squeezing her too tightly. "You look so small, though."

Andi chuckled. "I'm only two months along. The baby isn't due until early December. But I don't want to risk riding and getting hurt in any way."

"I'm so excited," Colt said, sitting down again. "I'm going to be an uncle. I can't wait."

"What do you mean, you can't wait? I'm finally going to be a grandmother," Ginny said, laughing.

"I'll have to call Carly tomorrow and tell her," Andi said. "I don't want her to feel left out."

They all sat at the table a while longer, discussing the cattle drive and joking and teasing each other. Glen showed up while they were all talking and he welcomed Colt home. Colt noticed his mom's eyes lit up when Glen entered the room. He watched the way Luke and Andi looked at each other, too. Their eyes were filled with so much warmth and tenderness for each other. *That's what true love looks like.* He realized he'd never seen Carly look at him that way. That thought made him sad.

After a while, everyone started yawning and got up to leave. Luke took Andi back home to the cabin. She'd mentioned she'd been having morning sickness and it made her very tired. Beth gave her some suggestions for tea and different spices that might safely help relieve the nausea, and Andi said she'd try them. Randy took off, and Ginny and Glen sat at the table sipping their last cup of coffee. Colt remembered how Luke had told him that Glen stayed the night often now, so he decided to go up to his room before things got awkward. He said goodnight to his mom and Glen, then patted Bree as he passed her pillow by the staircase. He then led Beth upstairs to show her to her room.

"The bathroom is here," he pointed out. "Looks like you're stuck sharing with me again."

Beth grinned. "I think I can handle it."

He walked her to the guest room, down the hall from his. It was the same room Carly had stayed in just a few months before. Beth opened the door and glanced inside.

"It's adorable. I just love this house," Beth said. "Everything is so warm and inviting. And your mom is the sweetest person I've ever met. I feel like I'm at home."

Colt nodded. "Yeah, my mom is pretty amazing. I'm still getting used to the idea of her and Glen together, though. Some things have changed since I've been gone."

Beth looked up at Colt, her eyes searching his. "You've changed, too," she said softly.

Colt's brows rose. "I have?"

Beth nodded. "You're not as shy as you were when I first met you. And you seem more confident." Beth grinned wickedly. "And you don't walk around the townhouse shirtless anymore, either."

Colt laughed. "Maybe I should start doing that again," he said with a glint in his eyes. "For old time's sake."

Beth shrugged. "You won't get any complaints from me."

Colt smiled down at Beth, noting how the gold flecks in her eyes sparkled tonight. She was so sweet, and so pretty. He had an overwhelming urge to kiss her. It was that same feeling he'd had the night of Carly's birthday party. *What in the world is wrong with me? I'm with Carly.*

"Goodnight, Colt," Beth said, stepping inside the bedroom. "See you in the morning."

Her words broke the spell that had overtaken Colt. "Goodnight, Beth." He watched as she shut the door, and then he went into his own bedroom.

* * *

Carly moaned when her phone rang early on Saturday morning. She looked at her clock and saw it was only eight a.m. Who in their right mind called this early on a Saturday morning? Certainly, not her friends. They'd all been out late the night before and every one of them would be sleeping like she was trying to do.

The phone stopped ringing and Carly sighed. *Good!* Then it started up again and she groaned. Her head hurt and her mouth felt dry. She definitely shouldn't have had those last two drinks at last call.

The persistent ringing of the phone was driving her crazy. Then a thought occurred to her—it could be Jordan. She hadn't seen him since Thursday night, so maybe he wanted to make plans for tonight. Excited now, Carly grabbed her phone from the nightstand and looked at the screen. It wasn't Jordan, it was Andi. With a sigh, Carly fell back on her pillows and answered, "Hello, Sis."

"Good morning," Andi said cheerfully. "Hope I didn't wake you."

Carly rolled her eyes. "No. I was getting up anyway," she lied. She hated for her sister to know just how often she went out drinking. Andi had always frowned upon her partying, and it had increased since Andi left last summer. She hoped Colt hadn't told her how often she went out.

"I called to tell you some exciting news," Andi said. "I had meant to wait a while longer, but since we've already told Colt and Beth, I thought you'd want to hear it, too."

"What is it?" Carly asked, not sure what could be this important.

"Luke and I are having a baby. You're going to be an Auntie!"

Carly sat there a moment, absorbing the news. "A baby? You're having a baby?"

"Yes," Andi squealed. "Isn't it exciting?"

"Sure, yeah, it is. I'm just surprised at how soon you decided to have children. You two just got married."

"I know, but we're both ready to start our family. Luke is ecstatic about it. And I'm so happy," Andi said. "Be happy for me, okay?"

"Oh, I am. I'm just a little shocked, that's all. When is the baby due?"

"Not until December. Just think, by Christmas this year we will have a cute little baby. I hope you plan on coming out, because you have to see your niece or nephew."

"Of course," Carly said, still feeling dazed. "So, you already told Colt and Beth?"

"Yeah, sorry you didn't hear first. I had hoped you'd come out here with Colt for the cattle drive. But then, I guess I knew it wasn't something you'd enjoy. Beth sure is nice, though. I'm happy I finally met her."

"Yeah, she is," Carly said. "Glad you two get along."

"She fits in perfectly around here. She even gave me some ideas on how to quell my morning sickness. She's great. I guess Colt is going to teach her how to ride this weekend before we leave. I'm sure she'll do fine."

"Sure. She'll do fine," Carly repeated. She frowned. It hadn't really occurred to her how much time Beth and Colt would spend together on their trip to the ranch. She didn't know why, but she felt a twinge of jealousy.

"You know, Carly, I feel like you're responsible for all the good things that have happened to me this past year. It was your advice that sparked everything."

Carly was confused. "My advice? What are you talking about?"

Andi laughed. "You were the one who said, "Kiss a cowboy for me," last summer when I was staying here at the ranch after my car broke down. Well, I took your advice, and I haven't stopped kissing my cowboy ever since."

Carly smiled. "See. I do have good ideas once in a while."

"You sure do. Well, I've got to go. I'm eating breakfast later since I feel so sick in the morning. I just wanted to share the great news with you. I love you, Carly. Take care."

"I love you, too," Carly said. "Congratulate Luke for me and say hi to Ginny. I really am happy for you, Big Sis."

Carly hung up and lay in bed staring at the ceiling. Andi was having a baby. Things were changing so fast. She thought about Colt teaching Beth to ride, and actually envied Beth for getting to ride the trails around the ranch with Colt. It was beautiful there, and she adored Ginny and Luke, and didn't even mind grouchy Randy. But she didn't want to move there and become Colt's wife and have babies yet. She knew deep in her heart, she and Colt didn't have the same type of relationship that Luke and Andi had. It made her sad, because she adored her hot cowboy, but it was the truth.

Since she was already awake, Carly decided to shower and call Chelle and Everly to see if they wanted to go to breakfast and shopping. She wanted to buy a new dress to wear in case Jordan called again.

Chapter Twenty

The next morning, Colt was up bright and early just as he'd always been before moving to Seattle. He ate breakfast with Randy and his mom, and then headed outdoors with Randy to help with the chores, even though Jake was there to do his usual work. Usually, Andi would be up at the house early to have breakfast, but Ginny said she'd been eating later because of her morning sickness. Ginny would make sure that Beth and Andi ate later when they were both up.

Colt worked alongside Jake, cleaning stalls, feeding the cattle and the horses, and all the other chores that needed to be done.

He walked to the fence by the barn and studied the horses out in the two fields. Luke's stallion and Randy's gelding were kept in one area and the mares and fillies were kept in the other. Colt preferred his mare, Maddie, which was a Tennessee Walker/Quarter Horse mix, to a stallion or gelding. She was almost seventeen hands tall and had a sweet disposition, but could run like the wind. Maddie was beautiful with brown and white markings and a dark brown mane and tail. Standing there, watching her in the field, Colt realized just how much he'd missed riding her. He'd broken her six years ago and she'd been his personal horse ever since. In fact, he'd broken nearly all the horses in the field. He knew everything about each of their personalities and how they handled. His eyes finally settled on

Sadie, a light brown Quarter Horse. She was seven years old and very easy to handle, but still had the stamina and power to go herding. She'd be perfect for Beth. Smiling, Colt strode out into the field to collect the two horses so he could start riding lessons with Beth.

Beth was awake and eating breakfast in the kitchen with Andi when Colt entered the house. He stood in the mudroom doorway so he wouldn't track dirt into the kitchen and said good morning to both women.

"When you're done eating, Beth, we can go riding. I brought the horses up to the barn."

Beth smiled up at him. She wore one of her loose sweatshirts, jeans, and sneakers, and her silky brown hair was pulled back into a ponytail. Her face was clear of makeup and her skin looked fresh and healthy. Just looking at her made Colt happy.

"I'm almost finished," she told him. "And you were right. You're mom makes the best jam I've ever tasted. We have to bring some home with us."

Colt nodded. *Home.* This was home to him, not the townhouse. But when Beth said it, it almost made him feel like Seattle was home, too.

"I'll wait outside for you. Don't rush. Enjoy your breakfast," Colt said before leaving.

Beth showed up in the barn wearing her new cowboy boots and one of Andi's cowboy hats that was hanging in the mudroom. "So, do I look like a genuine cowgirl?" she asked Colt when he glanced up and saw her.

Colt smiled wide. "I'd say so. You're all decked out, so let's get you riding. Do you want to learn how to saddle your own horse or do you want me to do it?"

"I'll learn how," Beth said cheerfully. "Teach me everything you know."

Colt chuckled. "Well, that won't take long. I don't know all that much. But I'll teach you what I can."

Beth's expression turned serious. "Don't put yourself down, Colt. You obviously know a lot about riding, horses, and ranching. That's something to be proud of."

Colt nodded. Beth always made him feel good about himself. Sometimes, Carly made him feel inferior, not on purpose, but just because she was so much more sophisticated than he was. But Beth was different. She saw who he was on the inside and appreciated it.

"Okay. Let's get started. First off, I'd like you to meet your new best friend, Sadie. She's perfect for a new rider. She's sweet, gentle, and smart, but has enough spunk to keep her interesting."

"Hmm. Sounds like a certain cowboy I know," Beth said, her eyes twinkling mischievously.

Colt grinned.

She walked up to Sadie's stall. "Hi, Sadie. Nice to meet you."

"You can pet her nose and run your hand along her neck. That way she'll get to know you," Colt instructed.

Beth raised her hand to pet Sadie, but hesitated. "She's so, big. It's kind of intimidating."

"Here," Colt said, gently taking Beth's hand. "Like this." He placed her hand up high on the center of Sadie's nose and slowly moved it down to her nostrils.

"She's so soft," Beth said with delight.

Colt moved Beth's hand slowly over the side of Sadie's face and then up on her neck. "See, she likes it. Don't let her size scare you. She's just a big puppy dog." Colt stood close behind Beth as he watched her pet Sadie. He caught the scent of orange blossoms, the same scent he'd smelled before when he danced with her at Carly's birthday party. It was sweet yet soft, just like her. Shaking his head to keep his thoughts clear, he backed away and set to work.

Beth pet Sadie awhile longer while Colt set the saddle and bridle over a post by the stall. Then he pointed out his horse in the next stall.

"This is my horse, Maddie, over here," he said, gently rubbing his hand over her face. "I broke her, and Sadie, too. Actually, I broke and trained almost all the horses on the ranch, except for Luke's stallion, Chance. He did that himself."

Beth glanced over at Colt, clearly impressed. "That's amazing. So, are you the ranch's horse whisperer?"

Colt chuckled. "No. Not hardly. But I love working with horses."

"Does that mean you name them, too?" Beth asked.

Colt nodded. "I've named most of them."

"Hmm. Sadie. Maddie. Abby. Let me guess. You named them after all your old girlfriends," Beth teased.

"Smartass," Colt said softly, making Beth laugh out loud. "Come on. Let's start saddling up. You have a lot to learn in a very short time."

Colt hooked a lead rope to Sadie's halter and let Beth lead her out of the stall, and then he showed her how to tie a slip knot so the horse would stay put. They worked together, placing the blanket, then the saddle onto Sadie. Colt showed her how to cinch and knot it so it held firm. When it came time to place the bridle over Sadie's head and the bit into her mouth, Beth hesitated. "Will she bite? That's an awfully big mouth."

Colt shook his head. "Sadie hasn't ever bitten anyone. I doubt if she'll start now. Just put the bit gently up to her mouth and she'll open up. Believe it or not, horses like going for a ride. And they know the minute you saddle them, they're going. They like the exercise."

Beth glanced at Colt suspiciously. "You're making that up, right?"

"Which part?" Colt asked innocently.

"Never mind." Beth held the top of the bridle with her right hand and the bit with her left. Just as Colt had said, the minute the metal bit came close to Sadie's mouth, she opened and Beth slid it into place. "I did it," she said excitedly.

Colt nodded and smiled warmly. "Yes, you did. Now, let's go do the fun part—riding." He had Beth climb up on the horse and made sure the stirrups fit her properly, and then showed her how to work the reins. He also told her that kicking in on both sides of the horse would make Sadie run, but they weren't going to try that right away.

"So, how does it feel up there?" he asked.

"High," Beth replied, grimacing.

"You'll be fine. Just hang on. We're just going to walk, and maybe trot. No running."

Colt untied Sadie and slipped up into Maddie's saddle easily. Then he held onto the lead rope and led Sadie out of the barn. "Are you doing okay?"

"I'm still on her," Beth said.

"Good. No falling off on my watch." He moved Maddie beside Sadie, reached down, and unclipped the lead rope.

"What are you doing?" Beth asked, panic rising in her voice. "I thought you'd lead me for a while."

Colt chuckled. "You'll never learn how to pick up the rhythm of the horse if you're led everywhere. We'll go slow. Just try to keep your balance, keep your feet tight in the stirrups, and you'll be fine. Ready?"

Beth took a deep breath. "I guess so."

"Don't worry," Colt said, leaning close to Beth. "Sadie will follow Maddie's lead. You can trust me."

Colt walked Maddie away from the barn and up the trail in the center of the property that led to the back pastures. This was the same trail they would all take on Monday when the cattle drive began. As promised, Sadie followed Maddie at a leisurely pace.

They rode up the trail a bit with Colt in the lead, although he kept looking over his shoulder to make sure Beth was okay. He saw she was trying to get a feel for the horse's movements. After a while he slowed Maddie so he could ride side-by-side with Beth.

"How's it going?" he asked.

"Fine, so far. At first it was kind of rocky, but now I'm getting a feel for it."

"Good. See, riding isn't so hard," Colt said. He tossed her a wink. "It's just like riding a bike."

Beth rolled her eyes. "Yeah. A bike that has four legs and a mind of its own. But you were right. Sadie is a pretty mellow horse." They rode along until they made it to the top of the trail. Colt turned his horse around and directed Beth on how to turn hers. After she did, Beth gasped with delight.

"Look at that view," she said, gazing out over the ranch and across the road to the river and the hills in the distance. It wasn't yet noon, and the sun was nearly straight up in the sky. The river sparkled and the trees and grass were a bright, spring green.

Colt grinned. "I thought you'd like it. Andi painted a picture of this view at sunset. It's amazing. I'll have to bring you up here at sunset so you can see it yourself."

They turned and continued on up the trail, and then took a right onto the trail that circled Luke's horse pasture and stable and connected with the driveway in front of his cabin.

"Oh, is this Luke and Andi's place? It's so cute," Beth said, admiring the log cabin. There were several big pots around the outer area of the covered front porch that were waiting for flowers to be planted. A bench swing hung on one side of the porch and a small table with two chairs sat on the other side. A hitching post stood near the porch, too, where horses could be tied up.

"Yep. Do you want to go inside and look around?"

"Would that be okay? It doesn't look like either of them is here."

"He's my brother. Of course, it's okay," Colt said. He slid out of the saddle and tied the reins around the hitching post, before taking the reins from Beth. Coming to stand beside her, he said, "Slide on down."

Beth did, not as expertly as Colt had, but she landed with her feet on the ground. Colt had put his hands around her waist to steady her. Under her heavy sweatshirt, he felt how small her waist actually was. He always forgot she had a great figure, because she seemed so intent upon hiding it all the time.

They walked up the steps and Colt knocked loudly on the door before turning the handle and entering. "Hey? Is anyone here?" he hollered. When no one answered, he wiped his boots on the doormat and then entered. Beth did the same.

"Oh, my goodness," Beth said, surveying the room. "This is adorable. I love that huge rock fireplace. And all the windows in front. They give the room so much light."

Colt nodded. "Yeah. Luke did a good job of designing this. I'm going to ask him to draw up plans for my house, too."

Beth turned to Colt. "Luke drew up the plans? Did he go to school for that?"

"Nope. He went to college for engineering and he worked for Boeing in Southern California for a couple of years before moving home. But he has a talent for designing buildings, too. He built this house for his first wife."

Beth looked intrigued. "Luke was married once before?"

Colt nodded. "Yep. She left though. She couldn't stand living so far out in the country."

"Wow. I had no idea he'd been married before. And what

was wrong with her that she didn't love it here? It's beautiful, and everyone is so nice. I've never lived in the country before and I love it."

Colt glanced at Beth. He remembered how Andi had taken to the ranch so easily. It was as if she was meant to be here. Carly enjoyed riding and loved the family, but she didn't necessarily like being so far away from the city. He liked that Beth was already falling in love with the ranch.

Colt took her around the cabin, showing her all the rooms. The guest room was being used as an artist studio for Andi, but they'd soon be turning it into a nursery. Luke had promised Andi they'd add on next year so she could have a real art studio with plenty of windows for light. Colt pointed out the painting of the sunset over the ranch. It stood on an easel in the corner of the room, waiting to be framed.

"She's so talented," Beth said, staring at the painting in awe. "I wonder what it's like to have talent like that."

"You have talents," Colt said.

Beth shook her head. "Not like this. I can't paint, sing, dance, or even play sports very well. That's why I walk. It's the only exercise I can do that doesn't take talent."

Colt stared at her. "You help people get well. You make sick children smile. You cook like a pro, and you make me smile. Those are amazing talents."

Beth looked up at Colt. "That's so sweet. I never thought of it that way."

Colt grinned. "And what's this about not being able to dance? You dance just fine. Remember, we danced at Carly's party."

"I remember," Beth said softly. "But that was just one dance. You can't judge a person's skill from just one time."

"Then I guess we'll have to dance some more," Colt said happily. "There's a band every Saturday night at The Depot down the road. After supper, we'll go dancing."

Beth laughed. "I don't know how to dance to cowboy music."

"Don't worry," Colt told her. "If I can teach you how to ride a horse, I can teach you how to dance. That's my specialty."

* * *

That evening after supper, Colt talked Luke and Andi into joining him and Beth at The Depot. He tried getting his mother and Glen to come along, too, but they declined. "You young people go ahead," Ginny said. "We old people will stay home."

Everyone laughed. Ginny and Glen were only in their fifties. They had years before they'd be considered old.

They took two separate trucks in case Andi started to feel sick and needed to go home. "That means you'll have to watch how much you drink," Luke had warned Colt, reminding him of the days when his big brother always drove him home.

"You don't have to worry about that," Colt had told him, and Luke nodded approval. Colt felt he'd come a long way in just a few months. Before, he would have drunk as much as he wanted because someone was always looking out for him. Now, he looked after himself.

A short distance from the ranch, Colt followed Luke down an off ramp to where The Depot was located. The bar/restaurant/casino/gas station was the only place there, and already the parking lot was full. They parked, and Colt hopped out of the truck and ran around to open Beth's door.

Beth smiled. "My gentleman cowboy at work again," she teased as she slid out of the high truck with Colt giving her a hand.

Colt's heart warmed. He liked hearing her say "my

gentleman cowboy." It just sounded nice.

They walked inside the building and Colt watched as Beth's eyes sparkled with delight. The place was large, with wooden booths lining the walls, tables in the middle of the floor, a stage and dance floor on one end, and an old fashioned western bar on the other end. Off in another room were pool tables where men were crowded around holding cues, waiting their turn. Almost everyone in the place wore boots, cowboy hats, and jeans. Plaid shirts were very popular, too. Some of the women wore short skirts, tight T-shirts, and boots.

Beth laughed and looked at Colt. "I see now why you plopped this cowboy hat on my head. I would have been out of place without it."

"Yeah, they do like their cowboy styles around here," Andi said. "You'll get used to it after a while, though."

"I love it," Beth said gleefully. "It's all so warm and cozy in here. It's so different from the places in Seattle where it's wall-to-wall people smashed up against each other on the dance floor."

"That's for sure," Colt agreed. He hadn't enjoyed many of the places he and Carly had gone to.

They found an empty booth and a waitress came and took their order. They had a round of beers except for Andi. She ordered an iced tea instead.

The band members were setting up and tuning their guitars in preparation of playing. Several people saw Colt and came over to say hello. Colt introduced Beth to everyone who stopped by the table. From a table across the room near the pool tables, Randy nodded to them. They waved him over, but he declined with a wave. Randy was like family, but he was also a loner who liked to be by himself a lot.

"How did your first riding lesson go?" Andi asked Beth after everyone had their drinks and a basket of pretzels was placed on the table.

"Really well," Beth answered. "I was a little intimidated at first by the size of the horse, but she was easy to ride, until we trotted." Beth grimaced.

"Trotting is the worst," Andi said. "I'd rather gallop than trot any day. All that bouncing up and down jars your teeth out."

The men laughed and Beth blew out a sigh of relief. "Good, then it isn't just me. I thought I was going to fall right off, until I found the rhythm. We haven't tried galloping, yet. I guess we'll do that tomorrow."

"Yep," Colt said. "You have to be an expert by tomorrow night or else you'll learn along the way."

"I'm just hoping I can walk tomorrow," Beth said, laughing. "No one told me that riding makes your legs so sore. I'm not even sure I'll be able to get out of this booth."

"I'll get you warmed up with some dancing," Colt said, grinning.

"Yeah. If you're tired now, wait until Colt takes you for a spin around the floor. He taught me to dance to country music, but I could never keep up with him. He's got energy to spare," Andi said.

Colt smiled proudly. He'd always enjoyed coming here and dancing on the weekends. He'd really missed it while he was in Seattle. Dancing in the bars there wasn't anything like here.

The band started playing a slow tune to warm up the crowd and Colt immediately grabbed Beth's hand and pulled her out onto the dance floor. Smiling down at her, he slipped his hand around her waist and held her other hand. Beth placed her free hand on his shoulder. They swayed slowly to the music, their bodies close, but not touching.

Colt had noticed how nice Beth looked tonight. She wore a simple royal blue shirt over a white tank top and a pair of dark blue jeans. She'd worn her boots because Colt had told her that's what everyone wore plus she could break them in some more. He'd placed a white hat on her head before they'd left, and it looked cute on her brown hair that she'd left down. He smelled the orange blossom scent again, and wondered how she was able to smell so good after a day of riding. He'd taken a shower to wash away the stink of horse sweat, but she smelled wonderful.

The song ended and the band started playing a livelier tune. Colt smiled wide. "It's a two-step. Just follow along."

Beth tried, but kept tripping over her feet or stepping on Colt's. They both laughed. By the time the song was over, she'd caught on and when the next one started up, she was ready. For two more songs, Colt and Beth stepped, twirled, spun, and dipped. Colt couldn't remember when he'd had this much fun in a long time. By the time they made it back to the table, they were both parched and drank down their beers.

Another slow song started up and Colt grinned over at Luke and Andi. "They're playing your song. Aren't you going to dance?"

Luke glanced over at Andi and smiled. "Shall we?" She nodded and they stepped out onto the dance floor.

"That's their song? 'Desperado'?" Beth asked.

"Yep. It's the first song they ever danced to, before they even knew they were in love," Colt told her. "Of course, we all knew they were in love, but they were fighting it. Look at them out there. That's what true love really looks like."

Beth looked over at Colt. "Colt, you're such a romantic."

Colt felt his face grow hot. He didn't usually talk like that and it surprised him he had in front of Beth.

Beth placed her hand on his arm. "Don't be embarrassed. I think it's sweet. And you're right. They do look adorable together. I hope someday a man will look at me like that. A good man like Luke is hard to find."

Colt gazed at Beth. "I'm surprised someone hasn't snatched you up already," he said seriously. "You're beautiful, sweet, smart, and a great cook. What's wrong with the men in Seattle?"

"That's sweet of you to say, Colt, but men don't want women like me. I'm practical and not that much fun to be around. And beautiful? Not like Carly. She attracts men like flies to honey. She's beautiful, not me."

Colt frowned. He touched Beth's chin and made her look up into his eyes. "Remember this morning when you told me not to put myself down? Well, don't you do it, either. You are beautiful. I've never seen eyes as lovely as yours with those thick lashes and those sparkling gold flecks in them. Your lovely eyes were the first things I saw the moment I met you. Your skin is so creamy and soft that you don't need makeup. And when you smile, it warms up a room. No, you're not Carly, but she's not you, either. You're beautiful on the inside and outside, and that's a great thing to be."

Beth drew in a breath as she stared up at Colt. The music played softly in the background, and it felt like all the noise around them faded away in the distance. For one brief moment, Colt wanted to kiss her. But then Beth lifted her hand up to Colt's face and ran it gently across his cheek and down along his jawline. "Thank you, Colt. You're a good friend," she said softly.

The music stopped and the moment broke between them. Andi and Luke returned to the table just as the band started up with another snappy country song.

"There's your cue," Luke said. "Time to line dance."

"Line what?" Beth asked.

"You'll see," Colt said, grinning. He grabbed her hand and brought her out to the floor again.

Chapter Twenty-One

Colt awoke early the next morning, but lay in bed a while, thinking about last night. Not long after Luke and Andi had danced, they'd said goodnight and headed home. He and Beth stayed a while longer and danced or sat in the booth, talking. Randy had come over once and asked Beth to dance, and she did to a slow song. Colt had found himself simmering over their dancing together, although he had no idea why. He loved Carly. Why would he be jealous of Randy dancing with Beth?

Colt had pulled out his phone and tried to call Carly while Beth danced. It was his only chance to talk to her in private before the cattle drive. It rang several times, and then went to voice mail, so he'd hung up. He knew she was awake. After all, it was a Saturday night. Maybe it had just been too noisy in the bar she was at for her to hear her phone.

When Beth had come back to the table, she'd looked at him funny and asked, "What are you scowling at?"

"I didn't know I was. I just tried calling Carly, but she didn't answer," he'd told her.

"She's probably just out," Beth had said casually.

Yeah, she probably is. But with who? That's what worried Colt the most.

As Colt got out of bed to shower, he thought about the moment he'd shared with Beth last night. He'd meant every word he'd said to her. She was a wonderful person who thought of others and not just herself. He hated to admit it, but Carly was very self-involved. She could be thoughtful, but usually she wanted everything her way. Not Beth. She'd go out of her way to help others first. The difference between the two women was like night and day. Yet, he had feelings for both of them.

And there it was. He had feelings for Beth. Again, when he'd looked into her eyes, he'd wanted to kiss her. And when she'd touched his cheek, it was as if he'd been struck by lightning. His whole body had tingled. He'd never experienced that sensation before from a single touch. But then she'd said, "You're a good friend," and the magic was gone. Friend. That's all they were to each other. Friends.

Colt and Beth went riding again for several hours so she would feel comfortable on Sadie. They galloped and trotted and walked for miles. Colt even brought her into the cattle pasture to let her get a feel for how it was to ride beside them. He explained that they would ride as a pair and work together with one section of the herd. Luke would be in the lead and Randy would be at the rear. Jake and Glen were riding together and their neighbors, Ray and Jimmy, would pair up, too. And, of course, Bree would be where she was needed most, helping to keep the cattle in line.

"Bree has to work, too?" Beth asked.

"Yep. It's how she earns her keep. My mom and Andi baby her, but she's a working dog. Wait until you see her running around the herd, controlling the cattle. She loves it."

Just before sunset, they rode up the trail to the top of the hill to see the view. Beth gasped in delight as the sun touched the hilltops in the distance, turning everything a glorious golden red. The river sparkled in the fading light and the world seemed to come alive for that one brief moment before the sun fell behind the hills.

"It's so beautiful," Beth said, her eyes shining as she turned to Colt. "It's just like Andi's painting."

Colt smiled. Beth looked lovely sitting there, her eyes sparkling in the fading sunlight. *You're beautiful.* He panicked a moment, wondering if he'd said that aloud, but when Beth didn't react, he realized he'd only thought it. A part of him wished he had the nerve to say it aloud, because it was true. But he knew he had no right to say it.

That night, they all went to bed early since they'd be getting up before dawn to begin the process of gathering the cattle together before moving them. Colt gave Beth a set of saddlebags to pack her things in and told her they'd put them on Sadie in the morning. By nine o'clock that night, everyone was tucked away in their rooms, asleep.

The household arose before sunrise and ate a quick breakfast before heading out. Beth met Ray and Jimmy, two sturdy, suntanned cowboys, and Ray's wife, Amy, who volunteered to clean up the breakfast dishes so Ginny and Andi could leave before the herd started up the trail.

The two women took off with a truck loaded down with all the supplies they'd need to fix meals for the crew. Colt told Beth that they would set up camp in a spot they always stayed at for the night, and have food ready by the time they caught up to them. Each person was given a canteen full of fresh water and some food to put in their saddlebag to eat on the trail, because they wouldn't be stopping for lunch.

Colt saddled Maddie and then made sure Beth had saddled Sadie securely. Luke and the other men, along with Bree, were already in the field rounding up the cattle. As Colt climbed up on Maddie, Beth spied the holster attached to his belt, under his coat.

"Are you going to shoot something?" she asked.

Colt frowned a moment, then chuckled. "Oh, the handgun. Hopefully not, but it's best to carry one. All the men have either a rifle or pistol with them. Ma has one in the truck, too."

Beth's mouth dropped open. "Why?"

"There are wild animals up in the hills," Colt said. "Wolves, cougers, grizzlies. You name it, we have it. A man would be foolish to go up there without a gun."

"Oh," Beth said. "Guess I hadn't given that much thought."

Colt's eyes sparkled mischievously. "Don't worry. I know how to handle a gun. I won't accidently shoot you."

"Great. Thanks," Beth said dryly.

Colt left to help the men round up the herd. He told Beth to stay on the sidelines until they headed out so she wouldn't get caught in with the moving cattle.

By noon, Luke had the front of the herd moving up the trail and soon the bulk of the herd followed behind. Colt waved Beth over to the right flank of the herd to ride with him. Glen and Jake were manning the left flank, Ray and Jimmy were following toward the rear, and Randy stayed behind, keeping the back of the heard moving. Bree was up ahead with Luke, urging the cattle forward.

Cattle bellowed loudly and dust rose up from under the hundreds of hooves as they pounded the trail. Colt continually rode up and down the side of the herd and waved for Beth to follow. If a cow veered off the path, he was right there to nudge her back into the herd. Soon, Beth was doing the same, and they began working as a team, keeping the cattle together.

As the day grew warmer, Beth began peeling off the layers she'd worn until she was down to her T-shirt, but soon, as they rose higher in elevation, she began putting the layers back on. They didn't stop for lunch. Beth ate a protein bar and drank her water as they followed the herd. Colt did the same, except he had jerky packed in his bag. As the sun slowly settled in the west, they spotted the camp Andi and Ginny had set up and everyone sighed with relief. Their day wasn't over, but food was coming soon.

They moved the herd into a natural pasture, and then roped off several sections around the trees to try to contain the herd as much as possible. There was a pond for water and a stream that ran near the campsite, so the men watered the horses and then staked them so they could graze. The men would take turns watching the herd overnight to make sure they didn't stray too far or predators didn't attack.

Beth stumbled when she finally stepped down from her horse, and Colt caught her before she fell. "Oh, my goodness," she exclaimed. "My legs feel like rubber."

"Yeah, they will after a full day in the saddle," he told her. Colt slipped his arm around her waist and helped her hobble to the campsite so she could sit down.

"You're walking just fine," Beth noted.

"I'm a cowboy. I'm used to riding all day," Colt teased.

That night they ate stew cooked over a fire, pan corn bread, and some of Ginny's homemade peach preserves. Beth exclaimed it was the best meal she'd ever tasted, and everyone laughed.

"After riding all day, anything tastes good," Ginny said.

Three small tents were set up around the campfire and sleeping bags were provided. Luke and Andi took one tent and Ginny and Glen took another. Colt led Beth to the third one.

"I feel bad about sleeping in a tent when you have to sleep outdoors," Beth said as they stood beside her small tent.

"I don't mind sleeping under the stars," Colt told her. "Besides, if I slept in a tent the other men would rib me about being soft."

"Luke and Glen are sleeping in a tent and no one's making fun of them."

"That's because they have someone to sleep with," Colt said. "They'd give them heck if they didn't sleep in the tent with their ladies."

Beth reached out and squeezed Colt's arm. "You'd never be soft," she said. "You're the hardest working man I've ever met."

Colt smiled, and tipped his head so his hat brim hid his embarrassment. He never got used to being complimented by Beth.

Beth looked up at the sky. The moon was only half full, but it shone bright with stars glittering all around it. "This is a beautiful sky. It's so clear and the stars are glorious. I'm happy you invited me, Colt. I'd never have experienced something like this without having met you."

Colt tilted his head up and stared at the sky. Beth was right. It was beautiful. He'd lived here his whole life, so he was used to its beauty. But after being in Seattle, he had a greater appreciation for home. "I'm glad you came, too," he said softly. Then he grinned. "But wait a while before you thank me. There's still a whole lot of work left."

"Bring it on, Cowboy," Beth said, laughing. "Carly was right about one thing, though."

"What?"

"You smell terrible after a day of riding," Beth teased. "And I'm sure I do, too."

Colt let out a howl of laughter. "It'll get worse," he said. Then he leaned in close to Beth and caught her eyes with his. "But you still smell lovely," he whispered.

Beth smiled. She stood up on tiptoe and gave Colt a soft kiss on the cheek, then went inside her tent.

Colt stood there, letting the moment envelop him. That single kiss warmed his heart. Slowly, he turned and headed back to the campfire.

"Is Beth all tucked in for the night?" Luke asked as Colt rolled out his sleeping bag on the ground near the fire. Ray and Jimmy were watching the cattle for the first shift and Randy was already snoring softly in his own bag.

"Yep. I thought you went to bed already. You and I have the next shift."

"I know," Luke said. "I was just stoking the fire." He stared at Colt with his intense blue eyes. "Beth sure is nice. And she's a fast learner and a hard worker. She fits right in here with everyone."

Colt nodded. His saddle was at the head of the sleeping bag so he could lay his head on it. He sat on the ground and slipped off his boots, then slid into the bag. "She's enjoying it here. Beth loves the outdoors, so this is perfect for her."

"I was surprised Carly didn't want to come along. She loves to ride."

Colt chuckled. "Carly loves riding, but not camping and certainly not sleeping in a tent with no running water or a hair dryer."

"Hmm."

Colt glanced up at Luke. "What's that supposed to mean?"

Luke sat down in a camp chair near Colt. He leaned over and placed his elbows on his knees. "Nothing. Is everything all right with you and Carly?"

"Yep. We're fine," Colt said.

"That's good. Do you think you'll be coming home in September? Or are you going to stay in Seattle longer?"

Colt stared up into the sky. "I'll be coming home in September." He trained his eyes on his brother. Luke's expression didn't betray whether he was surprised or not. "I wanted to talk to you about something."

"Shoot," Luke said.

"I think it's time I had a place of my own. I'd like to build a house on the property just east of the main house."

Luke's brows rose. "Really? What brought this on?"

Colt shrugged. "It's just time I move into my own place. Now that Ma and Glen are together, I'm sure they'd like their privacy. Besides, I'm almost twenty-six. It's about time I moved out of my childhood bedroom, don't you think?"

Luke nodded. "What kind of place were you thinking of?"

"Nothing fancy. A cabin like yours, except I have a couple of different ideas for it. Would you be willing to draw up the plans for me? I'd like to start building it this fall so the outside is done and I can work on the inside all winter."

"Wow, you really are serious," Luke said. "I'd be happy to draw it up for you. Just give me a list of what you want in it and I'll see what I can come up with."

"Great. Then we could order the materials to build it so they're here and ready when I get home in September," Colt said. "I have money saved, and I'm sure I can get a loan for the rest."

"Well. Your own place. That's exciting," Luke said, smiling. "Does this mean that Carly might be coming home with you in the fall?"

Colt took a breath, and then let out a sigh. He doubted that Carly would follow him out here, but he didn't want to stay in Seattle forever, either. He'd have to see what happened when the time came. "I don't know," he told Luke honestly. "Carly's still finding her way. We'll see."

Luke nodded. He said goodnight to Colt and headed for his tent.

Colt lay under the stars, staring at the sky for a long time. Bree came and curled up beside him, and he ran his fingers though her silky fur. He wondered where Carly was right now, and if she was out with friends. He wondered who she was dancing with. It bothered him that he had to worry about that at all. He should be able to trust her, but deep in his heart, he wasn't completely sure he could.

As he lay there, his mind replayed the sweet kiss Beth had given him tonight, and he fell asleep smiling.

* * *

"My goodness. If I'd have known telling you that you stink would make you take your shirt off, I'd have told you sooner," Beth said, standing beside the stream early the next morning.

Colt stood and looked up in surprise at Beth grinning down at him. He'd taken off his shirt and T-shirt so he could wash some of the grime off from the day before. The water was ice cold and the air was chilly, yet he felt the warmth of embarrassment rise up his neck. "Sorry," he said, brushing his wet hair back with his hand.

Beth laughed. "No need to be. Every guy should look as good as you without a shirt."

Colt quickly grabbed the towel he'd brought along and dried off, then slipped his T-shirt on. "What are you doing down here?"

"Same thing you are," Beth said, walking over to the stream. "I figured I should wash up a bit. It sure is dusty riding along with a herd of cattle." She slipped off her outer shirt, revealing a tank top underneath. Then she kneeled down beside the stream and splashed water on her face.

Colt stood there, mesmerized. He was used to seeing Beth in her big sweatshirts or baggie scrubs. He'd never seen her in a skimpy tank top before. Her skin was creamy white and the tight top accentuated her small waist. He wondered why she was always trying to hide her figure.

"Is something wrong?" Beth asked.

Colt was jolted out of his thoughts. "No, no. Just thinking."

Beth stood and wiped her face and hands on a towel Ginny had given her. She slipped on her shirt, tucking it in. "I think I'll wait on washing my hair," she said. "It'll never dry in this cold air."

Colt nodded. He couldn't stop staring at Beth.

Beth walked over and ran her hand back and forth in front of Colt's eyes. "Earth to Colt."

Colt shook his head. "Sorry. I must be tired from being up half the night, watching the cattle," he lied.

"That's some pretty good scruff you've got going there," Beth teased. "You'll have a full beard by the time we get back."

Colt reached up and ran his hand over the side of his face. He was usually clean shaven.

"See you in a bit," Beth said, walking up the small hill toward camp. She stopped and turned. "Oh, and Colt?"

He looked up at her. "Huh?"

"You're T-shirt is inside-out. Again." Beth chuckled and walked away.

Colt looked down at his shirt. Sure enough, Beth was right. This was becoming a habit. He laughed at himself and fixed it.

Chapter Twenty-Two

The time went by quickly as they expertly moved the herd up into the hills toward the summer pasture. The second day it rained on them for a couple of hours, and Colt helped Beth into her poncho to keep her from getting soaked. She didn't complain and when the sun finally came out, she took off her poncho and shook out her hair so it would dry.

"Looks like I don't have to wash it, now," Beth had yelled over to Colt with a grin.

Colt thought of how upset Carly would have been if she'd been rained on compared to Beth's cavalier attitude. He knew he shouldn't compare the two, but it was hard not to.

Beth had a chance to see Bree in action, running back and forth, urging the cattle on and keeping them in line. Bree fearlessly nudged and bumped them and snapped at their heels. She never seemed to tire out.

"I wish the people I work with worked as hard as Bree," Beth called over to Colt. He nodded and smiled with pride.

As the third day came near its end, Colt found a calf that had wandered off from the herd and was tangled in some underbrush in a ditch. He waved Beth on and she continued to follow the herd. He knew if he needed help that Ray or Jimmy would be along shortly.

Colt dismounted and walked over to the bellowing calf. He

slipped on his work gloves and started pulling at the brittle brush that had tangled around one of the calves' legs. As he reached down to pick up the calf, his right arm scraped on a thick branch and it tore into the top of his arm. Colt swore and pulled away quickly. The sleeve of his shirt was spit open and there was a nasty gash about four inches long. It burned and was bleeding. He reached down again and pulled out the calf, then carried it out of the ditch. Setting it down, he pushed it in the direction of the herd. The calf ran off, following the sounds of the noisy herd.

By the time Colt caught up to Beth, camp was in sight. As they rode side-by-side, Beth suddenly gasped and pointed at Colt's arm.

"You're bleeding," she said. "What happened?"

Colt glanced down at the cut. It didn't burn anymore and he'd forgotten about it. But Beth was right, it was still bleeding. "Got cut on some brush is all," he said casually. "I'll take care of it at camp."

But long after they'd stopped for the night, Beth noticed that Colt hadn't bandaged his arm yet. She pulled him aside.

"You sit right there while I get the first aid kit," she commanded. "What's wrong with you? Do you want it to get infected?"

Ginny gave Beth the kit and she returned to where Colt sat and kneeled down beside him.

"It's really not all that bad," Colt began to say, but Beth cut him off as she rolled up his sleeve.

"It is bad. Look at it. It's deep. And it's dirty." She cleaned the wound with fresh water from her canteen, gently rubbing all around it with a clean towel.

Colt flinched. "Careful. It hurts."

"Don't be such a big baby," Beth told him. "I thought you were a tough cowboy."

"It can still hurt," Colt mumbled.

Beth pulled out the bottle of alcohol and soaked a cotton ball with it. "This is what's going to hurt," she said. She patted the wound with the alcohol soaked cotton and Colt winced, but he kept his mouth shut.

"I hope your shots are current," Beth said sharply. "The last thing you need is tetanus."

"I just had a tetanus shot last year," Colt said, still gritting his teeth from the burning pain.

"Good." Beth pulled out gauze from the kit and taped it down over the wound. Then she wrapped up his arm and taped it so it wouldn't unravel. "Don't get that wet," she warned, looking up at Colt sternly. "It should be okay until tomorrow night. I'll rewrap it then."

Colt watched as Beth replaced the supplies into the little metal kit. When she turned to face him again, he was smiling at her.

"What are you grinning at?" Beth asked.

"You. You can be a little frightening when you're mad. I hope you don't talk to your patients that way," he teased.

Beth glared at him and stood up, but before she could walk away, Colt gently grabbed her arm.

"Hey, I was just teasing."

"I know, but it wasn't funny. You should have taken this more seriously. You shouldn't let a deep cut like that go unattended."

"You're right. I'm sorry."

Beth sighed. "It scared me. Infection can come on quickly. I've seen people lose arms and legs from an infection that started with a smaller cut than that."

Colt reached up and ran a finger across the side of Beth's face and around her ear, pushing a strand of loose hair back. There were dirt smudges on her face from riding all day, but she still looked adorable. "Thanks," he said softly. "I'm glad I have you to look after me."

Beth gave him a small smile, then turned and headed back to the truck to put the first aid kit away. As Colt watched her leave, he realized that Beth had been taking care of him in one way or another since the day they met. She'd helped him with directions, fed him, went shopping with him for boots after he'd been hired at the market, and even sympathized with him when Carly banned him to the den for proposing to her. She was a good friend. No, she was more than a good friend. He'd never had anyone other than family care about him the way she seemed to. Colt sighed. It was a nice feeling, but this only made his feelings for her more confusing.

* * *

The next day was their last on the trail. When they finally reached the summer pasture, everyone cheered. It had only been four days, but it seemed like a long haul moving so slowly with the herd.

Once at the summer pasture, they had the small cabin at their disposal and an outhouse, too. The cabin was equipped with a generator for electricity so they had a stove, and a working refrigerator. There was also a hand pump in the sink for water. The cabin was used periodically during the summer months by Luke, Randy, or Colt when they went up to check on the cattle and work on the fences. The one room structure with two bunk beds, a sofa, and a small kitchen wasn't large enough to accommodate everyone who'd helped move the herd, but it was nice for Ginny and Andi to have a real stove to cook on.

"This is so adorable," Beth said when she looked inside the cabin. "What a wonderful retreat."

"Hmm," Colt murmured. "I never thought of it that way. We use it when we're working up here, not for a vacation home."

Beth gave him a sideways glance. "I'm surprised at you, Colt. With all your romantic notions, you never thought to bring a girl up here to woo."

Colt broke out laughing. "Woo? Heck, I don't even know what that means."

"Well, you do it quite well, Mr. Gentleman Cowboy," Beth told him.

Everyone ate a late lunch at the cabin and then Ray, Jimmy, Jake, and Randy headed back home. It was only a three-hour ride back to the main house when they weren't moving cattle along, and the sun wouldn't be going down for another three hours.

"You mean to tell me it took us four days to get here, but it won't take more than three hours to get home?" Beth asked.

"Goes a lot faster when you're not moving a herd of slow cattle," Colt said.

Colt asked Beth if she wanted to stay the night at the cabin and rest the horses or follow everyone else back to the ranch. Ginny and Andi were riding back in the truck and Glen and Luke were following on horseback. Beth said either way was fine with her, so Colt opted for them to stay at the cabin that night.

"There's a beautiful view not far from here. I think you'd enjoy seeing it," Colt explained. "We can go there in the morning before we head back."

Ginny left food for them for later that night and for breakfast. Luke looked at Colt oddly when he heard they were staying, but didn't say anything. Colt figured he thought it was strange they'd stay up here alone when they were only friends. Colt didn't think it was strange at all. Luke and Andi had stayed up here before they were a couple, and no one thought a thing about it. Of course, they did end up together after all.

After everyone left, Beth pumped water into a pan and started warming it on the stove. "It'll feel good to wash up with warm water for a change," she told Colt. He sat at the small table in the kitchen, watching her. "And we can clean your wound again and re-bandage it."

Colt groaned. "I think you like to torture me," he teased. "I'm going out to make sure there's enough water in the trough for the horses, and then I'll be back. You can have a little privacy."

He went outside to the small corral beside the cabin and checked on Sadie and Maddie. Both horses were lazily eating grass. The evening was chilly and he wouldn't be surprised if it got down into the forties tonight. He decided he'd bring in wood from the shed beside the house so they could start a fire and keep the little cabin warm.

Colt walked over to the trough and pumped the hand pump several times until fresh, cold well water came out and filled it up. He rolled his sleeves up, and being careful not to wet the bandage, washed his hands and face, feeling how thick his beard had become in only a few days. Then he ran the water over his head to clean his hair. He shook the water from his hair and ran his hands through it to smooth is back. He couldn't wait to get home and shave and shower. He knew he still smelled like the trail.

Colt went to the shed and stacked a few logs across his right arm, then carried them into the side door of the cabin. Beth stood by the sink in her tank top and jeans, her hair damp and her face and hands scrubbed clean. She frowned at Colt when she saw the heavy logs he carried.

"You'd better not be opening up that wound," she warned.

Colt chuckled. "I'm being careful," he said. He set the logs down beside the stone fireplace and started stacking them inside it in a crisscross fashion. "Would you mind bringing me some papers we have stacked in the broom closet over there?" he asked.

Beth went over to a small, narrow closet and saw papers stacked up on the floor. A broom hung on a hook on the wall, and a few other cleaning supplies were on a shelf up above. She brought over a handful of papers to Colt.

"I suppose it will get cold tonight," she said.

"Already is getting cold. Figured a fire would feel nice," Colt said.

He opened the draft and then stuffed a few pieces of paper under the wood. The strike of a match caught the paper on fire and the dry wood started burning quickly.

Beth walked closer to the fireplace. "Oh, that does feels good," she said, warming her hands in front of her.

Colt retrieved more wood and stacked it safely away from the flames. "Do you need to use the outhouse? It's best to go out before it gets completely dark," Colt said.

Beth nodded and Colt followed her outside with a flashlight.

"You don't have to come with me," Beth said, taking the light. "I don't want you standing right outside while I use it."

"I'll just watch from here," Colt told her. "Just in case some critter comes along." He patted the pistol on his hip.

"Well, don't mistake me for an animal and shoot me, okay?"

Colt grinned. "I won't."

Beth went inside, and then Colt sent her into the cabin while he used it. By the time they were both back inside the cabin, the fire had warmed up the little room.

"Okay, time to change that bandage," Beth said. "Sit down here. Ginny said there was a first aid kit in the cupboard." She retrieved it and placed it on the table. Then she brought the bowl of warm water she'd put aside to clean his arm with, and a clean washcloth. She pulled out a chair and sat knee-to-knee with Colt. As she unwrapped his bandage, she said, "Tell me about this cabin. How old is it?"

Colt watched her carefully unwrap the bandage as he spoke. "It was built in the 1860s by my four times great grandfather and his brother. It was one of their homestead cabins. Our house where Ma lives is the other cabin they built."

"Cabin? It's a huge house," Beth said, carefully working off the tape on the gauze.

"Yeah, it is now. But the house was originally just a one-room cabin with the fireplace, like this place. The sitting room at the house was the original structure, although it's changed a lot over the years. The ceiling was raised, and the rest of the house was added on throughout the years to accommodate a growing family."

"So, you're family has worked this land since the 1860s? That's so cool," Beth said. The bandage was off, and now she started washing it carefully so as not to break the scab open.

"Yep. But we didn't own as much back then as we do now. They started with the original three-hundred and twenty acres and grew it from there."

"Amazing," Beth said. She soaked a cotton ball in alcohol and began dabbing it on the cut. "You should be proud, owning and working a ranch that your ancestors started from the ground up. Not many people can say that, you know."

Colt nodded. He watched Beth work carefully on his arm. The alcohol stung a little, but not as bad as yesterday. She began putting fresh gauze on it and taping it down. "I am proud," he said softly. "That's why I'm coming back. You know, I couldn't wait to go out to Seattle to be with Carly, and I still want to be with her, but I need to come home. I love the ranch and working outdoors. And I realize now how much I missed my family. Even my horse," he said, grinning.

Beth looked up into his eyes. "I'd miss this place, too, if I were you. It's beautiful. And your family is amazing. You're so lucky, Colt. And now, you're going to start another generation of Brennans by building your cabin and someday raising a family. You're part of a legacy."

Colt hadn't thought about it that way, but it was true. He was a part of a legacy that he hoped to continue. Luke and Andi were already having the next Brennan generation. And someday, he would, too.

Beth rolled the outer bandage over the gauze and then taped it securely. "There you go. All done."

Colt looked down at his arm. "How'd you do that?"

"What?" Beth asked innocently. She started putting everything back into the first aid kit.

"I hardly even noticed you working on my arm, and then it was finished."

"It's a little trick we nurses use. I get patients to start talking about something they're interested in and they forget I'm working on them. It helps, especially with young children, who may panic at the sight of a wound."

Colt reached down and put his hand under Beth's chin, gently lifting her eyes up to his. They stared back at him, the gold flecks sparkling. "You're amazing at what you do, you know that? I feel so lucky that you're in my life."

Beth smiled warmly. "I feel the same way," she whispered.

Colt slowly ran his hand up the side of her face and behind her neck. His fingers slipped through her damp hair as his gaze touched her full lips. He thought of nothing else, only the two of them, so close, here in this cabin as the fire crackled nearby. Unable to resist any longer, he pulled Beth close and covered her lips with his.

Colt's passion grew as his lips met Beth's. She responded in kind, raising her hands up around his neck. Her touch caused

Colt's heart to beat faster and their tongues met and danced as beautifully as they'd danced together just a few days ago. Colt relished Beth's touch and the delicious taste of her. He stood, bringing her up with him and pulled her close, all the while kissing her, not wanting the kiss to end. His hands caressed her back and slid down to the curves of waist. She felt warm and soft, and all he wanted was to stay this way, and never stop.

Slowly, they pulled apart, their arms still wrapped around each other. Colt looked down into Beth's face and saw a look of sadness cross over it. Before he could say a word, she moved out of his embrace, busying herself with putting the things away.

"Beth?" he said softly.

Beth stopped still at the counter, her back to him. He saw the reflection of her face in the window glass above it. He couldn't tell if her expression was one of sadness, or regret.

Beth turned and gave him a small smile. "And you said you didn't know how to woo a woman."

Colt knew she was trying to lighten the heaviness in the room, but it fell flat on the floor. "Are you mad at me?" he asked.

Beth shook her head. "No."

"Should I apologize?"

Beth dropped her eyes to the floor. "No. That would only make it worse."

Colt swallowed hard. He wanted to walk over to Beth and pull her into his arms. *But I'm supposed to be in love with Carly. Remember?* Instead, he just stood there, feeling lost.

"It's been a long day," Beth said. "A long week of hard work. We're both tired. It's just one of those things that happen. Nothing more. We should get some sleep."

Colt watched as Beth walked across the room and pulled back the blankets on the bottom bunk. He sighed and went over to put more wood on the fire. After lighting an oil lamp, he took the flashlight outside and turned off the generator, then went back inside.

Beth was already under the covers, her back turned toward him. Colt sat on the chair and pulled off his boots, blew out the lamp, then climbed up into the bunk above Beth's. He lay there several minutes listening to the crackle of the fire. Finally, he asked, "Are we okay?"

"We're okay," Beth said softly. "Goodnight, Colt."

"Goodnight, Beth," Colt said.

Chapter Twenty-Three

They left for Seattle two days later. The morning after the kiss, Beth acted like it had never happened and Colt followed her lead. As promised, he'd shown her the beautiful view of the valley alight with the morning sun and Beth had been delighted by it. Then they'd ridden back to the ranch house, mostly in silence.

Colt left the ranch with a heavy heart. If working at the market had taught him anything, it was how lucky he'd been all these years to work outdoors in the fresh air instead of in a hot, noisy warehouse. He knew he'd miss his family even more now that he'd spent time with them. Everything was changing here. His mother and Glen were growing closer and Andi and Luke were having a baby, and he wasn't going to be around to be a part of it. At least he knew he was coming home in September, with or without Carly. He would love for her to change her mind and decide to marry him, but he didn't really see that happening. Either way, he was coming home, building his house, and working the ranch. He'd reminded Luke before leaving about the house plans and Luke had said he'd start to work on them right away.

"Anything to get you home," Luke had said with a grin.

They arrived at the townhouse around seven that evening and both immediately started unpacking and putting their things away. Colt had plenty of laundry to do, as well as Beth, so she started hers right away so he could do his in the morning. Beth was thrilled at all the jams and preserves Ginny had sent home with them, and she promptly put them up in the kitchen cupboard.

Carly wasn't home. It was Saturday night, so Colt figured she was out with her friends. He'd tried calling her several times as they drove home, but she never answered. He tried again as soon as he arrived at the townhouse and she still didn't answer. He texted her that he and Beth were home and he'd love to see her. An hour after the text had been delivered, she still hadn't answered him.

Colt stayed up until midnight, but Carly wasn't home yet so he gave up and went to bed in the den. He wanted so badly to see her to reinforce that they were still a couple. Maybe they could spend time together tomorrow, he thought, as he fell asleep from exhaustion.

Colt awoke the next morning to the smell of pancakes cooking and coffee brewing. He looked at the time. It was a little after eight. He hurried into the shower and dressed, his stomach growling with hunger. There was no way he wanted to miss out on the food that he was sure Beth was cooking.

When he came out to the kitchen, he found Beth sitting at the counter eating pancakes spread with Ginny's homemade strawberry jam. She grinned up at him. "I knew the smell of pancakes would wake you up. There's a plate of them in the oven, keeping warm."

Colt got the plate and filled a mug with coffee. He sat down next to Beth and dug right in.

"I can't get enough of your mom's jam," Beth said, stuffing her mouth with pancake. "It's so delicious."

"Hmm, sexy," he said, laughing at her for talking with her mouth full.

"I don't care. I think I'm going to eat everything with jam on it from now on."

Colt raised his brows. "Everything?"

Beth laughed and nearly choked on her food. "You have a dirty mind, Cowboy."

They were joking and laughing when Carly came out, wearing a silky blue robe and looking lovely. "Well, aren't you two chummy," she said, going over to the counter and pouring a mug of coffee. She walked with her mug around the counter and up to Colt, giving him a light kiss on the lips. "I'm sorry I missed your homecoming last night," she said, pouting with her pink lips. "My phone wasn't working very well. Your text didn't come through until this morning."

"That's okay," Colt said, eager to believe her excuse. "I was tired last night anyway. Here," he broke off a piece of pancake and jam with his fork and offered it to Carly. "We brought back mom's jam. It's heavenly."

Carly glanced at Beth, and then smiled and let Colt feed her the pancake. "Ahh. It is heavenly," she said, sighing.

Beth stood and walked to the counter. "I can make you some of your own, if you'd like," she said, dryly.

Carly sat on the stool that Beth had vacated and ran her hand up Colt's leg. "No, thanks," she told Beth. "I'm meeting the gang for brunch later." She turned her gaze to Colt. "Do you want to join us, even though you've already eaten?"

Colt's stomach was doing flips over Carly's hand rubbing up and down his thigh. She hadn't touched him in weeks, and all of a sudden she was cuddling up to him. He wasn't sure why, but he wasn't going to complain. *Maybe she missed me. Maybe we have a chance, after all.* His face brightened at that thought.

"Sure. I'll go with," he said.

Carly smiled wide and leaned over. Colt could see down her half-open robe. "Good. I'll go shower and get dressed," she said sweetly. "I think Quinn will be there, too, with Chelle. They're still going strong. You can tell us all about your cattle drive." She stood and walked into her bedroom, mug in hand. Colt's eyes followed her, and then he turned and caught Beth rolling her eyes before leaving the kitchen. Colt frowned. *What was that all about?*

Colt and Carly spent the afternoon with Chelle, Quinn, Everly, Adam, and Adam's new friend, Jeremy. Colt entertained them with stories about the cattle drive, which interested Quinn the most, and Carly snuggled up to Colt throughout the meal. Colt noticed that Chelle frowned at Carly quite often, but he had no idea why. After they left the restaurant, Carly said she wanted to go shopping at the mall. Colt was happy to oblige. He felt like he and Carly were almost back to the way they'd been at the start, and it made him very happy.

It was late when they returned home after eating a quick supper in a restaurant at the mall. Colt immediately smelled the delicious aroma of food and figured Beth had made up meals for the week while they were gone. He stopped by Beth's room a moment to say hi while Carly put her purchases away.

"I'm sorry I didn't help you with the food," he told Beth. "I'm afraid I forgot all about it."

Beth waved her hand through the air. "Don't worry about it. I still made up enough for you, too." She barely looked at him, keeping her eyes on her book.

Colt hesitated. He felt bad he'd abandoned Beth today, yet, he was happy Carly wanted to spend time with him again. He felt torn.

As if reading his mind, Beth said, "Don't worry about me, Colt. Go spend time with Carly."

Colt felt like he'd been dismissed. He said goodnight and gently closed Beth's door.

He walked down to Carly's room and poked his head in.

"Hey," he said softly.

Carly looked up at him and smiled. She'd been hanging up her new clothes. "Hey," she said.

He walked into the room and stopped only inches behind Carly. Gently pushing her hair aside, he kissed her neck, and then slipped his arms around her waist.

Carly turned and put her arms around his neck. Their kiss began gentle and sweet, but soon became more demanding. Colt pulled her closer to him, wanting to feel her body pressed against his. It had been so long since they'd been together, his body craved hers.

Carly gently pulled away and gave Colt a small smile. "I did miss you," she said sweetly. "But I'm so tired tonight. Do you mind if we wait until another night?"

Colt backed away, confused. Carly had been touching him and flirting with him all day. Had he misread her signals? "Are you sure?" he asked huskily. "I've really missed you."

Carly ran her hands over his perfectly chiseled face and down his neck to his shoulders. "You are my handsome Cowboy," she whispered. "And I did miss you, but I really need my sleep tonight. I'm sorry, Colt."

Colt nodded, and then kissed her tenderly on the cheek. "Okay. I understand." He walked to the doorway before turning around. "Goodnight, Carly."

Carly gave him a sweet smile. "Goodnight, Colt."

Colt went to the den to sleep in his small bed, alone.

* * *

Colt went to work as usual on Monday and started back into the routine of unloading freight and moving it around the warehouse. The day was warm and the warehouse was stuffy, and he ended up wearing only his T-Shirt by mid-morning.

Quinn was abnormally quiet today, but Colt just marked it down to a busy Monday.

At lunchtime, Colt went to the break room and heated up a container of lasagna Beth had made. It was delicious, and Colt felt guilty again for not helping Beth with the meals. She was always doing nice things for him, and how did he repay her? By running off with Carly the moment she paid the slightest bit of attention to him. Beth had even re-bandaged his arm yesterday morning. And before he'd left for work this morning, he'd bumped into her and she'd reminded him to be careful with his arm. Carly had noticed the large bandage and hadn't even asked him what had happened.

He thought back to yesterday and the way Carly had acted, and then how she'd refused his advances last night. It made no sense. How could he have misread her? Was she still afraid of going too fast? Or was there another reason she didn't want to sleep with him? He hated that he wondered it, yet, he didn't know what to think.

"Something smells good in here," Quinn said, entering the lunch room. "What's that? Homemade lasagna?"

Colt nodded. "Yeah. It's wonderful. Our roommate, Beth, cooks it up and freezes it so I have a lunch to bring every day. She makes all kinds of different meals."

"That's nice," Quinn said, sitting in a chair opposite of Colt. "I knew it couldn't be Carly. She doesn't seem like the type who would cook. I'd say that Beth is a keeper."

Colt cocked his head. It seemed like a strange thing for him to say about Beth. He chose to ignore the comment and said, "You were quiet this morning. Is anything wrong?"

Quinn sat up in his chair and ran his hand around the back of his neck. "I've just had a lot to think about."

"Is everything okay between you and Chelle?"

"Yes. I really like her. At first, I thought she was a little snobbish, but now that I know her, she's actually sweet."

"That's good. I like Chelle. I'm happy for you both," Colt told him. "Chelle was giving Carly a few strange looks yesterday. Do you know if they had a fight or something?"

Colt watched as Quinn ran his hand nervously over the back of his neck again. He wondered what was going on.

"Can I be honest with you?" Quinn asked.

"Sure," Colt said, sitting up straighter.

"Chelle was upset with Carly for putting on that act yesterday. At least, that's what Chelle called it. She said she hadn't seen Carly for almost two weeks, and then out of the blue Carly wants to meet for brunch and she's hanging all over you."

"Why does she think it's an act?" Colt asked. "Carly and I are together."

"Okay, don't get mad at me for saying this. Chelle said that Carly had told her you and she were slowing things down. And, well, she thought she saw Carly out with another guy last week."

Colt's heart dropped. "Really? Is she sure?"

Quinn shrugged. "I don't think she would have said it if she wasn't sure. Chelle thinks Carly put on a show yesterday to try to make everyone believe she's still with you. I'm sorry, Colt. Personally, I hope none of this is true and it's all a mistake. You know how women can be sometimes. The only reason I told you is because I like you. You're a nice guy, and you only deserve good things. And if any of this is true, I just wanted you to know so it doesn't come as a complete surprise."

Colt sat back in his chair, trying to process it all. It sounded like a lot of speculation to him. Yet, somewhere deep inside him, he did have to wonder if Carly was seeing another guy. She was such a sexual person, yet she'd denied him for the past few weeks and even last night. Obviously, something was going on.

"It's okay, Quinn. Thanks for mentioning it. Maybe I should talk to Carly before I jump to any conclusions, though," Colt said.

Quinn nodded. "That's a good idea. And I am sorry, Colt."

"Don't worry about it," Colt told him.

But Colt worried about it all day. Chelle was a pretty serious person and he doubted she'd say she saw Carly out with another man just to be catty. Maybe it had been one of Carly's gay friends, or even a client from the gallery. Colt thought back to the night he'd seen Carly dancing with the man wearing the suit, and how close they'd danced. Everly had said he'd been in the shop earlier that day. Could he be the man Chelle had seen Carly with?

Colt went directly home after work. He didn't want to talk to Carly about this at the gallery. He'd wait until she came home and then they could have a calm discussion.

Beth wasn't home yet from work, and Colt had a pile of laundry to do. He started a load of jeans and then folded the towels that were sitting in the dryer from the day before. The towels reminded him of how Carly left wet towels all over the bathroom, so he walked through her bedroom and into her bathroom to check. He grinned. Sure enough, there was a pile of wet towels on the floor. He picked them up, and then headed into the bedroom and looked around to make sure there weren't any on the floor. Carly had a lot of great attributes, but keeping her room clean wasn't one of them. Once he was sure there were no more towels, he turned to leave the room, and that's when his eyes touched on a jacket hanging over the desk's chair. A man's suit jacket.

Colt took a deep breath. *Don't jump to conclusions.* He set down the pile of towels and picked up the jacket. He hoped it was just one of hers that looked like menswear. But he knew immediately that it wasn't. The shoulders of the jacket were broad, almost wide enough to fit him, and the label inside was definitely a men's brand.

Colt stared at the man's jacket a long time, trying to come up with an excuse for it being here. Someone loaned it to her, because she was cold one night. Maybe. But who? And why hadn't she returned it? And why was it in her bedroom?

Colt's stomach turned sour. He quickly dropped the jacket onto the chair and picked up the pile of towels, then headed out of the room.

Everything was falling into place. How Carly backed away from their relationship and hadn't slept with him in a while. How she hadn't come to the ranch with him so she could be home, alone. That Chelle had seen her out with another man, and that Carly hadn't been hanging out with her regular friends for the past couple of weeks. All signs pointed to her seeing another man.

Colt's heart shattered.

Chapter Twenty-Four

Colt busied himself with his laundry, but he couldn't stop his thoughts from racing. When Beth came home a while later, she asked him if he'd be eating at home with her or out with Carly so she could take enough food out to heat up. Colt wasn't sure what he'd be doing. All he could think about was Carly and another man in her room. In her bed. The bed he'd recently shared with her for three months.

"Don't worry about me tonight," he told Beth. "I'll see what Carly is doing."

Beth nodded, but looked at him strangely. "Is everything okay?"

"I don't know, yet," Colt said honestly. He left it at that and Beth didn't pry.

At five-thirty, Carly came through the door complaining about traffic and rude customers, but when she saw Colt sitting on the sofa, she stopped and smiled. "At least I get to come home to my cute cowboy," Carly cooed. She walked over and dropped a kiss on Colt's lips, but when he didn't respond, she pulled away and looked at him quizzically. "Did you have a bad day?"

"We need to talk," Colt said seriously.

Carly studied him a moment, then glanced over at Beth who was working in the kitchen. She turned and walked toward her room. "Sure," she threw over her shoulder. "Let me just change and we can talk on our way to dinner. We're meeting up with Adam and his new boyfriend, you know, the guy from last night. I guess they're an item now."

Colt stood and followed Carly into her bedroom. When Carly turned and saw him directly behind her, she frowned.

"Just give me a few minutes, okay?" she said. "I won't be long."

Colt walked over to the jacket lying across the chair and pointed at it. "Why is there a man's jacket in your bedroom, Carly?"

Carly's mouth dropped open for only a second as she stared at the jacket. She regained her composure quickly. "Were you in my room, snooping around?" she asked incredulously.

"No, I was in your room picking up your wet towels, because I was doing laundry. Who does that jacket belong to?"

Carly waved her hand though the air as if it were nothing and walked over to her closet. "It's probably Adam's, silly. What does it matter?"

Colt held the jacket up. "This is too big for Adam," he said. "It's practically big enough for me. Carly, tell me the truth. Did you have a man here while I was in Montana?"

Carly's eyes flashed angrily. "So what if I did? It's not like we're completely exclusive. I told you I wanted to slow down our relationship."

Colt's face fell. She'd admitted another man was here. "You said you wanted to slow down, not that you wanted to date other men. You told me we were still a couple."

"Well, that doesn't mean I can't see other men," she screeched. "And what about you? You were off to Montana for a week with Beth. Why was that okay and this isn't?"

Colt stared at her, dumbfounded. "I was on a cattle drive with my family," he said, raising his voice in frustration. "And it was your idea that I ask Beth to come along, remember? You could have come, too. I asked you to come along."

Carly waved her hands angrily in the air. "I don't have to defend myself to you. This is my townhouse and I can have whoever I want here. I'm not talking about this anymore. Get out of my room," she yelled. "Get out!"

Colt's face hardened. He turned stiffly and strode out of the room. Carly slammed her bedroom door shut.

With his heart pounding, Colt walked into the den, pulled on his boots, and began tossing everything he owned into his duffle bag. He grabbed his hat and swung the heavy bag over his shoulder, and then headed for the door.

"Colt? What happened? Where are you going?" Beth called out as he opened the front door.

Colt stopped for only a second, but his anger ran too deep. He walked outside and slammed the door. He could faintly hear Beth calling after him as he headed for his truck.

* * *

Carly leaned against her bedroom door after slamming it shut. She couldn't catch her breath and felt sick in the pit of her stomach. Hot tears formed in her eyes and fell down her face. *Oh, my God. What have I done?*

Slowly, she made her way to the bed and sat down. The look of utter devastation in Colt's eyes had torn her apart. She hadn't meant to hurt him like this. He didn't deserve it.

When Colt came back from Montana, she'd had every intention of telling him that she felt they were in different stages of their lives and they should end their relationship. Crap, she hadn't even expected him to want to come back after being home, but he had. Then she went and made it worse by flirting with him yesterday and giving him hope that they were still together. It had been a lousy thing to do, and she knew it. But that morning when she'd come out from her room and saw

Colt and Beth laughing and talking, jealousy had overtaken her. She'd seen Colt look at Beth the way he'd once looked at her. With pure joy and admiration. It had made her so angry, she'd flirted with him to get his attention. And then there was Chelle, who'd told her she'd seen her out one night with Jordan. Carly had explained that she and Jordan were just friends, but Chelle hadn't believed her. The entire show she put on at brunch on Sunday was so Chelle would believe she was still with Colt. She was trying to fool everyone, and now she knew she'd only been fooling herself. She was a terrible person and she'd just hurt Colt, deeply.

Carly stood, picked up the jacket, rolled it into a ball, and threw it across the room. Stupid jacket. Why hadn't she taken it to work with her that morning so she could give it back to Jordan? At the very least, she should have put it in her car. Jordan had given it to her to wear one chilly evening as he walked her to her door and had forgotten to take it back. He hadn't spent the night, but now Colt thought he had.

Carly wiped the tears from her eyes. She got up and changed her clothes. She'd meet up with Adam as planned. She had to talk to someone, and she trusted Adam the most. He'd know how she could fix this. He'd help her.

As Carly walked past the kitchen, she stopped when Beth called out. "Is there anything I can do to help?"

Carly turned and looked at her. She slowly shook her head. "Thanks, but this is my mess. I have to clean it up."

Beth nodded. "He left," she said sadly. "Colt packed his bag and walked out."

Carly's shoulders sagged. She hadn't realized he'd left. She turned and walked out the door, closing it silently behind her.

* * *

Colt sat on the bench under a streetlamp outside the townhouse and took another swig of his bottle. The night air was cold, but he barely felt it, because the whiskey warmed him up from the inside. He had no idea what time it was. All he knew was the moon was high in the sky and dampness filled the night air.

He took another drink from the bottle and tried to sort out the day. He'd been so devastated by Carly's admission that she'd had a man there, that he'd actually seen red. Never in his life had anyone made him so angry that he felt out of control. He didn't even realize he'd packed his things and left until he'd driven miles out of Seattle, heading east. His basic instinct had been to go home, and for a few more miles, he'd thought that maybe he should. But then he'd remembered his promise to Gerard about working until September. He'd never broken a promise in his life, and he certainly wasn't going to break one now.

And then there was Beth. She'd been so good to him and he didn't want to leave without saying goodbye to her. So, he'd turned around and driven back.

Beth. Colt sat on the bench, drinking his whiskey and thinking about her. She was so sweet and thoughtful, yet such a strong person, too. He thought about how he'd had an overwhelming desire to kiss her several times, and had finally given in to that urge at the cabin that night. He'd really enjoyed kissing her.

What a hypocrite I am. I kissed her and yet I'm angry at Carly for seeing another man.

But then, it had only been a kiss. Carly had actually had a man in the townhouse doing God knows what.

Colt took another long drink from the bottle, enjoying the sting of the booze as it slid down his throat. Everything around him looked fuzzy, but he didn't know if it was the fog rolling in or if he was that drunk. He guessed it didn't matter either way.

"Colt? Is that you?" a soft voice asked from behind him.

Colt turned unsteadily, and over his shoulder he saw the outline of a woman. "Beth? What are you doing out here so late?"

Beth walked over to the bench and looked down at Colt. She wore sweats with a coat wrapped around her. "I could ask you the same question."

"You shouldn't have come out here if you didn't know it was me," Colt said, slurring his words. "I could have been a robber or something."

Beth smiled and sat down on the bench beside him. "I figured it was you. I saw the outline of your hat. I don't know too many people around here who wear cowboy hats."

"Ah." Colt lifted the bottle and took another drink.

Beth frowned. "Where have you been? I was worried about you."

Colt shrugged. "Mostly just here," he said. "I started for home, but then remembered my promise to the O'Hannans, so I came back. I stopped in a bar for a while and then realized that wasn't a smart idea. So, I picked up a bottle and parked out on the street by the townhouse and sat there for a while. Figured that might not be smart either, being found in my truck, drinking, so I came to this bench and have been here ever since."

Beth sighed. "At least you're being a safe drunk," she said. After Colt took another swig from his bottle, Beth gently took it from him. It was less than half full.

"Colt? Did you drink all of this?" she asked, a worried frown creasing her brow.

"Not yet," Colt said, grinning crookedly. "But I plan on it." He reached for the bottle, but Beth pulled it away.

"I think you've had plenty," she said. "I don't know what

happened between you and Carly, but if you want to talk, I'm a good listener."

Colt turned and looked at her, his eyes sad. "You know, everyone told me this would happen. They said, "Don't move out there. Carly goes through men like crazy." But I didn't believe them. Shit, even Andi, her own sister tried to warn me. But I thought I knew Carly better than all of them. And they were right. Here I am, only three months later and she's already found someone else. I should've listened, but I was just some stupid hayseed who didn't know a damned thing."

"You're not a stupid hayseed, Colt," Beth said gently. "You're a sweet man who fell in love. It's not your fault that Carly didn't appreciate you the way she should have."

Colt dropped back against the bench and rolled his head in Beth's direction. "I thought she loved me. How could I have ever believed that someone like her would love me? I feel like an idiot."

Beth scooted over beside Colt and placed her hand on his arm. "You're not an idiot, Colt. You're a pretty amazing guy. And right now we need to get you inside and into bed. It's one a.m., and by the looks of this bottle, you're not going to feel all that well in the morning."

Colt's eyes popped open. "One o'clock? Crap, I have to get to bed. How will I ever get up for work in the morning?"

"Don't worry about that now," Beth said, standing up and pulling Colt to his feet. He swayed and Beth grabbed him tightly to keep him from falling. She wrapped his arm around her shoulders and held him around the waist while carrying the whiskey bottle in her other hand. "Just lean on me, Colt. We don't need you to fall down and get hurt."

They managed to get inside the door and Beth led him into the den. He dropped down on the bed and sat there, dazed.

"Here," Beth said. "Let's get those boots off. Lift your leg."

Colt lifted his leg and fell backwards, catching himself on his elbows. "I can do it myself," he said, but he could barely sit up. Beth pulled off his boots, took his hat off his head, and then stacked his pillows up high so he wouldn't sleep lying down flat.

"Lie down and try to get some sleep," she said gently, pulling the covers up over him. "I'll check on you later. That's an awful lot of alcohol you drank on an empty stomach."

Colt's eyes were already closed. "I'll be fine," he said.

Beth turned to leave the room, but Colt spoke again.

"Beth?"

She walked back over to the bed. "Yes?"

Colt gazed up at her. "Why are you so nice to me?"

Beth smiled. She reached down and gently brushed the hair across his forehead. "I've already told you. It's easy to be nice to you."

Colt reached up and took her hand in his. "Thanks."

"You're welcome," Beth whispered. She gently let go of his hand. "Goodnight, Colt."

"Goodnight," Colt said. He was asleep before she even turned out the light.

Chapter Twenty-Five

Sunlight streamed in through the window over Colt's bed, waking him. Slowly, he opened his eyes, and then winced. Drums were beating in his head and his stomach rolled like a carnival ride. He tried sitting up, but immediately lay back down. Not only did his head hurt like hell, but it felt like it weighed a hundred pounds. *Oh, God. I think I'm dead.* He squeezed his eyes shut tight and lay there, waiting for the drummer in his head to stop playing.

"You awake yet?" a cheery voice asked.

Colt squinted and saw Beth walking in with a glass of water and her other hand cupped.

At least I made it to Heaven. Beth is here.

"Colt? I brought you some water and Tylenol. I figured you'd need it by now. The water will help hydrate you and make you feel a little better." Beth sat on the side of the bed and waited.

"You mean I'm not dead?" Colt asked, opening his eyes just a little bit more.

Beth chuckled. "No, but I'll bet you wish you were after all that whiskey you drank. Here," she handed him the Tylenol. "Take this. It'll help."

Colt pushed himself up as high as he could manage, took the pills, and then washed them down with the water. His stomach churned and he felt dizzy. He handed the water glass back to Beth, afraid he'd drop it. "What time is it?"

"It's almost noon, sleepyhead."

Colt's eyes popped open. "Noon? I'm late for work." He tried getting up, but Beth placed a hand on his chest and pushed him back down.

"Don't worry, I called Quinn and told him you didn't feel well. There was no way you were ever going to get up this morning. And you shouldn't get up, yet, either. Lay there a while and let the Tylenol do its job. As soon as your head stops pounding, you may be able to eat something and feel better."

Colt frowned. "Aren't you supposed to be at work?"

"I traded with another nurse. I couldn't leave you here all alone after all you drank last night. I was afraid I'd need to take you to the emergency room and have your stomach pumped. Have you never heard of alcohol poisoning, Cowboy?"

"I'm sorry, Beth. I didn't mean to make you lose a day of work. I hardly ever drink whiskey. I don't know why I thought it was a good idea last night, because it doesn't feel like a good idea today."

Beth squeezed his arm. "Don't worry about it. Just do what I say and stay in bed until your head stops pounding. Once you're able to get up, we'll get you fed."

Colt managed a grin. "Yes, ma'am. If I'm good, will you give me a lollipop?"

Beth stood and shook her head. "No. That will make you barf all over the place."

Colt chuckled, even though it made his head hurt even more. Beth headed for the door.

"Beth?"

She turned around. "Yes."

"Thanks for being here for me."

Beth nodded. "Get some more sleep. That's an order." She

disappeared out the door.

Colt closed his eyes, a smile on his lips despite how badly he felt. Beth had put that smile there. She usually made him smile. Right now, he needed all the warm, happy feelings he could get.

Colt slept for another hour and when he awoke, he realized the drummer had finally left his head. He slowly stood, and even though he felt lightheaded and his legs were wobbly, he made it to the bathroom. He turned on the shower and stood under the warm water for a long time. It felt good, even if his stomach continued to roll.

When he stepped out of the shower, he realized he hadn't brought in any clean clothes. *Crap, my duffle bag is still in the truck with all my clothes.* He was about to put on his dirty ones when he spied a T-shirt, underwear, jeans, and socks, neatly folded and lying on the back of the toilet. Colt grinned and shook his head. His little nurse at work, again. What would he do without her?

Colt dressed and dried his hair and then put his dirty clothes in his room. There, lying on his neatly made bed was his duffle bag. He found a clean shirt and put it on over his T-shirt, then walked out to the kitchen. His legs felt steadier after the shower, but he needed some food to calm his stomach.

Beth was already cooking up scrambled eggs and toast. Colt's heart melted. She was too good to him. He walked over and wrapped his arms around her from behind and gave her a kiss on the cheek.

"What is this all about?" Beth asked, laughing.

"It's a big thank you for everything. For getting my duffle bag, for making my bed, for the pills this morning, and for making me breakfast. Most of all, for being so nice to me. I can't tell you how much I appreciate you," Colt said.

"It's nothing," Beth said, stirring the eggs. "Although that duffle bag was pretty heavy. I'm afraid I had to drag it on the ground on the way in here."

Colt laughed. "You should have let me get it."

"Oh, no. I was afraid you'd walk around shirtless again," Beth teased.

Colt sat and ate breakfast while Beth sat with him, drinking coffee. The food was delicious and it did help make him feel better. He looked up at Beth and her brown eyes sparkled back at him. *How wonderful to wake up to her sweet face.* Colt stopped chewing a moment as that thought resonated with him. Beth had managed to make him smile all morning despite his hangover, and despite the fact that less than twenty-four hours ago, Carly had crushed his heart. That was how amazing Beth was.

The thought of Carly dampened his mood. "I suppose Carly went to work, as usual," he said.

Beth nodded. "I didn't talk to her this morning, but last night she said she needed to fix her mess. I'm not sure what she meant by that."

Colt sighed. "I think it's too late to fix anything."

"What are you going to do?" Beth asked, biting her lip.

Colt shrugged. "I'm not sure. I should stay and finish out the summer like I promised Gerard I would. But, if I can't live here, I don't know where I'd go. I don't want to rent a place for only three months. I guess I have to find out what Carly wants."

"If it means anything at all, I'd be happy if you stayed for the summer," Beth said softly.

"Thanks, Beth. I'd still like to stay, but it would be hard seeing Carly with another man. Do you think she'd bring him home if I'm here?"

Beth grimaced. "Geez, I'd hope not. She's never brought that many men around here, and no one ever lived here before you. I think she's sensitive enough not to strut another man in front of you."

"Yeah, I suppose," Colt said. But as they cleaned up the kitchen, Colt thought he wouldn't be surprised at anything Carly did after what she'd done to him.

Colt felt better and Beth said a little fresh air might be good for him. They went for a walk around the neighborhood, and then Colt finished washing the dirty laundry he hadn't finished the day before. By the time Carly came through the door at five-thirty, he almost felt human.

She stopped when she saw Colt on the sofa with Beth. They'd been watching House Hunters International, drooling over beach homes in the Caribbean. Both sets of eyes looked up when Carly walked in.

"Hi," Carly said, tentatively. She slipped off her heels and walked over to the sofa, her eyes on Colt.

Beth turned off the television. "I'll give you guys some privacy." She stood and headed to her room.

"Thanks, Beth," Carly said softly. Beth waved acknowledgment and shut her door.

Carly looked down at Colt and he thought he saw relief in her eyes. "I thought you'd left."

"I almost did, but I came back."

Carly sat down gingerly on the other side of the sofa, curling her legs up under her. "I'm glad you did. Can we talk?"

Colt sighed. He turned and faced her. "Guess we should. Last night we just yelled at each other."

"No, I yelled. I'm sorry. I was embarrassed for having been caught, and frustrated," Carly said. "I met with Adam last night and we talked for hours. He told me I needed to tell you the truth. And I need to apologize. And that I'm an idiot for not choosing you."

Colt frowned. "Adam said that? I didn't think he even liked me."

Carly slid closer to Colt. "Of course, he likes you. Everyone likes you, Colt."

"Except you," Colt said sadly.

"That's not true." Carly reached out and laid her hand on Colt's arm. "I adore you and I've always been attracted to you. That's why it was so hard for me to tell you the truth. I had meant to break it off with you when you came back from Montana, but then I lost the nerve. I hated more than anything the thought of hurting you. But now, you hate me."

"I don't hate you, Carly. I'm just trying to understand. If you wanted to break up, why were you leading me on all day Sunday? It doesn't make sense."

Carly dropped her eyes. "I shouldn't have done that, and I'm sorry about that, too. It's just that when I came out that morning and saw you and Beth eating breakfast together and joking and laughing, I suddenly felt jealous. You and Beth seemed so close. I didn't want to be left out. I had to prove to myself that I was still special to you. I realize that was stupid of me."

Colt leaned forward. "Beth and I are just friends. Why would that make you feel jealous?"

Carly looked up at him, her blue eyes sad. "Are you sure you're just friends, Colt? You were looking at her the same way you used to look at me. Your eyes were sparkling and you were hanging on every word she said. It made me jealous. I'll admit, I'm shallow that way. But it did."

Colt stared at her, trying to imagine what she'd seen in his eyes. He did admire Beth and he felt close to her. And then there was that kiss. He'd longed to kiss her, and finally did. It hadn't been planned, and they stopped at just the kiss. But, he had to admit, he did have feelings for Beth, yet he'd thought his feelings for Carly were stronger. Now, everything had changed.

Carly took his hand and held it in her small one. "None of that matters now, anyway. I know I shouldn't have been involved with another man while I was still with you. But you need to know that I didn't sleep with him. We've gone out to eat and dance a few times, but we aren't intimate, yet. I had his jacket, because he'd given it to me to wear one night when it was chilly and I forgot to give it back. Still, I know I shouldn't have been seeing him at all when you thought we were still together. I'm sorry I hurt you so badly. I never meant to do that."

Colt's brow creased. The fact that Carly said they hadn't been intimate *yet* told him that she planned on being so at some point. "I still don't understand why, Carly. I thought you had strong feelings for me. You said we were slowing things down a little, not running off to see other people. I loved you. I wanted to marry you."

Carly sighed. "That's just it, Colt. You want so much more than I want right now. I thought you and I were just having fun. I wanted to explore a relationship with you, but I'm not ready to get married. I want to see other people and enjoy myself. When you proposed, you scared me. I realized that you were taking us more seriously than I was. That's why I said we should slow things down. I hadn't planned on meeting Jordan, or having feelings for him, too. It just happened."

"But how can you say you had strong feelings for me and then have feelings for him at the same time?" Colt asked, perplexed.

Tears formed in Carly's eyes and fell one by one down her cheeks. "I can't explain it. I'm sorry. I do care about you, but I was attracted to him as well. Haven't you ever had feelings for two people at once, Colt? It's not something a person can shut off or control."

Colt reached up and gently wiped the tears away from Carly's cheeks with the side of his thumb. His thoughts returned to when he'd kissed Beth. He thought back to the night of Carly's birthday party and how his desire to kiss Beth had started then. He'd been confused about his feelings for both women at the same time. Suddenly, he realized that he couldn't blame Carly for the same thing he'd been feeling all along.

"So, this is it," Colt said, already knowing the answer.

"Yes, I guess it is. I really do care about you, Colt. Please believe that. But I want to explore a relationship with Jordan. I'm sorry."

Colt nodded. "I suppose you want me to move out."

Carly sat up and looked at Colt quizzically. "Don't you want to go home, back to the ranch? I know how much you miss it."

"I promised Gerard O'Hannan that I'd work until September. I never break a promise. I'm just not sure what to do about it."

"Stay here," Carly told him. "I don't mind you staying, if you can stand to be around me. We are still friends, aren't we? At least I hope we can still be friends." She gave him a small grin. "After all, we're both going to share a little niece, so we have to get along."

Colt grinned. "Maybe it's going to be a little nephew."

"Nope," Carly said adamantly. "It's going to be a girl. A little girl with red hair, just like Andi."

"Well, that wouldn't be so bad," Colt said. "And I'd like to stay, if you're sure you don't mind."

"Good," Carly placed a soft kiss on his cheek. "I'm glad you're staying. Maybe we can work on being friends again. I'd hate to have you leave here, hating me."

Colt shook his head. "I could never hate you, Carly. But I am going to miss us being together."

Carly raised her hand and gently caressed the side of Colt's face. "You are so cute and sweet and downright sexy, Colt Brennan," she said wistfully. "Life would be so much easier if I could fall in love with you and marry you and do all those normal things that people do. I wish I were more like Andi, or even Beth. But I'm not. I'm not ready to commit to anyone yet. I just know that someday, I'm going to be very sorry I gave you up, and very jealous of whoever you end up with."

Colt took her hand and kissed her palm and they sat there a moment in silence, each lost in their own thoughts.

Carly gently pulled away and stood up. "I'm meeting the gang for dinner. I think Quinn and Chelle will be there. Do you want to join us?"

Colt shook his head. "I think I'll stay here and eat with Beth tonight."

Carly nodded and then went into her room.

Colt stood and walked out the sliding glass door to the patio. It was still light out, but it was cloudy and a soft mist was in the air. He breathed in the fresh air and thought about the ranch and how much he wished he were there right now. If he were, he'd be riding Maddie up the trail, possibly heading to the summer pasture cabin so he could brood for days by himself.

At the thought of the cabin, Colt was again reminded of Beth. Carly had said she'd seen something special in his eyes when he looked at Beth. Was that true? He hadn't realized his feelings for Beth were so transparent. But then, he hadn't yet sorted out what he felt for her, either. She made him laugh and smile and he was always happy around her. And sometimes he felt the urge to be close to Beth. To touch her hand, brush her hair behind her ear, and to kiss her. All so simple, yet intimate gestures. With Carly, things were hot and steamy from the moment they'd met, so he'd confused that with true love. But Beth? She was different. A woman like Beth would need to be romanced, cherished, and respected. Beth would need to be wooed. *Wooed? I must be going crazy if I'm using that word now.*

"Hey, Cowboy. You want to eat, yet?" A gentle voice

interrupted Colt's thoughts and he turned to see Beth standing in the doorway. "Or do you want to stand out there in the rain?"

Colt looked up. He'd been so deep in thought, he hadn't even noticed that it had started raining. "Supper sounds great. I'll help you make it," he said, coming back inside.

"You're going to make someone a very good wife someday," Beth said over her shoulder on the way to the kitchen.

"Smartass," Colt said, grinning. Beth turned and gave him that genuine smile that he loved so much and they began making supper, together.

Chapter Twenty-Six

The next few weeks went by quickly for Colt as he split his time between working and spending time with Beth. Carly came and went, but there was never any sign of Jordan, and for that, Colt was grateful. When he'd returned to work the day after he and Carly broke it off, Quinn had said he'd heard about their break-up, and if Colt felt he wanted to go home to the ranch, he and his father would understand. But Colt told him he was going to stay. "I always keep my word," he'd told Quinn. Since then, he, Beth, Quinn, and Chelle had gone out several times for supper or to the movies. The foursome always had a good time together and Carly's name was never mentioned.

As June slipped into July, Colt was surprised one Sunday evening when he opened his email and saw a message from Luke and Andi. Colt whooped with glee when he saw a file attached named Colt's Cabin. He ran out to the kitchen with his computer in hand where Beth was finishing loading the dishes into the dishwasher from supper and told her the good news.

"Luke sent my house plans. Come take a look."

Beth quickly dried her hands and came to the counter, sitting down close to Colt.

Colt opened the file and there was a picture of his house

design plans. Luke owned software to create 3D designs as well as basic plans used by contractors, and he'd sent Colt copies of those. The design included everything Colt had always wanted in a house. An open kitchen and living room with a vaulted ceiling, a large dining room, a river rock fireplace just like the one in Luke's house, and large glass windows all around. A loft built over the kitchen area was also included. Colt had wanted a walk-in laundry room in the hallway as well as two large bedrooms, one being the master suite with an attached bathroom. Luke had done it all, and it looked amazing.

"Colt. I'm so excited for you," Beth squealed, giving him a hug. "I wish I could see it when it's done. This is so exciting."

Colt smiled over at Beth. He loved that she was excited for him. "Remember, you promised you'd help me pick out cabinets, countertops, light fixtures, and everything else. I'm going to hold you to that promise."

Beth's smiled faded. "I wish I could. But I'll be here and you'll be in Montana. Besides, I'll bet Andi is wonderful at picking out those things. After all, she is an artist."

"Who's an artist?" Carly asked. She'd been in her room changing before going out to dinner.

"Andi," Beth said. "Come look at the plans for Colt's house. Luke designed them."

Carly's face registered surprise. "House? I didn't know you were building a house. When did all this happen?" She walked over and glanced at the plans on the computer screen.

"I decided it was time I had my own place. I had asked Luke to draw up plans when I was home in May. If we're lucky, we can build the shell of the house in September when I get back and then I can finish the inside during the winter months."

"Oh." Carly looked unsure of what to say. "It looks really nice. I like the loft. It looks a lot like Luke's cabin."

"It is, just with a few changes," Colt said.

"Well, congratulations, Colt," Carly said, placing a quick kiss on his cheek. "You deserve it. Ginny is sure going to be lonely when you move out, though."

Colt shook his head. "She has Glen to keep her company now, and a new grandbaby on the way. I'm sure she won't even miss me."

Carly waved goodbye and Colt picked up his phone to call Luke and tell him how much he loved the plans. He wanted him to order the supplies as soon as possible so they could get started on the house. He also needed a contractor to come in and lay the foundation first.

"Hey, Luke," Colt said as soon as his brother answered. "I love the house design. When can we start?"

Luke laughed. "I'm glad you like them. We can start anytime. I already talked to the man who set up the foundation for my house and got a quote for you. He also suggested the perfect spot on the property where the drainage would be the best. Plus, you have to think about where the well and septic will go. All that is done before you actually build the house."

"Then let's get started," Colt said. "I have enough money to start and I'll get a loan for the rest when I come back home. Can you set up the well and septic companies for me? And send me a picture of the building site he chose. I want to make sure I like it. Then, we can order the lumber for when I get home."

"Oh, and I can also run a ranch during that time, too," Luke said, chuckling. "No problem."

Colt laughed. He knew Luke was just teasing. "How's that beautiful sister-in-law of mine?"

"She's doing pretty well. She's at four months now and still as slender as always. I keep asking her if she's really pregnant. She's not as sick feeling anymore, either. You should see her and Ma. They're already doing up the nursery and buying baby things. It's crazy."

"That's nice to hear. I can't wait to see everyone again. And I can't wait to get started on my house," Colt said.

"How's Carly?" Luke asked. "And Beth? We really enjoyed having her along on the cattle drive. She's a hard worker and a sweet gal."

Colt hesitated. He figured Carly hadn't told Andi yet that they'd broken up. "Beth is fine. She just made me supper, again. It's almost like being at home."

"That's good. What about Carly?"

Colt took a deep breath. "Carly and I aren't together any longer. But I'm going to stay here until September."

There was a long pause on the other end. Colt figured Luke was letting this news sink in. He waited for the 'I told you so'.

"I'm sorry to hear that, Colt," Luke said seriously. "Do you want to talk about it?"

"No, I'm okay. It happened in May and we're getting along fine. But thanks for offering."

"Well, again, I'm sorry. I guess Carly hasn't told Andi, yet. Do you mind if I tell her?" Luke asked.

"That's fine. Everyone will know soon enough," Colt said.

"Okay. Well, I'll get started on that house and we'll go from there. And Colt?"

"Yeah?"

"I'm really proud of you. You followed your heart and even though it didn't work out, at least you tried. And you're keeping your promise to your employer. You're a good man. And truth be told, I'm very happy you're coming back. Jake is a good hand, but there's no replacement for you."

A lump formed in Colt's throat. Luke had always treated him like his baby brother and had never referred to him as a man before. It was as if they were now both equals. It warmed his heart.

When he hung up, he swiped his eyes with the sleeve of his shirt.

"Is everything okay?" Beth asked, concerned.

Colt nodded, and then turned to her with a huge smile. "Everything is great. Luke's getting things started. How about you and I go to the home improvement stores tomorrow after work and look at all the stuff I'll need? I'll buy you supper."

Beth's face lit up. "I can't wait."

The rest of the week, Colt and Beth went from store to store after work, looking at everything from cabinets to tile, flooring to faucets. They looked at appliances, too. Colt liked the black stove and refrigerator, but Beth liked the stainless steel ones. "They're more up-to-date," she told him. Since Colt was never going to sell his house, it didn't matter which he had. They joked and laughed and teased, pointing out the ugly finishes and drooling over the expensive ones. Colt kept a list of what he liked and a running total of what everything would cost. Most of all, he just enjoyed spending the time with Beth.

Even though Colt was no longer attached to Carly, neither he nor Beth spoke of the kiss at the cabin or had made a move to become anything more than friends. Often, Colt would be close to Beth when they were working together in the kitchen, eating, or out walking, and he'd have an overwhelming urge to hold her hand and even pull her to him and kiss her. But he refrained. He knew starting a relationship so soon after breaking up with Carly wasn't a good idea, yet, he had strong feelings for Beth. He understood, though, that it would be best to give himself a little time before exploring a new relationship with anyone. So, he held back.

* * *

Colt came home from work one afternoon in late July and

found Beth on the sofa, curled up in the corner with a box of tissues. Her face was streaked with tears. He went to her immediately.

"What happened? Are you okay? Are you sick?" Colt asked.

Beth shook her head and wiped her eyes. She still wore her scrubs and the front of her shirt was damp from tears.

Colt knelt down in front of her and pulled her to him, holding her close. He rocked her gently, side to side, running his strong hand comfortingly over her back. Beth clung to him, her tears falling as her shoulders shook.

"Tell me what I can do for you," Colt whispered in her ear.

Beth slowly pulled back, brushing away tears, and looked down into Colt's concerned eyes. "I'm sorry. I shouldn't be crying like this. It's been a rough day," she said, her voice shaky.

"Do you want to talk about it?" Colt asked.

"Give me a minute to calm down," Beth told him.

"Can I get you some tea? Coffee? A water?"

"Tea would be nice," Beth said, still wiping away tears.

Colt went into the kitchen and started the kettle, then pulled down a mug and selected one of the many herbal teas Beth enjoyed drinking. When the water began boiling, he poured it into the mug, over the tea bag. He let it steep for a couple of minutes, and then brought the warm mug over to Beth.

"Thanks," she said, still curled up in the corner. She wrapped her hands around the mug and took a sip. It reminded Colt of the very first time he met Beth, when he'd come out of Carly's room and she was curled up on the sofa just like this. That day seemed like ages ago.

Colt sat down beside her. "Feel better?"

Beth nodded. "It's so stupid of me to cry," she said.

"No, it's not. You're human. What happened?"

Beth took another sip of the warm tea. "One of our patients

died today. It was a little boy who comes in weekly for chemo treatments. He's been sick a long time, so he usually stays overnight to be monitored after treatment. Only an hour after his treatment, he went into cardiac arrest. It was so unexpected. And he was only eight years old." Fresh tears fell from Beth's eyes. Colt took the mug from her so she could wipe them away.

"That's terrible," Colt said softly, his heart breaking for the little boy. To have cancer so young was sad enough, but dying suddenly was terrible.

"I'm not supposed to get attached to patients. You can't work with patients properly if you become emotionally attached. But it was hard not to fall in love with this little guy. We all knew he was going to leave us someday. The treatment was only prolonging the inevitable. But no one ever imagined he'd go this way. All the nurses and even his doctor were in shock. And when I saw the devastation on his parents' faces, I lost it. I felt so sorry for them. It's just so, so sad."

Beth cried again and Colt slid over and wrapped his arm around her. She dropped her head on his shoulder and stayed that way until the tears subsided.

"I'm sorry, Beth. I can't even imagine how painful that must be to lose a patient, especially such a young one. That poor boy. And his parents. You'd have to be inhuman to not break down in tears."

"I had to leave the room. I didn't want his parents to see me crying and make it even worse. My supervisor sent me home. She was upset, too, but she held it in. I just couldn't."

"You have a kind heart, Beth," Colt said gently. "That's nothing to be ashamed of. It's one of my favorite things about you."

Beth turned her head and looked up at him. "But I'm supposed to be strong."

Colt gave her a small smile. "You are strong. You amaze me

with how strong you are. But you're kindhearted, too, and that's what makes you so wonderful."

Beth laid her head back on his shoulder and Colt pulled her closer. He liked how she felt up against him. It felt right.

"Hey, I'll make supper for us tonight, okay? You can just sit back and relax," Colt said.

"That would be nice. Thanks, Colt."

Colt kissed the top of her head and reluctantly pulled away and stood up. "Let me clean up first. I stink from working all day. Then I'll make supper. So, tell me. Do you want pepperoni on your pizza or just have it plain?"

Beth glanced up at him. "You call that making supper? Calling out for pizza?"

Colt grinned. "It's better than anything I'd cook."

Beth laughed heartily. "Then I want pepperoni. And breadsticks, too, since you're buying."

"You got it," Colt said, happy he'd made Beth smile.

He showered and ordered pizza and by the time they ate, Beth was feeling better. Afterwards, they took a walk in the cool evening. Halfway through their walk, Colt offered Beth his hand and she took it. When they got home, they watched a bit of television before going to bed.

After snapping off the television, Colt stood first and offered his hand to Beth, pulling her up off the sofa. They stood there, their bodies close, hands still clasped. "Tomorrow will be a better day," Colt said.

"Do you promise?" Beth asked, looking up at him.

Colt loved looking into her beautiful eyes. "I promise," he said softly.

He walked her to her room and stopped at the door.

"Thanks for being so sweet tonight, Colt," Beth told him. "I'm so happy that you're here. It's nice having someone to talk to."

"It's easy to be nice to you, Beth," Colt said, stealing her line. "I'm happy I'm here, too." He kissed her cheek, and Beth sighed.

"Goodnight, Beth."

"Goodnight, Colt."

Colt watched her enter her room and close the door before heading into his own room.

Chapter Twenty-Seven

August arrived and it occurred to Colt that he only had a month left before he headed home. Luke and he were in constant contact about the progress of the house, and so far they'd staked out the foundation and put in the sewer and well. Luke had ordered the lumber and other building materials and they were due to be delivered in mid-August. It was beginning to drain Colt's bank account, so he called his bank in Missoula and made arrangements for a home loan. The loan officer sent him the paperwork via email and didn't think there'd be a problem with Colt attaining a loan. The acreage that Colt was building on was deeded to him and was worth much more than the house he was building, so it would be his collateral. Plus, the Brennans had always done business with the bank and had good credit. Colt felt good about his decisions and couldn't wait until he could go home and begin building.

That Saturday night, he took Beth out to supper at a nice restaurant in downtown Seattle and afterwards they walked along near the water. The full moon shone on the bay and small boats in the private harbor had lights that twinkled in the dark. They stopped a moment, gazing out into the night, listening to music as if filtered out from nearby dance clubs.

Colt turned his head and looked up at the Ferris wheel, lit up against the dark sky. "You know. I've been here for months and I haven't really seen any of the tourist sites in Seattle," he told Beth.

Beth glanced up at him in surprise. "Didn't Carly take you to any of the popular sites?"

Colt chuckled. "Yep. All the popular bars and restaurants. And the mall. And you've shown me all the best home improvement stores."

Beth shook her head. "We're terrible. I'm sorry, Colt."

"It's no big deal," Colt said. "But it would be nice to see a few sites before I leave."

"Just name it and we'll go," Beth said. "We have five weekends this month and we can do something new every Saturday and Sunday."

"That would be great," Colt said. He looked over again at the Ferris wheel. "What about that?"

Beth glanced in the direction he was looking and smiled wide. "They're still open tonight. Let's go now. It's the most beautiful at night anyway."

"Really?" Colt asked. "Right now?"

"Why not?" Beth grabbed his hand and pulled him in the direction of the Ferris wheel.

They walked to the end of Pier 57 where the Ferris wheel, officially called the Seattle Great Wheel, was located, past brightly lit shops, restaurants, and an arcade. There was a line for tickets, so they waited their turn. The light breeze off the water was chilly, and Beth shivered as she stood in front of Colt. She'd worn a short-sleeved dress and low-heeled sandals and both of them had left their jackets in the car since it had been warm earlier.

Colt noticed her shiver. He stepped up close behind her and wrapped his arms around her crossed ones, sharing his warmth. "Better?"

Beth turned her head and smiled up at him. "Much better."

When they got to the front of the line, Colt took out his wallet to pay, but Beth stopped him. "This is my treat. You bought supper," she said as she opened her purse.

Colt gave her a worried frown. He wasn't used to women paying when he was out with them.

"It's okay, Cowboy," Beth teased, seeming to read his mind. "Women today pay their way, too." She paid for the tickets and then they walked over to wait in line again.

Colt stood beside her, wrapping his arm around her waist and pulling her close. "I don't want you to get cold," he said as an excuse to hold her.

Beth chuckled, but she snuggled up beside him.

Colt looked up into the sky at the top of the Ferris wheel. "This sure is a lot taller than I thought. It looked a lot smaller from a distance."

"Are you afraid to go up now?" Beth teased.

Colt shook his head. "Nope. I'm game if you are."

When their turn came, they were given a gondola all to themselves. The attendant gave Beth a hand up into it and Colt stepped in, ducking his head. Once they were seated, the man smiled and said, "Have a good ride." Then he closed the door.

They felt the wheel begin to move backwards.

Colt looked over at Beth. "Here we go."

They moved only a short distance and then stopped so more people could get on. The stopping and starting continued until they were near the very top, almost two hundred feet in the sky.

Colt looked around him with wide eyes. The lights on the buildings and piers reflected on the water, giving off a spectacular view. He saw the Space Needle, and many other tall buildings. Above them, the full moon glowed brightly in the inky blue sky. It was one of the most incredible sites he'd ever seen.

He looked down at Beth, who was also taking in the view.

"Isn't it beautiful?" she asked, gazing up at him. Her eyes sparkled and her face was alight with wonder. His heart swelled with affection for this amazing woman beside him.

"It is beautiful," he said softly. "Almost as beautiful as you." Colt reached up and caressed the side of her face, running his hand through the back of her loose hair. Slowly, he bent his head and lightly touched his lips to hers. When he pulled away slightly and looked into Beth's eyes, they were warm and inviting. Dipping his head again, his lips met hers with more passion than before, opening her mouth with his. Beth ran her hand up around the back of his neck, sending delicious chills down his spine. Their tongues met as their breathing quickened. Suddenly, the wheel moved and they both pulled away in surprise. Beth laughed and Colt smiled at their both being startled from the movement of the wheel.

Colt wrapped his arm around Beth and pulled her close as the wheel spun a full turn around. After two full revolutions, it stopped again at the top. Behind them was the skyline, so Beth took out her phone and they posed with their heads together and the lights shining behind them. Colt kissed her again, enjoying the feel of her wrapped in his arms.

Beth looked up at Colt with tenderness in her eyes. "So, has this turned into an official date or are you just taking advantage of me, Cowboy?" she asked, tugging at his hat.

Colt smiled down warmly at her. "I think it's now officially a date."

"Well, if I'd known that, I would have let you pay for the tickets," she said, giving him a mischievous grin.

Colt's eyes sparkled. "How 'bout I just kiss you again?" he said, lowering his head and pulling her close.

"Only if you promise not to stop," Beth whispered as their lips touched once more.

Their kiss did finally end when their gondola made its last

stop on the platform, and Colt stepped out, offering his hand to Beth. She accepted, and stepped out, smiling up at him. The attendant smiled and nodded to them as they walked away, but they barely noticed, because they only had eyes for each other.

They walked back to his truck, hand-in-hand, and when they climbed up into the cab, Colt couldn't resist kissing Beth one more time. Now that he could kiss her freely, he didn't want to stop. But he did, and drove them home as she sat beside him in the cab, her hand warm on his thigh.

It was dark in the townhouse when they entered. Only the light above the stove was on. Carly was still out for the night, so they had the place to themselves. Beth led Colt by the hand to the sofa, and after they sat, she slowly removed his hat and ran her hands through his hair, pushing it out of his eyes. She cupped his face in her small hands, studying him with her eyes, seemingly trying to memorize every angle of his face. Then she kissed him softly as he ran his hands around her waist.

Pulling back, Beth spoke quietly. "I've wanted to kiss you again ever since we kissed at the cabin. I've dreamt about it, even though I knew I shouldn't."

"Me, too," Colt said hoarsely. "I know it was wrong, because I thought I was with Carly, yet, I was so drawn to you. I couldn't stay angry at Carly for cheating on me when I had feelings for you, too."

Beth's eyes dropped. "Are you still in love with Carly?"

Colt tipped her chin up with his fingers. "No. To tell you the truth, I'm not sure what Carly and I had was love. I thought it was, but now I realize it was just physical and I mistook that for real love."

"So, what is this?" Beth asked.

"I don't know. I only know that I enjoy spending time with you and you make me laugh and smile all the time. I love how real you are, and how caring and warm you are to me and everyone." Colt grinned. "I love that you think a good day is walking through a home improvement center, looking at cabinets. I love how you enjoy simple things, like dinner at home and walks in the park. I love how the gold flecks in your eyes sparkle when you smile. Being with you just makes me incredibly happy."

"You're so sweet and kind and terribly handsome," Beth said, grinning up at Colt. "It would be impossible to resist you."

Colt pulled her to him. "Kiss me. Don't stop kissing me." He bent down and their lips met once more, their tongues dancing to their own silent tune. Colt ran his hands up her back and down again to her waist. He loved the feel of her in his arms. Her hands ran across his broad shoulders and down his back. His heart pounded as his desire grew. Colt slowly trailed kisses across her cheek and down to the base of her neck, her intake of breath when he hit the sweet spot on her throat spurring him on. He wanted to kiss every part of her. He wanted more than anything in this world to feel her soft skin under his fingers and to make love to her over and over again. But he reluctantly pulled away, despite his desire, knowing that they should take it slow.

"We should wait," he said, his breathing ragged.

Beth ran her hand along the square line of his jaw and smiled up at him. "We should," she agreed, breathing heavily. "This is new to us. Maybe we should slow it down."

Colt sat up straight and pulled Beth up against him. She dropped her head on his shoulder and sighed.

"I really don't want to stop," he said, chuckling.

"Me, either. But we should. We have a few more weeks together. Let's give ourselves some time." Beth looked up at him with worried eyes. "Colt, I want to make sure this is real. I don't want to be your rebound relationship. I'm not Carly. I can never compete with her, and I don't want to feel as if I have to."

Colt's brows furrowed. "I'd never compare you to Carly. This isn't a rebound thing. I promise you. You're worth more than a hundred Carlys, because I love everything about you that makes you special."

Beth smiled. "Then let's see what happens, okay?"

Colt nodded.

Beth leaned over and kissed him on the cheek, and then stood. "I should go to bed. We have to decide where we want to go tomorrow. Remember, we have to play tourist for the next few weekends."

Colt stood and they walked together to Beth's door. He kissed her again, a sweet, gentle kiss, and she pulled away and entered the room.

"Goodnight, Colt."

"Goodnight, Beth. Pleasant dreams."

She closed her door softly behind her.

Colt went to his own room knowing exactly who he'd be dreaming about tonight.

* * *

Colt and Beth were up early the next morning and had a big breakfast of pancakes, bacon, and Ginny's delicious strawberry jam. They were laughing and teasing each other as they were putting away the dishes when Carly came out of her room. She looked at them strangely as she poured herself a mug of coffee.

"What are you two up to today?" Carly asked, settling down at the counter. "You seem awfully cheerful."

"We went up in the big Ferris wheel last night," Colt said, picking up Beth's phone and showing Carly the photo of them. "It was fun."

"Oh." Carly glanced at the picture, and then looked at the

two in the kitchen. "I'm sorry, Colt. I forgot you wanted to do that. Is there anywhere else you want to visit while you're here? You and I could go to a few places together."

Beth turned around to hang the dishtowel, but Colt caught her frown before she'd turned away.

"That's okay, Carly. I know you hate that kind of stuff. Beth is taking me all around. We're going to the aquarium today, and up in the Space Needle, and then next weekend we're going hiking around Mount Rainier. We're making plans for the next few weekends."

Carly's gaze moved between Colt and Beth. "Well, that sounds nice. I'm sure you'll have a good time." She stood and walked back to her bedroom with her mug in hand.

Beth looked up at Colt after Carly left. "She seemed a little miffed."

Colt shrugged. "She shouldn't be. I'm not a part of her life anymore, and she has another guy."

Beth looked worried. "Yeah, but I have to live with her long after you leave in September."

Colt pulled her close and kissed her. "Don't worry. She'll get over it." The both went off to their rooms to get ready to leave.

As Colt pulled on his boots and grabbed his hat, Beth's words rang out in his mind. When he left, he'd be leaving Beth behind. He wasn't happy with that thought. But had they known each other long enough for him to stay, or her to follow him to the ranch? He didn't want to make any more hasty decisions like when he'd decided to move here on a whim. Yet, he would miss Beth desperately. He hoped he'd have his answer by the time the month was through.

Chapter Twenty-Eight

Carly felt like a third wheel in her own townhouse. Something was going on between Colt and Beth, she knew it, but it wasn't her business anymore. She'd chosen Jordan over Colt, and now she had to mind her own business. But it still, for some odd reason, made her feel sad.

She called her friends to see if they wanted to go to Sunday brunch, but everyone was busy. Chelle didn't answer, Adam was busy with his new boyfriend, and Everly had a family gathering she had to attend. She tried calling Jordan for the hundredth time this week, but there was still no answer, only his voicemail. *Where in the hell is he?*

Carly dressed in a tight blue dress that showed off her eyes and put on a pair of high heels. She left her long blond hair down and put on her favorite pink lipstick. Looking through her jewelry, she spied the necklace and earrings that Colt had given her, and sighed. It wouldn't be right to wear them. She chose another necklace and earrings instead. Carly left the townhouse and hopped into her car. She was going to drive to Jordan's downtown apartment and see if he was home. He had to be. Even if he'd been gone on business this past week, he should be home by now.

As she drove into Seattle, she smiled when she thought back over the past two months with Jordan. Since she'd finally come clean to Colt, she and Jordan had taken their relationship to a whole new level. She'd spent many evenings with him in his apartment, sometimes staying overnight after an evening of dancing and bar hopping downtown. Jordan knew how to have fun and he had the money to spend on her. He was the perfect gentleman and he was also the most exciting lover she'd ever been with. Even though they had only been seeing each other for a few weeks, she felt like she'd become very close to him. Carly had never felt for a man the way she felt about Jordon. She'd never really been in love with a man before, not even with Colt. But falling in love with Jordan would be easy. Her heart fluttered just thinking about him as she pulled into a parking spot and headed into the modern, glass building where he lived.

Carly took the elevator up to the fifth floor, humming to the music playing over the speakers. With a smile on her lips, she stepped off and strode over to Jordan's door. She knocked, and waited, hoping to hear the sound of him walking to the door.

After a moment, she did hear someone unlock the door. Her heart soared. He was home. Maybe he'd had his phone off and hadn't seen her messages. She smiled wide as the door opened, but her smiled faded when she saw a woman standing there, holding a small child.

"Can I help you?" the woman asked, staring quizzically at Carly. The woman was dressed nicely in a designer dress and heels, a diamond pendent around her neck that matched the huge diamond studs in her ears. Her auburn hair was swept up into a French twist, and her face was done up impeccably. The child wore a red, frilly dress and little shiny, red leather shoes. Her little blond curls bounced when she turned her head to stare at Carly.

Carly's words caught in her throat. *Who was this well-dressed woman? A sister? A friend?*

The woman continued staring at Carly. "Was there something you wanted?" she asked.

Carly swallowed hard and took a breath, trying to regain her composure. "I'm sorry," she said, looking past the woman to see if anyone else was in the apartment. There were a few toys scattered on the floor, but otherwise it looked just as she remembered it. "I was looking for Jordan. Is he home?"

The woman tilted her head up a bit, looking Carly over. "I see. Are you a friend of his?"

Carly's heart began to pound. She didn't know who this woman was, and she suddenly felt trapped. "I know him from work," she lied.

The woman's beautifully painted lips formed a perfect O. She seemed relieved. "I see. Well, I'm sorry, but my husband isn't here. He's gone on business. He should be back on Monday, though, so you should see him then."

Carly's felt the blood drain from her face. *Husband*. The word spun around in her head. *This woman is married to Jordan. And they have a child.*

"I'm sorry," the woman continued. "I don't remember if we've ever met. I'm Katherine, and this is our daughter, Janie." She reached out her hand.

Carly had no choice but to shake her hand. "I'm Carly. I'm new at the firm, so we've never met," she managed to say.

"It's nice to meet you, Carly. I rarely see Jordan's fellow workers, except at the Christmas party once a year. We came into the city to stay at the apartment to do some shopping while Jordan was gone. Usually, we're at our house in the suburbs. It's a quieter place to raise children."

Carly's head spun. She had to get away. "It's nice to meet you. I'll catch up with Jordan at the office," she said, backing away.

Katherine nodded and began to close the door. The little girl waved, and Carly's heart ripped to shreds. That adorable little girl had just waved unknowingly at her father's mistress.

Carly stepped into the elevator and fell against the wall. Tears burned her eyes. She'd never in her life dated a married man. No matter what everyone thought of her, she'd never knowingly break up a family. But she had. Jordan was married. He'd lied to her and used her.

The elevator door opened and Carly walked quickly through the lobby and out into the fresh air. She felt sick to her stomach. *How could he do this to me? To them?*

Climbing into her car, she sat behind the wheel while tears blurred her vision. Her heart still pounded and her stomach rolled over. She had no one to call, no one to confide in. Her friends were busy and she certainly couldn't tell Beth or Colt. Or Andi. She could never tell her sister that she'd been seeing a married man, even if it hadn't been intentional. Andi would be so disappointed in her. She probably already was, for breaking Colt's heart.

Colt.

Carly's tears fell faster when she thought about how she'd left Colt for Jordan. She'd hurt one of the sweetest men she'd even known so she could be with a cheater. And now, she had neither man.

With a heavy heart, Carly drove home.

* * *

Colt and Beth spent half the day at the aquarium enjoying the antics of the otters and seals and marveling at the underwater dome where fish swam all around them. Colt bought Beth an adorable stuffed otter in the gift shop and her eyes lit up at the sweet gift. They walked around the piers downtown, ate a late lunch, and then went up into the Space

Needle just as dusk fell over the city. They stayed a while, watching day turn into night as the city lit up.

They were both surprised to see Carly at home when they returned to the townhouse. She sat on the sofa wearing comfy pajama pants and a sweatshirt, watching a sad movie on television. Colt frowned when he saw her there. He'd never once seen Carly dressed that way or just sitting at home. When he looked over at Beth, she shrugged. Apparently, this was new to her, too.

"Is everything okay?" Beth asked casually. "Are you feeling okay?"

Carly looked up at them and forced a smile. "I'm fine. Just relaxing."

Colt saw her eyes were red and he knew she'd been crying. "Are you sure you're okay?" he asked.

Carly waved her hand through the air as if to dismiss him. "I'm fine. You two just do what you do. Don't worry about me."

Colt and Beth looked at each other, and then went into the kitchen. Beth cut slices of apple pie she'd made the day before and they sat in front of the television with Carly and ate it. Even Carly accepted a piece. Whatever had happened, she was keeping it to herself, so they let her have her space.

Over the next few weekends Colt and Beth visited various sites around Seattle. They went on one of the shorter hikes near Mount Rainier, where they walked beside a beautiful crystal lake that was as smooth as glass. Colt loved it there, because it reminded him of home. And he was again in awe of Beth. She was a trooper, just as she'd been on the cattle drive. In fact, he thought she could probably out hike him. Another weekend they visited the underground city in Seattle, which completely fascinated Colt. He'd never seen anything like it before. They rode the ferry to Bainbridge Island and back, just so Colt could go on his first ferry ride. They had so much fun playing tourist, and even Beth hadn't visited many of the sites before and enjoyed it as much as Colt did.

As each day passed, Colt's affection for Beth grew deeper. He loved kissing Beth, holding her close, and having her by his side everywhere they went. He'd never felt this connected with Carly, or any other woman he'd ever dated, which he had to admit wasn't many. But in Beth he saw something different from all of them. They had been friends first, which had created a bond between them. As his time to leave drew near, he began to worry he might lose her when he drove away. He wasn't sure if he could bear that.

On the Saturday before Colt was due to go home, Beth told him she had a surprise for him and to be sure to wear his boots and hat. Since he usually did, he didn't think too much about it. They met up with Quinn and Chelle for supper in downtown Seattle and had a wonderful time. Colt really liked Quinn and he was glad that Beth enjoyed spending time with the couple as well. After they ate, Beth led the group up a street they'd never been on before and suddenly Colt realized what the surprise was. Drifting outside of a small bar were the sounds of country music.

"I found a place where you can dance the way you like," she told him, beaming with delight.

Colt grinned and the four of them went inside. It was decorated in western style and there was a four-piece band up on stage, playing country music. The place was packed with people, most of them wearing boots, jeans, and cowboy hats, dancing on the polished wooden floor in front of the band.

"See why I insisted you wear your boots and hat?" she said, her eyes sparkling up at him.

Colt pulled her close, dropping a kiss on her lips. "You're amazing, you know that?"

Beth laughed. "Come on, Cowboy. Let's dance."

They found a small space on the dance floor and joined right in, dancing a two-step, and then speeding it up with a livelier tune. When everyone got into position for a line dance, all four of them joined in, laughing at how badly they followed along. Quinn bought beers for the group and they found a small table to sit at.

"I've never been here before," Quinn said over the music. "This is fun."

Colt nodded. Beth had known, as she always seemed to, how to make him happy.

After a time the bar became so crowded that they decided to leave. They were surprised to see a line of people waiting to get in. They walked along the streets, enjoying the fresh night air, until they arrived at their cars.

Chelle gave Colt a hug before she and Quinn left. "I probably won't see you again before you leave, so I'll say goodbye now," she told him. "I'm so happy I got to know you, Colt. You're a sweet guy. Stay that way, okay?"

Colt hugged her back and said goodbye. He'd really started to like Chelle after getting to know her better. He waved to Quinn. He'd be seeing him at work the next week.

Beth and Colt stepped up into his truck and Colt drew her to him. "Thanks for tonight. I really enjoyed it. You always know how to make me happy." He kissed her lightly, and soon their kiss became more demanding. Beth was the one to pull away first.

"Let's go home," she said.

When they arrived at the townhouse, it was dark inside and Carly wasn't home yet. She was back to going out nightly, although they had no idea where she went or with whom. Colt figured she was out with Adam or Everly, or maybe even Jordan. He didn't know who Carly spent time with anymore.

Beth turned on a lamp in the living room and they both sat down on the sofa and snuggled close.

"I know it wasn't like The Depot in Montana," Beth said. "But it was fun dancing with you there."

"Maybe someday you can come out to the ranch again and we can go dancing," Colt said, hopeful.

"Maybe," Beth answered softly.

Colt leaned down and gently kissed Beth's neck. He ran kisses along her jaw, to her cheek, and then brushed her lips with his. Beth responded, pulling him closer. Their kiss deepened and their hands began to roam. When Colt touched her breast, Beth's breath drew in quickly. He pulled away, afraid he'd gone too far, but she looked at him with shimmering eyes and whispered, "Don't stop."

Their desire grew and became more urgent. Beth lay back on the sofa and Colt leaned over her, kissing her. He unbuttoned the top button of her blouse and kissed the hollow of her neck, then unbuttoned another and kissed her lower. He wanted her so much, needed her desperately. But not here, reason told him. Not on the sofa.

Drawing away, Colt stood and offered his hand to Beth. Confused, she reached up and he pulled her to him. "Let me love you," he whispered, gazing down into her eyes.

Beth looked up at him longingly and led him to her bedroom, shutting the door behind them. She lit a candle on her dresser and then turned to him. Colt reached up and slowly began unbuttoning her blouse until it opened up, her full breasts pushing against her silky bra. He trailed kisses down her neck and chest. Beth's hands roamed around the back of his neck and up through his hair, urging him on. He slipped her blouse off her shoulders and she dropped her arms, letting it fall to the floor. Gently, he reached around her and unhooked her bra, letting it drop to join the blouse.

Colt gasped when he looked down at her. "My God, you're so beautiful," he said hoarsely. He dipped down and kissed first one breast and then the other, before covering one of her nipples with his lips.

Beth arched her back, responding to Colt's touch. She began unbuttoning his shirt and pushed it away. Colt quickly pulled his T-shirt over his head and Beth ran her hands across his taut chest, his muscles flexing with every breath. They embraced, feeling the delicious warmth of skin against skin. She reached up and drew his head down, kissing him greedily. Neither one could contain their desire any longer. They shed their jeans and fell back on the bed, kissing each other urgently.

In a brief moment of clarity, Colt pulled away and asked, "Are you sure?"

Beth looked up at him, her eyes filled with desire. "Yes," she whispered.

Colt kissed her softly, but he could no longer hold back. They joined together, their fit perfect, their rhythm in harmony with each other. At that instant, Colt truly believe he'd found his true home.

Afterwards, they lay together with Beth's head on his chest and his arm around her. They were quiet for some time, absorbing the depth of their feelings for each other and what they'd just shared. The moon filtered in through the blinds of the window over Beth's bed and the candle flickered as it grew smaller, leaving dancing shadows on the ceiling.

Colt tenderly kissed the top of Beth's head. "I'm falling in love with you, Beth," he said softly.

"I'm falling in love with you, too," Beth whispered.

Colt rolled to his side and ran his hand up Beth's curves, stopping to cup her face. He kissed her lips once more, unable to get enough of her. "I can't stop kissing you," he said, grinning. "I never want to stop kissing you."

Beth smiled up at him. "Then don't stop."

Colt pulled her to him and very slowly made love to her again.

Chapter Twenty-Nine

Colt and Beth spent every moment possible together that last week before he left. After work each day, they'd come home and do what they'd always done, walked, ate supper, and watched television. But at night, Colt held Beth close in his arms after they made love, feeling content to have her warm body pressed up against his.

They were careful not to let on to Carly about their relationship, not because they were ashamed or afraid of what she might think, but because they wanted it to belong only to them for the short time they had.

The last day of work at the market, Gerard came up to Colt with an envelope that held his final paycheck. He shook his hand and thanked him for all his hard work and for keeping his promise.

"I know things didn't work out the way you wanted with your girl," Gerard said. "But I'm happy we had you with us for this short time."

"I really enjoyed working here and getting to know Quinn. I've met a new lifelong friend," Colt told him, and he meant it. Quinn was already planning on coming to the ranch in the fall to help move the cattle back down to the winter pasture.

"Quinn tells me you're building a house back home," Gerard said. "I put a little something extra in your paycheck to help you along. Good luck, Colt. We'll miss you."

Colt thanked him and watched the older man walk away. He opened his paycheck and his eyes grew wide. Gerard had added a thousand dollars to his paycheck. It was such an amazing gift, and Colt knew he'd put it to good use on his house.

Quinn reluctantly said goodbye to his friend. "I'm going to miss working with you. No one works as hard as you do. Chelle and I will also miss going out with you and Beth. We had a lot of fun."

Colt nodded. He'd miss them, too. "But you're coming in the fall, right?"

"You bet I am. I'm going to learn to be a cowboy," Quinn said, smirking.

Even Connor came to the warehouse to say goodbye to Colt. "Goodbye, Colt the Cowboy," he said with a mischievous grin. "You'll certainly be missed up front. There are a few girls up there who would have liked to have gotten to know you better," he teased.

Leaving the market was bittersweet for Colt. Even though he was happy to be going back to the ranch, he knew he'd miss everyone here.

His last night in Seattle, he and Beth ate out at a nice restaurant, and then took a romantic walk along the waterfront as the moon came up. They spoke very little, because neither of them was looking forward to saying goodbye.

Earlier, before they'd left the townhouse, Carly had pulled Colt aside and hugged him tight. "I probably won't see you again before you leave tomorrow," she'd told him, her eyes tearing up. "I'm sorry again for what happened. I did enjoy our time together, and I'll always have a place for you in my heart. You're such a good man, Colt. I wish I'd wanted what you did. It just didn't work out."

"It's okay," Colt said, smiling down at her. "We had fun,

right? Sometimes things aren't meant to be."

Carly nodded. "Goodbye, Colt. I'll see you in December when our little niece makes her appearance."

"Or nephew," Colt said, grinning.

Carly laughed and kissed him softly on the cheek before leaving to go out with her friends.

That night, Colt and Beth made love, slow and sweet, savoring every last moment together. Afterward, as they lay together in each other arms, Colt's mind was reeling. He didn't want to leave Beth. He was afraid if he did, he'd never see her again, and he couldn't bear to lose her.

"I don't want to leave you," Colt finally said. "Maybe I should stay a little longer."

Beth turned to him. "I don't want you to go, either," she told him honestly. "But you have to. You need to go home and build your house and be a rancher again. You missed it. I know you did. Seattle isn't the place for you. Montana is."

"But you're not in Montana," Colt said, his heart breaking. "I love you, Beth. I want to be with you." He hesitated a moment, then asked tentatively. "Would you ever considering moving to Montana?"

Beth raised her hand up to Colt's face and gently caressed his cheek. "Colt, we can't make hasty decisions about our lives. You gave up everything to follow Carly out here just a few months ago, and it didn't work out. You and I need to take a little time to make sure we know what we want."

"I already know what I want," Colt insisted. "I want you."

"Oh, Colt." Beth's eyes filled with tears. "Wanting you isn't the problem. Loving you is easy. But just a few short weeks ago, you thought you wanted to be with Carly, and look how that turned out. I don't want to be your second choice. I want you to know for certain that I'm the person you really love and want."

Colt's jaw tightened in frustration. "I'm not in love with Carly and I realize now that I never felt for her how I do for you. You're not my second choice, Beth. I want you, and only you. Please believe me."

Beth wiped away her tears. "Let's just give it some time. Go home. Build your house, be with your family, and do what you do. I'll stay here and do what I do. Let's see how you feel once we're no longer together every day. I need you to take the time to be sure you know exactly what you want, Colt."

"What about you?" Colt asked quietly. "What if you find you want someone other than me?"

Beth smiled wanly. "I'm not looking for anyone else, Colt. If we're meant to be together, we will be. Let's just make sure. Who knows? Maybe there's some cute little cowgirl just waiting for you back home. Maybe you'll find someone else."

Colt bent down and kissed her tenderly. "There's no one else," he said, close to her lips. "Only you."

Beth sighed. "I want to believe that. I really do. Let's make sure, though. Do this for me, Colt. Please?"

Reluctantly, Colt agreed. Beth rolled over and Colt drew her to him, curling his body around hers, memorizing every curve of her body against his for all the lonely nights ahead.

* * *

Colt left early the next morning with a heavy heart. Beth walked him out to his truck to say goodbye, wearing her baggy sweatshirt and jeans as she usually did and looking just as adorable as the first time he'd seen her. He kissed her tenderly on the lips before hopping behind the wheel, because if their goodbye had stretched out any longer, he was afraid he wouldn't be able to leave. As he drove away, he looked in the rearview mirror one last time and saw her standing there, smiling at him, being there for him just as she had been since that very first day.

As Colt made the long drive back to the ranch, he realized that Beth was only looking out for him as she had so many other times before. She wanted him to make the right decision and not rush into anything without truly thinking about it. He'd done that when he'd run off to Seattle to be with Carly. His hormones and desires had urged him to leave home and be with Carly and common sense had been thrown to the wind. Beth didn't want him to make another mistake like that one. And he didn't want to either, for fear of hurting her as badly as Carly had hurt him.

Beth knew him too well. Maybe even better than he knew himself.

By the time Colt turned into the ranch's driveway, he'd convinced himself into giving careful thought to his future. No more rash, immature decisions. He'd work the ranch, build his home, and live his life. If Beth had a place in that future, he'd do it the right way and not on a whim. She deserved that.

Everyone was at the main house and greeted him warmly when he entered. There were hugs and tears all around, they were all so happy to have Colt home. Even Bree danced happily around him until he'd petted her behind the ears. The kitchen smelled of his favorite fried chicken and his mom's apple pie and it didn't take Ginny long to serve up leftovers that she'd kept warm for him.

Colt couldn't believe how big Andi's belly had grown since May. Her face had filled out a little too, but she looked radiant. When he hugged her, he was careful not to squeeze her hard.

Andi laughed. "You aren't going to hurt me or this baby," she said, wrapping her arms around him. "I'm so happy you're finally home."

Even Luke hugged his little brother. "Have you grown

taller?" he asked, looking at Colt, eye to eye. "Weren't you supposed to have stopped growing by now?" he joked.

"I've always been nearly as tall as you," Colt said. "You'd just never admit it."

Randy and Glen were there also, and they all sat around the table joking and laughing and catching up. They asked about Carly and Beth, and told him what had been going on at the ranch. It was a warm, wonderful homecoming, and despite Colt's sadness at leaving Beth behind, he was thrilled to be home.

The next day Colt fell back easily into his chores around the ranch. He walked out into the field and greeted both Maddie and Sadie, running his hand down their smooth, shiny coats. He'd missed riding and working with the horses. Even simple tasks like feeding the animals and cleaning out stalls made him appreciate being back at the ranch. At least he was working outside in the fresh air and not stuck in a hot, stuffy warehouse. Luke had told him that Jake found another job on a ranch nearby so at least he didn't have to feel bad about Jake losing his job here. He and his wife had welcomed a new baby boy three months ago, so he'd needed the steady work.

Later that afternoon, Luke took Colt down to the building site about a half-mile east from the main house. Colt was amazed at all Luke had accomplished in the short time he'd given him. They'd secured the necessary building permits and had put in a gravel driveway from the highway up to the house. The sewer system and well were in place, and the cement foundation had been laid. Luke had talked Colt into having an electric radiant heating system laid in the slab foundation as an additional heat source. Luke had learned from experience that his wood fireplace wasn't enough and had to add electric baseboards this past year, which he wasn't too fond of. Colt appreciated Luke's input, because it would save him money in the long run.

Luke had given his design to a local log house building company and they had cut the specially preserved logs to fit the design and delivered everything necessary for them to put together Colt's home both outside and inside.

Colt marveled at the wood cut in various sizes piled high. "It's like playing with life-sized Lincoln logs," he said, laughing. They had done the very same thing for Luke's home, but it had been several years ago and Colt had forgotten just how much went into it.

"Greg will bring his crane to help us place logs as soon as we get too high to do it by hand," Luke told Colt. Another friend of theirs was an expert at building stone fireplaces, and Luke had contacted him to build Colt's. "All this is going to cost you a pretty penny," Luke said. "But it's too late to back out now. You're in knee deep."

Colt nodded. "I'll be okay. I've been saving money since I became a partner on the ranch after dad died. Ma did a good job of investing my earnings since I spent so little. Plus, I was able to get a bank loan for the balance, so I can afford it. Just promise me we'll have a profit for the next few years," he teased Luke.

Luke grinned. "I'd like to promise that to myself," he said. "But we're okay. The ranch is doing well and beef is still high. At least this year will be a good year."

Colt was relieved to hear that. He knew he'd work his hardest to keep the ranch in the black.

That weekend, they began work on the house and several weekends later, they had the shell up. Their neighbors, Ray and Jimmy, helped them with the heavier logs until it was time for Greg to bring his crane and lift logs up into position. Everyone happily pitched in because that was what neighbors here did. Colt knew he'd be forever grateful to his friends and neighbors for helping him build his house.

Colt and Luke worked on the roof and Randy helped shingle it. By late October, they had all the windows and doors installed and the fireplace was laid and ready for use. The first snow fell the day after it was complete, and everyone was thrilled they'd accomplished so much in so little time.

Of course, Colt had months of work ahead of him finishing the inside of the house, but he didn't mind. In fact, he couldn't wait to work on it.

Quinn came in early November and rode with them, moving the cattle down from the summer pasture. Some would be sold off for income while the younger cattle grew over the winter. This was the time of year they reaped the rewards of all their hard work, and as Luke predicted, it ended up being a very good income year. The whole family, including Quinn, Glen, and Randy, went to The Depot and celebrated with a round of beers while Andi drank iced tea. They were all in a good place in their lives, settled and happy, with a new generation of Brennans on the way. Life at the Brennan Ranch was good.

Except for one thing. Beth wasn't here to help Colt celebrate.

All throughout the building process, Colt had thought constantly of Beth. He took some time every Saturday night to drive down to The Depot parking lot and call her. They'd talk for an hour, maybe two, about the new house, her work, and everything in-between. Colt never pressed her about their relationship, and Beth didn't either. They just enjoyed talking to each other. But Colt wanted more. He wanted Beth to lie beside him every night and wake up with him every morning. He wanted someone to share his day with, ride the trails with, and most of all, share his new home with. And that someone for him was Beth.

One Sunday afternoon, Colt was inside his home laying the

oak plank floor over the subfloor. It wasn't difficult, just time consuming, but he saved a lot of money doing this work himself. He looked up in surprise when there was a knock on the door, and then it slowly opened.

"Hey, there. Can I come in?" Andi asked, walking over the threshold carefully. Bree followed her in. Bree had become attached to Andi from the very beginning and was often at her side.

Colt smiled and immediately stood up and stepped over to Andi. He moved away boards that were on the floor. She was very large at this point, only a month away from having the baby, and he was afraid she might trip and hurt herself. Luke would never forgive him if that happened, and he'd never forgive himself.

"Come in, but be careful," he told her seriously. He held out his arm for Andi to steady herself on and she looked up at him quizzically.

"I'm pregnant, Colt. Not senile," she teased. "But I love your concern."

Colt grinned. He couldn't help not watching over Andi. He adored her that much.

"I had to see how the house is coming along," Andi said, looking all around her. "Luke wouldn't let me near the building site when it was being put up for fear I'd get hurt. And now I'm as big as a house and I don't feel like going very far. But I wanted to see what you've done before this baby arrives and I'm too busy to come here."

As Bree lay curled up near the crackling fireplace, Colt took Andi on a tour of the rooms, telling her everything he planned on doing. "I'm laying the wood floor right now, but then I need to finish the walls and get the cabinets and light fixtures and everything else picked out."

Andi looked up at the two portable work lights he'd hung

from the beams and had plugged into the outlets. "Yeah, I think light fixtures should be the first thing on your list," she said, smiling. "You need to be able to see what you're doing."

Colt nodded. "I haven't decided what I want yet, though. Once I get the cabinets ordered, and the island, I'll know what will work around them. I'll have a light over the sink, of course, and I want pendant lights over the island. I'm thinking canister lights in the ceiling might be smart here in the living room, or maybe some sort of track lighting above the fireplace. I'm just not sure."

Andi's brows rose. "It sounds to me like you know a lot about these things. Most men don't even know what a pendent light is. Where'd you learn all that?"

Colt's expression softened. "I used to watch a lot of home decorating shows with Beth," he said. "And she loved walking around home improvement stores, picking out her favorite things for her dream home. It was fun."

"I liked Beth when she came out here for the cattle drive. She's a hard worker and a sweet person," Andi said. "Maybe you should have her come here and help you pick out fixtures. It sounds like she has a real knack for it."

Colt nodded. "I was going to call her later this week and ask her if she'd come out and help, once I get this flooring down."

Andi smiled. "That's wonderful. We'd all love to see her again." Andi moved closer to Colt, looking up into his blue eyes. "You know, Colt? You changed while you were in Seattle. You're more confident and less shy. You're no longer Luke's little brother. When I look at you now, I see that you are your own man."

Colt looked down at her, surprised by her words. He did feel more confident than he had been less than a year ago. And he was surer of who he was and what he wanted.

"Is that what a broken heart does?" Andi asked. "Make you

grow up? Or is it because you're in love?"

Colt stared at her, dumbfounded. *How does she know?*

Andi grinned mischievously. "I saw how you looked at Beth when she was here. And how well you both got along. If you two didn't fall in love, I'd be shocked."

Colt shook his head. "Sure can't hide anything from you," he told her. "I do love Beth. I don't know how you figured it out, but it's true."

Andi reached up and hugged him tight. "Call it intuition. Or maybe I just pay attention more than others do. Or maybe I'm a romantic and want to see you happy. I just knew. And I also know that if you don't call her and get her out here soon, you'll be sorry. She's definitely a keeper."

Colt nodded. He agreed completely.

Chapter Thirty

Colt drove to The Depot and sat in the parking lot that evening to call Beth. Andi was right—if he didn't do it soon, he'd lose her, and he didn't want that to happen.

Beth answered on the second ring, sounding surprised. "Hey, there, Cowboy. I didn't expect to hear from you so soon."

Colt smiled. He always loved hearing Beth's voice. It had a soothing quality to it and made him feel warm inside. "I know, but I just couldn't wait any longer. I'm working on putting down the wood floors in the house, and then I'll need to pick out all the other finishes. I'm holding you to your promise."

"What promise?" Beth asked, sounding confused.

"You said you wanted to come and help me pick out all my fixtures and finishes. I need your help, Beth. I can't do this myself. What do you say? Is there any chance you can get off of work for a few days and fly out here?" Colt held his breath. What if she said no? What if she no longer felt the same about him? A million what ifs ran through his mind in the ensuing silence.

"I'd really love to do that," Beth said hesitantly. "But are you sure you want me to help?"

"Of course, I want you to help," Colt said softly. "Beth, I know you wanted us to take time and figure out if what we feel for each other is real. I have taken the time, and still, all I think of is you. I'd love to have you come here and help me, whether or not you still feel the same way about me."

"Oh, Colt," Beth said, sighing.

"I'm not going to pressure you about us, Beth," Colt said gently. "All I'm asking is if you'd come help me with my house. No expectations. Just cabinets, countertops, light fixtures, and bedroom carpeting. Maybe even a faucet or two," he teased.

"I'd really like to do that," Beth said. "When did you want me to come?"

Colt's heart soared. "Anytime. As soon as you can."

"I'll see what I can do about taking a few days off at work," Beth said, noncommittally. "I may have to trade with a few people. I'll let you know as soon as I know anything, okay?"

"That's fine," Colt said, trying not to get his hopes up. He couldn't tell from Beth's tone if she really wanted to come or was just being nice. Maybe he'd already lost her.

They said their goodbyes and Colt headed home with an aching heart. He hoped Beth would give him another chance to show her how much he loved her. He didn't want anyone else but her. Ever.

* * *

Carly walked into the living room just as Beth clicked off her phone. Usually, she and Beth said very little to each other, but tonight, she noticed Beth looked sad. "What's that frown on your face for? Bad news?"

Beth glanced up at Carly from where she sat on the sofa. "I didn't realize I was frowning. That was Colt."

Carly cocked her head. "Why aren't you smiling, then? His calls usually make you happy. Is something wrong at the ranch?"

Beth shook her head. "No, everything is fine." She looked at Carly. "Colt invited me to come there and help him pick out fixtures for his home."

"So, what's the problem? You like that sort of thing."

Beth sighed. "I'm not sure if I should go."

Carly crossed her arms and looked at Beth sternly. "You mean, you're telling me that a hunky, adorable, sweet cowboy who has the biggest heart of anyone we know invited you to spend a few days with him, and you aren't sure you want to? What's wrong with you? I thought you liked Colt."

"That's the problem," Beth said.

Carly moved closer to Beth. "Listen, I know you two had something going on before he left." When Beth's eyes widened, Carly merely waved her hand through the air. "Don't be so surprised. I'm not an idiot. I saw the way he looked at you. Frankly, I'm the one who's surprised you didn't follow him there sooner."

"It's complicated."

"No, it's not. You're in love with him and he's definitely in love with you. You both want the same things out of life. What in the world is keeping you from being with him?"

Beth turned sad eyes to Carly. "He loved you first. How will I ever know if he fell for me on the rebound, or if he truly loves me?"

Carly took a breath. She walked over and dropped into the chair by the sofa, leaning forward towards Beth. "Yes, he thought he loved me. But the truth is, it wasn't truly love. He just thought we were in love, but we never really were. We had fun. And he doesn't have feelings for me any longer. He's yours, Beth. One-hundred percent. And if you don't book the next flight out of here to be with him, then you're crazy. He's handsome, reliable, sweet, charming, and downright sexy. He's also loyal and he'll love you until the day he dies. He's a

Brennan, for Pete's sake. That's how the Brennans are. And if I had my head screwed on right, I would have hung onto Colt with both hands." Carly gave a small smile and spoke softly. "He may have thought he loved me first, but it's you he loves now. He doesn't want me, Beth. He wants you."

Tears filled Beth's eyes. Carly was right. And hearing it from her seemed to change everything. "Thanks, Carly. I needed to hear that."

Carly stood and waved away her words. "Aw, it's nothing. Just remember though, I'll be around whether anyone wants me to be or not. My sister lives there and my little niece is coming soon, and I love that family, too. If you can live with that, then we're good."

Beth smiled, wiping away her tears. "If I can live with you, then I guess I can live with you being around once in a while."

Carly grinned and nodded. She grabbed her coat, waved goodbye, and headed out to meet up with her friends.

* * *

Colt stood in the Missoula International Airport awaiting the arrival of Beth's plane. It was a Wednesday afternoon on a sunny but chilly November day. It had only been ten days since he'd invited Beth to come out, but it had felt like a lifetime. He couldn't believe this day had finally arrived, and he paced impatiently, waiting for the flight to arrive.

As he paced, he remembered how almost a year ago he'd waited impatiently in this same spot for Carly to arrive. His life had changed greatly since then. He'd been a wet-behind-the-ears cowboy who knew nothing about love or relationships, but had thought he'd known everything. Now, he realized how much his ideas of life and love had changed, and the difference between a hot crush and true love. He wouldn't change any of this past year, not even the heartache he'd felt when Carly discarded him. He knew if he hadn't followed her to Seattle, he'd have never met Beth, and as far as he was concerned, their meeting had been fate. He only hoped she felt the same way.

In the days since Beth told him she was coming, he'd finished laying the wooden floors in the front part of the house and had started on the interior walls. He was trying to leave as much work undone as possible so he could get her input. She had a wonderful sense of style and he trusted her to help him create a warm, welcoming home that he, and he hoped someday his future family, would enjoy.

The plane finally arrived, and with his coat slung over his arm, he hurried over to the baggage carrousels to wait for her to appear. When she did, he smiled wide. She was as beautiful as ever, her brown eyes twinkling when they met his. Unable to control himself any longer, Colt strode up to her, dropped his coat, and wrapped his arms around her.

Beth laughed and hugged him back, giving him a light kiss on the lips.

"I can't believe you're finally here," Colt whispered in her ear. "I've missed you so much."

"Me, too," Beth told him.

Aware that people were staring, they separated. Colt found her bag among the others and then they headed for the truck, holding hands.

Once inside the warm truck cab, Colt wanted desperately to pull Beth to him and kiss her, but he thought better of it. He should take it slowly. He had to make sure she still felt the same as he did.

They rode the hour's drive back to the ranch, talking about Colt's friends in Seattle and his family here. Beth told him she'd gone to lunch a few times with Chelle, and that she enjoyed spending time with her. She described the Christmas stockings she was filling for the patients at the hospital, just as she'd done for Easter with the baskets. "Except this time we won't have a Christmas Cowboy to pass them out," she teased.

"Maybe I should come there and help," he said, half-serious. He'd had so much fun doing it last time.

Beth beamed at him. "I'd like that."

When they arrived at the ranch, Ginny and Andi greeted Beth warmly in the cozy kitchen. Bree also greeted her before returning to her pillow by the stairs. The men were out working, but would be in for supper. Ginny was quick to serve up sandwiches and cookies with mugs of hot chocolate. They all sat around the table, eating and talking for over an hour.

Beth exclaimed over how big Andi's belly had grown since she'd last seen her. "You must be ready to have that baby by now," she said.

Andi nodded. "Yes. I have three weeks to go, but it can't come soon enough for me."

"Well, at least we have a nurse in the house now if that baby decides to make a quick appearance," Ginny teased.

Beth shook her head. "I've never delivered a baby on my own, so try not to have it while I'm here, okay?"

They all laughed.

Colt took Beth's bag up to the spare room and reluctantly left her with the women. "I have a few chores to do, and then I'll be back," he said, wishing his could kiss her, but not wanting to do it in front of his family. "Tonight we can go see the house, okay?"

Beth nodded. "I can't wait."

"You go on and work," Ginny said. "We'll take good care of Beth."

Colt left and worked quickly. Right before suppertime, he hurried into the house and showered. He'd been in such a hurry to shower, he'd forgotten to bring clean clothes into the bathroom, and he certainly didn't want to put on his dirty ones. Cracking the door just a bit, he peeked out and saw the hallway was empty, so he wrapped a towel around his waist and stepped out.

Beth opened her bedroom door just as he came out and gave a small chuckle. "Still walking around without clothes on, I see," she teased.

Colt spun around, and then grinned. "Sorry."

Beth walked over to him, looking clean and fresh and wearing jeans and a long-sleeved T-shirt. She gazed up into his baby blue eyes. "Don't be sorry. I've missed this," she said softly.

Colt's heart pounded. He reached for her and they kissed, softly at first, and then more passionately. Beth pulled away and grinned. "Uh, maybe you should get dressed. That towel doesn't hide much."

Colt laughed. "Okay. But let's pick up where we left off later, okay?"

Beth winked and headed for the stairs. She turned and said, "Hey, Colt?"

Colt stood in the doorway of his room and glanced over at her. "What?"

"Don't put your T-shirt on inside out, okay?" Beth laughed and went down the steps.

Colt smiled. They were still the same as they'd always been. Almost three months apart hadn't changed a thing. His heart soared with delight.

* * *

After supper, Colt drove Beth down to his house. It was already dark out and he had to use a flashlight on the path up to the front door. There was only a wood platform acting as a step, but next year he planned on building a large, covered porch like Luke's house had. Until then, the platform would have to do.

He opened the door and stepped up inside, then gave Beth a hand up. "Stay here a moment," he said. He walked a short distance and clicked on both of the work lights that still hung from the beam overhead.

The lights gave the room a warm glow, giving the honey-colored floor a soft gleam. Beth gasped in delight as she slowly looked around.

"Oh, Colt. This is amazing," she exclaimed. "The floors are perfect, and I love the log interior walls. And that fireplace. It's so beautiful."

Colt beamed with pleasure. He quickly took her around, showing her what he'd done already and what he planned on doing. "The outer walls are round logs with insulation in-between each layer, and then there's a layer of insulation and then the inner wall. I chose the log interior for the living room, dining room, and kitchen, since they are wide open, and I'm going to use it upstairs in the loft, but I haven't decided on the bathrooms, bedrooms, and hallway. I could use sheetrock in those areas. I wanted to wait to see what you thought."

Beth looked at the walls in the living room where they were finished. "I love the log interior," she said. "I guess I never realized you could do it that way. It's so smart, considering how cold it gets here in the winter."

Colt nodded. "That's what I figured. Luke didn't do it this way and now he says he wished he had. His house stays warm, but this will be more energy efficient."

"I love it," Beth said. "And the big windows, and the loft. It's all so cozy. You did such a good job on this, Colt."

Colt grinned. He enjoyed hearing her praise. "I had a lot of help," he said. He took her on a tour of the rest of the house and they talked about ideas for all the rooms. He couldn't wait to go shopping with Beth. He loved all her ideas for the house.

When they came back into the living room, Colt took some wood he had stacked beside the fireplace and started a fire. It flickered and crackled, giving warmth to the room. There was nowhere to sit except the floor, so Colt laid out his sheepskin coat in front of the fire and they sat there together, watching the flames.

Beth turned to Colt. "I'm so proud of you, Colt. You've accomplished so much since coming home. You truly belong here in this beautiful home and with your family all around."

Colt raised his hand and ran his fingers through Beth's loose hair, pushing it behind her ear. He drew her to him and kissed her lightly on the lips.

Beth gave him a small smile. "Did you bring me here to seduce me, Cowboy?" she asked softly.

Colt looked into her shining eyes. He loved her long, thick lashes, the gold flecks that sparkled when she smiled, and the way her soft lips felt against his. He loved Beth. He knew it back in Seattle, and he knew it now, as sure as he was sitting here. Slowly, he shook his head.

"No. Actually, I have other plans for you," he said. He stood, pulling her up with him.

Beth looked at him quizzically. "What are you up to?"

Colt pulled his phone from his pocket and searched it a moment, then hit the screen. Music began to filter from the phone's speaker. He turned the sound up, and then set it on a sawhorse near them. Offering his hand to her, he asked, "Will you do me the honor of being the first woman to ever dance with me on this new floor?"

Beth's face softened. "I'd be honored." She took his hand and he pulled her to him, placing his other hand around her waist.

Their bodies touched as they moved slowly to the soulful tune. Beth cocked her head, turning her ear toward the music. "That isn't country music," she said, surprised.

Colt smiled. "No. Do you recognize this song? It's "All of Me" by John Legend. It's the very first song we ever danced to together. Remember?"

"Yes," Beth said wistfully. "At Carly's birthday party. You remembered."

"How could I forget?" Colt asked. "It's one of my most favorite memories. You remember when I walked you to your car that night?"

Beth nodded. "I do. For a moment, I thought you were going to kiss me. But that was crazy of me. You loved Carly."

Colt shook his head slowly. "No, it wasn't crazy of you. I wanted to kiss you. I almost did."

Beth sighed and nestled her head on Colt's chest. "I think I fell in love with you that night," she whispered.

Colt kissed the top of her head. "I know I fell for you that night. And I haven't stopped falling for you since."

Beth raised her eyes to Colt. He kissed her lips tenderly. As the music played on, he took a small box from his pocket and pulled away from Beth. Still holding her hand, knelt before her.

Beth's looked down at him in astonishment.

"Beth, will you do me the honor of being the only woman to ever dance with me on this floor? Forever. Will you marry me?" He opened the small box. Inside it was a delicate diamond ring set in white gold.

Beth's eyes filled with tears. "I can't believe this," she said. "Is this real, or a dream?"

Colt smiled. "Yes, it's real. Marry me, Beth. I promise I'll love you, and only you, forever."

"Yes," Beth said through her tears. "Yes, Colt. I love you so much."

Colt stood and slipped the ring on her finger. It fit perfectly, just as they'd fit perfectly together from the moment they met.

"I love you, Beth," Colt said, pulling her to him. They kissed again, and as the music played on, they finished the first of many dances they'd have for the rest of their lives.

Chapter Thirty-One

Colt and Beth were married on a chilly spring afternoon in April in front of the fireplace at the Brennan ranch house just as all the Brennans had before them. Their wedding and reception was small and elegant, with only close family and friends attending. Quinn and Chelle were there, as well as Beth's mother, Rose, and Beth's stepfather, Samuel. Luke was Colt's best man and Chelle was Beth's maid of honor. Andi stood and watched the ceremony with her beautiful baby girl in her arms. She'd given birth on December fourth and they'd named her Jessica Virginia Brennan after both of her grandmothers. Luke took great delight in calling his little girl Jessi, and even now, as he stood beside Colt, he smiled over at his beautiful wife and baby daughter.

Carly was not in attendance. She had made her excuses and had sent the couple a wedding gift. It was a beautiful sculpture made by Adam. Carly had explained to Colt that it would be in bad taste for her to be there, but he'd certainly be seeing a lot of her now that Jessi was born. In fact, she'd been there for Jessi's first Christmas, and everyone had a good time. Carly would always be a part of their family, and Beth understood that and didn't mind. After all, it was Carly who'd told her she'd be crazy not to run to Colt, and she'd been right.

After Colt had proposed to Beth, they spent the little time

she had there picking out items for the home they were going to share. Beth went back to Seattle and gave her notice at work, and then Colt arrived three weeks later and they packed up his truck and her car with the few items Beth wanted to take with her. They'd stopped in Spokane on the way back to the ranch to visit with Rose and Samuel and drop off Christmas gifts, including some of Ginny's best preserves. It didn't take long for Rose to fall for her future son-in-law. She saw right away what a good man he'd be for her daughter.

Colt had surprised Beth with the completed master suite in the house when she returned to Montana. He'd wanted them to be able to live in their house while they finished it, and she was so pleased he'd done this for her. They had the privacy they craved in the home they loved.

All through the winter and spring, Colt and Beth worked on their home together whenever they had a spare moment. Beth received her Registered Nursing license in Montana and was hired part-time at the local hospital in Superior. She filled her days with working on the house, helping out on the ranch, and working at the hospital. Beth had never felt happier or more fulfilled.

And Colt had never been more content. His days were filled with hard work on both the ranch and the house, and his nights were spent holding Beth in his arms. He had his family around him and the woman he loved. Nothing else could ever have made him happier.

As Beth and Colt repeated their vows, they only had eyes for each other.

"I now pronounce you husband and wife," the minister announced. "Colt, you may kiss your bride."

Colt smiled down at Beth, his love for her reflecting in his eyes. He bent his head and kissed her tenderly on the lips, sealing the promise of a lifetime together in the same way it had started, with one single kiss.

About the Author

Deanna Lynn Sletten grew up on the sunny coast of southern California before moving to northern Minnesota as a teenager. That's a story all its own. Her interest in writing novels was sparked in a college English class, and she has been writing in some form or another ever since. In 2011, Deanna discovered the world of self-publishing and published three novels she'd written over the years. After that, she was hooked.

Deanna's women's fiction novels, *Widow, Virgin, Whore* and *Maggie's Turn* have both made the top 100 bestselling book lists on both Amazon and Barnes & Noble in 2014. Her romance novels *Memories* and *Sara's Promise* both won semifinalist in The Kindle Book Review's Best Indie Books of 2012 and 2013 respectively. *Sara's Promise* was also a finalist in the 2013 National Indie Excellence Book Awards.

Deanna enjoys writing heartwarming women's fiction and romance novels with unforgettable characters. She has also written one middle-grade novel that takes you on the adventure of a lifetime. She believes in fate, destiny, love at first sight, soul mates, second chances, magic, and happily ever after, and these are all reflected in her novels.

Deanna is married and has two grown children. When not writing, she enjoys walking the wooded trails around her home with her beautiful Australian Shepherd or relaxing in the boat on the lake in the summer.

Deanna loves hearing from her readers. Connect with her at:

Blog: www.deannalynnsletten.com
Website: www.deannalsletten.com
Twitter: @DeannaLSletten
Facebook: http://www.facebook.com/DeannaLynnSletten
Goodreads: http://www.goodreads.com/dsletten

If you enjoyed **A Kiss for Colt,** you might also enjoy
these novels by Deanna Lynn Sletten

Kiss a Cowboy (Kiss a Cowboy Series, Book One)
(Romance)

Destination Wedding
(Romance)

Memories
(Romance)

Sara's Promise
(Romance)

Maggie's Turn
(Women's Fiction)

Summer of the Loon
(Women's Fiction)

Widow, Virgin Whore ~ A Novel
(Women's Fiction/Family Drama)

Please enjoy the follow excerpt from Deanna's next novel, **Kissing Carly (Kiss a Cowboy Series Book Three)** coming Spring 2015.

KISS A COWBOY SERIES BOOK THREE

Deanna Lynn Sletten

Chapter One

Carly Stevens slowly drove up the long driveway leading to the ranch house. With every crunch of gravel under her tires, her heart beat faster. As she comes to a stop near the familiar house, she brushed back her long, blond hair and bit her pretty, full bottom lip.

Well. Here I go.

Carly turned the key off and put the car in park as her blue eyes scanned the windows of the house. It was after one o'clock on a sunny June afternoon, but she didn't see any movement inside the house. She looked around at the red barn a short distance away and the pastures dotted with grazing horses and cattle. There are four trucks in the driveway, and a smaller SUV, so she knows people were here. She's surprised that no one is walking around or working.

Carly stepped out of her car and stretched. The day was warm and the sun felt good on her back. She'd driven to the Montana ranch from Seattle in two days, even though she could have easily made it in one. She hadn't been in a rush to arrive. No one was expecting her, and the longer she put off talking to her sister, Andi, the better. But now, here she was. She could no longer put off the inevitable.

Carly slowly spun around, taking in the beauty of the Brennan ranch. To her right was the classic red barn and fenced-in pastures. To the left was the trail that headed up into the hills where the summer pasture lay and where there was an amazing view of the ranch. As she continued turning left there was the house, then the highway, and across from that, the Clark Fork River sparkled just under the hill of pine trees that rose to the sky. Carly sighed. She was definitely a city girl, but she couldn't deny how beautiful it was here.

The sound of a door opening caught her attention and Carly looked up at the house in time to lock eyes with her handsome brother-in-law, Luke Brennan, as he stepped down the back stairs. Behind him was Randy Olson, Luke's longtime friend who worked here on the ranch.

Luke's dark blue eyes stared at Carly in surprise. "Carly?"

Carly took a breath and pasted a sweet smile on her face. "Luke!" she exclaimed as she sauntered over to wrap her arms around his broad shoulders. "Aren't you looking handsome as ever?" From the corner of her eye, she saw Randy behind them rolling his eyes. She ignored the crabby ranch hand and kept the smile on her face as she moved away from Luke.

"Where is everyone?" Carly asked. "It's like a ghost town around here."

"We were all inside, eating lunch," Luke said, still looking dazed by the fact that Carly had showed up out of nowhere. "Did Andi know you were coming?"

Carly shook her head. "No, but won't she be surprised?" she asked sweetly. Carly turned to Randy. "Hello, Randy. How have you been?"

Randy nodded. "Hello, Carly." He tapped Luke on the arm. "I'm heading off to the pasture. See you in a bit." Then he strode off toward the barn.

Carly frowned as she watched Randy walk away. He wasn't a bad looking man. Some might even call him ruggedly handsome. His dark brown hair was a bit shaggy, and he always looked like he'd forgotten to shave. But in the past she'd seen his brown eyes sparkle when he teased and she knew he could be sweet when he wanted to. He never paid a bit of attention to her, though, and that always irked her. Men fawned over Carly wherever she went. Everyone, except Randy.

The back door opened again and Carly's frown turned into a warm smile. "Colt, my hunky cowboy!" Carly said, running over to give Colt Brennan a hug. Colt stood there, stunned, but wrapped his arms around Carly and gave her a squeeze.

"Carly? I didn't know you were coming here," he said. He glanced over at his brother, but Luke just shrugged.

Carly pulled away and beamed up at him. "I'm surprising everyone," she said, running her hand down Colt's muscular arm. "You look gorgeous, as always," Carly told him. "Married life is treating you well." Carly sighed as she gazed up at Colt. A year ago, Colt had left the ranch to live with Carly in Seattle, but their relationship hadn't worked out. Carly just hadn't been ready to settle down with one man. However, Carly's roommate, Beth, fell for the sweet, hunky cowboy and she and Colt were married just two months ago, here at the ranch. As Carly looked up into Colt's baby blue eyes, she couldn't help but regret not wanting to marry him when he'd asked. But deep down, she knew it would never have worked.

"Thanks," Colt said, grinning. "You look just as beautiful as ever, Carly."

"You're such a sweetheart, Colt," Carly told him with a smile.

"What's all the commotion out here?" Virginia 'Ginny' Brennan asked from the top of the steps. Her eyes grew wide when she saw Carly. "Carly! My goodness, but what a wonderful surprise." Ginny hurried down the steps to hug Carly with Bree, their black and white Australian Shepherd cattle dog, bounding at her heels.

Carly hugged Ginny tight. She adored the older woman who always welcomed her at the ranch with open arms and never judged her no matter what awful stunts she pulled. Since her own parents had died in a car accident when Carly was only fourteen and Andi was eighteen, Carly had been missing a mother figure. But Ginny filled that role with ease, and Carly appreciated her for it.

Ginny stood back and looked Carly up and down with a smile. "You are just as cute as a bug as ever. Why, I'm surprised Andi didn't tell us you were coming."

Carly tried to look contrite. "I didn't tell her. I hope you don't mind my showing up like this."

"Oh, darling," Ginny said, pulling her close again. "You're family. You can come here whenever your heart desires."

Carly looked into Ginny's kind hazel eyes. With her dark blond hair always pulled back into a ponytail, and only a few wisps of grey running through it, she barely looked old enough to be Luke and Colt's mother. She was a bit taller than Carly, and stayed slender from working hard around the ranch. It was her kind heart, however, that won over everyone who came to the ranch. "Thanks, Ginny. You're just too good to me."

Ginny swiped her hand through the air to brush away her words. "It's easy being kind to you, Sweetie." She turned and called out toward the house. "Andi, come on out. There's a surprise waiting for you in the driveway."

A moment later, a young woman with long, dark red hair and brilliant green eyes came to the door, holding a small baby on her hip. The little girl in her arms was a tiny replica of her mother. Andi stood there, surprise clearly marked on her face. "Carly? What are you doing here?"

"Andi!" Carly cried with delight. She ran over and met her sister at the bottom of the steps, pulling her and the baby into a hug. "I'm so happy to see you. And Jessi. She's grown so much.

She's so adorable."

The baby backed away from Carly, her eyes big as saucers. Tears began to well in her little green eyes.

Carly pulled away. "Oh, no. I'm making her cry," she said, truly distressed. "My own little niece doesn't even know me."

"She's fine," Andi said as she bounced little Jessi on her hip. "She's only six months old, so of course, she doesn't know you. But she will, if you stay a few days."

Carly looked at her big sister, her eyes questioning. "Are you mad that I just showed up?"

Andi shook her head. "Of course not. I was just surprised. Whatever made you drive all this way without letting us know?"

Carly set her pretty pink lips into a pout. "I missed you. All of you. And my baby niece, too. Isn't that enough to make me want to come here for a visit?"

Andi looked at her in a way that made Carly think she didn't believe her. Andi knew her too well.

"Well, boys," Ginny said, turning to Luke and Colt. "Why don't you two carry Carly's things up to the guest room? Carly. Come on in and have some lunch. You must be starving." Ginny headed back into the house.

Carly turned to Luke and Colt and hit the unlock button on her car key. Luke opened up the back of her Honda CR-V and looked inside. A crease touched his brow when he saw all the luggage in the back. "You want all of this in the house?"

"Yes, please," Carly said sweetly. "Oh," she walked over to the car and retrieved her purse and a large handbag. "Thanks, guys," she said, walking back over to Andi.

Andi watched as Luke and Colt unloaded four large suitcases. "Why so many bags?" she asked her sister.

Carly shrugged. "A girl can never have enough clothes along with her."

Andi shook her head and headed back inside the house with

Carly on her heels.

* * *

Randy strode out into the pasture by the barn and retrieved his gelding, Black Jack. The horse came to him immediately, and Randy stroked his silky neck a moment before leading him into the barn to saddle him. Black Jack was a tall Tennessee Walker, seventeen hands, and was a sleek black with an even darker black mane and tail. He'd broke Black Jack himself, ten years ago, and trained him, and they'd been constant companions ever since.

As Randy saddled his horse, his thoughts turned to Carly and he rolled his eyes again. *What is that girl up to now?* Randy had a soft spot for Luke's wife Andi, and he also liked Colt's wife, Beth, very much. Both women were genuine, honest, and hardworking, and neither one had a phony bone in their bodies. But Carly was different. That girl put on a show wherever she went. Just because she had a curvy body, long, silky blond hair, and those big blue eyes, she thought she had every man wrapped around her perfectly manicured little finger. Every man, except Randy.

He chuckled when he thought of the many times she'd tried to win him over with her pouty lips or hip-swaying walk. He just ignored her as if she wasn't even there. He knew it drove her crazy, and that made it even more fun for him. Randy wasn't generally a mean spirited person, but he wasn't going to be had by a five foot, five inch tall spoiled brat. For the life of him, he couldn't understand how Carly and Andi could be sisters. Andi was so sweet, smart, and reliable, and Carly, well, she wasn't any of those things. He supposed losing her parents at such an early age hadn't been easy for her, but she'd had Andi to take care of her, so she had no excuse for her behavior.

A lot of people lose a parent when they're young, and they turn out fine. He did. So what was up with her?

Of course, Randy had been lucky enough to have the Brennans take him under their wing when he was eight years old. He lived with his mom in town, but he spent most weekends on the ranch learning everything he knew today under the tutelage of Luke's father, Jack. Jack had been a hard-working man who cared deeply for his family, and between him and Ginny, there had been enough love to spread around, even to a little boy whose own father hadn't cared enough about him to stick around. Every day of his life, Randy was thankful for the Brennans and all they'd done for him, because God only knew what would have happened to him without them.

Randy finished saddling Black Jack and then slipped on the bridle. The afternoon was heating up and it was hot in the barn. He lifted his black cowboy hat off his head, ran his hand through his hair, then replaced the hat. He knew he needed a haircut, but he just hadn't gotten around to it. He'd try to get one Saturday so he'd look respectable on Sunday, not that it mattered. His mother probably wouldn't notice anyway.

Randy led Black Jack out of the barn and then hopped up into the saddle and took off toward the trail that led to the back of the property. A few of the cows and calves had been left in the lower pasture instead of brought up to the higher summer pasture, and he was going to check on them. The calves had been born later than the others, and two of them weren't growing as fast as they should. If it was necessary for them to supplement their diet, then they would. He'd go see how they were faring first, and tomorrow he'd bring the barrel of grain up to them if he felt it was necessary.

Before he hit the trail, Randy turned back a moment and saw Luke and Colt walking into the barn. He waved and they waved back. Randy knew that Colt was heading back over to

Ray's place to help with the haying. The Brennans and their neighbor, Ray, shared the haying fifty/fifty. Ray had the equipment and the Brennans had the fields, so it worked out well for both of them. Luke was going to work on the riding lawn mower since it was acting up again. There was always work to be done on a spread as big as this.

Randy turned Black Jack back toward the trail, clicked his tongue, and off they galloped.